The Day of the Dragon

As seen through the eyes of bestselling Hugo, Nebula, and World Fantasy Award masters, including:

"St. Dragon and the George" by Gordon R. Dickson: Trapped in a dragon's body, a college professor must convince a dragon-slaying knight to help rescue his love from an ogre's clutches!

"A Plague of Butterflies" by Orson Scott Card: The hidden city was built not to keep the dragons out—but to keep them in. Now butterflies lead a sacred wanderer to the greatest dragon of all, who schemes to replace the forests destroyed by man . . .

"The George Business" by Roger Zelazny: Mutual dreams of wealth and death lead a dragon and a gigolo to reach a strange arrangement . . .

"Dragons' Teeth" by David Drake: Roman soldiers must battle a wizard who can raise monsters from the past . . .

"Two Yards of Dragon" by L. Sprague de Camp: These days a dragon slayer needs a strong horse, common sense—and a good lawyer!

"A Hiss of Dragon" by Gregory Benford and Marc Laidlaw: Biotechs created dragons; now surviving them is a growth industry . . .

A Dragon-Lover's Treasury Of The Fantastic

EDITED BY
MARGARET WEIS

ASPECT

WARNER BOOKS

A Time Warner Company

Introduction—Copyright © 1994 by Margaret Weis. Used by arrangement with the author.

"Weyr Search" by Anne McCaffrey—Copyright © 1967 by Anne McCaffrey. First appeared in ANALOG. Reprinted by permission of the author and the author's agent, Virginia Kidd.

"Cockfight" by Jane Yolen—Copyright © 1980 by Jane Yolen. Reprinted by permission of Curtis Brown, Ltd.

"The Storm King" by Joan D. Vinge—Copyright © 1980 by Joan D. Vinge. Reprinted by permission of the author.
Copyright information continued on page 422.

Warner Books, Inc., 1271 Avenue of the Americas, New York, NY 10020

 A Time Warner Company

Printed in the United States of America

First Printing: October 1994

10 9 8 7 6 5 4 3 2 1

Library of Congress Cataloging-in-Publication Data

A Dragon-lover's treasury of the fantastic/edited by Margaret Weis.
   p. cm.
  ISBN 0-446-67063-4
  1. Fantastic fiction, American.   2. Dragons—Fiction.   I. Weis, Margaret.
PS648.F3D66 1994
913'.0876608375—dc20   93-50918
                                                              CIP

Book design by H. Roberts
Cover design by Don Puckey
Cover illustration by Ciruelo Cabral
Hand-lettering by Carl Dellacroce

CONTENTS

Introduction

Margaret Weis

Of all the beasts in the Bestiary, the dragon is the most fascinating. Perhaps because it is—or has become over time and literature—the most human in its nature and characteristics. Dragons attract us with their beauty and grace, fascinate us with their magic, lure us with promises of fabulous wealth, ill-gotten booty, free for the taking, with nary a guilty thought or qualm of conscience, for, after all, we are ridding the world of evil.

Sometime around 1983, when I first started working as a book editor for TSR, Inc., producers of the Dungeons & Dragons® role-playing games, the marketing department conducted a survey. They asked the players what the company could do to make the game modules better.

The answer: The dungeons are fine. We want more dragons.

One would think battling dragons every Saturday would lose its thrill, but, being a "gamer" myself, I can assure you that nothing causes the heart of a player to quicken, the eye to brighten, than to discover a gigantic clawed footprint in the path or to hear the peasant relate in panicked tones how, "Yon great winged beast done lifted me daughter clean in the air and made off wit' her!"

We know that at least half the party won't survive the encounter, but the knowledge of treasure, of battle with a worthy and cunning foe, draws us on.

Yet, after the hard-fought battle, with a foe worthy of our steel, who among the party doesn't feel a pang of regret when the glorious creature falls from the air, mortally wounded. And as we sneak off, like thieves with the treasure, we talk in hushed, almost reverent tones, of the monster we slew, and we feel—deep inside—ashamed, unworthy.

We know we have felled something greater, more wondrous than ourselves.

In this volume I have collected some of my very favorite dragon stories, by some of the best-known authors in the science fiction and fantasy fields. Some, I'm sure, you will come to as old favorites, as interesting and exciting to read again as they were the first time. In others, you will find new and entertaining adventures.

Just exactly the sort of book to take along while posting guard on the king's treasure caravan. You are reading, enthralled, when suddenly from the sky above, you hear the creak and flap of huge leathery wings. . . .

A DRAGON-LOVER'S TREASURY
OF THE FANTASTIC

WEYR SEARCH

Anne McCaffrey

When is a legend legend? Why is a myth a myth? How old and disused must a fact be for it to be relegated to the category: Fairy tale? And why do certain facts remain incontrovertible, while others lose their validity to assume a shabby, unstable character?

Rukbat, in the Sagittarian sector, was a golden G-type star. It had five planets, plus one stray it had attracted and held in recent millennia. Its third planet was enveloped by air man could breathe, boasted water he could drink, and possessed a gravity which permitted man to walk confidently erect. Men discovered it, and promptly colonized it, as they did every habitable planet they came to and then—whether callously or through collapse of empire, the colonists never discovered, and eventually forgot to ask—left the colonies to fend for themselves.

When men first settled on Rukbat's third world, and named it Pern, they had taken little notice of the stranger-planet, swinging around its primary in a wildly erratic elliptical orbit. Within a few generations they had

1

forgotten its existence. The desperate path the wanderer pursued brought it close to its stepsister every two hundred [Terran] years at perihelion.

When the aspects were harmonious and the conjunction with its sister-planet close enough, as it often was, the indigenous life of the wanderer sought to bridge the space gap to the more temperate and hospitable planet.

It was during the frantic struggle to combat this menace dropping through Pern's skies like silver threads that Pern's contact with the mother-planet weakened and broke. Recollections of Earth receded further from Pernese history with each successive generation until memory of their origins degenerated past legend or myth, into oblivion.

To forestall the incursions of the dreaded Threads, the Pernese, with the ingenuity of their forgotten Yankee forebears and between first onslaught and return, developed a highly specialized variety of a life form indigenous to their adopted planet—the winged, tailed, and fire-breathing dragons, named for the Earth legend they resembled. Such humans as had a high empathy rating and some innate telepathic ability were trained to make use of and preserve this unusual animal whose ability to teleport was of immense value in the fierce struggle to keep Pern bare of Threads.

The dragons and their dragonmen, a breed apart, and the shortly re-newed menace they battled, created a whole new group of legends and myths.

As the menace was conquered the populace in the Holds of Pern settled into a more comfortable way of life. Most of the dragon Weyrs eventually were abandoned, and the descendants of heroes fell into disfavor, as the legends fell into disrepute.

This, then, is a tale of legends disbelieved and their restoration. Yet—how goes a legend? When is myth?

> Drummer, beat, and piper, blow,
> Harper, strike, and soldier, go.
> Free the flame and sear the grasses
> Till the dawning Red Star passes.

Lessa woke, cold. Cold with more than the chill of the everlastingly clammy stone walls. Cold with the prescience of a danger greater than when, ten full Turns ago, she had run, whimpering, to hide in the watch-wher's odorous lair.

Rigid with concentration, Lessa lay in the straw of the redolent cheese room, sleeping quarters shared with the other kitchen drudges. There was an urgency in the ominous portent unlike any other forewarning. She touched the awareness of the watch-wher, slithering on its rounds in the courtyard. It circled at the choke-limit of its chain. It was restless, but oblivious to anything unusual in the predawn darkness.

The danger was definitely not within the walls of Hold Ruath. Nor approaching the paved perimeter without the Hold where relentless grass had forced new growth through the ancient mortar, green witness to the deterioration of the once stone-clean Hold. The danger was not advancing up the now little used causeway from the valley, nor lurking in the craftsmen's stony holdings at the foot of the Hold's cliff. It did not scent the wind that blew from Tillek's cold shores. But still it twanged sharply through her senses, vibrating every nerve in Lessa's slender frame. Fully roused, she sought to identify it before the prescient mood dissolved. She cast outward, toward the Pass, farther than she had ever pressed. Whatever threatened was not in Ruatha . . . yet. Nor did it have a familiar flavor. It was not, then, Fax.

Lessa had been cautiously pleased that Fax had not shown himself at Hold Ruath in three full Turns. The apathy of the craftsmen, the decaying farmholds, even the green-etched stones of the Hold infuriated Fax, self-styled Lord of the High Reaches, to the point where he preferred to forget the reason why he had subjugated the once proud and profitable Hold.

Lessa picked her way among the sleeping drudges, huddled together for warmth, and glided up the worn steps to the kitchen-proper. She slipped across the cavernous kitchen to the stable-yard door. The cobbles of the yard were icy through the thin soles of her sandals and she shivered as the predawn air penetrated her patched garment.

The watch-wher slithered across the yard to greet her, pleading, as it always did, for release. Glancing fondly down at the awesome head, she promised it a good rub presently. It crouched, groaning, at the end of its chain as she continued to the grooved steps that led to the rampart over the Hold's massive gate. Atop the tower, Lessa stared toward the east where the stony breasts of the Pass rose in black relief against the gathering day.

Indecisively she swung to her left, for the sense of danger issued from that direction as well. She glanced upward, her eyes drawn to the red star which had recently begun to dominate the dawn sky. As she stared, the star radiated a final ruby pulsation before its magnificence was lost in the brightness of Pern's rising sun.

For the first time in many Turns, Lessa gave thought to matters beyond Pern, beyond her dedication to vengeance on the murderer Fax for the annihilation of her family. Let him but come within Ruath Hold now and he would never leave.

But the brilliant ruby sparkle of the Red Star recalled the Disaster Ballads—grim narratives of the heroism of the dragonriders as they braved the dangers of *between* to breathe fiery death on the silver Threads that dropped through Pern's skies. Not one Thread must fall to the rich soil, to burrow deep and multiply, leaching the earth of minerals and fertility. Straining her eyes as if vision would bridge the gap between periol and person, she stared intently eastward. The watch-wher's thin, whistled question reached her just as the prescience waned.

Dawnlight illumined the tumbled landscape, the unplowed fields in the valley below. Dawnlight fell on twisted orchards, where the sparse herds of milchbeasts hunted stray blades of spring grass. Grass in Ruatha grew where it should not, died where it should flourish. An odd brooding smile curved Lessa's lips. Fax realized no profit from his conquest of Ruatha . . . nor would he, while she, Lessa, lived. And he had not the slightest suspicion of the source of this undoing.

Or had he? Lessa wondered, her mind still reverberating from the savage prescience of danger. East lay Fax's ancestral and only legitimate Hold. Northeast lay little but bare and stony mountains and Benden, the remaining Weyr, which protected Pern.

Lessa stretched, arching her back, inhaling the sweet, untainted wind of morning.

A cock crowed in the stableyard. Lessa whirled, her face alert, eyes darting around the outer Hold lest she be observed in such an uncharacteristic pose. She unbound her hair, letting it fall about her face concealingly. Her body drooped into the sloppy posture she affected. Quickly she thudded down the stairs, crossing to the watch-wher. It lurred piteously, its great eyes blinking against the growing daylight. Oblivious to the stench of its rank breath, she hugged the scaly head to her, scratching its ears and eye ridges. The watch-wher was ecstatic with pleasure, its long body trembling, its clipped wings rustling. It alone knew who she was or cared. And it was the only creature in all Pern she trusted since the day she had blindly sought refuge in its dark stinking lair to escape Fax's thirsty swords that had drunk so deeply of Ruathan blood.

Slowly she rose, cautioning it to remember to be as vicious to her as to all should anyone be near. It promised to obey her, swaying back and forth to emphasize its reluctance.

The first rays of the sun glanced over the Hold's outer wall. Crying out, the watch-wher darted into its dark nest. Lessa crept back to the kitchen and into the cheese room.

> From the Weyr and from the Bowl
> Bronze and brown and blue and green
> Rise the dragonmen of Pern,
> Aloft, on wing, seen, then unseen.

F'lar on bronze Mnementh's great neck appeared first in the skies above the chief Hold of Fax, so-called Lord of the High Reaches. Behind him, in proper wedge formation, the wingmen came into sight. F'lar checked the formation automatically; as precise as at the moment of entry to *between*.

As Mnementh curved in an arc that would bring them to the perimeter of the Hold, consonant with the friendly nature of this visitation, F'lar surveyed with mounting aversion the disrepair of the ridge defenses. The firestone pits were empty and the rock-cut gutters radiating from the pits were green-tinged with a mossy growth.

Was there even one lord in Pern who maintained his Hold rocky in observance of the ancient Laws? F'lar's lips tightened to a thinner line. When this Search was over and the Impression made, there would have to be a solemn, punitive Council held at the Weyr. And by the golden shell of the queen, he, F'lar, meant to be its moderator. He would replace lethargy with industry. He would scour the green and dangerous scum from the heights of Pern, the grass blades from its stoneworks. No verdant skirt would be condoned in any farmhold. And the tithings which had been so miserly, so grudgingly presented would, under pain of firestoning, flow with decent generosity into the Dragon weyr.

Mnementh rumbled approvingly as he vaned his pinions to land lightly on the grass-etched flagstones of Fax's Hold. The bronze dragon furled his great wings, and F'lar heard the warning claxon in the Hold's Great Tower. Mnementh dropped to his knees as F'lar indicated he wished to dismount. The bronze rider stood by Mnementh's huge wedgeshaped head, politely awaiting the arrival of the Hold lord. F'lar idly gazed down the valley, hazy with warm spring sunlight. He ignored the furtive heads that peered at the dragonman from the parapet slits and the cliff windows.

F'lar did not turn as a rush of air announced the arrival of the rest of the wing. He knew, however, when F'nor, the brown rider, his half-brother, took the customary position on his left, a dragon-length to the rear. F'lar caught a glimpse of F'nor's boot-heel twisting to death the grass crowding up between the stones.

An order, muffled to an intense whisper, issued from within the great court, beyond the open gates. Almost immediately a group of men marched into sight, led by a heavy-set man of medium height.

Mnementh arched his neck, angling his head so that his chin rested on the ground. Mnementh's many faceted eyes, on a level with F'lar's head, fastened with disconcerting interest on the approaching party. The dragons could never understand why they generated such abject fear in common folk. At only one point in his life span would a dragon attack a human and that could be excused on the grounds of simple ignorance. F'lar could not explain to the dragon the politics behind the necessity of inspiring awe in the holders, lord and craftsman alike. He could only observe that the fear and apprehension showing in the faces of the advancing squad which troubled Mnementh was oddly pleasing to him, F'lar.

*   *   *

"Welcome, Bronze Rider, to the Hold of Fax, Lord of the High Reaches. He is at your service," and the man made an adequately respectful salute.

The use of the third person pronoun could be construed, by the meticulous, to be a veiled insult. This fit in with the information F'lar had on Fax; so he ignored it. His information was also correct in describing Fax as a greedy man. It showed in the restless eyes which flicked at every detail of F'lar's clothing, at the slight frown when the intricately etched sword-hilt was noticed.

F'lar noticed, in his own turn, the several rich rings which flashed on Fax's left hand. The overlord's right hand remained slightly cocked after the habit of the professional swordsman. His tunic, of rich fabric, was stained and none too fresh. The man's feet, in heavy wher-hide boots, were solidly planted, weight balanced forward on his toes. A man to be treated cautiously, F'lar decided, as one should the conqueror of five neighboring Holds. Such greedy audacity was in itself a revelation. Fax had married into a sixth . . . and had legally inherited, however unusual the circumstances, the seventh. He was a lecherous man by reputation.

Within these seven Holds, F'lar anticipated a profitable Search. Let R'gul go southerly to pursue Search among the indolent, if lovely, women there. The Weyr needed a strong woman this time; Jora had been worse than useless with Nemorth. Adversity, uncertainty: those were the conditions that bred the qualities F'lar wanted in a weyrwoman.

"We ride in Search," F'lar drawled softly, "and request the hospitality of your Hold, Lord Fax."

Fax's eyes widened imperceptibly at mention of Search.

"I had heard Jora was dead," Fax replied, dropping the third person abruptly as if F'lar had passed some sort of test by ignoring it. "So Nemorth has a new queen, hm-m-m?" he continued, his eyes darting across the rank of the ring, noting the disciplined stance of the riders, the healthy color of the dragons.

F'lar did not dignify the obvious with an answer.

"And, my Lord—" Fax hesitated, expectantly inclining his head slightly toward the dragonman.

For a pulse beat, F'lar wondered if the man were deliberately pro-voking him with such subtle insults. The name of bronze riders should be as well known throughout Pern as the name of the Dragonqueen and her Weyrwoman. F'lar kept his face composed, his eyes on Fax's.

Leisurely, with the proper touch of arrogance, F'nor stepped for-ward, stopping slightly behind Mnementh's head, one hand negli-gently touching the jaw hinge of the huge beast.

"The Bronze Rider of Mnementh, Lord F'lar, will require quarters for himself. I, F'nor, brown rider, prefer to be lodged with the wingmen. We are, in number, twelve."

F'lar liked that touch of F'nor's, totting up the wing strength, as if Fax were incapable of counting. F'nor had phrased it so adroitly as to make it impossible for Fax to protest the insult.

"Lord F'lar," Fax said through teeth fixed in a smile, "the High Reaches are honored with your Search."

"It will be to the credit of the High Reaches," F'lar replied smoothly, "if one of its own supplies the Weyr."

"To our everlasting credit," Fax replied as suavely. "In the old days, many notable weyrwomen came from my Holds."

"Your Holds?" asked F'lar, politely smiling as he emphasized the plural. "Ah, yes, you are now overlord of Ruatha, are you not? There have been many from that Hold."

A strange tense look crossed Fax's face. "Nothing good comes from Ruath Hold." Then he stepped aside, gesturing F'lar to enter the Hold.

Fax's troop leader barked a hasty order and the men formed two lines, their metal-edged boots flicking sparks from the stones.

At unspoken orders, all the dragons rose with a great churning of air and dust. F'lar strode nonchalantly past the welcoming files. The men were rolling their eyes in alarm as the beasts glided above to the inner courts. Someone on the high tower uttered a frightened yelp as Mnementh took his position on that vantage point. His great wings drove phosphoric-scented air across the inner court as he maneuvered his great frame onto the inadequate landing space.

Outwardly oblivious to the consternation, fear and awe the dragons inspired, F'lar was secretly amused and rather pleased by the effect. Lords of the Holds needed this reminder that they must deal with dragons, not just with riders, who were men, mortal and murderable. The ancient respect for dragonmen as well as dragonkind must be reinstilled in modern breasts.

"The Hold has just risen from the table, Lord F'lar, if . . ." Fax suggested. His voice trailed off at F'lar's smiling refusal.

"Convey my duty to your lady, Lord Fax," F'lar rejoined, noticing with inward satisfaction the tightening of Fax's jaw muscles at the ceremonial request.

"You would prefer to see your quarters first?" Fax countered.

F'lar flicked an imaginary speck from his soft wher-hide sleeve and shook his head. Was the man buying time to sequester his ladies as the old time lords had?

"Duty first," he said with a rueful shrug.

"Of course," Fax all but snapped and strode smartly ahead, his heels pounding out the anger he could not express otherwise. F'lar decided he had guessed correctly.

F'lar and F'nor followed at a slower pace through the double-doored entry with its massive metal panels, into the great hall, carved into the cliffside.

"They eat not badly," F'nor remarked casually to F'lar, appraising the remnants still on the table.

"Better than the Weyr, it would seem," F'lar replied dryly.

"Young roasts and tender," F'nor said in a bitter undertone, "while the stringy, barren beasts are delivered up to us."

"The change is overdue," F'lar murmured, then raised his voice to conversational level. "A well-favored hall," he was saying amiably as they reached Fax. Their reluctant host stood in the portal to the inner Hold, which, like all such Holds, burrowed deep into stone, traditional refuge of all in time of peril.

Deliberately, F'lar turned back to the banner-hung Hall. "Tell me, Lord Fax, do you adhere to the old practices and mount a dawn guard?"

Fax frowned, trying to grasp F'lar's meaning.

"There is always a guard at the Tower."

"An easterly guard?"

Fax's eyes jerked toward F'lar, then to F'nor.

"There are always guards," he answered sharply, "on all the approaches."

"Oh, just the approaches," and F'lar nodded wisely to F'nor.

"Where else?" demanded Fax, concerned, glancing from one dragonman to the other.

"I must ask that of your harper. You do keep a trained harper in your Hold?"

"Of course. I have several trained harpers," and Fax jerked his shoulders straighter.

F'lar affected not to understand.

"Lord Fax is the overlord of six other Holds," F'nor reminded his wingleader.

"Of course," F'lar assented, with exactly the same inflection Fax had used a moment before.

The mimicry did not go unnoticed by Fax but as he was unable to construe deliberate insult out of an innocent affirmative, he stalked into the glow-lit corridors. The dragonmen followed.

The women's quarters in Fax's Hold had been moved from the traditional innermost corridors to those at cliff-face. Sunlight poured down from three double-shuttered, deep-casement windows in the outside wall. F'lar noted that the bronze hinges were well oiled, and the sills regulation spearlength. Fax had not, at least, diminished the protective wall.

The chamber was richly hung with appropriately gentle scenes of women occupied in all manner of feminine tasks. Doors gave off the main chamber on both sides into smaller sleeping alcoves and from these, at Fax's bidding, his women hesitantly emerged. Fax sternly gestured to a blue-gowned woman, her hair white-streaked, her face lined with disappointments and bitterness, her body swollen with pregnancy. She advanced awkwardly, stopping several feet from her lord. From her attitude, F'lar deduced that she came no closer to Fax than was absolutely necessary.

"The Lady of Crom, mother of my heirs," Fax said without pride or cordiality.

"My Lady—" F'lar hesitated, waiting for her name to be supplied. She glanced warily at her lord.

"Gemma," Fax snapped curtly.

F'lar bowed deeply. "My Lady Gemma, the Weyr is on Search and requests the Hold's hospitality."

"My Lord F'lar," the Lady Gemma replied in a low voice, "you are most welcome."

F'lar did not miss the slight slur on the adverb nor the fact that Gemma had no trouble naming him. His smile was warmer than courtesy demanded, warm with gratitude and sympathy. Looking at the number of women in these quarters, F'lar thought there might be one or two Lady Gemma could bid farewell without regret.

Fax preferred his women plump and small. There wasn't a saucy one in the lot. If there once had been, the spirit had been beaten out of her. Fax, no doubt, was stud, not lover. Some of the covey had not all winter long made much use of water, judging by the amount of sweet oil gone rancid in their hair. Of them all, if these were all, the Lady Gemma was the only willful one; and she, too old.

The amenities over, Fax ushered his unwelcome guests outside, and led the way to the quarters he had assigned the bronze rider.

"A pleasant room," F'lar acknowledged, stripping off gloves and wher-hide tunic, throwing them carelessly to the table. "I shall see to my men and the beasts. They have been fed recently," he commented, pointing up Fax's omission in inquiring. "I request liberty to wander through the crafthold."

Fax sourly granted what was a dragonman's traditional privilege.

"I shall not further disrupt your routine, Lord Fax, for you must have many demands on you, with seven Holds to supervise." F'lar inclined his body slightly to the overlord, turning away as a gesture of dismissal. He could imagine the infuriated expression on Fax's face from the stamping retreat.

F'nor and the men had settled themselves in a hastily vacated barrackroom. The dragons were perched comfortably on the rocky ridges above the Hold. Each rider kept his dragon in light, but alert, charge. There were to be no incidents on a Search.

As a group, the dragonmen rose at F'lar's entrance.

"No tricks, no troubles, but look around closely," he said laconically. "Return by sundown with the names of any likely prospects." He caught F'nor's grin, remembering how Fax had slurred over some names. "Descriptions are in order and craft affiliation."

The men nodded, their eyes glinting with understanding. They were flatteringly confident of a successful Search even as F'lar's doubts grew now that he had seen Fax's women. By all logic, the pick of the High Reaches should be in Fax's chief Hold—but they were not. Still, there were many large craftholds not to mention the six other High Holds to visit. All the same . . .

In unspoken accord F'lar and F'nor left the barracks. The men would follow, unobtrusively, in pairs or singly, to reconnoiter the crafthold and the nearer farmholds. The men were as overtly eager to be abroad as F'lar was privately. There had been a time when dragonmen were frequent and favored guests in all the great Holds throughout Pern, from southern Fort to high north Igen. This pleasant custom, too, had died along with other observances, evidence of the low regard in which the Weyr was presently held. F'lar vowed to correct this.

He forced himself to trace in memory the insidious changes. The Records, which each Weyrwoman kept, were proof of the gradual, but perceptible, decline, traceable through the past two hundred full Turns. Knowing the facts did not alleviate the condition. And F'lar was of that scant handful in the Weyr itself who did credit Records and Ballad alike. The situation might shortly reverse itself radically if the old tales were to be believed.

There was a reason, an explanation, a purpose, F'lar felt, for every one of the Weyr laws from First Impression to the Firestone: from the grass-free heights to ridge-running gutters. For elements as minor as controlling the appetite of a dragon to limiting the inhabitants of the Weyr. Although why the other five Weyrs had been abandoned, F'lar did not know. Idly he wondered if there were records, dusty and crumbling, lodged in the disused Weyrs. He must contrive to check when next his wings flew patrol. Certainly there was no explanation in Benden Weyr.

"There is industry but no enthusiasm," F'nor was saying, drawing F'lar's attention back to their tour of the crafthold.

They had descended the guttered ramp from the Hold into the crafthold proper, the broad roadway lined with cottages up to the imposing stone crafthalls. Silently F'lar noted moss-clogged gutters on the roofs, the vines clasping the walls. It was painful for one of his calling to witness the flagrant disregard of simple safety precautions. Growing things were forbidden near the habitations of mankind.

"News travels fast," F'nor chuckled, nodding at a hurrying craftsman, in the smock of a baker, who gave them a mumbled good day. "Not a female in sight."

His observation was accurate. Women should be abroad at this hour, bringing in supplies from the storehouses, washing in the river on such a bright warm day, or going out to the farmholds to help with planting. Not a gowned figure in sight.

"We used to be preferred mates," F'nor remarked caustically.

"We'll visit the Clothmen's Hall first. If my memory serves me right . . ."

"As it always does . . ." F'nor interjected wryly. He took no advantage of their blood relationship but he was more at ease with the bronze rider than most of the dragonmen, the other bronze riders included. F'lar was reserved in a close-knit society of easy equality. He flew a tightly disciplined wing but men maneuvered to serve under him. His wing always excelled in the Games. None ever floundered in *between* to disappear forever and no beast in his wing sickened, leaving a man in dragonless exile from the Weyr, a part of him numb forever.

"L'tol came this way and settled in one of the High Reaches," F'lar continued.

"L'tol?"

"Yes, a green rider from S'lel's wing. You remember."

An ill-timed swerve during the Spring Games had brought L'tol and his beast into the full blast of a phosphene emission from S'lel's bronze Tuenth. L'tol had been thrown from his beast's neck as the dragon tried to evade the blast. Another wingmate had swooped to catch the rider but the green dragon, his left wing crisped, his body scorched, had died of shock and phosphene poisoning.

"L'tol would aid our Search," F'nor agreed as the two dragonmen walked up to the bronze doors of the Clothmen's Hall. They paused on the threshold, adjusting their eyes to the dimmer light within. Glows punctuated the wall recesses and hung in clusters above the larger looms where the finer tapestries and fabrics were woven by master craftsmen. The pervading mood was one of quiet, purposeful industry.

Before their eyes had adapted, however, a figure glided to them, with a polite, if curt, request for them to follow him.

They were led to the right of the entrance, to a small office, curtained from the main hall. Their guide turned to them, his face visible in the wallglows. There was that air about him that marked him indefinably as a dragonman. But his face was lined deeply, one side seamed with old burn marks. His eyes, sick with a hungry yearning, dominated his face. He blinked constantly.

"I am now Lytol," he said in a harsh voice.

F'lar nodded acknowledgment.

"You would be F'lar," Lytol said, "and you, F'nor. You've both the look of your sire."

F'lar nodded again.

Lytol swallowed convulsively, the muscles in his face twitching as the presence of dragonmen revived his awareness of exile. He essayed a smile.

"Dragons in the sky! The news spread faster than Threads."

"Nemorth has a new queen."

"Jora dead?" Lytol asked concernedly, his face cleared of its nervous movement for a second.

F'lar nodded.

Lytol grimaced bitterly. "R'gul again, huh." He stared off in the middle distance, his eyelids quiet but the muscles along his jaw took up the constant movement. "You've the High Reaches? All of them?" Lytol asked, turning back to the dragonman, a slight emphasis on "all."

F'lar gave an affirmative nod again.

"You've seen the women." Lytol's disgust showed through the words. It was a statement, not a question, for he hurried on. "Well, there are no better in all the High Reaches," and his tone expressed utmost disdain.

"Fax likes his women comfortably fleshed and docile," Lytol rattled on. "Even the Lady Gemma has learned. It'd be different if he didn't need her family's support. Ah, it would be different indeed. So he keeps her pregnant, hoping to kill her in childbed one day. And he will. He will."

Lytol drew himself up, squaring his shoulders, turning full to the two dragonmen. His expression was vindictive, his voice low and tense.

"Kill that tyrant, for the sake and safety of Pern. Of the Weyr. Of the queen. He only bides his time. He spreads discontent among the other lords. He"—Lytol's laughter had an hysterical edge to it now—"he fancies himself as good as dragonmen."

"There are no candidates then in this Hold?" F'lar said, his voice sharp enough to cut through the man's preoccupation with his curious theory.

Lytol stared at the bronze rider. "Did I not say it?"

"What of Ruath Hold?"

Lytol stopped shaking his head and looked sharply at F'lar, his lips curling in a cunning smile. He laughed mirthlessly.

"You think to find a Torene, or a Moreta, hidden at Ruath Hold in these times? Well, all of that Blood are dead. Fax's blade was thirsty that day. He knew the truth of those harpers' tales, that Ruathan lords gave full measure of hospitality to dragonmen and the Ruathan were a breed apart. There were, you know," Lytol's voice dropped to a confiding whisper, "exiled Weyrmen like myself in that Line."

F'lar nodded gravely, unable to contradict the man's pitiful attempt at self-esteem.

"No," and Lytol chuckled softly. "Fax gets nothing from that Hold but trouble. And the women Fax used to take . . ." his laugh turned nasty in tone. "It is rumored he was impotent for months afterward."

"Any families in the holdings with Weyr blood?"

Lytol frowned, glanced surprised at F'lar. He rubbed the scarred side of his face thoughtfully.

"There were," he admitted slowly. "There were. But I doubt if any live on." He thought a moment longer, then shook his head emphatically.

F'lar shrugged.

"I wish I had better news for you," Lytol murmured.

"No matter," F'lar reassured him, one hand poised to part the hanging in the doorway.

Lytol came up to him swiftly, his voice urgent.

"Heed what I say, Fax is ambitious. Force R'gul, or whoever is Weyrleader next, to keep watch on the High Reaches."

Lytol jabbed a finger in the direction of the Hold. "He scoffs openly at tales of the Threads. He taunts the harpers for the stupid nonsense of the old ballads and has banned from their repertoire all dragonlore. The new generation will grow up totally ignorant of duty, tradition and precaution."

F'lar was surprised to hear that on top of Lytol's other disclosures. Yet the Red Star pulsed in the sky and the time was drawing near when they would hysterically reavow the old allegiances in fear for their very lives.

"Have you been abroad in the early morning of late?" asked F'nor, grinning maliciously.

"I have," Lytol breathed out in a hushed, choked whisper. "I have . . ." A groan was wrenched from his guts and he whirled away from the dragonmen, his head bowed between hunched shoulders. "Go," he said, gritting his teeth. And, as they hesitated, he pleaded, "Go!"

F'lar walked quickly from the room, followed by F'nor. The bronze rider crossed the quiet dim Hall with long strides and exploded into the startling sunlight. His momentum took him into the center of the square. There he stopped so abruptly that F'nor, hard on his heels, nearly collided with him.

"We will spend exactly the same time within the other Halls," he announced in a tight voice, his face averted from F'nor's eyes. F'lar's throat was constricted. It was difficult, suddenly, for him to speak. He swallowed hard, several times.

"To be dragonless . . ." murmured F'nor, pityingly. The encounter with Lytol had roiled his depths in a mournful way to which he was unaccustomed. That F'lar appeared equally shaken went far to dispel F'nor's private opinion that his half-brother was incapable of emotion.

"There is no other way once First Impression has been made. You know that," F'lar roused himself to say curtly. He strode off to the Hall bearing the Leathermen's device.

> The Hold is barred
> The Hall is bare.
> And men vanish.
> The soil is barren,
> The rock is bald.
> All hope banish.

Lessa was shoveling ashes from the hearth when the agitated messenger staggered into the Great Hall. She made herself as inconspicuous as possible so the Warder would not dismiss her. She had contrived to be sent to the Great Hall that morning, knowing that the Warder intended to brutalize the Head Clothman for the shoddy quality of the goods readied for shipment to Fax.

"Fax is coming! With dragonmen!" the man gasped out as he plunged into the dim Great Hall.

The Warder, who had been about to lash the Head Clothman, turned, stunned, from his victim. The courier, a farmholder from the edge of Ruatha, stumbled up to the Warder, so excited with his message that he grabbed the Warder's arm.

"How dare you leave your Hold?" and the Warder aimed his lash at the astonished holder. The force of the first blow knocked the man from his feet. Yelping, he scrambled out of reach of a second lashing. "Dragonmen indeed! Fax? Ha! He shuns Ruatha. There!" The Warder punctuated each denial with another blow, kicking the helpless wretch for good measure, before he turned breathless to glare at the clothman and the two underwarders. "How did he get in here with such a threadbare lie?" The Warder stalked to the great door. It was flung open just as he reached out for the iron handle. The ashenfaced guard officer rushed in, nearly toppling the Warder.

"Dragonmen! Dragons! All over Ruatha!" the man gibbered, arms

flailing wildly. He, too, pulled at the Warder's arm, dragging the stupefied official toward the outer courtyard, to bear out the truth of his
statement.

Lessa scooped up the last pile of ashes. Picking up her equipment,
she slipped out of the Great Hall. There was a very pleased smile on
her face under the screen of matted hair.

A dragonman at Ruatha! She must somehow contrive to get Fax
so humiliated, or so infuriated, that he would renounce his claim to the
Hold, in the presence of a dragonman. Then she could claim her
birthright.

But she would have to be extraordinarily wary. Dragonriders were
men apart. Anger did not cloud their intelligence. Greed did not sully
their judgment. Fear did not dull their reactions. Let the dense-witted
believe human sacrifice, unnatural lusts, insane revel. She was not so
gullible. And those stories went against her grain. Dragonmen were
still human and there was Weyr blood in *her* veins. It was the same
color as that of anyone else; enough of hers had been spilled to prove
that.

She halted for a moment, catching a sudden shallow breath. Was
this the danger she had sensed four days ago at dawn? The final encounter in her struggle to regain the Hold? No—there had been more
to that portent than revenge.

The ash bucket banged against her shins as she shuffled down the
low-ceilinged corridor to the stable door. Fax would find a cold welcome. She had laid no new fire on the hearth. Her laugh echoed back
unpleasantly from the damp walls. She rested her bucket and propped
her broom and shovel as she wrestled with the heavy bronze door that
gave into the new stables.

They had been built outside the cliff of Ruatha by Fax's first
Warder, a subtler man than all eight of his successors. He had achieved
more than all others and Lessa had honestly regretted the necessity of
his death. But he would have made her revenge impossible. He would
have caught her out before she had learned how to camouflage herself
and her little interferences. What had his name been? She could not
recall. Well, she regretted his death.

The second man had been properly greedy and it had been easy to set up a pattern of misunderstanding between Warder and craftsmen. That one had been determined to squeeze all profit from Ruathan goods so that some of it would drop into his pocket before Fax suspected a shortage. The craftsmen who had begun to accept the skillful diplomacy of the first Warder bitterly resented the second's grasping, high-handed ways. They resented the passing of the Old Line and, even more so, the way of its passing. They were unforgiving of insult to Ruatha, its now secondary position in the High Reaches, and they resented the individual indignities that holders, craftsmen and farmers alike suffered under the second Warder. It took little manipulation to arrange for matters at Ruatha to go from bad to worse.

The second was replaced and his successor fared no better. He was caught diverting goods, the best of the goods at that. Fax had had him executed. His bony head still hung in the main firepit above the great Tower.

The present incumbent had not been able to maintain the Hold in even the sorry condition in which he had assumed its management. Seemingly simple matters developed rapidly into disasters. Like the production of cloth . . . Contrary to his boasts to Fax, the quality had not improved, and the quantity had fallen off.

Now Fax was here. And with dragonmen! Why dragonmen? The import of the question froze Lessa, and the heavy door closing behind her barked her heels painfully. Dragonmen used to be frequent visitors at Ruatha, that she knew, and even vaguely remembered. Those memories were like a harper's tale, told of someone else, not something within her own experience. She had limited her fierce attention to Ruatha only. She could not even recall the name of Queen or Weyrwoman from the instructions of her childhood, nor could she recall hearing mention of any queen or weyrwoman by anyone in the Hold these past ten Turns.

Perhaps the dragonmen were finally going to call the lords of the Holds to task for the disgraceful show of greenery about the Holds. Well, Lessa was to blame for much of that in Ruatha but she defied even a dragonman to confront her with her guilt. Did all Ruatha fall to the Threads it would be better than remaining dependent to Fax! The heresy shocked Lessa even as she thought it.

Wishing she could as easily unburden her conscience of such blasphemy, she ditched the ashes on the stable midden. There was a sudden change in air pressure around her. Then a fleeting shadow caused her to glance up.

From behind the cliff above glided a dragon, its enormous wings spread to their fullest as he caught the morning updraft. Turning effortlessly, he descended. A second, a third, a full wing of dragons followed in soundless flight and patterned descent, graceful and awesome. The claxon rang belatedly from the Tower and from within the kitchens there issued the screams and shrieks of the terrified drudges.

Lessa took cover. She ducked into the kitchen where she was instantly seized by the assistant cook and thrust with a buffet and a kick toward the sinks. There she was put to scrubbing grease-encrusted serving bowls with cleansing sand.

The yelping canines were already lashed to the spitrun, turning a scrawny herdbeast that had been set to roast. The cook was ladling seasonings on the carcass, swearing at having to offer so poor a meal to so many guests, and some of them high-rank. Winter-dried fruits from the last scanty harvest had been set to soak and two of the oldest drudges were scraping roots.

An apprentice cook was kneading bread; another, carefully spicing a sauce. Looking fixedly at him, she diverted his hand from one spice box to a less appropriate one as he gave a final shake to the concoction. She added too much wood to the wall oven, insuring ruin for the breads. She controlled the canines deftly, slowing one and speeding the other so that the meat would be underdone on one side, burned on the other. That the feast should be a fast, the food presented found inedible, was her whole intention.

Above in the Hold, she had no doubt that certain other measures, undertaken at different times for this exact contingency, were being discovered.

Her fingers bloodied from a beating, one of the Warder's women came shrieking into the kitchen, hopeful of refuge there.

"Insects have eaten the best blankets to shreds! And a canine who had littered on the best linens snarled at me as she gave suck! And the rushes are noxious, the best chambers full of debris driven in by the winter wind. Somebody left the shutters ajar. Just a tiny bit, but it was enough . . ." the woman wailed, clutching her hand to her breast and rocking back and forth.

Lessa bent with great industry to shine the plates.

Watch-wher, watch-wher,
In your lair,
Watch well, watch-wher!
Who goes there?

"The watch-wher is hiding something," F'lar told F'nor as they consulted in the hastily cleaned Great Hall. The room delighted to hold the wintry chill although a generous fire now burned on the hearth.

"It was but gibbering when Canth spoke to it," F'nor remarked. He was leaning against the mantel, turning slightly from side to side to gather some warmth. He watched his wingleader's impatient pacing.

"Mnementh is calming it down," F'lar replied. "He may be able to sort out the nightmare. The creature may be more senile than aware, but . . ."

"I doubt it," F'nor concurred helpfully. He glanced with apprehension up at the webhung ceiling. He was certain he'd found most of the crawlers, but he didn't fancy their sting. Not on top of the discomforts already experienced in this forsaken Hold. If the night stayed mild, he intended curling up with Canth on the heights. "That would be more reasonable than anything Fax or his Warder have suggested."

"Hm-m-m," F'lar muttered, frowning at the brown rider.

"Well, it's unbelievable that Ruatha could have fallen to such disrepair in ten short Turns. Every dragon caught the feeling of power and it's obvious the watch-wher had been tampered with. That takes a good deal of control."

"From someone of the Blood," F'lar reminded him.

F'nor shot his wingleader a quick look, wondering if he could possibly be serious in the light of all information to the contrary.

"I grant you there is power here, F'lar," F'nor conceded. "It could easily be a hidden male of the old Blood. But we need a female. And

Fax made it plain, in his inimitable fashion, that he left none of the old Blood alive in the Hold the day he took it. No, no." The brown rider shook his head, as if he could dispel the lack of faith in his wingleader's curious insistence that the Search would end in Ruath with Ruathan blood.

"That watch-wher is hiding something and only someone of the Blood of its Hold can arrange that," F'lar said emphatically. He gestured around the Hall and toward the walls, bare of hangings. "Ruatha has been overcome. But she resists . . . subtly. I say it points to the old Blood, and power. Not power alone."

The obstinate expression in F'lar's eyes, the set of his jaw, suggested that F'nor seek another topic.

"The pattern was well-flown today," F'nor suggested tentatively. "Does a dragonman good to ride a flaming beast. Does the beast good, too. Keeps the digestive process in order."

F'lar nodded sober agreement. "Let R'gul temporize as he chooses. It is fitting and proper to ride a firespouting beast and these holders need to be reminded of Weyr power."

"Right now, anything would help our prestige," F'nor commented sourly. "What had Fax to say when he hailed you in the Pass?" F'nor knew his question was almost impertinent but if it were, F'lar would ignore it.

F'lar's slight smile was unpleasant and there was an ominous glint in his amber eyes.

"We talked of rule and resistance."

"Did he not also draw on you?" F'nor asked.

F'lar's smile deepened. "Until he remembered I was dragon-mounted."

"He's considered a vicious fighter," F'nor said.

"I am at some disadvantage?" F'lar asked, turning sharply on his brown rider, his face too controlled.

"To my knowledge, no," F'nor reassured his leader quickly. F'lar had tumbled every man in the Weyr, efficiently and easily. "But Fax kills often and without cause."

"And because we dragonmen do not seek blood, we are not to be feared as fighters?" snapped F'lar. "Are you ashamed of your heritage?"

"I? No!" F'nor sucked in his breath. "Nor any of our wing!" he added proudly. "But there is that in the attitude of the men in this progression of Fax's that . . . that makes me wish some excuse to fight."

"As you observed today, Fax seeks some excuse. And," F'lar added thoughtfully, "there is something here in Ruatha that unnerves our noble overlord."

He caught sight of Lady Tela, whom Fax had so courteously assigned him for comfort during the progression, waving to him from the inner Hold portal.

"A case in point. Fax's Lady Tela is some three months gone."

F'nor frowned at the insult to his leader.

"She giggles incessantly and appears so addlepated that one cannot decide whether she babbles out of ignorance or at Fax's suggestion. As she has apparently not bathed all winter, and is not, in any case, my ideal, I have"—F'lar grinned maliciously—"deprived myself of her kind offices."

F'nor hastily cleared his throat and his expression as Lady Tela approached them. He caught the unappealing odor from the scarf or handkerchief she waved constantly. Dragonmen endured a great deal for the Weyr. He moved away, with apparent courtesy, to join the rest of the dragonmen entering the Hall.

F'lar turned with equal courtesy to Lady Tela as she jabbered away about the terrible condition of the rooms which Lady Gemma and the other ladies had been assigned.

"The shutters, both sets, were ajar all winter long and you should have seen the trash on the floors. We finally got two of the drudges to sweep it all into the fireplace. And then that smoked something fearful 'till a man was sent up." Lady Tela giggled. "He found the access blocked by a chimney stone fallen aslant. The rest of the chimney, for a wonder, was in good repair."

She waved her handkerchief. F'lar held his breath as the gesture wafted an unappealing odor in his direction.

He glanced up the Hall toward the inner Hold door and saw Lady Gemma descending, her steps slow and awkward. Some subtle differ-

ence about her gait attracted him and he stared at her, trying to identify it.

"Oh, yes, poor Lady Gemma," Lady Tela babbled, sighing deeply.
"We are so concerned. Why Lord Fax insisted on her coming, I do not
know. She is not near her time and yet . . ." The lighthead's concern
sounded sincere.

F'lar's incipient hatred for Fax and his brutality matured abruptly.
He left his partner chattering to thin air and courteously extended his
arm to Lady Gemma to support her down the steps and to the table.
Only the brief tightening of her fingers on his forearm betrayed her
gratitude. Her face was very white and drawn, the lines deeply etched
around mouth and eyes, showing the effort she was expending.

"Some attempt has been made, I see, to restore order to the Hall,"
she remarked in a conversational tone.

"Some," F'lar admitted dryly, glancing around the grandly propor-
tioned Hall, its rafter festooned with the webs of many Turns. The inhabitants of those gossamer nests dropped from time to time, with ripe
splats, to the floor, onto the table and into the serving platters. Nothing replaced the old banners of the Ruathan Blood, which had been removed from the stark brown stone walls. Fresh rushes did obscure the
greasy flagstones. The trestle tables appeared recently sanded and
scraped, and the platters gleamed dully in the refreshed glows. Unfortunately, the brighter light was a mistake for it was much too unflatter-
ing.

"This was such a graceful Hall," Lady Gemma murmured for
F'lar's ears alone.

"You were a friend?" he asked, politely.

"Yes, in my youth." Her voice dropped expressively on the last
word, evoking for F'lar a happier girlhood. "It was a noble line!"

"Think you *one* might have escaped the sword?"

Lady Gemma flashed him a startled look, then quickly composed
her features, lest the exchange be noted. She gave a barely perceptible
shake of her head and then shifted her awkward weight to take her
place at the table. Graciously she inclined her head toward F'lar, both
dismissing and thanking him.

F'lar returned to his own partner and placed her at the table on his left. As the only person of rank who would dine that night at Ruath Hold, Lady Gemma was seated on his right; Fax would be beyond her. The dragonmen and Fax's upper soldiery would sit at the lower tables. No guildmen had been invited to Ruatha. Fax arrived just then with his current lady and two underleaders, the Warder bowing them effusively into the Hall. The man, F'lar noticed, kept a good distance from his overlord—as well as a Warder might whose responsibility was in this sorry condition. F'lar flicked a crawler away. Out of the corner of his eye, he saw Lady Gemma wince and shudder.

Fax stamped up to the raised table, his face black with suppressed rage. He pulled back his chair roughly, slamming it into Lady Gemma's before he seated himself. He pulled the chair to the table with a force that threatened to rock the none too stable trestle-top from its supporting legs. Scowling, he inspected his goblet and plate, fingering the surface, ready to throw them aside if they displeased him.

"A roast and fresh bread, Lord Fax, and such fruits and roots as are left. Had I but known of your arrival, I could have sent to Crom for . . ."

"Sent to Crom?" roared Fax, slamming the plate he was inspecting into the table so forcefully the rim bent under his hands. The Warder winced again as if he himself had been maimed.

"The day one of my Holds cannot support itself *or* the visit of its rightful overlord, I shall renounce it."

Lady Gemma gasped. Simultaneously the dragons roared. F'lar felt the unmistakable surge of power. His eyes instinctively sought F'nor at the lower table. The brown rider—all the dragonmen—had experienced that inexplicable shaft of exultation.

"What's wrong, Dragonman?" snapped Fax.

F'lar, affecting unconcern, stretched his legs under the table and assumed an indolent posture in the heavy chair.

"Wrong?"

"The dragons!"

"Oh, nothing. They often roar . . . at the sunset, at a flock of passing wherries, at mealtimes," and F'lar smiled amiably at the Lord of the High Reaches. Beside him his tablemate gave a squeak.

"Mealtimes? Have they not been fed?"

"Oh, yes. Five days ago."

"Oh. Five . . . days ago? And are they hungry . . . now?" Her voice trailed into a whisper of fear, her eyes grew round.

"In a few days," F'lar assured her. Under cover of his detached amusement, F'lar scanned the Hall. That surge had come from nearby. Either in the Hall or just outside. It must have been from within. It came so soon upon Fax's speech that his words must have triggered it. And the power had had an indefinably feminine touch to it.

One of Fax's women? F'lar found that hard to credit. Mnementh had been close to all of them and none had shown a vestige of power. Much less, with the exception of Lady Gemma, any intelligence.

One of the Hall women? So far he had seen only the sorry drudges and the aging females the Warder had as housekeepers. The Warder's personal woman? He must discover if that man had one. One of the Hold guards' women? F'lar suppressed an intense desire to rise and search.

"You mount a guard?" he asked Fax casually.

"Double at Ruath Hold!" he was told in a tight, hard voice, ground out from somewhere deep in Fax's chest.

"Here?" F'lar all but laughed out loud, gesturing around the sadly appointed chamber.

"Here! Food!" Fax changed the subject with a roar.

Five drudges, two of them women in brown-gray rags such that F'lar hoped they had had nothing to do with the preparation of the meal, staggered in under the emplattered herdbeast. No one with so much as a trace of power would sink to such depths, unless . . .

The aroma that reached him as the platter was placed on the serving table distracted him. It reeked of singed bone and charred meat. The Warder frantically sharpened his tools as if a keen edge could somehow slice acceptable portions from this unlikely carcass.

Lady Gemma caught her breath again and F'lar saw her hands curl tightly around the armrests. He saw the convulsive movement of her throat as she swallowed. He, too, did not look forward to this repast.

The drudges reappeared with wooden trays of bread. Burnt crusts had been scraped and cut, in some places, from the loaves before serving. As other trays were borne in, F'lar tired to catch sight of the faces of the servitors. Matted hair obscured the face of the one who presented a dish of legumes swimming in greasy liquid. Revolted, F'lar poked through the legumes to find properly cooked portions to offer Lady Gemma. She waved them aside, her face ill-concealing her discomfort.

As F'lar was about to turn and serve Lady Tela, he saw Lady Gemma's hand clutch convulsively at the chair arms. He realized that she was not merely nauseated by the unappetizing food. She was seized with labor contractions.

F'lar glanced in Fax's direction. The overlord was scowling blackly at the attempts of the Warder to find edible portions of meat to serve.

F'lar touched Lady Gemma's arm with light fingers. She turned just enough to look at F'lar from the corner of her eye. She managed a socially correct half-smile.

"I dare not leave just now, Lord F'lar. He is always dangerous at Ruatha. And it may only be false pangs."

F'lar was dubious as he saw another shudder pass through her frame. The woman would have been a fine weyrwoman, he thought ruefully, were she but younger.

The Warder, his hands shaking, presented Fax the sliced meats. There were slivers of overdone flesh and portions of almost edible meats, but not much of either.

One furious wave of Fax's broad fist and the Warder had the plate, meats and juice, square in the face. Despite himself, F'lar sighed, for those undoubtedly constituted the only edible portions of the entire beast.

"You call this food? *You call this food?*" Fax bellowed. His voice boomed back from the bare vault of the ceiling, shaking crawlers from their webs as the sound shattered the fragile strands. "Slop! *Slop!*"

F'lar rapidly brushed crawlers from Lady Gemma who was helpless in the throes of a very strong contraction.

"It's all we had on such short notice," the Warder squealed, juices streaking down his cheeks. Fax threw the goblet at him and the wine went streaming down the man's chest. The steaming dish of roots followed and the man yelped as the hot liquid splashed over him.

"My lord, my lord, had I but known!"

"Obviously, Ruatha *cannot* support the visit of its Lord. You must renounce it," F'lar heard himself saying.

His shock at such words issuing from his mouth was as great as that of everyone else in the Hall. Silence fell, broken by the splat of falling crawlers and the drip of root liquid from the Warder's shoulders to the rushes. The grating of Fax's boot-heel was clearly audible as he swung slowly around to face the bronze rider.

As F'lar conquered his own amazement and rapidly tried to predict what to do next to mend matters, he saw F'nor rise slowly to his feet, hand on dagger hilt.

"I did not hear you correctly?" Fax asked, his face blank of all expression, his eyes snapping.

Unable to comprehend how he could have uttered such an arrant challenge, F'lar managed to assume a languid pose.

"You did mention," he drawled, "that if any of your Holds could not support itself and the visit of its rightful overlord, you would renounce it."

Fax stared back at F'lar, his face a study of swiftly suppressed emotions, the glint of triumph dominant. F'lar, his face stiff with the forced expression of indifference, was casting swiftly about in his mind. In the name of the Egg, had he lost all sense of discretion?

Pretending utter unconcern, he stabbed some vegetables onto his knife and began to munch on them. As he did so, he noticed F'nor glancing slowly around the Hall, scrutinizing everyone. Abruptly F'lar realized what had happened. Somehow, in making that statement, he, a dragonman, had responded to a covert use of the power. F'lar, the bronze rider, was being put into a position where he would *have* to fight Fax. Why? For what end? To get Fax to renounce the Hold? Incredible! But, there could be only one possible reason for such a turn of events. An exultation as sharp as pain swelled within F'lar. It was all he could do to maintain his pose of bored indifference, all he could do to turn his attention to thwarting Fax, should he press for a duel. A duel would serve no purpose. He, F'lar, had no time to waste on it.

A groan escaped Lady Gemma and broke the eye-locked stance of the two antagonists. Irritated, Fax looked down at her, fist clenched and half-raised to strike her for her temerity in interrupting her lord and master. The contraction that contorted the swollen belly was as obvious as the woman's pain. F'lar dared not look toward her but he wondered if she had deliberately groaned aloud to break the tension.

Incredibly, Fax began to laugh. He threw back his head, showing big, stained teeth, and roared.

"Aye, renounce it, in favor of her issue, if it is male . . . and lives!" he crowed, laughing raucously.

"Heard and witnessed!" F'lar snapped, jumping to his feet and pointing to the riders. They were on their feet in the instant. "Heard and witnessed!" they averred in the traditional manner.

With that movement, everyone began to babble at once in nervous relief. The other women, each reacting in her way to the imminence of birth, called orders to the servants and advice to each other. They converged toward Lady Gemma, hovering undecidedly out of Fax's range, like silly wherries disturbed from their roosts. It was obvious they were torn between their fear of the lord and their desire to reach the laboring woman.

He gathered their intentions as well as their reluctance and, still stridently laughing, knocked back his chair. He stepped over it, strode down to the meatstand and stood hacking off pieces with his knife, stuffing them, juice dripping, into his mouth without ceasing his guffawing.

As F'lar bent toward Lady Gemma to assist her out of her chair, she grabbed his arm urgently. Their eyes met, hers clouded with pain. She pulled him closer.

"He means to kill you, Bronze Rider. He loves to kill," she whispered.

"Dragonmen are not easily killed, but I am grateful to you."

"I do not want you killed," she said, softly, biting at her lip. "We have so few bronze riders."

F'lar stared at her, startled. Did she, Fax's lady, actually believe in the Old Laws?

F'lar beckoned to two of the Warder's men to carry her up into the Hold. He caught Lady Tela by the arm as she fluttered past him.

"What do you need?"

"Oh, oh," she exclaimed, her face twisted with panic; she was distractedly wringing her hands. "Water, hot. Clean cloths. And a birthing-woman. Oh, yes, we must have a birthing-woman."

F'lar looked about for one of the Hold women, his glance sliding over the first disreputable figure who had started to mop up the spilled food. He signaled instead for the Warder and peremptorily ordered him to send for the woman. The Warder kicked at the drudge on the floor.

"You . . . you! Whatever your name is, go get her from the crafthold. You must know who she is."

The drudge evaded the parting kick the Warder aimed in her direction with a nimbleness at odds with her appearance of extreme age and decrepitude. She scurried across the Hall and out the kitchen door.

Fax sliced and speared meat, occasionally bursting out with a louder bark of laughter as his inner thoughts amused him. F'lar sauntered down to the carcass and, without waiting for invitation from his host, began to carve neat slices also, beckoning his men over. Fax's soldiers, however, waited until their lord had eaten his fill.

> Lord of the Hold, your charge is sure
> In thick walls, metal doors and no verdure.

Lessa sped from the Hall to summon the birthing-woman, seething with frustration. So close! So close! How could she come so close and yet fail? Fax should have challenged the dragonman. And the dragonman was strong and young, his face that of a fighter, stern and controlled. He should not have temporized. Was all honor dead in Pern, smothered by green grass?

And why, oh why, had Lady Gemma chosen that precious moment to go into labor? If her groan hadn't distracted Fax, the fight would have begun and not even Fax, for all his vaunted prowess as a vicious fighter, would have prevailed against a dragonman who had her—Lessa's—support! The Hold must be secured to its rightful Blood again. Fax must not leave Ruatha, alive, again!

Above her, on the High Tower, the great bronze dragon gave forth a weird croon, his many-faceted eyes sparkling in the gathering darkness.

Unconsciously she silenced him as she would have done the watch-wher. Ah, that watch-wher. He had not come out of his den at her passing. She knew the dragons had been at him. She could hear him gibbering in panic.

The slant of the road toward the crafthold lent impetus to her flying feet and she had to brace herself to a sliding stop at the birthing-woman's stone threshold. She banged on the closed door and heard the frightened exclamation within.

"A birth. A birth at the Hold," Lessa cried.

"A birth?" came the muffled cry and the latches were thrown up on the door. "At the Hold?"

"Fax's lady and, as you love life, hurry! For if it is male, it will be Ruatha's own lord."

That ought to fetch her, thought Lessa, and in that instant, the door was flung open by the man of the house. Lessa could see the birthing-woman gathering up her things in haste, piling them into her shawl. Lessa hurried the woman out, up the steep road to the Hold, under the Tower gate, grabbing the woman as she tried to run at the sight of a dragon peering down at her. Lessa drew her into the Court and pushed her, resisting, into the Hall.

The woman clutched at the inner door, balking at the sight of the gathering there. Lord Fax, his feet up on the trestle table, was paring his fingernails with his knife blade, still chuckling. The dragonmen in their wher-hide tunics were eating quietly at one table while the soldiers were having their turn at the meat.

The bronze rider noticed their entrance and pointed urgently toward the inner Hold. The birthing-woman seemed frozen to the spot. Lessa tugged futilely at her arm, urging her to cross the Hall. To her surprise, the bronze rider strode to them.

"Go quickly, woman, Lady Gemma is before her time," he said, frowning with concern, gesturing imperatively toward the Hold entrance. He caught her by the shoulder and led her, all unwilling, Lessa tugging away at her other arm.

When they reached the stairs, he relinquished his grip, nodding to Lessa to escort her the rest of the way. Just as they reached the massive inner door, Lessa noticed how sharply the dragonman was looking at them—at her hand, on the birthing-woman's arm. Warily, she glanced at her hand and saw it, as if it belonged to a stranger: the long fingers, shapely despite dirt and broken nails; her small hand, delicately boned, gracefully placed despite the urgency of the grip. She blurred it and hurried on.

> Honor those the dragons heed,
> In thought and favor, word and deed.
> Worlds are lost or worlds are saved
> By those dangers dragonbraved.
>
> Dragonman, avoid excess;
> Greed will bring the Weyr distress;
> To the ancient Laws adhere,
> Prospers thus the Dragon weyr.

An unintelligible ululation raised the waiting men to their feet, startled from private meditations and diversion of Bonethrows. Only Fax remained unmoved at the alarm, save that the slight sneer, which had settled on his face hours past, deepened to smug satisfaction.

"Dead-ed-ed," the tidings reverberated down the rocky corridors of the Hold. The weeping lady seemed to erupt out of the passage from the inner Hold, flying down the steps to sink into an hysterical heap at Fax's feet. "She's dead. Lady Gemma is dead. There was too much blood. It was too soon. She was too old to bear more children."

F'lar couldn't decide whether the woman was apologizing for, or exulting in, the woman's death. She certainly couldn't be criticizing her Lord for placing Lady Gemma in such peril. F'lar, however, was sincerely sorry at Gemma's passing. She had been a brave, fine woman.

And now, what would be Fax's next move? F'lar caught F'nor's identically quizzical glance and shrugged expressively.

"The child lives!" a curiously distorted voice announced, penetrating the rising noise in the Great Hall. The words electrified the atmosphere. Every head slewed round sharply toward the portal to the inner Hold where the drudge, a totally unexpected messenger, stood poised on the top step.

"It is male!" This announcement rang triumphantly in the still Hall.

Fax jerked himself to his feet, kicking aside the wailer at his feet, scowling ominously at the drudge. "What did you say, woman?"

"The child lives. It is male," the creature repeated, descending the stairs.

Incredulity and rage suffused Fax's face. His body seemed to coil up.

"Ruatha has a new lord!" Staring intently at the overlord, she advanced, her mien purposeful, almost menacing.

The tentative cheers of the Warder's men were drowned by the roaring of the dragons.

Fax erupted into action. He leaped across the intervening space, bellowing. Before Lessa could dodge, his fist crashed down across her face. She fell heavily to the stone floor, where she lay motionless, a bundle of dirty rags.

"Hold, Fax!" F'lar's voice broke the silence as the Lord of the High Reaches flexed his leg to kick her.

Fax whirled, his hand automatically closing on his knife hilt.

"It was heard and witnessed, Fax," F'lar cautioned him, one hand outstretched in warning, "by dragonmen. Stand by your sworn and witnessed oath!"

"Witnessed? By Dragonmen?" cried Fax with a derisive laugh. "Dragonwomen, you mean," he sneered, his eyes blazing with contempt, as he made one sweeping gesture of scorn.

He was momentarily taken aback by the speed with which the bronze rider's knife appeared in his hand.

"Dragonwomen?" F'lar queried, his lips curling back over his teeth, his voice dangerously soft. Glowlight flickered off his circling knife as he advanced on Fax.

"Women! Parasites on Pern. The Weyr power is over. Over!" Fax roared, leaping forward to land in a combat crouch.

*   *   *

The two antagonists were dimly aware of the scurry behind them, of tables pulled roughly aside to give the duelists space. F'lar could spare no glance at the crumpled form of the drudge. Yet he was sure, through and beyond instinct sure, that she was the source of power. He had felt it as she entered the room. The dragons' roaring confirmed it. If that fall had killed her . . . He advanced on Fax, leaping high to avoid the slashing blade as Fax unwound from the crouch with a powerful lunge.

F'lar evaded the attack easily, noticing his opponent's reach, deciding he had a slight advantage there. But not much. Fax had had much more actual hand-to-hand killing experience than had he whose duels had always ended at first blood on the practice floor. F'lar made due note to avoid closing with the burly lord. The man was heavy-chested, dangerous from sheer mass. F'lar must use agility as his weapon, not brute strength.

Fax feinted, testing F'lar for weakness, or indiscretion. The two crouched, facing each other across six feet of space, knife hands weaving, their free hands, spread-fingered, ready to grab.

Again Fax pressed the attack. F'lar allowed him to close, just near enough to dodge away with a backhanded swipe. Fabric ripped under the tip of his knife. He heard Fax snarl. The overlord was faster on his feet than his bulk suggested and F'lar had to dodge a second time, feeling Fax's knife score his wher-hide jerkin.

Grimly the two circled, each looking for an opening in the other's defense. Fax plowed in, trying to corner the lighter, faster man between raised platform and wall.

F'lar countered, ducking low under Fax's flailing arm, slashing obliquely across Fax's side. The overlord caught at him, yanking savagely, and F'lar was trapped against the other man's side, straining desperately with his left hand to keep the knife arm up. F'lar brought up his knee, and ducked away as Fax gasped and buckled from the pain in his groin, but Fax struck in passing. Sudden fire laced F'lar's left shoulder.

Fax's face was red with anger and he wheezed from pain and shock. But the infuriated lord straightened up and charged. F'lar was forced to sidestep quickly before Fax could close with him. F'lar put the meat table between them, circling warily, flexing his shoulder to assess the extent of the knife's slash. It was painful, but the arm could be used.

Suddenly Fax scooped up some fatty scraps from the meat tray and hurled them at F'lar. The dragonman ducked and Fax came around the table with a rush. F'lar leaped sideways. Fax's flashing blade came within inches of his abdomen, as his own knife sliced down the outside of Fax's arm. Instantly the two pivoted to face each other again, but Fax's left arm hung limply at his side.

F'lar darted in, pressing his luck as the Lord of the High Reaches staggered. But F'lar misjudged the man's condition and suffered a terrific kick in the side as he tried to dodge under the feinting knife. Doubled with pain, F'lar rolled frantically away from his charging adversary. Fax was lurching forward, trying to fall on him, to pin the lighter dragonman down for a final thrust. Somehow F'lar got to his feet, attempting to straighten to meet Fax's stumbling charge. His very position saved him. Fax over-reached his mark and staggered off balance. F'lar brought his right hand over with as much strength as he could muster and his blade plunged through Fax's unprotected back until he felt the point stick in the chest plate.

The defeated lord fell flat to the flagstones. The force of his descent dislodged the dagger from his chestbone and an inch of bloody blade re-emerged.

F'lar stared down at the dead man. There was no pleasure in killing, he realized, only relief that he himself was still alive. He wiped his forehead on his sleeve and forced himself erect, his side throbbing with the pain of that last kick and his left shoulder burning. He half-stumbled to the drudge, still sprawled where she had fallen.

He gently turned her over, noting the terrible bruise spreading across her cheek under the dirty skin. He heard F'nor take command of the tumult in the Hall.

The dragonman laid a hand, trembling in spite of an effort to control himself, on the woman's breast to feel for a heartbeat . . . It was there, slow but strong.

A deep sigh escaped him for either blow or fall could have proved fatal. Fatal, perhaps, for Pern as well.

Relief was colored with disgust. There was no telling under the filth how old this creature might be. He raised her in his arms, her light body no burden even to his battle-weary strength. Knowing F'nor would handle any trouble efficiently, F'lar carried the drudge to his own chamber.

Putting the body on the high bed, he stirred up the fire and added more glows to the bedside bracket. His gorge rose at the thought of touching the filthy mat of hair but nonetheless and gently, he pushed it back from the face, turning the head this way and that. The features were small, regular. One arm, clear of rags, was reasonably clean above the elbow but marred by bruises and old scars. The skin was firm and unwrinkled. The hands, when he took them in his, were filthy but well-shaped and delicately boned.

F'lar began to smile. Yes, she had blurred that hand so skillfully that he had actually doubted what he had first seen. And yes, beneath grime and grease, she was young. Young enough for the Weyr. And no born drab. There was no taint of common blood here. It was pure, no matter whose the line, and he rather thought she was indeed Ruathan. One who had by some unknown agency escaped the massacre ten Turns ago and bided her time for revenge. Why else force Fax to renounce the Hold?

Delighted and fascinated by this unexpected luck, F'lar reached out to tear the dress from the unconscious body and found himself constrained not to. The girl had roused. Her great, hungry eyes fastened on his, not fearful or expectant; wary.

A subtle change occurred in her face. F'lar watched, his smile deepening, as she shifted her regular features into an illusion of disagreeable ugliness and great age.

"Trying to confuse a dragonman, girl?" he chuckled. He made no further move to touch her but settled against the great carved post of the bed. He crossed his arms sternly on his chest, thought better of it immediately, and eased his sore arm. "Your name, girl, and rank, too."

She drew herself upright slowly against the headboard, her features no longer blurred. They faced each other across the high bed.

"Fax?"

"Dead. Your name!"

A look of exulting triumph flooded her face. She slipped from the bed, standing unexpectedly tall. "Then I reclaim my own. I am of the Ruathan Blood. I claim Ruath," she announced in a ringing voice.

F'lar stared at her a moment, delighted with her proud bearing. Then he threw back his head and laughed.

"This? This crumbling heap?" He could not help but mock the disparity between her manner and her dress. "Oh, no. Besides, Lady, we dragonmen heard and witnessed Fax's oath renouncing the Hold in favor of his heir. Shall I challenge the babe, too, for you? And choke him with his swaddling cloth?"

Her eyes flashed, her lips parted in a terrible smile.

"There is no heir. Gemma died, the babe unborn. I lied."

"Lied?" F'lar demanded, angry.

"Yes," she taunted him with a toss of her chin. "I lied. There was no babe born. I merely wanted to be sure you challenged Fax."

He grabbed her wrist, stung that he had twice fallen to her prodding.

"You provoked a dragonman to fight? To kill? *When he is on Search?*"

"Search? Why should I care about a Search? I've Ruatha as my Hold again. For ten Turns, I have worked and waited, schemed and suffered for that. What could your Search mean to me?"

F'lar wanted to strike that look of haughty contempt from her face. He twisted her arm savagely, bringing her to her knees before he released his grip. She laughed at him, and scuttled to one side. She was on her feet and out the door before he could give chase.

Swearing to himself, he raced down the rocky corridors, knowing she would have to make for the Hall to get out of the Hold. However, when he reached the Hall, there was no sign of her fleeing figure among those still loitering.

"Has that creature come this way?" he called to F'nor who was, by chance, standing by the door to the Court.

"No. Is she the source of power after all?"

"Yes, she is," F'lar answered, galled all the more. "And Ruathan Blood at that!"

"Oh ho! Does she depose the babe, then?" F'nor asked, gesturing

toward the birthing-woman who occupied a seat close to the now blazing hearth.

F'lar paused, about to return to search the Hold's myriad passages.
He stared, momentarily confused, at this brown rider.

"Babe? What babe?"

"The male child Lady Gemma bore," F'nor replied, surprised by
F'lar's uncomprehending look.

"It lives?"

"Yes. A strong babe, the woman says, for all that he was premature
and taken forcibly from his dead dame's belly."

F'lar threw back his head with a shout of laughter. For all her
scheming, she had been outdone by truth.

At that moment, he heard Mnementh roar in unmistakable elation and the curious warble of other dragons.

"Mnementh has caught her," F'lar cried, grinning with jubilation.
He strode down the steps, past the body of the former Lord of the High
Reaches and out into the main court.

He saw that the bronze dragon was gone from his Tower perch
and called him. An agitation drew his eyes upward. He saw Mnementh
spiraling down into the Court, his front paws clasping something.
Mnementh informed F'lar that he had seen her climbing from one of
the high windows and had simply plucked her from the ledge, knowing
the dragonman sought her. The bronze dragon settled awkwardly onto
his hind legs, his wings working to keep him balanced. Carefully he set
the girl on her feet and formed a precise cage around her with his huge
talons. She stood motionless within that circle, her face toward the
wedge-shaped head that swayed above her.

The watch-wher, shrieking terror, anger and hatred, was lunging
violently to the end of its chain, trying to come to Lessa's aid. It
grabbed at F'lar as he strode to the two.

"You've courage enough, girl," he admitted, resting one hand casually on Mnementh's upper claw. Mnementh was enormously pleased
with himself and swiveled his head down for his eye ridges to be
scratched.

"You did not lie, you know," F'lar said, unable to resist taunting
the girl.

Slowly she turned toward him, her face impassive. She was not afraid of dragons, F'lar realized with approval.

"The babe lives. And it is male."

She could not control her dismay and her shoulders sagged briefly before she pulled herself erect.

"Ruatha is mine," she insisted in a tense low voice.

"Aye, and it would have been, had you approached me directly when the wing arrived here."

Her eyes widened. "What do you mean?"

"A dragonman may champion anyone whose grievance is just. By the time we reached Ruath Hold, I was quite ready to challenge Fax given any reasonable cause, despite the Search." This was not the whole truth but F'lar must teach this girl the folly of trying to control dragonmen. "Had you paid any attention to your harper's songs, you'd know your rights. And," F'lar's voice held a vindictive edge that surprised him, "Lady Gemma might not now lie dead. She suffered far more at that tyrant's hand than you."

Something in his manner told him that she regretted Lady Gemma's death, that it had affected her deeply.

"What good is Ruatha to you now?" he demanded, a broad sweep of his arm taking in the ruined court yard and the Hold, the entire unproductive valley of Ruatha. "You have indeed accomplished your ends; a profitless conquest and its conqueror's death." F'lar snorted: "All seven Holds will revert to their legitimate Blood, and time they did. One Hold, one lord. Of course, you might have to fight others, infected with Fax's greed. Could you hold Ruatha against attack . . . now . . . in her decline?"

"Ruatha is mine!"

"Ruatha?" F'lar's laugh was derisive. "When you could be Weyrwoman?"

"Weyrwoman?" she breathed, staring at him.

"Yes, little fool. I said I rode in Search . . . it's about time you attended to more than Ruatha. And the object of my Search is . . . you!"

She stared at the finger he pointed at her as if it were dangerous.

"By the First Egg, girl, you've power in you to spare when you can turn a dragonman, all unwitting, to do your bidding. Ah, but never again, for now I am on guard against you."

Mnementh crooned approvingly, the sound a soft rumble in his throat. He arched his neck so that one eye was turned directly on the girl, gleaming in the darkness of the court.

F'lar noticed with detached pride that she neither flinched nor blanched at the proximity of an eye greater than her own head.

"He likes to have his eye ridges scratched," F'lar remarked in a friendly tone, changing tactics.

"I know," she said softly and reached out a hand to do that service.

"Nemorth's queen," F'lar continued, "is close to death. This time we must have a strong Weyrwoman."

"This time—the Red Star?" the girl gasped, turning frightened eyes to F'lar.

"You understand what it means?"

"There is danger . . ." she began in a bare whisper, glancing apprehensively eastward.

F'lar did not question by what miracle she appreciated the imminence of danger. He had every intention of taking her to the Weyr by sheer force if necessary. But something within him wanted very much for her to accept the challenge voluntarily. A rebellious Weyrwoman would be even more dangerous than a stupid one. This girl had too much power and was too used to guile and strategy. It would be a calamity to antagonize her with injudicious handling.

"There is danger for all Pern. Not just Ruatha," he said, allowing a note of entreaty to creep into his voice. "And *you* are needed. Not by Ruatha," a wave of his hand dismissed that consideration as a negligible one compared to the total picture. "We are doomed without a strong Weyrwoman. Without you."

"Gemma kept saying *all* the bronze riders were needed," she murmured in a dazed whisper.

What did she mean by that statement? F'lar frowned. Had she heard a word he had said? He pressed his argument, certain only that he had already struck one responsive chord.

"You've won here. Let the babe," he saw her startled rejection of that idea and ruthlessly qualified it, ". . . Gemma's babe . . . be reared at Ruatha. You have command of all the Holds as Weyrwoman, not ruined Ruatha alone. You've accomplished Fax's death. Leave off vengeance."

She stared at F'lar with wonder, absorbing his words.

"I never thought beyond Fax's death," she admitted slowly. "I never thought what should happen then."

Her confusion was almost childlike and struck F'lar forcibly. He had had no time, or desire, to consider her prodigious accomplishment. Now he realized some measure of her indomitable character. She could not have been much over ten Turns of age herself when Fax had murdered her family. Yet somehow, so young, she had set herself a goal and managed to survive both brutality and detection long enough to secure the usurper's death. What a Weyrwoman she would be! In the tradition of those of Ruathan blood. The light of the paler moon made her look young and vulnerable and almost pretty.

"You can be Weyrwoman," he insisted gently.

"Weyrwoman," she breathed, incredulous, and gazed round the inner court bathed in soft moonlight. He thought she wavered.

"Or perhaps you enjoy rags?" he said, making his voice harsh, mocking. "And matted hair, dirty feet and cracked hands? Sleeping in straw, eating rinds? You are young . . . that is, I assume you are young," and his voice was frankly skeptical. She glared at him, her lips firmly pressed together. "Is this the be-all and end-all of your ambition? What are you that this little corner of the great world is *all* you want?" He paused and with utter contempt added, "The blood of Ruatha has thinned, I see. You're afraid!"

"I am Lessa, daughter of the Lord of Ruath," she countered, stung. She drew herself erect. Her eyes flashed. "I am afraid of nothing!"

F'lar contented himself with a slight smile.

Mnementh, however, threw up his head, and stretched out his sinuous neck to its whole length. His full-throated peal rang out down the valley. The bronze dragon communicated his awareness to F'lar that Lessa had accepted the challenge. The other dragons answered back, their warbles shriller than Mnementh's bellow. The watch-wher which had cowered at the end of its chain lifted its voice in a thin, un-nerving screech until the Hold emptied of its startled occupants.

"F'nor," the bronze rider called, waving his wingleader to him. "Leave half the flight to guard the Hold. Some nearby lord might think to emulate Fax's example. Send one rider to the High Reaches with the glad news. You go directly to the Cloth Hall and speak to L'tol . . . Lytol." F'lar grinned. "I think he would make an exemplary Warder and Lord Surrogate for this Hold in the name of the Weyr and the babe."

The brown rider's face expressed enthusiasm for his mission as he began to comprehend his leader's intentions. With Fax dead and Ruatha under the protection of dragonmen, particularly that same one who had dispatched Fax, the Hold would have wise management.

"She caused Ruatha's deterioration?" he asked.

"And nearly ours with her machinations," F'lar replied but having found the admirable object of his Search, he could not be magnani-mous. "Suppress your exultation, brother," he advised quickly as he took note of F'nor's expression. "The new queen must also be Im-pressed."

"I'll settle arrangements here. Lytol is an excellent choice," F'nor said.

"Who is this Lytol?" demanded Lessa pointedly. She had twisted the mass of filthy hair back from her face. In the moonlight the dirt was less noticeable. F'lar caught F'nor looking at her with an all too easily read expression. He signaled F'nor, with a peremptory gesture, to carry out his orders without delay.

"Lytol is a dragonless man," F'lar told the girl, "no friend to Fax. He will ward the Hold well and it will prosper." He added persuasively with a quelling stare full on her, "Won't it?"

She regarded him somberly, without answering, until he chuckled softly at her discomfiture.

"We'll return to the Weyr," he announced, proffering a hand to guide her to Mnementh's side.

The bronze one had extended his head toward the watch-wher who now lay panting on the ground, its chain limp in the dust.

"Oh," Lessa sighed, and dropped beside the grotesque beast. It raised its head slowly, lurring piteously.

"Mnementh says it is very old and soon will sleep itself to death."

Lessa cradled the bestial head in her arms, scratching it behind the ears.

"Come, Lessa of Pern," F'lar said, impatient to be up and away.

She rose slowly but obediently. "It saved me. It knew me."

"It knows it did well," F'lar assured her, brusquely, wondering at such an uncharacteristic show of sentiment in her.

He took her hand again, to help her to her feet and lead her back to Mnementh. As they turned, he glimpsed the watch-wher, launching itself at a dead run after Lessa. The chain, however, held fast. The beast's neck broke, with a sickening audible snap.

Lessa was on her knees in an instant, cradling the repulsive head in her arms.

"Why, you foolish thing, why?" she asked in a stunned whisper as the light in the beast's green-gold eyes dimmed and died out.

Mnementh informed F'lar that the creature had lived this long only to preserve the Ruathan line. At Lessa's imminent departure, it had welcomed death.

A convulsive shudder went through Lessa's slim body. F'lar watched as she undid the heavy buckle that fastened the metal collar about the watch-wher's neck. She threw the tether away with a violent motion. Tenderly she laid the watch-wher on the cobbles. With one last caress to the clipped wings, she rose in a fluid movement and walked resolutely to Mnementh without a single backward glance. She stepped calmly to the dragon's raised leg and seated herself, as F'lar directed, on the great neck.

F'lar glanced around the courtyard at the remainder of his wing which had reformed there. The Hold folk had retreated back into the safety of the Great Hall. When his wingmen were all astride, he vaulted to Mnementh's neck, behind the girl.

"Hold tightly to my arms," he ordered her as he took hold of the smallest neck ridge and gave the command to fly.

Her fingers closed spasmodically around his forearm as the great bronze dragon took off, the enormous wings working to achieve height from the vertical takeoff. Mnementh preferred to fall into flight from a cliff or tower. Like all dragons, he tended to indolence. F'lar glanced behind him, saw the other dragonmen form the flight line, spread out to cover those still on guard at Ruatha Hold.

When they had reached a sufficient altitude, he told Mnementh to transfer, going *between* to the Weyr.

Only a gasp indicated the girl's astonishment as they hung *between*. Accustomed as he was to the sting of the profound cold, to the awesome utter lack of light and sound, F'lar still found the sensations unnerving. Yet the uncommon transfer spanned no more time than it took to cough thrice.

Mnementh rumbled approval of this candidate's calm reaction as they flicked out of the eerie *between*.

And then they were above the Weyr, Mnementh setting his wings to glide in the bright daylight, half a world away from night-time Ruatha.

As they circled above the great stony trough of the Weyr, F'lar peered at Lessa's face, pleased with the delight mirrored there; she showed no trace of fear as they hung a thousand lengths above the high Benden mountain range. Then, as the seven dragons roared their incoming cry, an incredulous smile lit her face.

The other wingmen dropped into a wide spiral, down, down while Mnementh elected to descend in lazy circles. The dragonmen peeled off smartly and dropped, each to his own tier in the caves of the Weyr. Mnementh finally completed his leisurely approach to their quarters, whistling shrilly to himself as he braked his forward speed with a twist of his wings, dropping lightly at last to the ledge. He crouched as F'lar swung the girl to the rough rock, scored from thousands of clawed landings.

"This leads only to our quarters," he told her as they entered the corridor, vaulted and wide for the easy passage of great bronze dragons.

As they reached the huge natural cavern that had been his since Mnementh achieved maturity, F'lar looked about him with eyes fresh from his first prolonged absence from the Weyr. The huge chamber was unquestionably big, certainly larger than most of the halls he had visited in Fax's procession. Those halls were intended as gathering places for men, not the habitations of dragons. But suddenly he saw his own quarters were nearly as shabby as all Ruatha. Benden was, of a certainty, one of the oldest dragon weyrs, as Ruatha was one of the oldest Holds, but that excused nothing. How many dragons had bedded in that hollow to make solid rock conform to dragon proportions! How many feet had worn the path past the dragon's weyr into the sleeping chamber, to the bathing room beyond where the natural warm spring provided ever-fresh water! But the wall hangings were faded and unraveling and there were grease stains on lintel and floor that should be sanded away.

He noticed the wary expression on Lessa's face as he paused in the sleeping room.

"I must feed Mnementh immediately. So you may bathe first," he said, rummaging in a chest and finding clean clothes for her, discards of other previous occupants of his quarters, but far more presentable than her present covering. He carefully laid back in the chest the white wool robe that was traditional Impression garb. She would wear that later. He tossed several garments at her feet and a bag of sweetsand, gesturing to the hanging that obscured the way to the bath.

He left her, then, the clothes in a heap at her feet, for she made no effort to catch anything.

Mnementh informed him that F'nor was feeding Canth and that he, Mnementh, was hungry, too. *She* didn't trust F'lar but she wasn't afraid of himself.

"Why should she be afraid of you?" F'lar asked. "You're cousin to the watch-wher who was her only friend."

Mnementh informed F'lar that he, a fully matured bronze dragon, was no relation to any scrawny, crawling, chained, and wing-clipped watch-wher.

F'lar, pleased at having been able to tease the bronze one, chuckled to himself. With great dignity, Mnementh curved down to the feeding ground.

> By the Golden Egg of Faranth
> By the Weyrwoman, wise and true,
> Breed a flight of bronze and brown wings,
> Breed a flight of green and blue.

Breed riders, strong and daring,
Dragon-loving, born as hatched,
Flight of hundreds soaring skyward,
Man and dragon fully matched.

Lessa waited until the sound of the dragonman's footsteps proved he had really gone away. She rushed quickly through the big cavern, heard the scrape of claw and the *whoosh* of the mighty wings. She raced down the short passageway, right to the edge of the yawning entrance. There was the bronze dragon circling down to the wider end of the mile-long barren oval was the Benden Weyr. She had heard of the Weyrs, as any Pernese had, but to be in one was quite a different matter.

She peered up, around, down that sheer rock face. There was no way off but by dragon wing. The nearest cave mouths were an unhandy distance above her, to one side, below her on the other. She was neatly secluded here.

Weyrwoman, he had told her. His woman? In his weyr? Was that what he had meant? No, that was not the impression she got from the dragon. It occurred to her, suddenly, that it was odd she had understood the dragon. Were common folk able to? Or was it the dragonman blood in her line? At all events, Mnementh had inferred something greater, some special rank. She remembered vaguely that, when dragonmen went on Search, they looked for certain women. Ah, certain women. She was one, then, of several contenders. Yet the bronze rider had offered her the position as if she and she, alone, qualified. He had his own generous portion of conceit, that one, Lessa decided. Arrogant he was, though not a bully like Fax.

She could see the bronze dragon swoop down to the running herdbeasts, saw the strike, saw the dragon wheel up to settle on a far ledge to feed. Instinctively she drew back from the opening, back into the dark and relative safety of the corridor.

The feeding dragon evoked scores of horrid tales. Tales at which she had scoffed but now . . . Was it true, then, that dragons did eat human flesh? Did . . . Lessa halted that trend of thought. Dragonkind was no less cruel than mankind. The dragon, at least, acted from bestial need rather than bestial greed.

Assured that the dragonman would be occupied a while, she crossed the larger cave into the sleeping room. She scooped up the clothing and the bag of cleansing sand and proceeded to the bathing room.

To be clean! To be completely clean and to be able to stay that way. With distaste, she stripped off the remains of the rags, kicking them to one side. She made a soft mud with the sweetsand and scrubbed her entire body until she drew blood from various half-healed cuts. Then she jumped into the pool, gasping as the warm water made the sweetsand foam in the lacerations.

It was a ritual cleansing of more than surface soil. The luxury of cleanliness was ecstasy.

Finally satisfied she was as clean as one long soaking could make her, she left the pool, reluctantly. Wringing out her hair she tucked it up on her head as she dried herself. She shook out the clothing and held one garment against her experimentally. The fabric, a soft green, felt smooth under her water-shrunken fingers, although the nap caught on her roughened hands. She pulled it over her head. It was loose but the darker-green over-tunic had a sash which she pulled in tight at the waist. The unusual sensation of softness against her bare skin made her wriggle with voluptuous pleasure. The skirt, no longer a ragged hem of tatters, swirled heavily around her ankles. She smiled. She took up a fresh drying cloth and began to work on her hair.

A muted sound came to her ears and she stopped, hands poised, head bent to one side. Straining, she listened. Yes, there were sounds without. The dragonman and his beast must have returned. She grimaced to herself with annoyance at this untimely interruption and rubbed harder at her hair. She ran fingers through the half-dry tangles, the motions arrested as she encountered snarls. Vexed, she rummaged on the shelves until she found, as she had hoped to, a coarse-toothed metal comb.

Dry, her hair had a life of its own suddenly, crackling about her hands and clinging to face and comb and dress. It was difficult to get the silky stuff under control. And her hair was longer than she had thought, for, clean and unmatted, it fell to her waist—when it did not cling to her hands.

She paused, listening, and heard no sound at all. Apprehensively, she stepped to the curtain and glanced warily into the sleeping room. It was empty. She listened and caught the perceptible thoughts of the sleepy dragon. Well, she would rather meet the man in the presence of a sleepy dragon than in a sleeping room. She started across the floor and, out of the corner of her eye, caught sight of a strange woman as she passed a polished piece of metal hanging on the wall.

Amazed, she stopped short, staring, incredulous, at the face the metal reflected. Only when she put her hands to her prominent cheekbones in a gesture of involuntary surprise and the reflection imitated the gesture, did she realize she looked at herself.

Why, that girl in the reflector was prettier than Lady Tela, than the clothman's daughter! But so thin. Her hands of their own volition dropped to her neck, to the protruding collarbones, to her breasts which did not entirely accord with the gauntness of the rest of her. The dress was too large for her frame, she noted with an unexpected emergence of conceit born in that instant of delighted appraisal. And her hair . . . it stood out around her head like an aureole. It wouldn't lie contained. She smoothed it down with impatient fingers, automatically bringing locks forward to hang around her face. As she irritably pushed them back, dismissing a need for disguise, the hair drifted up again.

A slight sound, the scrape of a boot against stone, caught her back from her bemusement. She waited, momentarily expecting him to appear. She was suddenly timid. With her face bare to the world, her hair behind her ears, her body outlined by a clinging fabric, she was stripped of her accustomed anonymity and was, therefore, in her estimation, vulnerable.

She controlled the desire to run away—the irrational fear. Observing herself in the looking metal, she drew her shoulders back, tilted her head high, chin up; the movement caused her hair to crackle and cling and shift about her head. She was Lessa of Ruatha, of a fine old Blood. She no longer needed artifice to preserve herself; she must stand proudly bare-faced before the world . . . and that dragonman.

Resolutely she crossed the room, pushing aside the hanging on the doorway to the great cavern.

He was there, beside the head of the dragon, scratching its eye ridges, a curiously tender expression on his face. The tableau was at variance with all she had heard of dragonmen.

She had, of course, heard of the strange affinity between rider and dragon but this was the first time she realized that love was part of that bond. Or that this reserved, cold man was capable of such deep emotion.

He turned slowly, as if loath to leave the bronze beast. He caught sight of her and pivoted completely round, his eyes intense as he took note of her altered appearance. With quick, light steps, he closed the distance between them and ushered her back into the sleeping room, one strong hand holding her by the elbow.

"Mnementh has fed lightly and will need quiet to rest," he said in a low voice. He pulled the heavy hanging into place across the opening.

Then he held her away from him, turning her this way and that, scrutinizing her closely, curious and slightly surprised.

"You wash up . . . pretty, yes, almost pretty," he said, amused condescension in his voice. She pulled roughly away from him, piqued. His low laugh mocked her. "After all, how could one guess what was under the grime of . . . ten full Turns?"

At length he said, "No matter. We must eat and I shall require your services." At her startled exclamation, he turned, grinning maliciously now as his movement revealed the caked blood on his left sleeve. "The least you can do is bathe wounds honorably received fighting your battle."

He pushed aside a portion of the drape that curtained the inner wall. "Food for two!" he roared down a black gap in the sheer stone.

She heard a subterranean echo far below as his voice resounded down what must be a long shaft.

"Nemorth is nearly rigid," he was saying as he took supplies from another drape-hidden shelf, "and the Hatching will soon begin anyhow."

A coldness settled in Lessa's stomach at the mention of a Hatching. The mildest tales she had heard about that part of dragonlore were chilling, the worst dismayingly macabre. She took the things he handed her numbly.

"What? Frightened?" the dragonman taunted, pausing as he stripped off his torn and bloodied shirt.

With a shake of her head, Lessa turned her attention to the wide-shouldered, well-muscled back he presented her, the paler skin of his body decorated with random bloody streaks. Fresh blood welled from the point of his shoulder for the removal of his shirt had broken the tender scabs.

"I will need water," she said and saw she had a flat pan among the items he had given her. She went swiftly to the pool for water, wondering how she had come to agree to venture so far from Ruatha. Ruined though it was, it had been hers and was familiar to her from Tower to deep cellar. At the moment the idea had been proposed and insidiously prosecuted by the dragonman, she had felt capable of anything, having achieved, at last, Fax's death. Now, it was all she could do to keep the water from slopping out of the pan that shook unaccountably in her hands.

She forced herself to deal only with the wound. It was a nasty gash, deep where the point had entered and torn downward in a gradually shallower slice. His skin felt smooth under her fingers as she cleansed the wound. In spite of herself, she noticed the masculine odor of him, compounded not unpleasantly of sweat, leather, and an unusual muskiness which must be from close association with dragons.

She stood back when she had finished her ministration. He flexed his arm experimentally in the constricting bandage and the motion set the muscles rippling along side and back.

When he faced her, his eyes were dark and thoughtful.

"Gently done. My thanks." His smile was ironic.

She backed away as he rose but he only went to the chest to take out a clean, white shirt.

A muted rumble sounded, growing quickly louder.

Dragons roaring? Lessa wondered, trying to conquer the ridiculous fear that rose within her. Had the Hatching started? There was no watch-wher's lair to secrete herself in, here.

As if he understood her confusion, the dragonman laughed good-humoredly and, his eyes on hers, drew aside the wall covering just as some noisy mechanism inside the shaft propelled a tray of food into sight.

Ashamed of her unbased fright and furious that he had witnessed it, Lessa sat rebelliously down on the fur-covered wall seat, heartily wishing him a variety of serious and painful injuries which she could dress with inconsiderate hands. She would not waste future opportunities.

He placed the tray on the low table in front of her, throwing down a heap of furs for his own seat. There was meat, bread, a tempting yellow cheese and even a few pieces of winter fruit. He made no move to eat nor did she, though the thought of a piece of fruit that was ripe, instead of rotten, set her mouth to watering. He glanced up at her, and frowned.

"Even in the Weyr, the lady breaks bread first," he said, and inclined his head politely to her.

Lessa flushed, unused to any courtesy and certainly unused to being first to eat. She broke off a chunk of bread. It was nothing she remembered having tasted before. For one thing, it was fresh baked. The flour had been finely sifted, without trace of sand or hull. She took the slice of cheese he proffered her and it, too, had an uncommonly delicious sharpness. Made bold by this indication of her changed status, Lessa reached for the plumpest piece of fruit.

"Now," the dragonman began, his hand touching hers to get her attention.

Guiltily she dropped the fruit, thinking she had erred. She stared at him, wondering at her fault. He retrieved the fruit and placed it back in her hand as he continued to speak. Wide-eyed, disarmed, she nibbled, and gave him her full attention.

"Listen to me. You must not show a moment's fear, whatever happens on the Hatching Ground. And you must not let her overeat." A wry expression crossed his face. "One of our main functions is to keep a dragon from excessive eating."

Lessa lost interest in the taste of the fruit. She placed it carefully back in the bowl and tried to sort out not what he had said, but what his tone of voice implied. She looked at the dragonman's face, seeing him as a person, not a symbol, for the first time.

There was a blackness about him that was not malevolent; it was a brooding sort of patience. Heavy black hair, heavy black brows; his eyes, a brown light enough to seem golden, were all too expressive of cynical emotions, or cold hauteur. His lips were thin but well-shaped and in repose almost gentle. Why must he always pull his mouth to one side in disapproval or in one of those sardonic smiles? At this moment, he was completely unaffected.

He meant what he was saying. He did not want her to be afraid. There was no reason for her, Lessa, *to* fear.

He very much wanted her to succeed. In keeping whom from overeating what? Herd animals? A newly hatched dragon certainly wasn't capable of eating a full beast. That seemed a simple enough task to Lessa . . . Main function? *Our* main function?

The dragonman was looking at her expectantly.

"Our main function?" she repeated, an unspoken request for more information inherent in her inflection.

"More of that later, first things first," he said, impatiently waving off other questions.

"But what happens?" she insisted.

"As I was told so I tell you. No more, no less. Remember these two points. No fear, and no overeating."

"But . . ."

"You, however, need to eat. Here." He speared a piece of meat on his knife and thrust it at her, frowning until she managed to choke it down. He was about to force more on her but she grabbed up her half-eaten fruit and bit down into the firm sweet sphere instead. She had already eaten more at this one meal than she was accustomed to having all day at the Hold.

"We shall soon eat better at the Weyr," he remarked, regarding the tray with a jaundiced eye.

Lessa was surprised. This was a feast, in her opinion.

"More than you're used to? Yes, I forgot you left Ruatha with bare bones indeed."

She stiffened.

"You did well at Ruatha. I mean no criticism," he added, smiling at her reaction. "But look at you," and he gestured at her body, that curious expression crossing his face, half-amused, half-contemplative. "I should not have guessed you'd clean up pretty," he remarked. "Nor with such hair." This time his expression was frankly admiring.

Involuntarily she put one hand to her head, the hair crackling over her fingers. But what reply she might have made him, indignant as she was, died aborning. An unearthly keening filled the chamber.

The sounds set up a vibration that ran down the bones behind her ear to her spine. She clapped both hands to her ears. The noise rang through her skull despite her defending hands. As abruptly as it started, it ceased.

Before she knew what he was about, the dragonman had grabbed her by the wrist and pulled her over to the chest.

"Take those off," he ordered, indicating dress and tunic. While she stared at him stupidly, he held up a loose white robe, sleeveless and beltless, a matter of two lengths of fine cloth fastened at shoulder and side seams. "Take it off, or do I assist you?" he asked, with no patience at all.

The wild sound was repeated and its unnerving tone made her fingers fly faster. She had no sooner loosened the garments she wore, letting them slide to her feet, than he had thrown the other over her head. She managed to get her arms in the proper places before he grabbed her wrist again and was speeding with her out of the room, her hair whipping out behind her, alive with static.

As they reached the outer chamber, the bronze dragon was standing in the center of the cavern, his head turned to watch the sleeping room door. He seemed impatient to Lessa; his great eyes, which fascinated her so, sparkled iridescently. His manner breathed an inner excitement of great proportions and from his throat a high-pitched croon issued, several octaves below the unnerving cry that had roused them all.

With a yank that rocked her head on her neck, the dragonman pulled her along the passage. The dragon padded beside them at such speed that Lessa fully expected they would all catapult off the ledge. Somehow, at the crucial stride, she was a-perch the bronze neck, the dragonman holding her firmly about the waist. In the same fluid movement, they were gliding across the great bowl of the Weyr to the higher wall opposite. The air was full of wings and dragon tails, rent with a chorus of sounds, echoing and re-echoing across the stony valley.

Mnementh set what Lessa was certain would be a collision course with other dragons, straight for a huge round blackness in the cliff-face, high up. Magically, the beasts filed in, the greater wingspread of Mnementh just clearing the sides of the entrance.

The passageway reverberated with the thunder of wings. The air compressed around her thickly. Then they broke out into a gigantic cavern.

Why, the entire mountain must be hollow, thought Lessa, incredulous. Around the enormous cavern, dragons perched in serried ranks, blues, greens, browns and only two great bronze beasts like Mnementh, on ledges meant to accommodate hundreds. Lessa gripped the bronze neck scales before her, instinctively aware of the imminence of a great event.

Mnementh wheeled downward, disregarding the ledge of the bronze ones. Then all Lessa could see was what lay on the sandy floor of the great cavern: dragon eggs. A clutch of ten monstrous, mottled eggs, their shells moving spasmodically as the fledglings within tapped their way out. To one side, on a raised portion of the floor, was a golden egg, larger by half again the size of the mottled ones. Just beyond the golden egg lay the motionless ochre hulk of the old queen.

Just as she realized Mnementh was hovering over the floor in the vicinity of that egg, Lessa felt the dragonman's hands on her, lifting her from Mnementh's neck.

Apprehensively, she grabbed at him. His hands tightened and inexorably swung her down. His eyes, fierce and gray, locked with hers.

"Remember, Lessa!"

Mnementh added an encouragement, one great compound eye turned on her. Then he rose from the floor. Lessa half-raised one hand in entreaty, bereft of all support, even that of the sure inner compulsion which had sustained her in her struggle for revenge on Fax. She saw the bronze dragon settle on the first ledge, at some distance from the other two bronze beasts. The dragonman dismounted and Mnementh curved his sinuous neck until his head was beside his rider. The man reached up absently, it seemed to Lessa, and caressed his mount.

Loud screams and wailings diverted Lessa and she saw more dragons descend to hover just above the cavern floor, each rider depositing a young woman until there were twelve girls, including Lessa. She remained a little apart from them as they clung to each other. She regarded them curiously. The girls were not injured in any way she could see, so why such weeping? She took a deep breath against the coldness within her. Let *them* be afraid. She was Lessa of Ruatha and did not need to be afraid.

Just then, the golden egg moved convulsively. Gasping as one, the girls edged away from it, back against the rocky wall. One, a lovely blonde, her heavy plait of golden hair swinging just above the ground, started to step off the raised floor and stopped, shrieking, backing fearfully toward the scant comfort of her peers.

Lessa wheeled to see what cause there might be for the look of horror on the girl's face. She stepped back involuntarily herself.

In the main section of the sandy arena, several of the handful of eggs had already cracked wide open. The fledglings, crowing weakly, were moving toward . . . and Lessa gulped . . . the young boys standing stolidly in a semi-circle. Some of them were no older than she had been when Fax's army had swooped down on Ruath Hold.

The shrieking of the women subsided to muffled gasps. A fledgling reached out with claw and beak to grab a boy.

Lessa forced herself to watch as the young dragon mauled the youth, throwing him roughly aside as if unsatisfied in some way. The boy did not move and Lessa could see blood seeping onto the sand from dragon-inflicted wounds.

A second fledgling lurched against another boy and halted, flapping its damp wings impotently, raising its scrawny neck and croaking a parody of the encouraging croon Mnementh often gave. The boy uncertainly lifted a hand and began to scratch the eye ridge. Incredulous, Lessa watched as the fledgling, its crooning increasingly more mellow, ducked its head, pushing at the boy. The child's face broke into an unbelieving smile of elation.

Tearing her eyes from this astounding sight, Lessa saw that another fledgling was beginning the same performance with another boy. Two more dragons had emerged in the interim. One had knocked a boy down and was walking over him, oblivious to the fact that its claws were raking great gashes. The fledgling who followed its hatch-mate stopped by the wounded child, ducking its head to the boy's face, crooning anxiously. As Lessa watched, the boy managed to struggle to his feet, tears of pain streaming down his cheeks. She could hear him pleading with the dragon not to worry, that he was only scratched a little.

It was over very soon. The young dragons paired off with boys. Green riders dropped down to carry off the unacceptable. Blue riders settled to the floor with their beasts and led the couples out of the cavern, the young dragons squealing, crooning, flapping wet wings as they staggered off, encouraged by their newly acquired weyrmates.

Lessa turned resolutely back to the rocking golden egg, knowing what to expect and trying to divine what the successful boys had, or had not done, that caused the baby dragons to single them out.

A crack appeared in the golden shell and was greeted by the terrified screams of the girls. Some had fallen into little heaps of white fabric, others embraced tightly in their mutual fear. The crack widened and the wedge-head broke through, followed quickly by the neck, gleaming gold. Lessa wondered with unexpected detachment how long it would take the beast to mature, considering its by no means small size at birth. For the head was larger than that of the male dragons and they had been large enough to overwhelm sturdy boys of ten full Turns.

Lessa was aware of a loud hum within the Hall. Glancing up at the audience, she realized it emanated from the watching bronze dragons, for this was the birth of their mate, their queen. The hum increased in volume as the shell shattered into fragments and the golden, glistening body of the new female emerged. It staggered out, dipping its sharp beak into the soft sand, momentarily trapped. Flapping its wet wings, it righted itself, ludicrous in its weak awkwardness. With sudden and unexpected swiftness, it dashed toward the terror-stricken girls.

Before Lessa could blink, it shook the first girl with such violence, her head snapped audibly and she fell limply to the sand. Disregarding her, the dragon leaped toward the second girl but misjudged the distance and fell, grabbing out with one claw for support and raking the girl's body from shoulder to thigh. The screaming of the mortally injured girl distracted the dragon and released the others from their horrified trance. They scattered in panicky confusion, racing, running, tripping, stumbling, falling across the sand toward the exit the boys had used.

As the golden beast, crying piteously, lurched down from the raised arena toward the scattered women, Lessa moved. Why hadn't that silly clunk-headed girl stepped side, Lessa thought, grabbing for the wedge-head, at birth not much larger than her own torso. The dragon's so clumsy and weak she's her own worst enemy.

Lessa swung the head round so that the many-faceted eyes were forced to look at her . . . and found herself lost in that rainbow regard.

A feeling of joy suffused Lessa, a feeling of warmth, tenderness, unalloyed affection and instant respect and admiration flooded mind and heart and soul. Never again would Lessa lack an advocate, a defender, an intimate, aware instantly of the temper of her mind and heart, of her desires. How wonderful was Lessa, the thought intruded into Lessa's reflections, how pretty, how kind, how thoughtful, how brave and clever!

Mechanically, Lessa reached out to scratch the exact spot on the soft eye ridge.

The dragon blinked at her wistfully, extremely sad that she had distressed Lessa. Lessa reassuringly patted the slightly damp, soft neck that curved trustingly toward her. The dragon reeled to one side and one wing fouled on the hind claw. It hurt. Carefully, Lessa lifted the erring foot, freed the wing, folding it back across the dorsal ridge with a pat.

The dragon began to croon in her throat, her eyes following Lessa's every move. She nudged at Lessa and Lessa obediently attended the other eye ridge.

The dragon let it be known she was hungry.

"We'll get you something to eat directly," Lessa assured her briskly and blinked back at the dragon in amazement. How could she be so

callous? It was a fact that this little menace had just now seriously injured, if not killed, two women.

She wouldn't have believed her sympathies could swing so alarm-
ingly toward the beast. Yet it was the most natural thing in the world
for her to wish to protect this fledgling.

The dragon arched her neck to look Lessa squarely in the eyes.
Ramoth repeated wistfully how exceedingly hungry she was, confined
so long in that shell without nourishment.

Lessa wondered how she knew the golden dragon's name and
Ramoth replied: Why shouldn't she know her own name since it was
hers and no one else's? And then Lessa was lost again in the wonder of
those expressive eyes.

Oblivious to the descending bronze dragons, uncaring of the presence of their riders, Lessa stood caressing the head of the most wonderful creature on all Pern, fully prescient of troubles and glories, but most
immediately aware that Lessa of Pern was Weyrwoman to Ramoth the
Golden, for now and forever.

COCKFIGHT

Jane Yolen

The pit-cleaners circled noisily, gobbling up the old fewmets with their iron mouths. They spat out fresh sawdust and moved on. It generally took several minutes between fights, and the mechanical clanking of the cleaners was matched by the roars of the pit-wise dragons and the last-minute betting calls of their masters.

Jakkin heard the noises through the wooden ceiling as he groomed his dragon in the under-pit stalls. It was the first fight for both of them, and Jakkin's fingers reflected his nervousness. He simply could not keep them still. They picked off bits of dust and flicked at specks on the dragon's already gleaming scales. They polished and smoothed and polished again. The red dragon seemed oblivious to first-fight jitters and arched up under Jakkin's hands.

Jakkin was pleased with his dragon's color. It was a dull red. Not the red of the holly berry or the red of the wild-flowering trillium, but the red of life's blood spilled upon the sand. It was a fighter's color, and

59

he had known it from the first. That was why he had sneaked the dragon from its nest, away from its hatchlings, when the young worm had emerged from its egg in the sand of the nursery.

The dragon had looked then like any lizard, for it had not yet shed its eggskin, which was wrinkled and yellow, like custard scum. But Jakkin had sensed, beneath the skin, a darker shadow and had known it would turn red. Not many would have known, but Jakkin had, though he was only fourteen.

The dragon was not his, not really, for it had belonged to his master's nursery, just as Jakkin did. But on Austar IV there was only one way to escape from bond, and that was with gold. There was no quicker way to get gold than as a bettor in the dragon pits. And there was nothing Jakkin wanted more than to be free. He had lived over half his life bonded to the nursery, from the time his parents had died when he was four. And most of that time he had worked as a stallboy, no better than a human pit-cleaner, for Sarkkhan's Dragonry. What did it matter that he lived and slept and ate with his master's dragons? He was allowed to handle only their fewmets and spread fresh sawdust for their needs. If he could not raise a fighting dragon himself and buy his way out of bond, he would end up an *old* stallboy, like Likkarn, who smoked blisterweed, dreamed his days away, and cried red tears.

So Jakkin had watched and waited and learned as much as a junior stallboy could about dragon ways and dragon lore, for he knew the only way out of bond was to steal that first egg and raise it up for fighting or breeding or, if need was great, for the stews. But Jakkin did not know eggs—could sense nothing through the elastic shell—and so he had stolen a young dragon instead. It was a greater risk, for eggs were never counted, but the new-hatched dragons were. At Sarkkhan's Dragonry old Likkarn kept the list of hatchlings. He was the only one of the bonders who could write, though Jakkin had taught himself to read a bit.

Jakkin had worried all through the first days that Likkarn would know and, knowing, tell. He kept the hatchling in a wooden crate turned upside down way out in the sands. He swept away his footsteps to and from the crate, and reckoned his way to it at night by the stars.

And somehow he had not been found out. His reward had come as the young worm had grown.

First the hatchling had turned a dull brown and could trickle smoke through its nose slits. The wings on its back, crumpled and weak, had slowly stretched to a rubbery thickness. For days it had remained mud-colored. Another boy might have sold it then to the stews, keeping the small fee in his leather bond bag that swung from the metal bond chain around his neck. It would have been a laughable amount, a coin or two at the most, and the bag would have looked just as empty as before.

But Jakkin had waited, and the dragon finally molted, patchworking into a red. The nails on its foreclaws, which had been as brittle as jingle shells, were now as hard as golden oak and the same color. Its hindclaws were dull and strong as steel. Its eyes were two black shrouds. It had not roared yet, but Jakkin knew the roar would come, loud and full and fierce, when it was first blooded in the ring. The quality of the roar would start the betting rippling again through the crowd who judged a fighter by the timbre of its voice.

Jakkin could hear the cleaners clanking out of the ring through the mecho-holes. He ran his fingers through his straight brown hair and tried to swallow, then touched a dimple on his cheek that was as deep as a blood score. His hand found the bond bag and kneaded it several times for luck.

"Soon now," he promised the red dragon in a hoarse whisper, his hand still on the bag. "Soon. We will show them a first fight. They will remember us."

The red was too busy munching on blisterwort to reply.

A disembodied voice announced the next fight. "Jakkin's Red, Mekkle's Bottle O' Rum."

Jakkin winced. He knew a little about Mekkle's dragon already. He had heard about it that morning as they had come into the pit stalls. Dragon masters and trainers did not chatter while they groomed their fighters, but bettors did, gathering around the favorites and trading stories of other fights. Mekkle's Rum was a light-colored male that favored its left side and had won three of its seven fights—the last three. It would never be great, the whispers had run, but it was good enough, and a hard draw for a new dragon, possibly disastrous for a would-be dragon master. Jakkin knew his red could be good with time, given the luck of the draw. It had all the things a dragon fighter was supposed to have: it had heart, it listened well, it did all he asked of it. But just as Jakkin had never run a fighter before, the red had never been in a ring. It had never been blooded or given roar. It did not even have its true name yet. Already, he knew, the betting was way against the young red, and he could hear the murmur of new bets after the announcement. The odds would be so awful, he might never be able to get a sponsor for a second match. First fights were free, but seconds cost gold. And if he had no sponsor, that would leave only the stews for the dragon and a return to bond for himself.

Jakkin stroked the bond bag once more, then buttoned his shirt up over it to conceal it. He did not know yet what it felt like to be free, so he could stand more years as a bonder. And there might always be another chance to steal. But how could he ever give up the red to the stews? It was not any old dragon, it was his. They had already shared months of training, long nights together under the Austar moons. He knew its mind better than his own. It was a deep, glowing cavern of colors and sights and sounds. He remembered the first time he had really felt his way into it, lying on his side, winded from running, the red beside him, a small mountain in the sand. The red calmed him when he was not calm, cheered him when he thought he could not be cheered. Linked as he was with it now, how could he bear to hear its last screams in the stews and stay sane? Perhaps that was why Likkarn was always yelling at the younger bonders, why he smoked blisterweed that turned the mind foggy and made a man cry red tears. And perhaps that was why dragons in the stews were always yearlings or the untrained. Not because they were softer, more succulent, but because no one would hear them when they screamed.

Jakkin's skin felt slimed with perspiration and the dragon sniffed it on him, giving out a few straggles of smoke from its slits. Jakkin fought down his own fear. If he could not control it, his red would have no chance at all, for a dragon was only as good as its master. He took deep breaths and then moved over to the red's head. He looked into its black, unblinking eyes.

"Thou art a fine one, my Red," he whispered. "First fight for us both, but I trust thee." Jakkin always spoke *thou* to his dragon. He felt it somehow brought them closer. "Trust me?"

The dragon responded with slightly rounded smokes. Deep within its eyes Jakkin thought he detected small lights.

"Dragon's fire!" he breathed. "Thou *art* a fighter. I knew it!"

Jakkin slipped the ring from the red dragon's neck and rubbed its scales underneath. They were not yet as hard as a mature fighter's, and for a moment he worried that the older Bottle O' Rum might tear the young dragon beyond repair. He pulled the red's head down and whispered into its ear. "Guard thyself here," he said, rubbing with his fingers under the tender neck links and thinking danger at it.

The dragon shook its head playfully, and Jakkin slapped it lightly on the neck. With a surge, the red dragon moved out of the stall, over to the dragonlock, and flowed up into the ring.

"It's eager," the whisper ran around the crowd. They always liked that in young dragons. Time enough to grow cautious in the pit. Older dragons often were reluctant and had to be prodded with jumpsticks behind the wings or in the tender underparts of the tail. The bettors considered that a great fault. Jakkin heard the crowd's appreciation as he came up into the stands.

It would have been safer for Jakkin to remain below, guiding his red by mind. That way there would be no chance for Master Sarkkhan to find him here, though he doubted such a well-known breeder would enter a back-country pit-fight. And many trainers, Mekkle being one of them, stayed in the stalls drinking and smoking and guiding their dragons where the crowd could not influence them. But Jakkin needed to see the red as well as feel it, to watch the fight through his own eyes as well as the red's. They had trained too long at night, alone, in the sands. He did not know how another dragon in a real fight would respond. He had to see to understand it all. And the red was used to him being close by. He did not want to change that now. Besides, unlike many of the other bonders, he had never been to a fight, only read about them in books and heard about them from his bondmates. This might be his only chance. And, he further rationalized, up in the stands he might find out more about Mekkle's orange that would help him help the red.

Jakkin looked around the stands cautiously from the stairwell. He saw no one he knew, neither fellow bonders nor masters who had traded with Sarkkhan. He edged quietly into the stands, just one more boy at the fights. Nothing called attention to him but the empty bond bag beneath his shirt. He checked his buttons carefully to make sure they were closed. Then he leaned forward and watched as his red circled the ring.

It held its head high and measured the size of the pit, the height of the walls. It looked over the bettors as if it were counting them, and an appreciative chuckle went through the crowd. Then the red scratched in the sawdust several times, testing its depth. And still Bottle O' Rum had not appeared.

Then with an explosion, Bottle O' Rum came through the dragonlock and landed with all four feet planted well beneath the level of the sawdust, his claws fastened immovably to the boards.

"Good stance," shouted someone in the crowd, and the betting began anew.

The red gave a little flutter with its wings, a flapping that might indicate nervousness, and Jakkin thought at it: "He is a naught. A stander. But thy nails and wings are fresh. Do not be afraid. Remember thy training." At that the little red's head went high and its neck scales glittered in the artificial sun of the pit.

"Watch that neck," shouted a heckler. "There's one that'll be blooded soon."

"Too soon," shouted another from across the stands at him.

Bottle O' Rum charged the inviting neck.

It was just as Jakkin hoped, for charging from the fighting stance is a clumsy maneuver at best. The claws must be retracted simultaneously, and the younger the dragon the more brittle its claws. The orange, Rum, seven fights older than the red, was not yet fully mature. As Rum charged, one of the nails on his front right claw caught in the floorboards and splintered, causing him to falter for a second. The red shifted its position slightly. Instead of blooding the red on the vulnerable neck, Rum's charge brought him headlong onto the younger dragon's chest plates, the hardest and slipperiest part of a fighting dragon's armor. The screech of teeth on scale brought winces to the crowd. Only Jakkin was ready, for it was a maneuver he had taught his dragon out in the hidden sands.

"Now!" he cried out and thought at once.

The young red needed no urging. It bent its neck around in a fast, vicious slash, and blood spurted from behind the ears of Mekkle's Rum.

"First blood!" cried the crowd.

Now the betting would change, Jakkin thought with a certain pleasure, and touched the bond bag through the thin cloth of his shirt. Ear bites bleed profusely but are not important. It would hurt the orange dragon a little, like a pinprick or a splinter does a man. It would make the dragon mad and—more important—a bit more cautious. But first blood! It looked good.

Bottle O' Rum roared with the bite, loud and piercing. It was too high up in the throat, yet with surprising strength. Jakkin listened carefully, trying to judge. He had heard dragons roar at the nursery in mock battles or when the keepers blooded them for customers intent on hearing the timbre before buying. To him the roar sounded as if it had all its power in the top tones and none that resonated. Perhaps he was wrong, but if his red could *outlast* the orange, it might impress this crowd.

In his eagerness to help his dragon, Jakkin moved to the pit rail. He elbowed his way through some older men.

"Here, youngster, what do you think you're doing?" A man in a gray leather coverall spoke. He was obviously familiar with the pits. Anyone in leather knew his way around. And his face, what could be seen behind the gray beard, was scored with dragon-blood scars.

"Get back up in the stands. Leave ringside to the money men," said his companion, taking in Jakkin's leather-patched cloth shirt and trousers with a dismissing look. He ostentatiously jounced a full bag that hung from his wrist on a leather thong.

Jakkin ignored them, fingering his badge with the facs picture of the red on it. He leaned over the rail. "Away, away, good Red," he thought at his dragon, and smiled when the red immediately wheeled and winged up from its blooded foe. Only then did he turn and address the two scowling bettors. "Pit right, good sirs," he said with deference, pointing at the same time to his badge.

They mumbled, but moved aside for him.

The orange dragon in the pit shook its head, and the blood beaded its ears like a crown. A few drops spattered over the walls and into the stands. Each place a drop touched burned with that glow peculiar to the acidic dragon's blood. One watcher in the third row of the stands was not quick enough and was seared on the cheek. He reached up a hand to the wound but did not move from his place.

The orange Rum stood up tall again and dug back into the dust.

"Another stand," said the gray leather man to Jakkin's right.

"*Pah*, that's all it knows," said the dark man beside him. "That's how it won its three fights. Good stance, but that's it. I wonder why I bet on it at all. Let's go and get something to smoke. This fight's a bore."

Jakkin watched them leave from the corner of his eye, but he absorbed their information. If the orange was a stander—if the information was true—it would help him with the fight.

The red dragon's leap back had taken it to the north side of the pit. When it saw that Bottle O' Rum had chosen to stand, it circled closer warily.

Jakkin thought at it, "He's good in the stance. Do not force him there. Make him come to thee."

The dragon's thoughts, as always, came back clearly to Jakkin, wordless but full of color and emotion. The red wanted to charge; the dragon it had blooded was waiting. The overwhelming urge was to carry the fight to the foe.

"No, my Red. Trust me. Be eager, but not foolish," cautioned Jakkin, looking for an opening.

But the crowd, as eager as the young dragon, was communicating with it, too. The yells of the men, their thoughts of charging, overpowered Jakkin's single line of calm. The red started to move.

When it saw the red bunching for a charge, Rum solidified his stance. His shoulders went rigid with the strain. Jakkin knew that if his red dived at that standing rock, it could quite easily break a small bone in its neck. And rarely did a dragon come back to the pit once its neck-bones had been set. Then it was good only for the breeding nurseries—if it had a fine pit record—or the stews.

"Steady, steady," Jakkin said aloud. Then he shouted and waved a hand, "*No!*"

The red had already started its dive, but the movement of Jakkin's hand was a signal too powerful for it to ignore and, at the last possible minute, it pulled to one side. As it passed, Rum slashed at it with a gaping mouth and shredded its wingtip.

"Blood," the crowd roared and waited for the red dragon to roar back.

Jakkin felt its confusion, and his head swam with the red of dragon's blood as his dragon's thoughts came to him. He watched as it soared to the top of the building and scorched its wingtip on the artificial sun, cauterizing the wound. Then, still hovering, it opened its mouth for its first blooded roar.

There was no sound.

"A mute!" called a man from the stands. He spit angrily to one side. "Never heard one before."

A wit near him shouted back, "You won't hear this one, either."

The crowd laughed at this, and passed the quip around the stands.

But Jakkin only stared up at his red bitterly. "A mute," he thought at it. "You are as powerless as I."

His use of the distancing pronoun *you* further confused the young dragon, and it began to circle downward in a disconsolate spiral, closer and closer to the waiting Rum, its mind a maelstrom of blacks and grays.

Jakkin realized his mistake in time. "It does not matter," he cried out in his mind. "Even with no roar, thou wilt be great." He said it with more conviction than he really felt, but it was enough for the red. It broke out of its spiral and hovered, wings working evenly.

The maneuver, however, was so unexpected that the pit-wise Bottle O' Rum was bewildered. He came out of his stance with a splattering of dust and fewmets, stopped, then charged again. The red avoided him easily, landing on his back and raking the orange scales with its claws. That drew no blood, but it frightened the older dragon into a hindfoot rise. Balancing on his tail, Rum towered nearly eight feet high, his front claws scoring the air, a single shot of fire streaking from his slits.

The red backwinged away from the flames and waited.

"Steady, steady," thought Jakkin, in control again. He let his mind recall for them both the quiet sands and the cool nights when they had practiced with the wooden dragon form on charges and clawing. Then Jakkin repeated out loud, "Steady, steady."

A hard hand on his shoulder broke through his thoughts and the sweet-strong smell of blisterweed assailed him. Jakkin turned.

"Not so steady yourself," came a familiar voice.

Jakkin stared up at the ravaged face, pocked with blood scores and stained with tear lines.

"Likkarn," breathed Jakkin, suddenly and terribly afraid.

Jakkin tried to turn back to the pit where his red waited. The hand on his shoulder was too firm, the fingers like claws through his shirt.

"And how did *you* become a dragon trainer?" the man asked.

Jakkin thought to bluff. The old stallboy was often too sunk in his smoke dreams to really listen. Bluff and run, for the wild anger that came after blister dreams never gave a smoker time to reason. "I found . . . found an egg, Likkarn," he said. And it could be true. There were a few wild dragons, bred from escapes that had gone feral.

The man said nothing, but shook his head.

Jakkin stared at him. This was a new Likkarn, harder, full of purpose. Then Jakkin noticed. Likkarn's eyes were clearer than he had ever seen them, no longer the furious pink of the weeder, but a softer rose. He had not smoked for several days at least. It was useless to bluff or run. "I took it from the nursery, Likkarn. I raised it in the sands. I trained it at night, by the moons."

"That's better. Much better. Liars are an abomination," the man said with a bitter laugh. "And you fed it what? Goods stolen from the master, I wager. You born bonders know nothing. Nothing."

Jakkin's cheeks were burning now. "I am no born bonder. And I would never steal from the master's stores. I planted in the sands last year and grew blisterweed and burnwort. I gathered the rest in the swamps. *On my own time.*" He added that fiercely.

"Bonders have no time of their own," Likkarn muttered savagely. "And supplements?"

"The master says supplements are bad for a fighter. They make a fighter fast in the beginning, but they dilute the blood." Jakkin looked into Likkarn's eyes more boldly now. "I heard the master say that. To a buyer."

Likkarn's smile was wry and twisted. "And you eavesdrop as well." He gave Jakkin's shoulder a particularly vicious wrench.

Jakkin gasped and closed his eyes with the pain. He wanted to cry out, and thought he had, when he realized it was not his own voice he heard but a scream from the pit. He pulled away from Likkarn and stared. The scream was Bottle O' Rum's, a triumphant roar as he stood over the red, whose injured wing was pinioned beneath Rum's right front claw.

"*Jakkin . . .*" came Likkarn's voice behind him, full of warning. How often Jakkin had heard that tone right before old Likkarn had roused from a weed dream to the fury that always followed. Likkarn was old, but his fist was still solid.

Jakkin trembled, but he willed his focus onto the red, whose thoughts came tumbling back into his head now in a tangle of muted colors and whines. He touched his hand to the small lump under his shirt where the bond bag hung. He could feel his own heart beating through the leather shield. "Never mind, my Red," soothed Jakkin. "Never mind the pain. Recall the time I stood upon thy wing and we played at the Great Upset. Recall it well, thou mighty fighter. Remember. Remember."

The red stirred only slightly and made a flutter with its free wing. The crowd saw this as a gesture of submission. So did Rum and, through him, his master Mekkle. But Jakkin did not. He knew the red had listened well and understood. The game was not over yet. Pit-fighting was not all brawn; how often Master Sarkkhan had said that. The best fighters, the ones who lasted for years, were cunning gamesters, and it was this he had guessed about his red from the first.

The fluttering of the unpinioned wing caught Bottle O' Rum's eye, and the orange dragon turned toward it, relaxing his hold by a single nail.

The red fluttered its free wing again. Flutter and feint. Flutter and feint. It needed the orange's attention totally on that wing. Then its tail could do the silent stalking it had learned in the sands with Jakkin.

Bottle O' Rum followed the fluttering as though laughing for his own coming triumph. His dragon jaws opened slightly in a deadly grin. If Mekkle had been in the stands instead of below in the stalls, the trick might not have worked. But the orange dragon, intent on the fluttering wing, leaned his head way back and fully opened his jaws, readying for the kill. He was unaware of what was going on behind him.

"Now!" shouted Jakkin in his mind and only later realized that the entire stands had roared the word with him. Only the crowd had been roaring for the wrong dragon.

The red's tail came around with a snap, as vicious and as accurate as a driver's whip. It caught the orange on its injured ear and across an eye.

Rum screamed instead of roaring and let go of the red's wing. The red was up in an instant and leaped for Bottle O' Rum's throat.

One, two and the ritual slashes were made. The orange throat was coruscated with blood, and Rum instantly dropped to the ground.

Jakkin's dragon backed at once, slightly akilter because of the wound in its wing.

"Game to Jakkin's Red," said the disembodied voice over the speaker.

The crowd was strangely silent. Then a loud whoop sounded from one voice buried in the stands, a bettor who had taken a chance on the First Fighter.

That single voice seemed to rouse Bottle O' Rum. He raised his head from the ground groggily. Only his head and half his neck cleared the dust. He strained to arch his neck over, exposing the underside to the light. The two red slashes glistened like thin, hungry mouths. Then Rum began a strange, horrible humming that changed to a high-pitched whine. His body began to shake, and the shaking became part of the sound as the dust eddied around him.

The red dragon swooped down and stood before the fallen Rum, as still as stone. Then it, too, began to shake.

The sound changed from a whine to a high roar. Jakkin had never heard anything like it before. He put his hands to the bond bag, then to his ears.

"What is it? What is happening?" he cried out, but the men on either side of him had moved away. Palms to ears, they backed toward the exits. Many in the crowds had already gone down the stairs, setting the thick wood walls between themselves and the noise.

Jakkin tried to reach the red dragon's mind, but all he felt were storms of orange winds, hot and blinding, and a shaft of burning white light. As he watched, the red rose up on its hind legs and raked the air frantically with its claws, as if getting ready for some last deadly blow.

"Fool's Pride," came Likkarn's defeated voice behind him, close enough to his ear to hear. "That damnable dragon wants death. He has been shamed, and he'll scream your red into it. Then you'll know. All you'll have left is a killer on your hands. I lost three that way. *Three*. Fool's Pride." He shouted the last at Jakkin's back, for at his first words, Jakkin had thrown himself over the railing into the pit. He landed on all fours, but was up and running at once.

He had heard of Fool's Pride, that part of the fighting dragon's bloody past that was not always bred out. Fool's Pride that led some defeated dragons to demand death. It had nearly caused dragons to become extinct. If men had not carefully watched the lines, trained the fighters to lose with grace, there would have been no dragons left on Austar IV. A good fighter should have a love of blooding, yes. But killing made dragons unmanageable, made them feral, made them wild.

Jakkin crashed into the red's side. "No, no!" he screamed up at it, beating on its body with his fists. "Do not wet thy jaws in his death." He reached as high as he could and held on to the red's neck. The scales slashed one of his palms, but he did not let go.

It was his touch more than his voice or his thoughts that stopped the young red. It turned slowly, sluggishly, as if rousing from a dream. Jakkin fell from its neck to the ground.

The movement away shattered Bottle O' Rum's concentration. He slipped from screaming to unconsciousness in an instant.

The red nuzzled Jakkin, its eyes unfathomable, its mind still clouded. The boy stood up. Without bothering to brush the dust from his clothes, he thought at it, "*Thou mighty First.*"

The red suddenly crowded his mind with victorious sunbursts, turned, then streaked back through the hole to its stall and the waiting burnwort.

Mekkle and two friends came up the stairs, glowering, leaped into the pit and dragged the fainting orange out through a mecho-hole by his tail.

Only then did Jakkin walk back to ringside, holding his cut hand palm up. It had just begun to sting.

Likkarn, still standing by the railing, was already smoking a short strand of blisterweed. He stared blankly as the red smoke circled his head.

"I owe you," Jakkin said slowly up to him, hating to admit it. "I did not know Fool's Pride when I saw it. Another minute and the red would have been good for nothing but the stews. If I ever get a second fight, I will give you some of the gold. *Your bag is not yet full.*"

Jakkin meant the last phrase simply as ritual, but Likkarn's eyes suddenly roused to weed fury. His hand went to his throat. "You owe me nothing," said the old man. He held his head high, and the age lines on his neck crisscrossed like old fight scars. "*Nothing.* You owe the master everything. I need no reminder that I am a bonder. *I fill the bag myself.*"

Jakkin bowed his head under the old man's assault. "Let me tend the red's wounds. Then do with me as you will." He turned and, without waiting for an answer, ducked through the mecho-hole and slid down the shaft.

Jakkin came to the stall where the red was already at work grooming itself, polishing its scales with a combination of fire and spit. He slipped the ring around its neck and knelt down by its side. Briskly he put his hand out to touch its wounded wing, in a hurry to finish the examination before Likkarn came down. The red drew back at his touch, sending a mauve landscape into his mind, dripping with gray tears.

"Hush, little flametongue," crooned Jakkin, slowing himself down and using the lullaby sounds he had invented to soothe the hatchling of the sands. "I won't hurt thee. I want to help."

But the red continued to retreat from him, crouching against the wall.

Puzzled, Jakkin pulled his hand back, yet still the red huddled away, and a spurt of yellow-red fire flamed from its slits. "Not here, furnace-lung," said Jakkin, annoyed. "That will set the stall on fire."

A rough hand pushed him aside. It was Likkarn, no longer in the weed dream but starting into the uncontrollable fury that capped a weed sequence. The dragon, its mind open with the pain of its wound and the finish of the fight, had picked up Likkarn's growing anger and reacted to it.

"You don't know wounds," growled Likkarn. "I'll show you what a *real* trainer knows." He grabbed the dragon's torn wing and held it firmly; then with a quick motion, and before Jakkin could stop him, he set his mouth on the jagged tear.

The dragon reared back in alarm and tried to whip its tail around, but the stalls were purposely built small to curb such motion. Its tail scraped along the wall and barely tapped the man. But Jakkin grabbed at Likkarn's arm with both hands and furiously tore him from the red's wing.

"I'll kill you, you weeder," he screamed. "Can't you wait till a dragon is in the stews before you try to eat it. I'll kill you." He slammed at Likkarn with his fist and feet, knowing as he did it that the man's weed anger would be turned on him and he might be killed by it, and not caring. Suddenly Jakkin felt himself being lifted up from behind, his legs dangling, kicking uselessly at the air. A strong arm around his waist held him fast. Another pushed Likkarn back against the wall.

"Hold off, boy. He was a good trainer—once. And he's right about the best way to deal with a wing wound. An open part, filled with dragon's blood, might burn the tongue surely. But a man's tongue heals quickly, and there is something in human saliva that closes these small tears."

Jakkin twisted around as best he could and saw the man he had most feared seeing. It was Master Sarkkhan himself, in a leather suit of the red-and-gold nursery colors. His red beard was brushed out, and he looked grim.

Sarkkhan put the boy down but held on to him with one hand. With the other, he brushed his hair back from a forehead that was pitted with blood scores as evenly spaced as a bonder's chain. "Now promise me you will let Likkarn look to the red's wing."

"I will not. He's a weeder and he's as likely to rip the red as heal it, and the red hates him—just as I do," shouted Jakkin. There he stopped and put the back of his hand over his mouth, shocked at his own bold words.

Likkarn raised his hand to the boy and aimed a blow at his head, but before the slap landed, the dragon nosed forward and pushed the man to the ground.

Master Sarkkhan let go of Jakkin's shoulder and considered the red for a moment. "I think the boy is right, Likkarn. The dragon won't have you. It's too closely linked. I wouldn't have guessed that, but there it is. Best leave this to the boy and me."

Likkarn got up clumsily and brushed off his clothes. His bond bag had fallen over the top of his overall bib in the scuffle, and Jakkin was shocked to see that it was halfway plump, jangling with coins. Likkarn caught his look and angrily stuffed the bag back inside, then jabbed at the outline of Jakkin's bag under his shirt with a reddened finger. "And how much have *you* got there, boy?" He walked off with as much dignity as he could muster to slump by the stairwell and watch.

Sarkkhan ignored them both and crouched down by the dragon, letting it get the smell of him. He caressed its jaws and under its neck with his large, scarred hands. Slowly the big man worked his way back toward the wings, crooning at the dragon in low tones, smoothing its scales, all the while staring into its eyes. Slowly the membranes, top and bottom, shuttered the red's eyes, and it relaxed. Only then did Sarkkhan let his hand close over the wounded wing. The dragon gave a small shudder but was otherwise quite still.

"Your red did a good job searing its wound on the light. Did you teach it that?"

"No," the boy admitted.

"Of course not, foolish of me. How could you? No light in the sands. Good breeding, then," said Sarkkhan with a small chuckle of appreciation. "And I should know. After all, your dragon's mother is my best—Heart O' Mine."

"You . . . you knew all along, then." Jakkin felt as confused as a blooded First.

Sarkkhan stood up and stretched. In the confines of the stall he seemed enormous, a red-gold giant. Jakkin suddenly felt smaller than his years.

"*Fewmets*, boy. Of course I knew," Sarkkhan answered. "I know *everything* that happens at my nursery."

Jakkin collapsed down next to his dragon and put his arm over its neck. When he finally spoke, it was in a very small voice. "Then why did you let me do it? Why did you let me steal the dragon? Were you trying to get me in trouble? Do you want me in jail?"

The man threw back his head and roared, and the dragons in neighboring stalls stirred uneasily at the sound. Even Likkarn started at the laugh, and a trainer six stalls down growled in disapproval. Then Sarkkhan looked down at the boy, crouched by the red dragon. "I'm sorry, boy, I forget how young you are. Never known anyone quite that young to successfully train a hatchling. But every man gets a chance to steal one egg. It's a kind of test, you might say. The only way to break out of bond. Some men are meant to be bonders, some masters. How else can you tell? Likkarn's tried it—endless times, eh, old man?" The master glanced over at Likkarn with a look akin to affection, but Likkarn only glared back. "Steal an egg and try. The only things it is wrong to steal are a bad egg or your master's provisions." Sarkkhan stopped talking for a minute and mused, idly running a hand over the red dragon's back as it chewed contentedly now on its burnwort, little gray straggles of smoke easing from its slits. "Of course, most *do* steal bad eggs or are too impatient to train what comes out, and instead they make a quick sale to the stews for just a few coins to jangle in their bags. Then it's back to bond again before a month is out. It's only the ones who steal provisions that land in jail, boy."

"Then you won't put me in jail? Or the red in the stews? I couldn't let you do that, Master Sarkkhan. Not even you. I wouldn't let you. I . . ." Jakkin began to stutter, as he often did in his master's presence.

"Send a First Fighter, a *winner* to the stews? *Fewmets*, boy, where's your brain. Been smoking blisterweed?" Sarkkhan hunkered down next to him.

Jakkin looked down at his sandals. His feet were soiled from the dust of the stall. He ordered his stomach to calm down, and he felt an answering muted rainbow of calm from the dragon. Then a peculiar thought came to him. "Did *you* have to steal an egg, Master Sarkkhan?"

The big red-headed man laughed and thrust his hand right into Jakkin's face. Jakkin drew back, but Sarkkhan was holding up two fingers and wiggling them before his eyes.

"Two! I stole two. A male and a female. And it was not mere chance. Even then, I knew the difference. *In the egg* I knew. And that's why I'm the best breeder on Austar IV." He stood up abruptly and held out his hand to the boy. "But enough. The red is fine, and you are due upstairs." He yanked Jakkin to his feet and seemed at once to lose his friendliness.

"Upstairs?" Jakkin could not think what that meant. "You said I was not to go to jail. I want to stay with the red. I want . . ."

"*Wormwort*, boy, have you been listening or not? You have to register that dragon, give her a name, record her as a First Fighter, a winner."

"*Her?*" Jakkin heard only the one word.

"Yes, a her. Do you challenge *me* on that? And I want to come with you and collect my gold. I bet a bagful on that red of yours—on Likkarn's advice. He's been watching you train—my orders. He said she was looking good, and sometimes I believe him." Sarkkhan moved toward the stairwell where Likkarn still waited. "I owe him, you know. He taught me everything."

"Likkarn? Taught you?"

They stopped by the old man who was slumped again in another blisterweed dream. Sarkkhan reached out and took the stringy red weed ash from the old man's hand. He threw it on the floor and ground it savagely into the dust. "He wasn't born a weeder, boy. And he hasn't forgotten all he once knew." Then shaking his head, Master Sarkkhan moved up the stairs, impatiently waving a hand at the boy to follow.

A stray strand of color-pearls passed through Jakkin's mind, and he turned around to look at the dragon's stall. Then he gulped and said in a rush at Sarkkhan's back, "But she's a mute, Master. She may have won this fight by wiles, but she's a mute. No one will bet on a dragon that cannot roar."

The man reached down and grabbed Jakkin's hand, yanking him through the doorway and up the stairs. They mounted two at a time. "You really are lizard waste," said Sarkkhan, punctuating his sentences with another step. "Why do you think I sent a half-blind weeder skulking around the sands at night watching you train a snatchling? Because I'd lost my mind? *Fewmets*, boy. I want to know what is happening to every damned dragon I have bred, because I have had a hunch and a hope these past ten years, breeding small-voiced dragons together. I've been *trying* to breed a mute. Think of it, a mute fighter—why, it would give nothing away, not to pit foes or to bettors. A mute fighter and its trainer . . ." and Sarkkhan stopped on the stairs, looking down at the boy. "Why, they'd rule the pits, boy."

They finished the stairs and turned down the hallway. Sarkkhan strode ahead, and Jakkin had to doubletime in order to keep up with the big man's strides.

"Master Sarkkhan," he began at the man's back.

Sarkkhan did not break stride but growled, "I am no longer your master, Jakkin. *You* are a master now. A master trainer. That dragon will speak only to you, go only on your command. Remember that, and act accordingly."

Jakkin blinked twice and touched his chest. "But . . . but my bag is empty. I have no gold to fill it. I have no sponsor for my next fight. I . . ."

Sarkkhan whirled, and his eyes were fierce. "*I* am sponsor for your next fight. I thought that much, at least, was clear. And when your bag is full, you will pay me no gold for your bond. Instead, I want pick of the first hatching when the red is bred—to a mate of my choosing. If she is a complete mute, she may breed true, and *I* mean to have it."

"Oh, Master Sarkkhan," Jakkin cried, suddenly realizing that all his dreams were realities, "you may have the pick of the first *three* hatchings." He grabbed the man's hand and tried to shake his thanks into it.

"*Fewmets!*" the man yelled, startling some of the passersby. He shook the boy's hand loose. "How can you ever become a bettor if you offer it all up front. You have to disguise your feelings better than that. Offer me the pick of the *third* hatching. Counter me. Make me work for whatever I get."

Jakkin said softly, testing, "The pick of the third."

"First two," said Sarkkhan, softly back and his smile came slowly. Then he roared. "Or I'll have you in jail and the red in the stews."

A crowd began to gather around them, betting on the outcome of the uneven match. Sarkkhan was a popular figure at pit-fights, and the boy was leather-patched—obviously a bonder, an unknown, worm waste.

All at once Jakkin felt as if he were at pitside. He felt the red's mind flooding into his, a rainbow effect that gave him a rush of courage. It was a game, then, all a game. And he knew how to play. "The second," said Jakkin, smiling back. "After all, Heart's Blood is a First Fighter, and a winner. And," he hissed at Sarkkhan so that only the two of them could hear, "she's a mute." Then he stood straight and said loudly, so that it carried to the crowd, "You'll be lucky to have pick of the second."

Sarkkhan stood silently, as if considering both the boy and the crowd. He brushed his hair back from his forehead, then nodded. "Done," he said. "A hard bargain." Then he reached over and ruffled Jakkin's hair, and they walked off together.

The crowd, settling their bets, let them through.

"I *thought* you were a good learner," Sarkkhan said to the boy. "Second it is. Though," and he chuckled and said quietly, "you should remember this. There is never anything good in a first hatching. Second is the best by far."

"I didn't know," said Jakkin.

"Why should you?" countered Sarkkhan. "*You* are not the best breeder on Austar IV. I am. But I like the name you picked. Heart's Blood out of Heart O' Mine. It suits."

They went through the doorway together to register the red and to stuff Jakkin's bag with hard-earned dragon's gold.

THE STORM KING

Joan D. Vinge

They said that in those days the lands were cursed that lay in the shadow of the Storm King. The peak thrust up from the gently rolling hills and fertile farmlands like an impossible wave cresting on the open sea, a brooding finger probing the secrets of heaven. Once it had vomited fire and fumes, ash and molten stone had poured from its throat; the distant forerunners of the people who lived beneath it now had died of its wrath. But the Earth had spent Her fury in one final cataclysm, and now the mountain lay quiet, dark, and cold, its mouth choked with congealed stone.

And yet still the people lived in fear. No one among them remembered having seen its summit, which was always crowned by cloud; lightning played in the purple, shrouding robes, and distant thunder filled the dreams of the folk who slept below with the roaring of dragons.

For it was a dragon who had come to dwell among the crags: that elemental focus of all storm and fire carried on the wind, drawn to a place where the Earth's fire had died, a place still haunted by ancient grief. And sharing the spirit of fire, the dragon knew no law and obeyed no power except its own. By day or night it would rise on furious wings of wind and sweep over the land, inundating the crops with rain, blasting trees with its lightning, battering walls and tearing away rooftops; terrifying rich and poor, man and beast, for the sheer pleasure of destruction, the exaltation of uncontrolled power. The people had prayed to the new gods who had replaced their worship of the Earth to deliver them; but the new gods made Their home in the sky, and seemed to be beyond hearing.

By now the people had made Their names into curses, as they pried their oxcarts from the mud or looked out over fields of broken grain and felt their bellies and their children's bellies tighten with hunger. And they would look toward the distant peak and curse the Storm King, naming the peak and the dragon both; but always in whispers and mutters, for fear the wind would hear them, and bring the dark storm sweeping down on them again.

The storm-wracked town of Wyddon and its people looked up only briefly in their sullen shaking-off and shoveling-out of mud as a stranger picked his way among them. He wore the woven leather of a common soldier, his cloak and leggings were coarse and ragged, and he walked the planks laid down in the stinking street as though determination alone kept him on his feet. A woman picking through baskets of stunted leeks in the marketplace saw with vague surprise that he had entered the tiny village temple; a man putting fresh thatch on a torn-open roof saw him come out again, propelled by the indignant, orange-robed priest.

"If you want witchery, find yourself a witch! This is a holy place; the gods don't meddle in vulgar magic!"

"I can see that," the stranger muttered, staggering in ankle-deep mud. He climbed back onto the boards with some difficulty and obvious disgust. "Maybe if they did you'd have streets and not rivers of muck in this town." He turned away in anger, almost stumbled over a mud-colored girl blocking his forward progress on the boardwalk.

"You priests should bow down to the Storm King!" the girl postured insolently, looking toward the priest. "The dragon can change all our lives more in one night than your gods have done in a lifetime."

"Slut!" The priest shook his carven staff at her; its necklace of golden bells chimed like absurd laughter. "There's a witch for you, beggar. If you think she can teach you to tame the dragon, then go with her!" He turned away, disappearing into the temple. The stranger's body jerked, as though it strained against his control, wanting to strike at the priest's retreating back.

"You're a witch?" The stranger turned and glared down at the bony figure standing in his way, found her studying him back with obvious skepticism. He imagined what she saw—a foreigner, his straight black hair whacked off like a serf's, his clothes crawling with filth, his face grimed and gaunt and set in a bitter grimace. He frowned more deeply.

The girl shook her head. "No. I'm just bound to her. You have business to take up with her, I see—about the Storm King." She smirked, expecting him to believe she was privy to secret knowledge.

"As you doubtless overheard, yes." He shifted his weight from one leg to the other, trying fruitlessly to ease the pain in his back.

She shrugged, pushing her own tangled brown hair back from her face. "Well, you'd better be able to pay for it, or you've come a long way from Kwansai for nothing."

He started, before he realized that his coloring and his eyes gave that much away. "I can pay." He drew his dagger from its hidden sheath, the only weapon he had left, and the only thing of value. He let her glimpse the jeweled hilt before he pushed it back out of sight.

Her gray eyes widened briefly. "What do I call you, Prince of Thieves?" with another glance at his rags.

"Call me Your Highness," not lying, and not quite joking.

She looked up into his face again, and away. "Call me Nothing, Your Highness. Because I am nothing." She twitched a shoulder at him. "And follow me."

They passed the last houses of the village without further speech, and followed the mucky track on into the dark, dripping forest that lay at the mountain's feet. The girl stepped off the road and into the trees without warning; he followed her recklessly, half angry and half afraid that she was abandoning him. But she danced ahead of him through the pines, staying always in sight, although she was plainly impatient with his lagging pace. The dank chill of the sunless wood gnawed his aching back and swarms of stinging gnats feasted on his exposed skin; the bare-armed girl seemed as oblivious to the insects as she was to the cold.

He pushed on grimly, as he had pushed on until now, having no choice but to keep on or die. And at last his persistence was rewarded; he saw the forest rise ahead, and buried in the flank of the hillside among the trees was a mossy hut linteled by immense stones.

The girl disappeared into the hut as he entered the clearing before it. He slowed, looking around him at the clusters of carven images pushing up like unnatural growths from the spongy ground, or dangling from tree limbs. Most of the images were subtly or blatantly obscene. He averted his eyes and limped between them to the hut's entrance.

He stepped through the doorway without waiting for an invitation, to find the girl crouched by the hearth in the cramped interior, wearing the secret smile of a cat. Beside her an incredibly wrinkled, ancient woman sat on a three-legged stool. The legs were carved into shapes that made him look away again, back at the wrinkled face and the black, buried eyes that regarded him with flinty bemusement. He noticed abruptly that there was no wall behind her: the far side of the hut melted into the black volcanic stone, a natural fissure opening into the mountain's side.

"So, Your Highness, you've come all the way from Kwansai seeking the Storm King, and a way to tame its power?"

He wrapped his cloak closely about him and grimaced, the nearest thing to a smile of scorn that he could manage. "Your girl has a quick tongue. But I've come to the wrong place, it seems, for real power."

"Don't be so sure!" The old woman leaned toward him, shrill and spiteful. "You can't afford to be too sure of anything, Lassan-din. You were prince of Kwansai, you should have been king there when your father died, and overlord of these lands as well. And now you're nobody and you have no home, no friends, barely even your life. Nothing is what it seems to be . . . it never is."

Lassan-din's mouth went slack; he closed it, speechless at last. *Nothing is what it seems.* The girl called Nothing grinned up at him from the floor. He took a deep breath, shifting to ease his back again. "Then you know what I've come for, if you already know that much, witch."

The hag half-rose from her obscene stool; he glimpsed a flash of color, a brighter, finer garment hidden beneath the drab outer robe she wore—the way the inner woman still burned fiercely bright in her eyes, showing through the wasted flesh of her ancient body. "Call me no names, you prince of beggars! I am the Earth's Own. Your puny Kwansai priests, who call my sisterhood 'witch,' who destroyed our holy places and drove us into hiding, know nothing of power. They're fools, they don't believe in power and they are powerless, charlatans. You know it or you wouldn't be here!" She settled back, wheezing. "Yes, I could tell you what you want; but suppose you tell me."

"I want what's mine! I want my kingdom." He paced restlessly, two steps and then back. "I know of elementals, all the old legends. My people say that dragons are stormbringers, born from a joining of Fire and Water and Air, three of the four Primes of Existence. Nothing but the Earth can defy their fury. And I know that if I can hold a dragon in its lair with the right spells, it must give me what I want, like the heroes of the Golden Time. I want to use its power to take back my lands."

"You don't want much, do you?" The old woman rose from her seat and turned her back on him, throwing a surreptitious handful of something into the fire, making it flare up balefully. She stirred the pot that hung from a hook above it; spitting five times into the noxious brew as she stirred. Lassan-din felt his empty stomach turn over. "If you want to challenge the Storm King, you should be out there climbing, not here holding your hand out to me."

"Damn you!" His exasperation broke loose, and his hand wrenched her around to face him. "I need some spell, some magic, some way to pen a dragon up. I can't do it with my bare hands!"

She shook her head, unintimidated, and leered toothlessly at him.

"My power comes to me through my body, up from the Earth Our Mother. She won't listen to a man—especially one who would destroy her worship. Ask your priests who worship the air to teach you their empty prayers."

He saw the hatred rising in her, and felt it answered: The dagger was out of its hidden sheath and in his hand before he knew it, pressing the soft folds of her neck. "I don't believe you, witch. See this dagger—" quietly, deadly. "If you give me what I want, you'll have the jewels in its hilt. If you don't, you'll feel its blade cut your throat."

"All right, all right!" She strained back as the blade's tip began to bite. He let her go. She felt her neck; the girl sat perfectly still at their feet, watching. "I can give you something, a spell. I can't guarantee She'll listen. But you have enough hatred in you for ten men—and maybe that will make your man's voice loud enough to penetrate Her skin. This mountain is sacred to Her, She still listens through its ears, even if She no longer breathes here."

"Never mind the superstitious drivel. Just tell me how I can keep the dragon in without it striking me dead with its lightning. How I can fight fire with fire—"

"You don't fight fire with fire. You fight fire with water."

He stared at her; at the obviousness of it, and the absurdity— "The dragon is the creator of storm. How can mere water—?"

"A dragon is anathema. Remember that, prince who would be king. It is chaos, power uncontrolled; and power always has a price. That's the key to everything. I can teach you the spell for controlling the waters of the Earth; but you're the one who must use it."

He stayed with the women through the day, and learned as the hours passed to believe in the mysteries of the Earth. The crone spoke words that brought water fountaining up from the well outside her door while he looked on in amazement, his weariness and pain forgotten. As he watched she made a brook flow upstream; made crystal droplets beading the forest pines join in a diadem to crown his head, and then with a word released them to run cold and helpless as tears into the collar of his ragged tunic.

She seized the fury that rose up in him at her insolence, and chal-

lenged him to do the same. He repeated the ungainly, ancient spell-
words defiantly, arrogantly—and nothing happened. She scoffed, his
anger grew; she jeered and it grew stronger. He repeated the spell
again, and again, and again . . . until at last he felt the terrifying presence of an alien power rise in his body, answering the call of his blood.
The droplets on the trees began to shiver and commingle; he watched
an eddy form in the swift clear water of the stream—. The Earth had
answered him.

His anger failed him at the unbelievable sight of his success . . .
and the power failed him too. Dazed and strengthless, at last he knew
his anger for the only emotion with the depth or urgency to move the
body of the Earth, or even his own. But he had done the impossible—
made the Earth move to a man's bidding. He had proved his right to be
a king, proved that he could force the dragon to serve him as well. He
laughed out loud. The old woman moaned and spat, twisting her hands
that were like gnarled roots, mumbling curses. She shuffled away toward the woods as though she were in a trance; turned back abruptly as
she reached the trees, pointing past him at the girl standing like a
ghost in the hut's doorway. "You think you've known the Earth; that
you own Her, now. You think you can take anything and make it yours.
But you're as empty as that one, and as powerless!" And she was gone.

Night had fallen through the dreary wood without his realizing it.
The girl Nothing led him back into the hut, shared a bowl of thick,
strangely herbed soup and a piece of stale bread with him. He ate grate-
fully but numbly, the first warm meal he had eaten in weeks; his mind
drifted into waking dreams of banqueting until dawn in royal halls.

When he had eaten his share, wiping the bowl shamelessly with a
crust, he stood and walked the few paces to the hut's furthest corner.
He lay down on the hard stone by the cave mouth, wrapping his cloak
around him, and closed his eyes. Sleep's darker cloak settled over him.

And then, dimly, he became aware that the girl had followed
him, stood above him looking down. He opened his eyes unwillingly,
to see her unbelt her tunic and pull it off, kneel down naked at his
side. A piece of rock crystal, perfectly transparent, perfectly formed,
hung glittering coldly against her chest. He kept his eyes open, saying
nothing.

"The Old One won't be back until you're gone; the sight of a man calling on the Earth was too strong for her." Her hand moved insinuatingly along his thigh.

He rolled away from her, choking on a curse as his back hurt him sharply. "I'm tired. Let me sleep."

"I can help you. She could have told you more. I'll help you tomorrow . . . if you lie with me tonight."

He looked up at her, suddenly despairing. "Take my body, then; but it won't give you much pleasure." He pulled up the back of his tunic, baring the livid scar low on his spine. "My uncle didn't make a cripple of me—but he might as well have." When he even thought of a woman there was only pain, only rage . . . only that.

She put her hand on the scar with surprising gentleness. "I can help that too . . . for tonight." She went away, returned with a small jar of ointment and rubbed the salve slowly into his scarred back. A strange, cold heat sank through him; a sensuous tingling swept away the grinding ache that had been his only companion through these long months of exile. He let his breath out in an astonished sigh, and the girl lay down beside him, pulling at his clothes.

Her thin body was as hard and bony as a boy's, but she made him forget that. She made him forget everything, except that tonight he was free from pain and sorrow, tonight he lay with a woman who desired him, no matter what her reason. He remembered lost pleasure, lost joy, lost youth, only yesterday . . . until yesterday became tomorrow.

In the morning he woke, in pain, alone and fully clothed, aching on the hard ground. *Nothing* . . . He opened his eyes and saw her standing at the fire, stirring a kettle. A *dream*—? The cruel betrayal that was reality returned tenfold.

They ate together in a silence that was sullen on his part, and inscrutable on hers. After last night it seemed obvious to him that she was older than she looked—as obvious as the way he himself had changed from boy to old man in a span of months. And he felt an insubstantiality about her that he had not noticed before, an elusiveness that might only have been an echo of his dream. "I dreamed, last night . . ."

"I know." She climbed to her feet, cutting him off, combing her snarled hair back with her fingers. "You dream loudly." Her face was closed.

He felt a frown settle between his eyes again. "I have a long climb. I'd better get started." He pushed himself up and moved stiffly toward the doorway. The old hag still had not returned.

"Not that way," the girl said abruptly. "This way." She pointed as he turned back, toward the cleft in the rock.

He stood still. "That will take me to the dragon?"

"Only part way. But it's easier by half. I'll show you." She jerked a brand out of the fire and started into the maw of darkness.

He went after her with only a moment's uncertainty. He had lived in fear for too long; if he was afraid to follow this witch-girl into her Goddess's womb, then he would never have the courage to challenge the Storm King.

The low-ceilinged cleft angled steeply upward, a natural tube formed millennia ago by congealing lava. The girl began to climb confidently, as though she trusted some guardian power to place her hands and feet surely—a power he could not depend on as he followed her up the shaft. The dim light of day snuffed out behind him, leaving only her torch to guide them through utter blackness, over rock that was alternately rough enough to flay the skin from his hands and slick enough to give him no purchase at all. The tunnel twisted like a worm, widening, narrowing, steepening, folding back on itself in an agony of contortion. His body protested its own agony as he dragged it up handholds in a sheer rock face, twisted it, wrenched it, battered it against the unyielding stone. The acrid smoke from the girl's torch stung his eyes and clogged his lungs; but it never seemed to slow her own tireless motion, and she took no pity on his weakness. Only the knowledge of the distance he had come kept him from demanding that they turn back; he could not believe that this could possibly be an easier way than climbing the outside of the mountain. It began to seem to him that he had been climbing through this foul blackness for all of eternity, that this was another dream like his dream last night, but one that would never end.

The girl chanted softly to herself now; he could just hear her above his own labored breathing. He wondered jealously if she was drawing strength from the very stone around them, the body of the Earth. He could feel no pulse in the cold heart of the rock; and yet after yesterday he did not doubt its presence, even wondering if the Earth sapped his own strength with preternatural malevolence. *I am a man, I will be king!* he thought defiantly. And the way grew steeper, and his hands bled.

"Wait—!" He gasped out the word at last, as his feet went out from under him again and he barely saved himself from sliding back down the tunnel. "I can't go on."

The girl, crouched on a level spot above him, looked back and down at him and ground out the torch. His grunt of protest became a grunt of surprise as he saw her silhouetted against a growing gray-brightness. She disappeared from his view; the brightness dimmed and then strengthened.

He heaved himself up and over the final bend in the wormhole, into a space large enough to stand in if he had had the strength. He crawled forward hungrily into the brightness at the cave mouth, found the girl kneeling there, her face raised to the light. He welcomed the fresh air into his lungs, cold and cleansing; looked past her—and down.

They were dizzyingly high on the mountain's side, above the tree-line, above a sheer unscalable face of stone. A fast-falling torrent of water roared on their left, plunging out and down the cliff-face. The sun winked at him from the cloud-wreathed heights; its angle told him they had climbed for the better part of the day. He looked over at the girl.

"You're lucky," she said, without looking back at him. Before he could even laugh at the grotesque irony of the statement she raised her hand, pointing on up the mountainside. "The Storm King sleeps—another storm is past. I saw the rainbow break this sunrise."

He felt a surge of strength and hope, absorbed the indifferent blessing of the Holy Sun. "How long will it sleep?"

"Two more days, perhaps. You won't reach its den before night. Sleep here, and climb again tomorrow."

"And then?" He looked toward her expectantly.

She shrugged.

"I paid you well," not certain in what coin, anymore. "I want a fair return! How do I pen the beast?"

Her hand tightened around the crystal pendant hanging against her tunic. She glanced back into the cave mouth. "There are many waters flowing from the heights. One of them might be diverted to fall past the entrance of its lair."

"A waterfall? I might as well hold up a rose and expect it to cower!"

"Power always has its price; as the Old One said." She looked directly at him at last. "The storm rests here in mortal form—the form of the dragon. And like all mortals, it suffers. Its strength lies in the scales that cover its skin. The rain washes them away—the storm is agony to the stormbringer. They fall like jewels, they catch the light as they fall, like a trail of rainbow. It's the only rainbow anyone here has ever seen . . . a sign of hope, because it means an end to the storm; but a curse, too, because the storm will always return, endlessly."

"Then I could have it at my mercy . . ." He heard nothing else.

"Yes. If you can make the Earth move to your will." Her voice was flat.

His hands tightened. "I have enough hate in me for that."

"And what will you demand, to ease it?" She glanced at him again, and back at the sky. "The dragon is defiling this sacred place; it should be driven out. You could become a hero to my people, if you forced the dragon to go away—a god. They need a god who can do them some good . . ."

He felt her somehow still watching him, measuring his response, even though she had looked away. "I came here to solve my problem, not yours. I want my own kingdom, not a kingdom of mud-men. I need the dragon's power—I didn't come here to drive that away."

The girl said nothing, still staring at the sky.

"It's a simple thing for you to move the waters—why haven't you driven the dragon away yourself, then?" His voice rasped in his parched throat, sharp with unrecognized guilt.

"I'm Nothing. I have no power—the Old One holds my soul." She looked down at the crystal.

"Then why won't the Old One do it?"

"She hates, too. She hates what our people have become under the new gods, your gods. That's why she won't."

"I'd think it would give her great pleasure to prove the impotence of the new gods." His mouth stretched sourly.

"She wants to die in the Earth's time, not tomorrow." The girl folded her arms, and her own mouth twisted.

He shook his head. "I don't understand that . . . why you didn't destroy our soldiers, our priests, with your magic?"

"The Earth moves slowly to our bidding, because She is eternal. An arrow is small—but it moves swiftly."

He laughed once, appreciatively. "I understand."

"There's a cairn of stones over there." She nodded back into the darkness."Food is under it." He realized that this must have been a place of refuge for the women in times of persecution. "The rest is up to you." She turned, merging abruptly into the shadows.

"Wait!" he called, surprising himself. "You must be tired."

She shook her head, a deeper shadow against darkness.

"Stay with me—until morning." It was not quite a demand, not quite a question.

"Why?" He thought he saw her eyes catch light and reflect it back at him, like a wild thing's.

Because I had a dream. He did not say it, did not say anything else.

"Our debts have balanced." She moved slightly, and something landed on the ground at his feet: his dagger. The hilt was pockmarked with empty jewel settings; stripped clean. He leaned down to pick it up. When he straightened again she was gone.

"You need a light—!" He called after her again.

Her voice came back to him, from a great distance: "May you get what you deserve!" And then silence, except for the roaring of the falls.

He ate, wondering whether her last words were a benediction or a curse. He slept, and the dreams that came to him were filled with the roaring of dragons.

With the light of a new day he began to climb again, following the urgent river upward toward its source that lay hidden in the waiting crown of clouds. He remembered his own crown, and lost himself in memories of the past and future, hardly aware of the harsh sobbing of his breath, of flesh and sinew strained past a sane man's endurance. Once he had been the spoiled child of privilege, his father's only son—living in the world's eye, his every whim a command. Now he was as much Nothing as the witch-girl far down the mountain. But he would live the way he had again, his every wish granted, his power absolute—he *would* live that way again, if he had to climb to the gates of heaven to win back his birthright.

The hours passed, endlessly, inevitably, and all he knew was that slowly, slowly, the sky lowered above him. At last the cold, moist edge of clouds enfolded his burning body, drawing him into another world of gray mist and gray silences; black, glistening surfaces of rock; the white sound of the cataract rushing down from even higher above. Drizzling fog shrouded the distances any way he turned, and he realized that he did not know where in this layer of cloud the dragon's den lay. He had assumed that it would be obvious, he had trusted the girl to tell him all he needed to know . . . Why had he trusted her? That pagan slut—his hand gripped the rough hilt of his dagger; dropped away, trembling with fatigue. He began to climb again, keeping the sound of falling water nearby for want of any other guide. The light grew vaguer and more diffuse, until the darkness falling in the outer world penetrated the fog world and the haze of his exhaustion. He lay down at last, unable to go on, and slept beneath the shelter of an overhang of rock.

He woke stupefied by daylight. The air held a strange acridness that hurt his throat, that he could not identify. The air seemed almost to crackle; his hair ruffled, although there was no wind. He pushed himself up. He knew this feeling now: a storm was coming. A storm coming . . . a storm, here? Suddenly, fully awake, he turned on his knees, peering deeper beneath the overhang that sheltered him. And in the light of dawn he could see that it was not a simple overhang, but another opening into the mountain's side—a wider, greater one, whose depths the day could not fathom. But far down in the blackness a flickering of unnatural light showed. His hair rose in the electric breeze, he felt his skin prickle. *Yes . . . yes!* A small cry escaped him. He had found it! Without even knowing it, he had slept in the mouth of the dragon's lair all night. Habit brought a thanks to the gods to his lips, until he remembered—He muttered a *thank you* to the Earth beneath him before he climbed to his feet. A brilliant flash silhouetted him; a rumble like distant thunder made the ground vibrate, and he froze. Was the dragon waking—?

But there was no further disturbance, and he breathed again. Two days, the girl had told him, the dragon might sleep. And now he had reached his final trial, the penning of the beast. Away to his right he could hear the cataract's endless song. But would there be enough water in it to block the dragon's exit? Would that be enough to keep it prisoner, or would it strike him down in lightning and thunder, and sweep his body from the heights with torrents of rain? . . . Could he even move one droplet of water, here and now? Or would he find that all the thousand doubts that gnawed inside him were not only useless but pointless?

He shook it off, moving out and down the mist-dim slope to view the cave mouth and the river tumbling past it. A thin stream of water already trickled down the face of the opening, but the main flow was diverted by a folded knot of lava. If he could twist the water's course and hold it, for just long enough . . .

He climbed the barren face of stone at the far side of the cave mouth until he stood above it, confronting the sinuous steel and flashing white of the thing he must move. It seemed almost alive, and he felt weary, defeated, utterly insignificant at the sight of it. But the mountain on which he stood was a greater thing than even the river, and he knew that within it lay power great enough to change the water's course. But he was the conduit, his will must tap and bend the force that he had felt stir in him two days ago.

He braced his legs apart, gathered strength into himself, trying to recall the feel of magic moving in him. He recited the spell-words, the focus for the willing of power—and felt nothing. He recited the words again, putting all his concentration behind them. Again nothing. The Earth lay silent and inert beneath his feet.

Anger rose in him, at the Earth's disdain, and against the strange women who served Her—the jealous, demanding anger that had opened him to power before. And this time he did feel the power stir in him, sluggishly, feebly. But there was no sign of any change in the water's course. He threw all his conscious will toward change, *change, change*— but still the Earth's power faltered and mocked him. He let go of the ritual words at last, felt the tingling promise of energy die, having burned away all his own strength.

He sat down on the wet stone, listened to the river roar with laughter. He had been so sure that when he got here the force of his need would be strong enough . . . *I have enough hate in me*, he had told the girl. But he wasn't reaching it now. Not the real hatred that had carried him so far beyond the limits of his strength and experience. He began to concentrate on that hatred, and the reasons behind it: the loss, the pain, the hardship and fear . . .

His father had been a great ruler over the lands that his ancestors had conquered. And he had loved his queen, Lassan-din's mother. But when she died, his unhealing grief had turned him ruthless and iron-willed. He had become a despot, capricious, cruel, never giving an inch of his power to another man—even his spoiled and insecure son. Disease had left him wasted and witless in the end. And Lassan-din, barely come to manhood, had been helpless, unable to block his jealous uncle's treachery. He had been attacked by his own guard as he prayed in the temple (*In the temple*—his mouth pulled back), and maimed, barely escaping with his life, to find that his entire world had come to an end. He had become a hunted fugitive in his own land, friendless, trusting no one—forced to lie and steal and grovel to survive. He had eaten scraps thrown out to dogs and lain on hard stones in the rain, while the festering wound in his back kept him from any rest . . .

Reliving each day, each moment, of his suffering and humiliation, he felt his rage and his hunger for revenge grow hotter. The Earth hated this usurper of Her holy place, the girl had said . . . but no more than he hated the usurper of his throne. He climbed to his feet again, every muscle on fire, and held out his hands. He shouted the incantation aloud, as though it could carry all the way to his homeland. *His homeland:* he would see it again, make it his own again—

The power entered him as the final word left his mouth, paralyzing every nerve, stopping even the breath in his throat. Fear and elation were swept up together into the maelstrom of his emotions, and power exploded like a sun behind his eyes. But through the fiery haze that blinded him, he could still see the water heave up from its bed—a steely wall crowned with white, crumbling over and down on itself. It swept toward him, a terrifying cataclysm, until he thought that he would be drowned in the rushing flood. But it passed him by where he stood, plunging on over the outcropping roof of the cave below. Eddies of foam swirled around his feet, soaking his stained leggings.

The power left him like the water's surge falling away. He took a deep breath, and another, backing out of the flood. His body moved sluggishly; drained, abandoned, an empty husk. But his mind was full with triumph and rejoicing.

The ground beneath his feet shuddered, jarring his elation, dropping him giddily back into reality. He pressed his head with his hands as pain filled his senses, a madness crowding out coherent thought—a pain that was not his own.

(Water . . . !) Not a plea, but outrage and confusion, a horror of being trapped in a flood of molten fire. *The dragon.* He realized suddenly what had invaded his mind; realized that he had never stopped to wonder how a storm might communicate with a man: not by human speech, but by stranger, more elemental means. Water from the fall he had created must be seeping into its lair . . . His face twisted with satisfaction. "Dragon!" He called it with his mind and his voice together.

(Who calls? Who tortures me? Who fouls my lair? Show yourself, slave!)

"Show yourself to me, Storm King! Come out of your cave and destroy me—if you can!" The wildness of his challenge was tinged with terror.

The dragon's fury filled his head until he thought that it would burst; the ground shook beneath his feet. But the rage turned to frustration and died, as though the gates of liquid iron had bottled it up with its possessor. He gulped air, holding his body together with an effort of will. The voice of the dragon pushed aside his thoughts again, trampled them underfoot; but he knew that it could not reach him, and he endured without weakening.

(Who are you, and why have you come?) He sensed a grudging resignation in the formless words, the feel of a ritual as eternal as the rain.

"I am a man who should have been a king. I've come to you, who are King of Storms, for help in regaining my own kingdom."

(You ask me for that? Your needs mean nothing, human. You were born to misery, born to crawl, born to struggle and be defeated by the powers of Air and Fire and Water. You are meaningless, you are less than nothing to me!)

Lassan-din felt the truth of his own insignificance, the weight of the dragon's disdain. "That may be," he said sourly. "But this insignificant human has penned you up with the Earth's blessing, and I have no reason to ever let you go unless you pledge me your aid."

The rage of the storm beast welled up in him again, so like his own rage; it rumbled and thundered in the hollow of the mountain. But again a profound agony broke its fury, and the raging storm subsided. He caught phantom images of stone walls lit by shifting light, the smell of water.

(If you have the strength of the Earth with you, why bother me for mine?)

"The Earth moves too slowly," *and too uncertainly,* but he did not say that. "I need a fury to match my own."

(Arrogant fool,) the voice whispered, (you have no measure of my fury.)

"Your fury can crumble walls and blast towers. You can destroy a fortress castle—and the men who defend it. I know what you can do," refusing to be cowed. "And if you swear to do it for me, I'll set you free."

(You want a castle ruined. Is that all?) A tone of false reason crept into the intruding thoughts.

"No. I also want for myself a share of your strength—protection from my enemies." He had spent half a hundred cold, sleepless nights planning these words; searching his memory for pieces of dragon-lore, trying to guess the limits of its power.

(How can I give you that? I do not share my power, unless I strike you dead with it.)

"My people say that in the Golden Times the heroes wore mail made from dragon scales, and were invincible. Can you give me that?" He asked the question directly, knowing that the dragon might evade the truth, but that it was bound by immutable natural law, and could not lie.

(I can give you that,) grudgingly. (Is that all you ask of me?)

Lassan-din hesitated. "No. One more thing." His father had taught him caution, if nothing else. "One request to be granted at some future time—a request within your power, but one you must obey."

The dragon muttered, deep within the mountainside, and Lassan-din sensed its growing distress as the water poured into the cave. (If it is within my power, then, yes!) Dark clouds of anger filled his mind. (Free me, and you will have everything you ask!) *And more*—Did he hear that last, or was it only the echoing of his own mind? (Free me, and enter my den.)

"What I undo, I can do again." He spoke the warning more to reassure himself than to remind the dragon. He gathered himself mentally, knowing this time what he was reaching toward with all his strength, made confident by his success. And the Earth answered him once more. He saw the river shift and heave again like a glistening serpent, cascading back into its original bed; opening the cave mouth to his sight, fanged and dripping. He stood alone on the hillside, deafened by his heartbeat and the crashing absence of the river's voice. And then, calling his own strength back, he slid and clambered down the hillside to the mouth of the dragon's cave.

The flickering illumination of the dragon's fire led him deep into the maze of stone passageways, his boots slipping on the wet rock. His hair stood on end and his fingertips tingled with static charge, the air reeked of ozone. The light grew stronger as he rounded a final corner of rock; blazed up, echoing and reechoing from the walls. He shouted in protest as it pinned him like a creeping insect against the cave wall.

The light faded gradually to a tolerable level, letting him observe as he was observed, taking in the towering, twisted black-tar formations of congealed magma that walled this cavern . . . the sudden, heart-stopping vision they enclosed. He looked on the Storm King in silence for a time that seemed endless.

A glistening layer of cast-off scales was its bed, and he could scarcely tell where the mound ceased and the dragon's own body began. The dragon looked nothing like the legends described, and yet just as he had expected it to (and somehow he did not find that strange): Great mailed claws like crystal kneaded the shifting opalescence of its bed; its forelegs shimmered with the flexing of its muscles. It had no hindquarters, its body tapered into the fluid coils of a snake's form woven through the glistening pile. Immense segmented wings, as leathery as a bat's, as fragile as a butterfly's, cloaked its monstrous strength. A long sinuous neck stretched toward him, red faceted eyes shone with inner light from a face that was closest to a cat's face of all the things he knew, but fiercely fanged and grotesquely distorted. The horns of a stag sprouted from its forehead, and foxfire danced among the spines. The dragon's size was a thing that he could have described easily, and yet it was somehow immeasurable, beyond his comprehension.

This was the creature he had challenged and brought to bay with his feeble spell-casting . . . this boundless, pitiless, infinite demon of the air. His body began to tremble, having more sense than he did. But he *had* brought it to bay, taken its word-bond, and it had not blasted him the moment he entered its den. He forced his quavering voice to carry boldly, "I'm here. Where is my armor?"

(Leave your useless garments and come forward. My scales are my strength, lie among them and cover yourself with them. But remember when you do that if you wear my mail, and share my power, you may find them hard to put off again. Do you accept that?)

"Why would I ever want to get rid of power? I accept it! Power is the center of everything."

(But power has its price, and we do not always know how high it will be.) The dragon stirred restlessly, remembering the price of power as the water still pooling on the cavern's floor seeped up through its shifting bed.

Lassan-din frowned, hearing a deceit because he expected one. He stripped off his clothing without hesitation and crossed the vast, shadow-haunted chamber to the gleaming mound. He lay down below the dragon's baleful gaze and buried himself in the cool, scintillating flecks of scale. They were damp and surprisingly light under his touch, adhering to his body like the dust rubbed from a moth's wing. When he had covered himself completely, until even his hair glistened with myriad infinitesimal lights, the dragon bent its head until the horrible mockery of a cat's face loomed above him. He cringed back as it opened its mouth, showing him row behind row of inward-turning teeth, and a glowing forge of light. It let its breath out upon him, and his sudden scream rang darkly in the chamber as lightning wrapped his unprotected body.

But the crippling lash of pain was gone as quickly as it had come; and looking at himself he found the coating of scales fused into a film of armor as supple as his own skin, and as much a part of him now. His scale-gloved hands met one another in wonder, the hands of an alien creature.

(Now come.) A great glittering wing extended, inviting him to climb. (Cling to me as your armor clings to you, and let me do your bidding and be done with it.)

He mounted the wing with elaborate caution, and at last sat astride the reptilian neck, clinging to it with an uncertainty that did not fully acknowledge its reality.

The dragon moved under him without ceremony or sign, slithering down from its dais of scales with a hiss and rumble that trembled the closed space. A wind rose around them with the movement; Lassan-din felt himself swallowed into a vortex of cold, terrifying force that took his breath away, blinding and deafening him as he was sucked out of the cave-darkness and into the outer air.

Lightning cracked and shuddered, penetrating his closed lids, splitting apart his consciousness; thunder clogged his chest, reverberating through his flesh and bones like the crashing fall of an avalanche. Rain lashed him, driving into his eyes, swallowing him whole but not dissolving or dissipating his armor of scales.

In the first wild moments of storm he had been piercingly aware of an agony that was not his own, a part of the dragon's being tied into his consciousness, while the fury of rain and storm fed back on their creator. But now there was no pain, no awareness of anything tangible; even the substantiality of the dragon's existence beneath him had faded. The elemental storm was all that existed now, he was aware only of its raw, unrelenting power surrounding him, sweeping him on to his destiny.

After an eternity lost in the storm he found his sight again, felt the dragon's rippling motion beneath his hands. The clouds parted and as his vision cleared he saw, ahead and below, the gray stone battlements of the castle fortress that had once been his . . . and was about to become his again. He shouted in half-mad exultation, feeling the dragon's surging, unconquerable strength become his own. He saw from his incredible height the tiny, terrified forms of those men who had defeated and tormented him, saw them cowering like worms before the doom descending upon them. And then the vision was torn apart again in a blinding explosion of energy, as lightning struck the stone towers again and again, and the screams of the fortress's defenders were lost in the avalanche of thunder. His own senses reeled, and he felt the dragon's solidness dissolve beneath him once more; with utter disbelief felt himself falling, like the rain . . ."No! No—!"

But his reeling senses righted abruptly, and he found himself standing solidly on his own feet, on the smoking battlements of his castle. Storm and flame and tumbled stone were all around him, but the blackened, fear-filled faces of the beaten defenders turned as one to look up at his; their arms rose, pointing, their cries reached him dimly. An arrow struck his chest, and another struck his shoulder, staggering him; but they fell away, rattling harmlessly down his scaled body to his feet. A shaft of sunlight broke the clouds, setting afire the glittering carapace of his armor. Already the storm was beginning to dissipate; above him the dragon's retreat stained the sky with a band of rainbow scales falling. The voice of the storm touched his mind a final time, (You have what you desire. May it bring you the pleasure you deserve.)

The survivors began, one by one, to fall to their knees below him.

* * *

Lassan-din had ridden out of exile on the back of the whirlwind, and his people bowed down before him, not in welcome but in awe and terror. He reclaimed his birthright and his throne, purging his realm of those who had overthrown it with vengeful thoroughness, but never able to purge himself of the memories of what they had done to him. His treacherous uncle had been killed in the dragon's attack, robbing Lassan-din of his longed-for retribution, the payment in kind for his own crippling wound. He wore his bitterness like the glittering dragonskin, and he found that like the dragonskin it could never be cast off again. His people hated and feared him for his shining alienness; hated him all the more for his attempts to secure his place as their ruler, seeing in him the living symbol of his uncle's inhumanity, and his father's. But he knew no other way to rule them; he could only go on, as his father had done before him, proving again and again to his people that there was no escaping what he had become. Not for them, not for himself.

They called him the Storm King, and he had all the power he had ever dreamed of—but it brought him no pleasure, no ease, no escape from the knowledge that he was hated or from the chronic pain of his maimed back. He was both more and less than a man, but he was no longer a man. Lying alone in his chambers between silken sheets he dreamed now that he still slept on stones; and dreamed the dream he had had long ago in a witch's hut, a dream that might have been something more . . . And when he woke he remembered the witch-girl's last words to him, echoed by the storm's roaring—"May you get what you deserve."

At last he left his fortress castle, where the new stone of its mending showed whitely against the old; left his rule in the hands of advisers cowed by threats of the dragon's return; left his homeland again for the dreary, gray-clad land of his exile.

He did not come to the village of Wydden as a hunted exile this time, but as a conqueror gathering tribute from his subject lands. No one there recognized the one in the other, or knew why he ordered the village priest thrown bodily out of his wretched temple into the muddy street. But on the dreary day when Lassan-din made his way at last into the dripping woods beneath the ancient volcanic peak, he made the final secret journey not as a conqueror.

He came alone to the ragged hut pressed up against the brooding mountain wall, suffering the wet and cold, like a friendless stranger. He came upon the clearing between the trees with an unnatural suddenness, to find a figure in mud-stained, earth-brown robes standing by the well, waiting, without surprise. He knew instantly that it was not the old hag; but it took him a longer moment to realize who it was: The girl called Nothing stood before him, dressed as a woman now, her brown hair neatly plaited on top of her head and bearing herself with a woman's dignity. He stopped, throwing back the hood of his cloak to let her see his own glittering face—though he was certain she already knew him, had expected him.

She bowed to him with seeming formality. "The Storm King honors my humble shrine." Her voice was not humble in the least.

"Your shrine?" He moved forward. "Where's the old bitch?"

She folded her arms as though to ward him off. "Gone forever. As I thought you were. But I'm still here, and I serve in her place; I am Fallatha, the Earth's Own, now. And your namesake still dwells in the mountain, bringing grief to all who live in its cloud-shadow . . . I thought you'd taken all you could from us, and gained everything you wanted. Why have you come back, and come like a beggar?"

His mouth thinned. But this once he stopped the arrogant response that came too easily to his lips—remembering that he had come here the way he had, to remind himself that he must ask, and not demand. "I came because I need your help again."

"What could I possibly have to offer our great ruler? My spells are nothing compared to the storm's wrath. And you have no use for my poor body—"

He jerked at the mocking echo of his own thoughts. "Once I had, on that night we both remember—that night you gave me back the use of mine." He gambled with the words. His eyes sought the curve of her breasts, not quite hidden beneath her loose outer robe.

"It was a dream, a wish; no more. It never happened." She shook her head, her face still expressionless. But in the silence that fell between them he heard a small, uncanny sound that chilled him: somewhere in the woods a baby was crying.

Fallatha glanced unthinkingly over her shoulder, toward the hut, and he knew then that it was her child. She made a move to stop him as he started past her; let him go, and followed resignedly. He found the child inside, an infant squalling in a blanket on a bed of fragrant pine boughs. Its hair was midnight black, its eyes were dark, its skin dusky; his own child, he knew with a certainty that went beyond simply what his eyes showed him. He knelt, unwrapping the blanket—let it drop back as he saw the baby's form. "A girl-child," dull with disappointment.

Fallatha's eyes said that she understood the implications of his disappointment. "Of course. I have no more use for a boy-child than you have for this one. Had it been a male child, I would have left it in the woods."

His head came up angrily, and her gaze slapped him with his own scorn. He looked down again at his infant daughter, feeling ashamed. "Then it did happen . . ." His hands tightened by his knees. "Why?" looking up at her again.

"Many reasons, and many you couldn't understand . . . But one was to win my freedom from the Old One. She stole my soul, and hid it in a tree to keep me her slave. She might have died without telling me where it was. Without a soul I had no center, no strength, no reality. So I brought a new soul into myself—this one's," smiling suddenly at the wailing baby, "and used its focus to make her give me back my own. And then with two souls," the smile hardened, "I took hers away. She wanders the forest now searching for it. But she won't find it." Fallatha touched the pendant of rock crystal that hung against her breast; what had been ice clear before was now a deep, smoky gray color.

Lassan-din suppressed a shudder. "But why *my* child?" *My child.* His own gaze would not stay away from the baby for long. "Surely any village lout would have been glad to do you the service."

"Because you have royal blood, you were a king's son—you are a king."

"That's not necessarily proof of good breeding." He surprised himself with his own honesty.

"But you called on the Earth, and She answered you. I have never seen Her answer a man before, or since . . . And because you were in need." Her voice softened unexpectedly. "An act of kindness begets a kind soul, they say."

"And now you hope to beget some reward for it, no doubt." He spoke the words with automatic harshness. "Greed and pity—a fitting set of god-parents, to match her real ones."

She shrugged. "You will see what you want to see, I suppose. But even a blind man could see more clearly." A frown pinched her forehead. "You've come here to me for help, Lassan-din; I didn't come to you."

He rubbed his scale-bright hands together, a motion that had become a habit long since; they clicked faintly. "Does—does the baby have a name?"

"Not yet. It is not our custom to name a child before its first year. Too often they die. Especially in these times."

He looked away from her eyes. "What will you do with—our child?" Realizing suddenly that it mattered a great deal to him.

"Keep her with me, and raise her to serve the Earth, as I do."

"If you help me again, I'll take you both back to my own lands, and give you anything you desire." He searched her face for a response.

"I desire to be left in peace with my child and my goddess." She leaned down to pick the baby up, let it seek her breast.

His inspiration crystallized: "Damn it, I'll throw my own priests out, I'll make your goddess the only one and you her high priestess!"

Her eyes brightened, and faded. "A promise easily spoken, and difficult to keep."

"What do you want, then?" He got to his feet, exasperated.

"You have a boon left with the dragon, I know. Make it leave the mountain. Send it away."

He ran his hands through his glittering hair. "No, I need it. I came here seeking help for myself, not your people."

"They're your people now—they *are* you. Help them and you help yourself! Is that so impossible for you to see?" Her own anger blazed white, incandescent with frustration.

"If you want to be rid of the dragon so much, why haven't you sent it away yourself, witch?"

"I would have." She touched the baby's tiny hand, its soft black hair. "Long ago. But until the little one no longer suckles my strength away, I lack the power to call the Earth to my purpose."

"Then you can't help me, either." His voice was flat and hopeless.

"I still have the salve that eased your back; but it won't help you now, it won't melt away your dragon's skin . . . I couldn't help your real needs, even if I had all my power."

"What do you mean?" He thrust his face at her. "Are you saying you couldn't ever undo this scaly hide of mine, that protects me from my people's hatred—and makes me a monster in their eyes? You think that's really why I've come to you? What makes you think I'd ever want to give up *my* power, my protection?" He clawed at his arms.

"It's not a man's skin that makes him a monster, or a god." Fallatha said quietly. "It's what lies beneath the skin, behind the eyes— his actions, not his face. You've lost your soul, as I lost mine; and only you know where to find it . . . But perhaps it would do you good to shed that skin that keeps you safe from hatred; and from love and joy and mercy, all the other feelings that might pass between human beings, between your people and their king."

"Yes! Yes, I want to be free of it, by the Holy Sun!" His face collapsed under the weight of his despair. "I thought my power would give me everything. But behind this armor I'm still nothing; less than that crippled wretch you took pity on!" He realized at last that he had come here this time to rid himself of the same things he had come to rid himself of—and to find—before. "I have a last boon due me from the dragon. It made me as I am; it can unmake me." He ran his hands down his chest, feeling the slippery, unyielding scales hidden beneath the rich cloth of his shirt.

"You mean to seek it out again, then?"

He nodded, and his hands made fists.

She carried the baby with her to the shelf above the crooked window, took down a small earthenware pot. She opened it and held it close to the child's face still buried at her breast; the baby sagged into sleep in the crook of her arm. She turned back to his uncomprehending face. "The little one will sleep now until I wake her. We can take the inner way, as we did before."

"You're coming? Why?"

"You didn't ask me that before. Why ask it now?"

He wasn't sure whether it was a question or an answer. Feeling as though not only his body but his mind was an empty shell, he only shrugged and kept silent.

They made the nightmare climb into blackness again, worming their way upward through the mountain's entrails; but this time she did not leave him where the mountain spewed them out, close under the weeping lid of the sky. He rested the night with the mother of his only child, the two of them lying together but apart. At dawn they pushed on, Lassan-din leading now, following the river's rushing torrent upward into the past.

They came to the dragon's cave at last, gazed on it for a long while in silence, having no strength left for speech.

"Storm King!" Lassan-din gathered the rags of his voice and his concentration for a shout. "Hear me! I have come for my last request!"

There was an alien stirring inside his mind; the charge in the air and the dim flickering light deep within the cave seemed to intensify.

(So you have returned to plague me.) The voice inside his head cursed him, with the weariness of the ages. He felt the stretch and play of storm-sinews rousing; remembered suddenly, dizzily, the feel of his ride on the whirlwind. (Show yourself to me.)

They followed the winding tunnel as he had done before to an audience in the black hall radiant with the dust of rainbows. The dragon crouched on its scaly bed, its glowering ruby eye fixed on them. Lassan-din stopped, trying to keep a semblance of self-possession. Fallatha drew her robes close together at her throat and murmured something unintelligible.

(I see that this time you have the wisdom to bring your true source of power with you . . . though she has no power in her now. Why have you come to me again? Haven't I given you all that you asked for?)

"All that and more," he said heavily. "You've doubled the weight of the griefs I brought with me before."

(I?) The dragon bent its head; its horns raked them with claw-fingered shadows in the sudden, swelling brightness. (I did nothing to you. Whatever consequences you've suffered are no concern of mine.)

Lassan-din bit back a stinging retort; said, calmly, "But you remember that you owe me one final boon. You know that I've come to collect it."

(Anything within my power.) The huge cat-face bowed ill-humoredly; Lassan-din felt his skin prickle with the static energy of the moment.

"Then take away these scales you fixed on me, that make me invulnerable to everything human!" He pulled off his drab, dark cloak and the rich royal clothing of red and blue beneath it, so that his body shone like an echo of the dragon's own.

The dragon's faceted eyes regarded him without feeling. (I cannot.)

Lassan-din froze as the words out of his blackest nightmares turned him to stone. "What—what do you mean, you cannot? You did this to me—you can undo it!"

(I cannot. I can give you invulnerability, but I cannot take it away from you. I cannot make your scales dissolve and fall away with a breath any more than I can keep the rain from dissolving mine, or causing me exquisite pain. It is in the nature of power that those who wield it must suffer from it, even as their victims suffer. That is power's price—I tried to warn you. But you didn't listen . . . none of them have ever listened.) Lassan-din felt the sting of venom, and the ache of an ageless empathy.

He struggled to grasp the truth, knowing that the dragon could not lie. He swayed, as belief struck him at last like a blow. "Am I . . . am I to go through the rest of my life like this, then? Like a monster?" He rubbed his hands together, a useless, mindless washing motion.

(I only know that it is not in my power to give you freedom from yourself.) The dragon wagged its head, its face swelling with light, dazzling him. (Go away, then,) the thought struck him fiercely, (and suffer elsewhere!)

Lassan-din turned away, stumbling, like a beaten dog. But Fallatha caught at his glittering, naked shoulder, shook him roughly. "Your boon! It still owes you one—ask it!"

"Ask for what?" he mumbled, barely aware of her. "There's nothing I want."

"There is! Something for your people, for your child—even for you. Ask for it! Ask!"

He stared at her, saw her pale, pinched face straining with suppressed urgency and desire. He saw in her eyes the endless sunless days, the ruined crops, the sodden fields—the mud and hunger and misery the Storm King had brought to the lands below for three times her lifetime. And the realization came to him that even now, when he had lost control of his own life, he still had the power to end this land's misery. Understanding came to him at last that he had been given an opportunity to use his power positively, unselfishly, for the good of the people he ruled . . . for his own good. That it meant a freer choice, and perhaps a truer humanity, than anything he had ever done. That his father had lost something many years ago which he had never known was missing from his own life, until now. He turned back into the view of the dragon's hypnotically swaying head. "My last boon, then, is something else; something I know to be within your power, stormbringer. I want you to leave this mountain, leave these lands, and never return. I want you to travel seven days on your way before you seek a new settling place, if you ever do. Travel as fast as you can, and as far, without taking retribution from the lands below. That is the final thing I ask of you."

The dragon spat in blinding fury. He shut his eyes, felt the ground shudder and roll beneath him. (You dare to command me to leave my chosen lands? You dare?)

"I claim my right!" He shouted it, his voice breaking. "Leave these lands alone—take your grief elsewhere and be done with them, and me!"

(As you wish, then—) The Storm King swelled above them until it filled the cave-space, its eyes a garish hellshine fading into the night-blackness of storm. Lightning sheeted the closing walls, thunder rumbled through the rock, a screaming whirlwind battered them down against the cavern floor. Rain poured over them until there was no breathing space, and the Storm King roared its agony inside their skulls as it suffered for its own revenge. Lassan-din felt his senses leaving him, with the knowledge that the storm would be the last thing he ever knew, the end of the world . . .

But he woke again, to silence. He stirred sluggishly on the wet stone floor, filling his lungs again and again with clear air, filling his empty mind with the awareness that all was quiet now, that no storm raged for his destruction. He heard a moan, not his own, and coughing echoed hollowly in the silence. He raised his head, reached out in the darkness, groping, until he found her arm. "Fallatha—?"

"Alive . . . praise the Earth."

He felt her move, sitting up, dragging herself toward him. The Earth, the cave in which they lay, had endured the storm's rage with sublime indifference. They helped each other up, stumbled along the wall to the entrance tunnel, made their way out through the blackness onto the mountainside.

They stood together, clinging to each other for support and reassurance, blinking painfully in the glaring light of early evening. It took him long moments to realize that there was more light than he remembered, not less.

"Look!" Fallatha raised her arm, pointing. Water dripped in a silver line from the sleeve of her robe. "The sky! The sky—" She laughed, a sound that was almost a sob.

He looked up into the aching glare, saw patches that he took at first for blackness, until his eyes knew them finally for blue. It was still raining lightly, but the clouds were parting, the tyranny of gray was broken at last. For a moment he felt her joy as his own, a fleeting, wild triumph—until looking down, he saw his hands again, and his shimmering body still scaled, monstrous, untransformed . . . "Oh, gods—!" His fists clenched at the sound of his own curse, a useless plea to useless deities.

Fallatha turned to him, her arm still around his shoulder, her face sharing his despair. "Lassan-din. I always knew that you were a good man, even though you have done evil things . . . You have reclaimed your soul today—remember that, and remember that my people will love you for your sacrifice. The world exists beyond yourself, and you will see that how you make your way through it matters." She touched his scaled cheek hesitantly, a promise.

"But all they'll ever see is how I look! And no matter what I do from now on, when they see the mark of damnation on me, they'll only remember why they hated me." He caught her arms in a bruising grip. "Fallatha, help me, please—I'll give you anything you ask!"

She shook her head, biting her lips, "I can't, Lassan-din. No more than the dragon could. You must help yourself, change yourself—I can't do that for you."

"How? How can I rid myself of this skin, if all the magic of Earth and Sky can't do it?" He sank to his knees, feeling the rain strike the opalescent scales and trickle down—feeling it dimly, barely, as though the rain fell on someone else. Remorse and regret filled him now, as rage had filled him on this spot once before. Tears welled in his eyes and spilled over, in answer to the calling-spell of grief; ran down his face, mingling with the rain. He put up his hands, sobbing uncontrollably, unselfconsciously, as though he were the last man alive in the world, and alone forever.

And as he wept he felt a change begin in the flesh that met there, face against hands. A tingling and burning, the feel of skin sleep-deadened coming alive again. He lowered his hands wonderingly, saw the scales that covered them dissolving, the skin beneath them his own olive-brown, supple and smooth. He shouted in amazement, and wept harder, pain and joy intermingled, like the tears and rain that melted the cursed scales from his body and washed them away.

He went on weeping until he had cleansed himself in body and spirit, freed himself from the prison of his own making. And then, exhausted and uncertain, he climbed to his feet again, meeting the calm, gray gaze of the Earth's gratitude in Fallatha's eyes. He smiled and she smiled; the unexpectedness of the expression, and the sight of it, resonated in him.

Sunlight was spreading across the patchwork land far below, dressing the mountain slope in royal greens, although the rain still fell around them. He looked up almost unthinkingly, searching—found what he had not realized he sought. Fallatha followed his glance and found it with him. Her smile widened at the arching band of colors, the rainbow; not a curse any longer, or a mark of pain, but once again a promise of better days to come.

THE FELLOWSHIP
OF THE DRAGON

Patricia A. McKillip

A great cry rose throughout the land: Queen Celandine had lost her harper. She summoned north, south, east, west; we rode for days through mud and rain to meet, the five of us, at Trillium; from there we rode to Carnelaine. The world had come to her great court, for though we lived too far from her to hear her fabled harper play, we heard the rumor that at each full moon she gave him gloves of cloth of gold and filled his mouth with jewels. As we stood in the hall among her shining company, listening to her pleas for help, Justin, who is the riddler among us, whispered, "What is invisible but everywhere, swift as wind but has no feet, and has as many tongues that speak but never has a face?"

"Easy," I breathed. "Rumor."

"Rumor, that shy beast, says she valued his hands far more than his harping, and she filled his mouth with more than jewels."

I was hardly surprised. Celandine is as beautiful close as she is at a distance; she has been so for years, with the aid of a streak of sorcery she inherited through a bit of murkiness, an imprecise history on the distaff side, and she is not one to waste her gifts. She had married honorably, loved faithfully, raised her heirs well. When her husband died a decade ago, she mourned him with the good-hearted efficiency she had brought to marriage and throne. Her hair showed which way the wind was blowing, and the way that silver, ash and gold worked among the court was magical. But when we grew close enough to kneel before her, I saw that the harper was no idle indulgence, but had sung his way into her blood.

"You five," she said softly, "I trust more than all my court. I rely on you." Her eyes, green as her name, were grim; I saw the tiny lines of fear and temper beside her mouth. "There are some in this hall who—because I have not been entirely wise or tactful—would sooner see the harper dead than rescue him."

"Do you know where he is?"

She lowered her voice; I could scarcely hear her, though the jealous knights behind me must have stilled their hearts to catch her answer. "I looked in water, in crystal, in mirror: every image is the same. Black Tremptor has him."

"Oh, fine."

She bent to kiss me: we are cousins, though sometimes I have been more a wayward daughter, and more often, she a wayward mother. "Find him, Anne," she said. We five rose as one and left the court.

"What did she say?" Danica asked as we mounted. "Did she say Black Tremptor?"

"Sh!"

"That's a mountain," Fleur said.

"It's a bloody dragon," Danica said sharply, and I bellowed in a whisper, "Can you refrain from announcing our destination to the entire world?"

Danica wheeled her mount crossly; peacocks, with more haste than grace, swept their fine trains out of her way. Justin looked intrigued by the problem. Christabel, who was nursing a cold, said stoically, "Could be worse." What could be worse than being reduced to a cinder by an irritated dragon, she didn't mention. Fleur, who loved good harping, was moved.

"Then we must hurry. Poor man." She pulled herself up, cantered after Danica. Riding more sedately through the crowded yard, we found them outside the gate, gazing east and west across the gray, billowing sky as if it had streamed out of a dragon's nostrils.

"Which way?" Fleur asked. Justin, who knew such things, pointed. Christabel blew her nose. We rode.

Of course we circled back through the city and lost the knights who had been following us. We watched them through a tavern window as they galloped purposefully down the wrong crossroad. Danica, whose moods swung between sun and shadow like an autumn day, was being enchanted by Fleur's description of the object of our quest.

"He is a magnificent harper, and we should spare no pains to rescue him, for there is no one like him in all the world, and Queen Celandine might reward us with gold and honor, but he will reward us forever in a song."

Christabel waved the fumes of hot spiced wine at her nose. "Does anyone know this harper's name?"

"Kestral," I said. "Kestral Hunt. He came to court a year ago, at old Thurlow's death."

"And where," Christabel asked sensibly, "is Black Tremptor?"

We all looked at Justin, who for once looked uncomfortable. "North," she said. She is a slender, dark-haired, quiet-voiced woman with eyes like the storm outside. She could lay out facts like an open road, or mortar them into a brick wall. Which she was building for us now, I wasn't sure.

"Justin?"

"Well, north," she said vaguely, as if that alone explained itself. "It's fey, beyond the border. Odd things happen. We must be watchful."

We were silent. The tavern keeper came with our supper. Danica, pouring wine the same pale honey as her hair, looked thoughtful at the warning instead of cross. "What kinds of things?"

"Evidently harpers are stolen by dragons," I said. "Dragons with some taste in music."

"Black Tremptor is not musical," Justin said simply. "But like that, yes. There are so many tales, who knows which of them might be true? And we barely know the harper any better than the northlands."

"His name," I said, "and that he plays well."

"He plays wonderfully," Fleur breathed. "So they say."

"And he caught the queen's eye," Christabel said, biting into a chicken leg. "So he might look passable. Though with good musicians, that hardly matters."

"And he went north," Justin pointed out. "For what?"

"To find a song," Fleur suggested; it seemed, as gifted as he was, not unlikely.

"Or a harp," I guessed. "A magical harp."

Justin nodded. "Guarded by a powerful dragon. It's possible. Such things happen, north."

Fleur pushed her dish aside, sank tableward onto her fists. She is straw-thin, with a blacksmith's appetite; love, I could tell, for this fantasy, made her ignore the last of her parsnips. She has pale, curly hair like a sheep, and a wonderful, caressing voice; her eyes are small, her nose big, her teeth crooked, but her passionate, musical voice has proved Christabel right more times than was good for Fleur's husband to know. How robust, practical Christabel, who scarcely seemed to notice men or music, understood such things, I wasn't sure.

"So," I said. "North."

And then we strayed into the country called "Remember-when," for we had known one another as children in the court at Carnelaine, and then as members of the queen's company, riding ideals headlong into trouble, and now, as long and trusted friends. We got to bed late, enchanted by our memories, and out of bed far too early, wondering obviously why we had left hearth and home, husband, child, cat and goosedown bed for one another's surly company. Christabel sniffed, Danica snapped, Fleur babbled, I was terse. As always, only Justin was bearable.

We rode north.

The farther we travelled, the wilder the country grew. We moved quickly, slept under trees or in obscure inns, for five armed women riding together are easily remembered, and knights dangerous to the harper as well as solicitous of the queen would have known to track us.

Slowly the great, dark crags bordering the queen's marches came closer and closer to meet us, until we reached, one sunny afternoon, their shadow.

"Now what?" Danica asked fretfully. "Do we fly over that?" They were huge, barren thrusts of stone pushing high out of forests like bone out of skin. She looked at Justin; we all did. There was a peculiar expression on her face, as if she recognized something she had only seen before in dreams.

"There will be a road," she said softly. We were in thick forest; old trees marched in front of us, beside us, flanked us. Not even they had found a way to climb the peaks.

"Where, Justin?" I asked.

"We must wait until sunset."

We found a clearing, where the road we followed abruptly turned to amble west along a stream. Christabel and Danica went hunting. Fleur checked our supplies and mended a tear in her cloak. I curried the horses. Justin, who had gone to forage, came back with mushrooms, nuts and a few wild apples. She found another brush and helped me.

"Is it far now?" I asked, worried about finding supplies in the wilderness, about the horses, about Christabel's stubbornly lingering cold, even, a little, about the harper. Justin picked a burr out of her mount's mane. A line ran across her smooth brow.

"Not far beyond those peaks," she answered. "It's just that—"

"Just what?"

"We must be so careful."

"We're always careful. Christabel can put an arrow into anything that moves, Danica can—"

"I don't mean that. I mean: the world shows a different face beyond those peaks." I looked at her puzzledly; she shook her head; gazing at the mountains, somehow wary and entranced at once. "Sometimes real, sometimes unreal—"

"The harper is real, the dragon is real," I said briskly. "And we are real. If I can remember that, we'll be fine."

She touched my shoulder, smiling. "I think you're right, Anne. It's your prosaic turn of mind that will bring us all home again."

But she was wrong.

The sun, setting behind a bank of sullen clouds, left a message: a final shaft of light hit what looked like solid stone ahead of us and parted it. We saw a faint, white road that cut out of the trees and into the base of two great crags: the light seemed to ease one wall of stone aside, like a gate. Then the light faded, and we were left staring at the solid wall, memorizing the landscape.

"It's a woman's profile," Fleur said. "The road runs beneath the bridge of her nose."

"It's a one-eared cat," Christabel suggested.

"The road is west of the higher crag," Danica said impatiently. "We should simply ride toward that."

"The mountains will change and change again before we reach it," I said. "The road comes out of that widow's peak of trees. It's the highest point of the forest. We only need to follow the edge of the trees."

"The widow," Danica murmured, "is upside-down."

I shrugged. "The harper found his way. It can't be that difficult."

"Perhaps," Fleur suggested, "he followed a magical path."

"He parted stone with his harping," Christabel said stuffily. "If he's that clever, he can play his way out of the dragon's mouth, and we can all turn around and go sleep in our beds."

"Oh, Christabel," Fleur mourned, her voice like a sweet flute. "Sit down. I'll make you herb tea with wild honey in it; you'll sleep on clouds tonight."

We all had herb tea, with brandy and the honey Fleur had found, but only Fleur slept through the thunderstorm. We gathered ourselves wetly at dawn, slogged through endless dripping forest, until suddenly there were no more trees, there was no more rain, only the unexpected sun illumining a bone-white road into the great upsweep of stone ahead of us.

We rode beyond the land we knew.

I don't know where we slept that first night: wherever we fell off our horses, I think. In the morning we saw Black Tremptor's mountain, a dragon's palace of cliffs and jagged columns and sheer walls ascending into cloud. As we rode down the slope toward it, the cloud wrapped itself down around the mountain, hid it. The road, wanting nothing to do with dragons, turned at the edge of the forest and ran off the wrong direction. We pushed into trees. The forest on that side was very old, the trees so high, their green boughs so thick, we could barely see the sky, let alone the dragon's lair. But I have a strong sense of direction, of where the sun rises and sets, that kept us from straying. The place was soundless. Fleur and Christabel kept arrows ready for bird or deer, but we saw nothing on four legs or two: only spiders, looking old as the forest, weaving webs as huge and intricate as tapestry in the trees.

"It's so still," Fleur breathed. "As if it is waiting for music."

Christabel turned a bleary eye at her and sniffed. But Fleur was right: the stillness did seem magical, an intention out of someone's head. As we listened, the rain began again. We heard it patter from bough to bough a long time before it reached us.

Night fell the same way: sliding slowly down from the invisible sky, catching us without fresh kill, in the rain without a fire. Silent, we rode until we could barely see. We stopped finally, while we could still imagine one another's faces.

"The harper made it through," Danica said softly; what Celandine's troublesome, faceless lover could do, so could we.

"There's herbs and honey and more brandy," Christabel said. Fleur, who suffered most from hunger, having a hummingbird's energy, said nothing. Justin lifted her head sharply.

"I smell smoke."

I saw the light then: two square eyes and one round among the distant trees. I sighed with relief and felt no pity for whoever in that quiet cottage was about to find us on the doorstep.

But the lady of the cottage did not seem discomfitted to see five armed, dripping, hungry travellers wanting to invade her house.

"Come in," she said. "Come in." As we filed through the door, I saw all the birds and animals we had missed in the forest circle the room around us: stag and boar and owl, red deer, hare and mourning dove. I blinked, and they were motionless: things of thread and paint and wood, embroidered onto curtains, carved into the backs of chairs, painted on the rafters. Before I could speak, smells assaulted us, and I felt Fleur stagger against me.

"You poor children." Old as we were, she was old enough to say that. "Wet and weary and hungry." She was a bird-like soul herself: a bit of magpie in her curious eyes, a bit of hawk's beak in her nose. Her hair looked fine and white as spider web, her knuckles like swollen tree boles. Her voice was kindly, and so was her warm hearth, and the smells coming out of her kitchen. Even her skirt was hemmed with birds. "Sit down. I've been baking bread, and there's a hot meat pie almost done in the oven." She turned, to give something simmering in a pot over the fire a stir. "Where are you from and where are you bound?"

"We are from the court of Queen Celandine," I said. "We have come searching for her harper. Did he pass this way?"

"Ah," she said, her face brightening. "A tall man with golden hair and a voice to match his harping?"

"Sounds like," Christabel said.

"He played for me, such lovely songs. He said he had to find a certain harp. He ate nothing and was gone before sunrise." She gave the pot another stir. "Is he lost?"

"Black Tremptor has him."

"Oh, terrible." She shook her head. "He is fortunate to have such good friends to rescue him."

"He is the queen's good friend," I said, barely listening to myself as the smell from the pot curled into me, "and we are hers. What is that you are cooking?"

"Just a little something for my bird."

"You found a bird?" Fleur said faintly, trying to be sociable. "We saw none . . . Whatever do you feed it? It smells good enough to eat."

"Oh, no, you must not touch it; it is only bird-fare. I have delicacies for you."

"What kind of bird is it?" Justin asked. The woman tapped the spoon on the edge of the pot, laid it across the rim.

"Oh, just a little thing. A little, hungry thing I found. You're right: the forest has few birds. That's why I sew and paint my birds and animals, to give me company. There's wine," she added. "I'll get it for you."

She left. Danica paced; Christabel sat close to the fire, indifferent to the smell of the pot bubbling under her stuffy nose. Justin had picked up a small wooden boar and was examining it idly. Fleur drifted, pale as cloud; I kept an eye on her to see she did not topple into the fire. The old woman had trouble, it seemed, finding cups.

"How strange," Justin breathed. "This looks so real, every tiny bristle."

Fleur had wandered to the hearth to stare down into the pot. I heard it bubble fatly. She gave one pleading glance toward the kitchen, but still there was nothing to eat but promises. She had the spoon in her hand suddenly, I thought to stir.

"It must be a very strange bird to eat mushrooms," she commented. "And what looks like—" Justin put the boar down so sharply I jumped, but Fleur lifted the spoon to her lips. "Lamb," she said happily. And then she vanished: there was only a frantic lark fluttering among the rafters, sending plea after lovely plea for freedom.

The woman reappeared. "My bird," she cried. "My pretty." I was on my feet with my sword drawn before I could even close my mouth. I swung, but the old witch didn't linger to do battle. A hawk caught the lark in its claws; the door swung open, and both birds disappeared into the night.

We ran into the dark, stunned and horrified. The door slammed shut behind us like a mouth. The fire dwindled into two red flames that stared like eyes out of the darkened windows. They gave no light; we could see nothing.

"That bloody web-haired old spider," Danica said furiously. "That horrible, putrid witch." I heard a thump as she hit a tree; she cursed painfully. Someone hammered with solid, methodical blows at the door and windows; I guessed Christabel was laying siege. But nothing gave. She groaned with frustration. I felt a touch and raised my sword; Justin said sharply, "It's me." She put her hand on my shoulder; I felt myself tremble.

"Now what?" I said tersely. I could barely speak; I only wanted action, but we were blind and bumbling in the dark.

"I think she doesn't kill them," Justin said. "She changes them. Listen to me. She'll bring Fleur back into her house eventually. We'll find someone to tell us how to free her from the spell. Someone in this wilderness of magic should know. And not everyone is cruel."

"We'll stay here until the witch returns."

"I doubt she'll return until we're gone. And even if we find some way to kill her, we may be left with an embroidered Fleur."

"We'll stay."

"Anne," she said, and I slumped to the ground, wanting to curse, to weep, wanting at the very least to tear the clinging cobweb dark away from my eyes.

"Poor Fleur," I whispered. "She was only hungry . . . Harper or no, we rescue her when we learn how. She comes first."

"Yes," she agreed at that, and added thoughtfully, "The harper eluded the witch, it seems, though not the dragon."

"How could he have known?" I asked bitterly. "By what magic?"

"Maybe he had met the witch first in a song."

Morning found us littered across tree roots like the remains of some lost battle. At least we could see again. The house had flown itself away; only a couple of fiery feathers remained. We rose wordlessly, feeling the empty place where Fleur had been, listening for her morning chatter. We fed the horses, ate stone-hard bread with honey, and had a swallow of brandy apiece. Then we left Fleur behind and rode.

The great forest finally thinned, turned to golden oak, which parted now and then around broad meadows where we saw the sky again, and the high dark peak. We passed through a village, a mushroom patch of a place, neither friendly nor surly, nor overly curious. We found an inn, and some supplies, and, beyond the village, a road to the dragon's mountain that had been cleared, we were told, before the mountain had become the dragon's lair. Yes, we were also told, a harper had passed through . . . He seemed to have left little impression on the villagers, but they were a hard-headed lot, living under the dragon's shadow. He, too, had asked directions, as well as questions about Black Tremptor, and certain tales of gold and magic harps and other bits of country lore. But no one else had taken that road for decades, leading, as it did, into the dragon's mouth.

We took it. The mountain grew clearer, looming high above the trees. We watched for dragon wings, dragon fire, but if Black Tremptor flew, it was not by day. The rain had cleared; a scent like dying roses and aged sunlit wood seemed to blow across our path. We camped on one of the broad, grassy clearings where we watched the full moon rise, turn the meadow milky, and etch the dragon's lair against the stars.

But for Fleur, the night seemed magical. We talked of her, and then of home; we talked of her, and then of court gossip; we talked of her, and of the harper, and what might have lured him away from Celandine into a dragon's claw. And as we spoke of him, it seemed his music fell around us from the stars, and that the moonlight in the oak wood had turned to gold.

"Sh!" Christabel said sharply, and, drowsy, we quieted to listen. Danica yawned.

"It's just harping." She had an indifferent ear: Fleur was more persuasive about the harper's harping than his harping would have been. "Just a harping from the woods."

"Someone's singing," Christabel said. I raised my brows, feeling that in the untroubled, sweetly scented night, anything might happen.

"Is it our missing Kestral?"

"Singing in a tree?" Danica guessed. Christabel sat straight.

"Be quiet," she said sharply. Justin, lying on her stomach, tossing twigs into the fire, glanced at her surprisedly. Danica and I only laughed, at Christabel in a temper.

"You have no hearts," she said, blowing her nose fiercely. "It's so beautiful and all you can do is gabble."

"All right," Justin said soothingly. "We'll listen." But, moonstruck, Danica and I could not keep still. We told raucous tales of old loves while Christabel strained to hear, and Justin watched her curiously. She seemed oddly moved, did Christabel; feverish, I thought, from all the rain.

A man rode out of the trees into the moonlight at the edge of the meadow. He had milky hair, broad shoulders; a gold mantle fanned across his horse's back. The crown above his shadowed face was odd: a circle of uneven gold spikes, like antlers. He was unarmed; he played the harp.

"Not our harper," Danica commented. "Unless the dragon turned his hair white."

"He's a king," I said. "Not ours." For a moment, just a moment, I heard his playing, and knew it could have parted water, made birds speak. I caught my breath; tears swelled behind my eyes. Then Danica said something and I laughed.

Christabel stood up. Her face was unfamiliar in the moonlight. She took off her boots, unbraided her hair, let it fall loosely down her back; all this while we only watched and laughed and glanced now and then, indifferently, at the waiting woodland harper.

"You're hopeless boors," Christabel said, sniffing. "I'm going to speak to him, ask him to come and sit with us."

"Go on then," Danica said, chewing a grass blade. "Maybe we can take him home to Celandine instead." I rolled over in helpless laughter. When I wiped my eyes, I saw Christabel walking barefoot across the meadow to the harper.

Justin stood up. A little, nagging wind blew through my thoughts. I stood beside her, still laughing a little, yet poised to hold her if she stepped out of the circle of our firelight. She watched Christabel. Danica watched the fire dreamily, smiling. Christabel stood before the harper. He took his hand from his strings and held it out to her.

In the sudden silence, Justin shouted, "Christabel!"

All the golden light in the world frayed away. A dragon's wing of cloud brushed the moon; night washed toward Christabel, as she took his hand and mounted; I saw all her lovely, red-gold hair flowing freely in the last of the light. And then freckled, stolid, courageous, snuffling Christabel caught the harper-king's shoulders and they rode down the fading path of light into a world beyond the night.

We searched for her until dawn.

At sunrise, we stared at one another, haggard, mute. The great oak had swallowed Christabel; she had disappeared into a harper's song.

"We could go to the village for help," Danica said wearily.

"Their eyes are no better than ours," I said.

"The queen's harper passed through here unharmed," Justin mused. "Perhaps he knows something about the country of the woodland king."

"I hope he is worth all this," Danica muttered savagely.

"No man is," Justin said simply. "But all this will be worth nothing if Black Tremptor kills him before we find him. He may be able to lead us safely out of the northlands, if nothing else."

"I will not leave Fleur and Christabel behind," I said sharply. "I will not. You may take the harper back to Celandine. I stay here until I find them."

Justin looked at me; her eyes were reddened with sleeplessness, but they saw as clearly as ever into the mess we had made. "We will not leave you, Anne," she said. "If he cannot help us, he must find his own way back. But if he can help us, we must abandon Christabel now to rescue him."

"Then let's do it," I said shortly and turned my face away from the oak. A little wind shivered like laughter through their golden leaves.

We rode long and hard. The road plunged back into forest, up low foothills, brought us to the flank of the great dark mountain. We pulled up in its shadow. The dragon's eyrie shifted under the eye; stone pillars opened into passages, their granite walls split and hollowed like honey-combs, like some palace of winds, open at every angle yet with every passage leading into shadow, into the hidden dragon's heart.

"In there?" Danica asked. There was no fear in her voice, just her usual impatience to get things done. "Do we knock, or just walk in?" A wind roared through the stones then, bending trees as it blasted at us. I heard stones thrum like harp-strings; I heard the dragon's voice. We turned our mounts, flattened ourselves against them, while the wild wind rode over us. Recovering, Danica asked more quietly, "Do we go in together?"

"Yes," I said, and then, "No. I'll go first."

"Don't be daft, Anne," Danica said crossly. "If we all go together at least we'll know where we all are."

"And fools we will look, too," I said grimly, "caught along with the harper, waiting for Celandine's knights to rescue us as well." I turned to Justin. "Is there some secret, some riddle for surviving drag-ons?"

She shook her head helplessly. "It depends on the dragon. I known nothing about Black Tremptor, except that he most likely has not kept the harper for his harping."

"Two will go," I said. "And one wait."

They did not argue; there seemed no foolproof way, except for none of us to go. We tossed coins: two peacocks and one Celandine. Justin, who got the queen, did not look happy, but the coins were adamant. Danica and I left her standing with our horses, shielded within green boughs, watching us. We climbed the bald slope quietly, trying not to scatter stones. We had to watch our feet, pick a careful path to keep from sliding. Danica, staring groundward, stopped suddenly ahead of me to pick up something.

"Look," she breathed. I did, expecting a broken harp string, or an ivory button with Celandine's profile on it.

It was an emerald as big as my thumbnail, shaped and faceted. I stared at it a moment. Then I said, "Dragon-treasure. We came to find a harper."

"But Anne—there's another—" She scrabbled across loose stone to retrieve it. "Topaz. And over there a sapphire—"

"Danica," I pleaded. "You can carry home the entire mountain after you've dispatched the dragon."

"I'm coming," she said breathlessly, but she had scuttled crab-wise across the slope toward yet another gleam. "Just one more. They're so beautiful, and just lying here free as rain for anyone to take."

"Danica! They'll be as free when we climb back down."

"I'm coming."

I turned, in resignation to her sudden magpie urge. "I'm going up."

"Just a moment, don't go alone. Oh, Anne, look there, it's a diamond. I've never seen such fire."

I held my breath, gave her that one moment. It had been such a long, hard journey I found it impossible to deny her an unexpected pleasure. She knelt, groped along the side of a boulder for a shining as pure as water in the sunlight. "I'm coming," she assured me, her back to me. "I'm coming."

And then the boulder lifted itself up off the ground. Something forked and nubbled like a tree root, whispering harshly to itself, caught her by her hand and by her honey hair and pulled her down into its hole. The boulder dropped ponderously, earth shifted close around its sides as if it had never moved.

I stared, stunned. I don't remember crossing the slope, only beat-

ing on the boulder with my hands and then my sword hilt, crying furiously at it, until all the broken shards underfoot undulated and swept
me in a dry, rattling, bruising wave back down the slope into the trees.

Justin ran to help me. I was torn, bleeding, cursing, crying; I took
a while to become coherent. "Of all the stupid, feeble tricks to fall for!
A trail of jewels! They're probably not even real, and Danica got herself trapped under a mountain for a pocketful of coal or dragon
fewmets—"

"She won't be trapped quietly," Justin said. Her face was waxen.
"What took her?"

"A little crooked something—an imp, a mountain troll—Justin,
she's down there without us in a darkness full of whispering things—I
can't believe we were so stupid!"

"Anne, calm down, we'll find her."

"I can't calm down!" I seized her shoulders, shook her. "Don't you
disappear and leave me searching for you, too—"

"I won't, I promise. Anne, listen." She smoothed my hair with
both her hands back from my face. "Listen to me. We'll find her. We'll
find Christabel and Fleur, we will not leave this land until—"

"How?" I shouted. "How? Justin, she's under solid rock!"

"There are ways. There are always ways. This land riddles constantly, but all the riddles have answers. Fleur will turn from a bird into
a woman, we will find a path for Christabel out of the wood-king's
country, we will rescue Danica from the mountain imps. There are
ways to do these things, we only have to find them."

"How?" I cried again, for it seemed the farther we travelled in that
land, the more trouble we got into. "Every time we turn around one of
us disappears! You'll go next—"

"I will not, I promise—"

"Or I will."

"I know a few riddles," someone said. "Perhaps I can help."

We broke apart, as startled as if a tree had spoken: perhaps one
had, in this exasperating land. But it was a woman. She wore a black
cloak with a silver edging; her ivory hair and iris eyes and her grave,
calm face within the hood were very beautiful. She carried an odd staff
of gnarled black wood inset with a jewel the same pale violet as her

eyes. She spoke gently, unsurprised by us; perhaps nothing in this place surprised her anymore. She added, at our silence, "My name is Yrecros. You are in great danger from the dragon; you must know that."

"We have come to rescue a harper," I said bitterly. "We were five, when we crossed into this land."

"Ah."

"Do you know this dragon?"

She did not answer immediately; beside me, Justin was oddly still. The staff shifted; the jewel glanced here and there, like an eye. The woman whose name was Yrecros said finally, "You may ask me anything."

"I just did," I said bewilderedly. Justin's hand closed on my arm; I looked at her. Her face was very pale; her eyes held a strange, intense light I recognized: she had scented something intangible and was in pursuit. At such times she was impossible.

"Yrecros," she said softly. "My name is Nitsuj."

The woman smiled.

"What are you doing?" I said between my teeth.

"It's a game," Justin breathed. "Question for answer. She'll tell us all we need to know."

"Why must it be a game?" I protested. She and the woman were gazing at one another, improbable fighters about to engage in a delicate battle of wits. They seemed absorbed in one another, curious, stonedeaf. I raised my voice. "Justin!"

"You'll want the harper, I suppose," the woman said. I worked out her name then and closed my eyes.

Justin nodded. "It's what we came for. And if I lose?"

"I want you," the woman said simply, "for my apprentice." She smiled again, without malice or menace. "For seven years."

My breath caught. "No." I could barely speak. I seized Justin's arm, shook her. "Justin, Justin, please!" For just a moment I had, if not her eyes, her attention.

"It's all right, Anne," she said softly. "We'll get the harper without a battle, and rescue Fleur and Christabel and Danica as well."

"Justin!" I shouted. Above us all the pillars and cornices of stone echoed her name; great, barbed-winged birds wheeled out of the trees. But unlike bird and stone, Justin did not hear.

"You are a guest in this land," the woman said graciously. "You may ask first."

"Where is the road to the country of the woodland king?"

"The white stag in the oak forest follows the road to the land of the harper king," Yrecros answered, "if you follow from morning to night, without weapons and without rest. What is the Song of Ducirc, and on what instrument was it first played?"

"The Song of Ducirc was the last song of a murdered poet to his love, and it was played to his lady in her high tower on an instrument of feathers, as all the birds in the forest who heard it sang her his lament," Justin said promptly. I breathed a little then; she had been telling us such things all her life. "What traps the witch in the border woods in her true shape, and how can her power be taken?"

"The border witch may be trapped by a cage of iron; her staff of power is the spoon with which she stirs her magic. What begins with fire and ends with fire and is black and white between?"

"Night," Justin said. Even I knew that one. The woman's face held, for a moment, the waning moon's smile. "Where is the path to the roots of this mountain, and what do those who dwell there fear most?"

"The path is fire, which will open their stones, and what they fear most is light. What is always coming yet never here, has a name but does not exist, is longer than day but shorter than day?"

Justin paused a blink. "Tomorrow," she said, and added, "in autumn." The woman smiled her lovely smile. I loosed breath noiselessly. "What will protect us from the dragon?"

The woman studied Justin, as if she were answering some private riddle of her own. "Courtesy," she said simply. "Where is Black Tremptor's true name hidden?"

Justin was silent; I felt her thoughts flutter like a bird seeking a perch. The silence lengthened; an icy finger slid along my bones.

"I do not know," Justin said at last, and the woman answered, "The dragon's name is hidden within a riddle."

Justin read my thoughts; her hand clamped on my wrist. "Don't fight," she breathed.

"That's not—"

"The answer's fair."

The woman's brows knit thoughtfully. "Is there anything else you need to know?" She put her staff lightly on Justin's shoulder, turned the jewel toward her pale face. The jewel burned a sudden flare of amethyst, as if in recognition. "My name is Sorcery and that is the path I follow. You will come with me for seven years. After that, you may choose to stay."

"Tell me," I pleaded desperately, "how to rescue her. You have told me everything else."

The woman shook her head, smiling her brief moon-smile. Justin looked at me finally; I saw the answer in her eyes.

I stood mute, watching her walk away from me, tears pushing into my eyes, unable to plead or curse because there had been a game within a game, and only I had lost. Justin glanced back at me once, but she did not really see me, she only saw the path she had walked toward all her life.

I turned finally to face the dragon.

I climbed the slope again alone. No jewels caught my eye, no voice whispered my name. Not even the dragon greeted me. As I wandered through columns and caverns and hallways of stone, I heard only the wind moaning through the great bones of the mountain. I went deeper into stone. The passageways glowed butterfly colors with secretions from the dragon's body. Here and there I saw a scale flaked off by stone; some flickered blue-green-black, others the colors of fire. Once I saw a chip of claw, hard as horn, longer than my hand. Sometimes I smelled sulphur, sometimes smoke, mostly wind smelling of the stone it scoured endlessly.

I heard harping.

I found the harper finally, sitting ankle-deep in jewels and gold, in a shadowy cavern, plucking wearily at his harp with one hand. His other hand was cuffed and chained with gold to a golden rivet in the cavern wall. He stared, speechless, when he saw me. He was, as rumored, tall and golden-haired, also unwashed, unkempt and sour from captivity. Even so, it was plain to see why Celandine wanted him back.

"Who are you?" he breathed, as I trampled treasure to get to him.

"I am Celandine's cousin Anne. She sent her court to rescue you."

"It took you long enough," he grumbled, and added, "You couldn't have come this far alone."

"You did," I said tersely, examining the chain that held him. Even Fleur would have had it out of the wall in a minute. "It's gold, malleable. Why didn't you—"

"I tried," he said, and showed me his torn hands. "It's dragon magic." He jerked the chain fretfully from my hold. "Don't bother trying. The key's over near that wall." He looked behind me, bewilderedly, for my imaginary companions. "Are you alone? She didn't send her knights to fight this monster?"

"She didn't trust them to remember who they were supposed to kill," I said succinctly. He was silent, while I crossed the room to rummage among pins and cups and necklaces for the key. I added, "I didn't ride from Carnelaine alone. I lost four companions in this land as we tracked you."

"Lost?" For a moment, his voice held something besides his own misery. "Dead?"

"I think not."

"How did you lose them?"

"One was lost to the witch in the wood."

"Was she a witch?" he said, astonished. "I played for her, but she never offered me anything to eat, hungry as I was. I could smell food but she only said that it was burned and unfit for company."

"And one," I said, sifting through coins and wondering at the witch's taste, "to the harper-king in the wood."

"You saw him?" he breathed. "I played all night, hoping to hear his fabled harping, but he never answered with a note."

"Maybe you never stopped to listen," I said, in growing despair over the blind way he blundered through the land. "And one to the imps under the mountain."

"What imps?"

"And last," I said tightly, "in a riddle-game to the sorceress with the jewelled staff. You were to be the prize."

He shifted, chain and coins rattling. "She only told me where to find what I was searching for, she didn't warn me of the dangers. She could have helped me! She never said she was a sorceress."

"Did she tell you her name?"

"I don't remember—what difference does it make? Hurry with the key before the dragon smells you here. It would have been so much easier for me if your companion had not lost the riddle-game."

I paused in my searching to gaze at him. "Yes," I said finally, "and it would have been easier than that for all of us if you had never come here. Why did you?"

He pointed. "I came for that."

"That" was a harp of bone. Its strings glistened with the same elusive, shimmering colors that stained the passageways. A golden key lay next to it. I am as musical as the next, no more, but when I saw those strange, glowing strings I was filled with wonder at what music they might make and I paused, before I touched the key, to pluck a note.

It seemed the mountain hummed.

"No!" the harper cried, heaving to his feet in a tide of gold. Wind sucked out of the cave, as at the draw of some gigantic wing. "You stupid, blundering— How do you think I got caught? Throw me the key! Quickly!"

I weighed the key in my hand, prickling at his rudeness. But he was, after all, what I had promised Celandine to find, and I imagined that washed and fed and in the queen's hands, he would assert his charms again. I tossed the key; it fell a little short of his outstretched hand.

"Fool!" he snapped. "You are as clumsy as the queen."

Stone-still, I stared at him, as he strained, groping for the key. I turned abruptly to the harp and ran my hand down all the strings.

What travelled down the passages to find us shed smoke and fire and broken stone behind it. The harper groaned and hid behind his arms. Smoke cleared; great eyes like moons of fire gazed at us near the high ceiling. A single claw as long as my shin dropped within an inch of my foot. Courtesy, I thought frantically. Courtesy, she said. It was like offering idle chatter to the sun. Before I could speak, the harper cried,

"She played it! She came in here searching for it, too, though I tried to stop her—"

Heat whuffed at me; I felt the gold I wore burn my neck. I said, feeling scorched within as well, "I ask your pardon if I have offended you. I came, at my queen's request, to rescue her harper. It seems you do not care for harping. If it pleases you, I will take what must be an annoyance out of your house." I paused. The great eyes sank a little toward me. I added, for such things seemed important in this land, "My name is Anne."

"Anne," the smoke whispered. I heard the harper jerk in his chain. The claw retreated slightly; the immense flat lizard's head lowered, its fiery scales charred dark with smoke, tiny sparks of fire winking between its teeth. "What is his name?"

"Kestral," the harper said quickly. "Kestral Hunt."

"You are right," the hot breath sighed. "He is an annoyance. Are you sure you want him back?"

"No," I said, my eyes blurring in wonder and relief that I had finally found, in this dangerous land, something I did not need to fear. "He is extremely rude, ungrateful and insensitive. I imagine that my queen loves him for his hair or for his harper's hands; she must not listen to him speak. So I had better take him. I am sorry that he snuck into your house and tried to steal from you."

"It is a harp made of dragon bone and sinew," the dragon said. "It is why I dislike harpers, who make such things and then sing songs of their great cleverness. As this one would have." Its jaws yawned; a tongue of fire shot out, melted gold beside the harper's hand. He scuttled against the wall.

"I beg your pardon," he said hastily. A dark curved dragon's smile hung in the fading smoke; it snorted heat.

"Perhaps I will keep you and make a harp of your bones."

"It would be miserably out of tune," I commented. "Is there something I can do for you in exchange for the harper's freedom?"

An eye dropped close, moon-round, shadows of color constantly disappearing through it. "Tell me my name," the dragon whispered. Slowly I realized it was not a challenge but a plea. "A woman took my name from me long ago, in a riddle-game. I have been trying to remember it for years."

"Yrecros?" I breathed. So did the dragon, nearly singeing my hair.

"You know her."

"She took something from me: my dearest friend. Of you she said: the dragon's name is hidden within a riddle."

"Where is she?"

"Walking paths of sorcery in this land."

Claws flexed across the stones, smooth and beetle-black. "I used to know a little sorcery. Enough to walk as man. Will you help me find my name?"

"Will you help me find my friends?" I pleaded in return. "I lost four, searching for this unbearable harper. One or two may not want my help, but I will never know until I see them."

"Let me think . . ." the dragon said. Smoke billowed around me suddenly, acrid, ash-white. I swallowed smoke, coughed it out. When my stinging eyes could see again, a gold-haired harper stood in front of me. He had the dragon's eyes.

I drew in smoke again, astonished. Through my noise, I could hear Kestral behind me, tugging at his chain and shouting.

"What of me?" he cried furiously. "You were sent to rescue me! What will you tell Celandine? That you found her harper and brought the dragon home instead?" His own face gazed back at him, drained the voice out of him a moment. He tugged at the chain frantically, desperately. "You cannot harp! She'd know you false by that, and by your ancient eyes."

"Perhaps," I said, charmed by his suggestion, "she will not care."

"Her knights will find me. You said they seek to kill me! You will murder me."

"Those that want you dead will likely follow me," I said wearily, "for the gold-haired harper who rides with me. It is for the dragon to free you, not me. If he chooses to, you will have to find your own way back to Celandine, or else promise not to speak except to sing."

I turned away from him. The dragon-harper picked up his harp of bone. He said, in his husky, smoky voice,

"I keep my bargains. The key to your freedom lies in a song."

We left the harper chained to his harping, listening puzzledly with his deaf ear and untuned brain, for the one song, of all he had ever played and never heard, that would bring him back to Celandine. Outside, in the light, I led dragon-fire to the stone that had swallowed Danica, and began my backward journey toward Yrecros.

The Champion
of Dragons

Mickey Zucker Reichert

The rising sun haloed a red-tiered fortress on the mountain's highest peak. Far below, in a glade partially covered by mats of woven grass, Miura Usashibo and Otake Nakamura knelt in silence, chests rising and falling from the strain of mock combat. Nearby, their Sensei watched, stroking his wispy beard.

Usashibo closed his eyes, and a familiar quiet darkness overcame his world. His heart pounded from a mixture of exertion and excitement. Sweat rolled down his face. The reed mats cut their regular pattern into his knees, and the euphoric afterglow of combat consumed him. Victory no longer granted him the unbridled sense of triumph it had scarcely a year ago. Winning had become mundane. But the physical and emotional peak attained in combat never dulled. It seemed as if no reality existed beyond the feelings of inner peace and power he could reach only through all-consuming violence.

Usashibo turned his thoughts to the dragon that Sensei had chosen and trained him to fight. Sensei either would not or could not describe the creature and its method of combat. His initial explanation detailed all he would reveal of Usashibo's enemy. "Every ten years the Master and I select a champion to seek out and slay the dragon. We train him to reach beyond his limitations and drive him until he surpasses even the Master. We have chosen you, Miura Usashibo, as the fourteenth champion of dragons. The others never returned." Yet, despite this grim appraisal, the possibility of failure never occurred to Usashibo. *In the quiet of my soul, I am invincible. I will return.*

A sharp handclap snapped Usashibo's attention back to his surroundings. Sensei bowed, signaling an end to Usashibo's last practice session before setting out to destroy the dragon. As the old man turned, his linen jacket and pants hissed gently. Pausing, he bowed to the shrine of the mountain's spirit and climbed the long flight of stone steps which led to the Master's fortress.

Otake Nakamura remained kneeling where Usashibo had landed what Sensei had judged a killing blow. The interlocking squares of his abdominal muscles rose and fell, and blood beaded from the vertical red line where the champion of dragons' wooden sword had cut his stomach. Silently, he stared at the mats before him. Usashibo searched Nakamura's face for signs of the friendship they had shared a little over a year ago, but none survived. Usashibo studied his old companion, hungry for recognition that he was still a human being if no longer a friend.

Nakamura touched his forehead to the ground, then rose. "May you return from tomorrow's battle victorious and the gods of the winds and the mountains watch over you." Etiquette demanded Nakamura remain until Usashibo responded to his overly formal gesture.

Usashibo shifted uncomfortably, recalling the many times he had tried to force Nakamura to acknowledge how close they had been in friendship. But the mountains they had climbed together, the girls they had known, and the fights they had started became distant memories. Early in his training, Usashibo vented his frustration and loneliness on Nakamura during their practice sessions, battering him until he could barely walk. As he withdrew further, Usashibo's anger lessened. But the feeling of betrayal remained. The soul mate who would have urged

Usashibo to rip the dragon's ugly head off was gone, and Usashibo missed him.

Usashibo rose and pressed wrinkles from his pants with the palms of his hands. He replied with exaggerated formality. "Thank you, Otake." Usashibo dismissed his sparring partner, anxious for the solace of being alone.

Nakamura turned and followed Sensei up the stone staircase, apparently unable to understand the inspired madness that goaded Usashibo to consecrate his life to a goal no one had ever achieved and the fleeting glance at immortality it offered. As boys, Nakamura and Usashibo had shared visions of greatness, but it seemed Nakamura dreamed with his mouth instead of his heart.

Over the years of training, Usashibo had paid a high price for his dream. He denied himself many of the indulgences of youth, gradually surrendering pieces of himself to his art until only the warrior survived. Only one aspect of life remained inviolate: his love for his wife, Rumiko. He knew she fought to maintain the spark of desire within him. He wished her task was easier. Usashibo turned toward the narrow path which led to the village of Miyamoto and resolved to grant Rumiko the only gift which remained his to give: the last night he knew he would be alive.

At the edge of the rice mats, Usashibo slipped his feet into his sandals and slid his swords through his belt. Despite his melancholia, his mind entered his familiar regimen of imaginary combat. As he walked, he consciously controlled each step and shift of balance. His left hand rested on his scabbarded sword, draped over the handguard. He recalled Sensei's words at times when he had doubted his purpose: *Once a raindrop begins to fall, it must continue to fall or it is no longer even a drop of rain. A man must finish his journey once the first step is taken.* Usashibo laughed to himself and wished Sensei spoke more directly.

As Usashibo entered Miyamoto, he tried to close his mind against the ordeal mingling with its citizenry presented. The townspeople regarded him as the epitome of virtue or the target of envy, not as human. Soon, peasants and the rough wooden huts of the village surrounded him. Although people jammed the streets, the throng parted before him. Young girls leered invitations, and men he had known since childhood pretended not to notice him with exaggerated indifference. A child asked him if he could really slay the dragon, only to be snatched away by an embarrassed mother before Usashibo could answer. He felt the tension of hastily averted stares.

Stories of Usashibo's feats, provided and embellished by Nakamura, endeared the teller but not the subject. Many attributed Usashibo's prowess to magic or unwholesome herbs. Others sought tricks to make his accomplishments fall within their narrow view of possibility. Even those people who dismissed Nakamura's tales as lies managed to attribute the blame for the deception to Usashibo.

Quickly, Usashibo crossed the town and traversed the white gravel path through his garden to his cottage. He paused before the faded linen door and removed his sandals. Closing his eyes to help escape the cruel reality of Miyamoto, he stepped through the curtain. The starchy smell of boiling rice mingled with the pine scent of charcoal and the musky aroma of freshly cut reeds. Rice paper walls shielded him from the attentions of people who believed him either more or less than human. Gradually, Sensei's demands and the unattainable goals the peasants projected onto him were borne away on the breeze as wisps of smoke. His own aspirations still burned obsessively in his mind like an endless fire in a swordsmith's forge. He basked in the feeling of power it inspired. He accepted the flame he knew he could never entirely escape or extinguish. Without the desire it inspired, he would not be Miura Usashibo. He opened his eyes.

A ceramic pot rested on a squat, black hibachi. Steam and smoke rose, darkening the tan walls and ceiling. Rumiko knelt on the polished wood floor, and the brush in her hand darted over a sheet of paper. The soft beauty in her round face and dark eyes belied a wit that could cut as quickly and deeply as his sword and a strength which, in many ways, surpassed his own. The rice pot's lid rattled. White froth poured over the sides and hissed as it struck the charcoal. Rumiko rose, turned toward the hibachi, removed the lid, and stared into the boiling rice. Quietly, Usashibo waited for her to meet his gaze.

The steam freed several strands from Rumiko's tightly coiffed hair. Her face reddened. Droplets of sweat beaded on her upper lip, but she did not look up.

Tension filled the room. It seemed almost tangible, as it does when a delicate glass bottle has fallen but not yet shattered on the floor. He could deal with Rumiko momentarily, but Usashibo knew his swords demanded their proper respect. In four strides, he crossed the room and knelt before a black, lacquered stand. He withdrew the longer sword from his cloth belt, applied a thin coating of clove oil, blotted it nearly dry with powder, and delicately placed it in the stand. He slid the companion sword free, repeated the process, and hung it above its mate. Respectfully, he bowed, then rose.

Rumiko stood, stiff-backed, stirring the rice. Her wooden spoon moved in precise circles.

As Usashibo walked, the green reed mats crackled beneath his feet. He stopped behind Rumiko, swearing he would allow nothing to spoil this night for her. With a finger, he traced a stray lock of hair along her neck and trailed off across her shoulder. His hand discovered taut muscles beneath her thin robe. Confusion and concern mingled within Usashibo. "Rumiko?"

The faint, hissing explosions of Rumiko's tears striking the charcoal punctuated the silence. Usashibo's grip on her arms hardened, as if to lend her his own strength.

Rumiko shifted uneasily in his grasp. "Always the swords first. If you loved me as much as you love them, you'd stay. Let someone else try to kill the dragon."

Usashibo snapped Rumiko toward him and wrapped his arms around her. She braced her elbows against his chest. Carefully, Usashibo pulled her to him, despite her resistance, and buried his face in her hair. "Ah, Rumiko. I will return. You must believe."

Rumiko ceased struggling. Usashibo relaxed his arms and dropped them to her waist. She leaned away from him and stared through red-laced eyes. "Do you really believe the thirteen others thought they would lose? Why risk your life here with me to fight a dragon that never hurts anyone who doesn't attack it? Stay. Please."

Usashibo had never questioned his reason to slay the dragon. The thought of surrendering his dream seemed so alien it did not merit consideration, but her words raised doubt. *Perhaps the dragon could kill me as it did all the others.* After so many consecutive victories, the thought of defeat appalled Usashibo. He knew he must fight the dragon, if only to prove himself invincible. If he quit now, all his striving and sacrifice meant nothing. One moment of weakness would make him and everything he believed in a deadly joke. *Ideals are worth dying for. I have trained my entire life for this one fight. If I cannot win, I deserve to die. Once a raindrop begins to fall, it must continue to fall, or it is no longer even a drop of rain. I've lied to myself; Rumiko never understood my dream. She is the same as all the others.*

Usashibo recalled a clear winter day half a year and a lifetime ago. His first Sensei, the consummate warrior in action and spirit, had died in his sleep. He had much left to teach, and Usashibo had much he still wanted to learn. It seemed unfair for Sensei to die as quietly as a peasant. Shortly after learning of his teacher's death, Usashibo fought with Rumiko over how the rice was prepared and left her.

Then, distraught, Usashibo had walked to the falls north of Miyamoto and sat on the crest, watching water crash to the rocks below. Mist swirled around him as he folded a small square of paper into a swan. He tossed the bird over the precipice as a gift to the god of the cascade. It spiraled gently downward until it struck the water. Then it plummeted and disappeared beneath the foam. He had seen his future as a warrior perish with old Sensei, and he had lost Rumiko, too. At that time, he realized he wanted to follow his swan over the falls.

A hand had touched Usashibo's arm. He spun, drew his sword instinctively, stood, and faced Rumiko. Resheathing his sword, he had turned back to the waterfall. She stood beside him, and forced him to face her. He felt tears run down his face, and Rumiko smiled sadly. Her presence spoke more deeply than words. He thought he sensed an understanding and similarity of purpose that transcended love.

But the love Usashibo had believed in was a lie. Now, the muscles at the corners of his jaw tightened as well as his grip. Rumiko winced and twisted, pushing desperately at his hands. He released her, and she retreated, kneading bruised arms. "Go now. I refuse to spend the night with a man who would rather die alone than live with me."

Rage and self-pity warred within Usashibo. His stomach clenched, and thoughts raced through his mind. He was truly alone.

Sweat formed on his forehead, and he walked mechanically from Rumiko. He stooped, lifted the swords from their stand, and returned each to his belt. The familiarity of his weapons became an anchor for his troubled thoughts. In the past year they had cost him much, but they had returned far more in a way no one seemed to understand. While the world changed, they remained reassuringly constant. Though they tested him unmercifully, they never doubted or judged. *Rumiko cannot force me to give up the direction that shaped my life. I refuse to become her servant.* He dropped his left hand to his long sword and sprinted for the door.

The linen curtain enwrapped Usashibo like a net. His momentum carried him blindly through, tearing cloth from the doorway. Anger and frustration exploded within him. He shredded the faded linen. When the cloth fell away, he snatched up his sandals and resumed running.

Stones crunched beneath Usashibo's tread. Their sharp edges bit into his feet, and he sought the physical pain to replace the hurt Rumiko's betrayal had caused. He burst from his garden and into the street. He crashed into a young man and both sprawled in the dust. The man rose, swearing viciously. But when he recognized Usashibo, he broke off and apologized for his own clumsiness. *The bastards won't even curse me.* Unconsciously, Usashibo placed his right hand on his hilt. *The dragon won't single me out as different.*

Usashibo leapt to his feet and raced down the street, knocking peasants aside when they did not dodge quickly enough. Soon, they cleared a lane before him, and he ran between walls of people to meet the dragon.

The damp warmth of the pine forest surrounded Usashibo. He scrambled across a small waterfall. Thick boughs shielded him from the sun and freed the ground from undergrowth. The terrain remained level, and Usashibo quickly neared the isolated clearing where legend claimed the dragon lived. In the three days since he had left Rumiko, he existed only to slay the dragon. The rigor of solitary sword practice and travel occupied every waking moment, though Rumiko haunted his dreams.

Stray beams of sunlight pierced the forest's canopy. In the distance, a head-high wall of brambles signaled an end to the trees, the edge of the dragon's clearing. Usashibo squatted near the base of a tree. The muscles at the nape of his neck tightened. A wave of warmth passed through him. His chest prickled with the first drops of sweat.

The scene was a sharp contrast to Usashibo's imaginings. The hollow whistle of a songbird echoed from the edge of the clearing. A brown and black beetle peered cautiously from beneath a loose curl of bark above his shoulder. No evil presence exerted its control over the woodlands. But perhaps the clearing would be different.

Usashibo's left hand rested on the mouth of his scabbard, and his thumb overlapped the sword's guard. He crept from tree to tree, paused, and peeked through the wall of briars. In the center of the clearing stood a cottage surrounded by a garden similar to his own. Usashibo stared, unable to believe that anyone would dare to live this close to the dragon.

Usashibo circled the clearing, searching for a gap in the wall of thorns. At the far edge, he found a path that led through the garden to the cottage. He pushed through the briars and emerged into the sun. As he blinked, eyes adjusting to the light, a man stepped through the cottage's door. Although Usashibo had never seen this man before, much about him seemed familiar. The powerful shoulders and mocking eyes marked him as a warrior, even without the two swords resting in his belt. Usashibo's left hand resumed its position at the mouth of his scabbard. The two men stared at each other in silence, mirror images separated by clusters of red and gold blossoms.

Wind ruffled the strange man's wide black pants. Slowly, he moved toward Usashibo, feet skimming the ground but never losing contact. Just beyond sword range, he stopped and met Usashibo's stare. He grinned, and the creases that formed at the corners of his eyes made him look immeasurably older. "A champion of dragons. Ten years so soon."

Usashibo forced himself to relax; tension would slow his reactions. From the combination of ease and precision that permeated the man's movements, Usashibo knew he followed the way of the sword with a dedication most men cannot imagine. He knew this man shared his obsession to master his sword and himself and the isolation it brought. Curiosity broke through the strange feelings of companion-ship welling in Usashibo's mind. "How did you know I am a champion of dragons?"

A smile again crossed the man's face."The way you walk, the way you hold your shoulders, and the unconquerable look in your eye. The last man I fought recognized me as I now recognize you. I was the last champion of dragons."

Usashibo's eyes narrowed accusingly. He feigned wiping sweat from his palm on the left side of his jacket to bring his hand nearer the hilt of the sword. "The last champion died fighting the dragon. He never returned."

The man's hand also casually drifted to his sword. "And you saw the body? Why should I return to people who inspired me, drove me to achieve beyond their dreams, then condemned me as different. They made me become the dragon, as shall you if you survive me." The man unsheathed his sword slowly and raised the blade, hilt gripped two-handed near his shoulder. "You cannot escape them. I've lived many places. All people are the same. It's easier being alone."

Usashibo drew both his swords and retreated two steps. His short blade hovered at waist height, the long one poised above it. The thought of killing the only person who truly understood the hell he survived appalled him. "I don't want to fight you."

The man lowered the tip of his sword until it nearly touched the ground. "You don't need to know who'd win? If you're afraid, you're a disgrace to the swords you carry."

The possibility of losing this combat had never occurred to Usashibo. Surrender would render the years of training and self-denial meaningless. The minutes of immortality during this fight had cost too much to be given up now. After sacrificing Rumiko's love, one man's life would not keep Usashibo from his goal. Despite the bond he shared with this man, or because of it, Usashibo knew he must kill the dragon he faced. *In the quiet of my soul, I am invincible.*

Usashibo thrust with both swords. The man dodged and retreated. The two men circled. They probed each other's defenses without fully attacking. The man struck for Usashibo's forward leg. Usashibo leapt above the attack. The man lunged again. Usashibo batted the blade aside with his short sword. He countercut at the man's wrists. The man jerked his sword back and caught Usashibo's blow near his hilt. Spinning away, he cut beneath Usashibo's guard. Pain seared Usashibo's thigh. Reflexively, he lowered both swords to block the blow which had already landed. The man's sword arched toward Usashibo's undefended head.

Usashibo dropped his short sword and pivoted away. As the blow descended, Usashibo blended with the man's movement. His free hand caught his opponent's hilt and continued the forward motion. Pulled off-balance, the man stumbled. Usashibo drove his long sword into his opponent's chest. He continued the cut as his blade slid free. The man dropped to the ground.

Red froth bubbled from the man's mouth as he clutched the wound. "Brother, you did not disappoint me." A final smile crossed his face before death glazed his features.

A horse's whicker snapped Usashibo's attention from the man he had killed. Snatching up his short sword, he whirled, poised for combat.

Rumiko sat astride a dun stallion at the edge of the clearing, bow in hand, arrow nocked. She answered Usashibo's question before he asked it. "If he'd won, I'd have killed him."

Usashibo lowered his swords and stared at his wife, puzzled. The entire situation confounded him, and the burning cut on his thigh clouded thought further. One question pressed foremost in his thoughts. "Why didn't you shoot him before the fight?"

A shy smile lit Rumiko's face. "When I heard him talk, I knew he was right. You had to fight." She shrugged. "That's the way Miura Usashibo is."

Suddenly, Usashibo realized the force that had driven and shaped his life had disappeared. The dragon was dead. The joy he should have felt at Rumiko's revelation lost itself in the void the dragon had filled. For the first time in Usashibo's life, he experienced panic. Tears welled in his eyes.

Rumiko's grin broadened as her horse danced sideways. "I understand Mimasaka has been plagued by a demon for three hundred years."

An inner warmth and new sense of purpose suffused Usashibo. *There are many dragons and only one Rumiko.* "Let's go home."

Two Yards of Dragon

L. Sprague de Camp

Eudoric Damberton, Esquire, rode home from his courting of Lusina, daughter of the enchanter Baldonius, with a face as long as an olifant's nose. Eudoric's sire, Sir Dambert, said:

"Well, how fared thy suit, boy? Ill, eh?"

"I—" began Eudoric.

"I told you 'twas an asinine notion, eh? Was I not right? When Baron Emmerhard has more daughters than he can count, any one of which would fetch a pretty parcel of land with her, eh? Well, why answerest not?"

"I—" said Eudoric.

"Come on, lad, speak up!"

"How can he, when ye talk all the time?" said Eudoric's mother, the Lady Aniset.

"Oh," said Sir Dambert. "Your pardon, son. Moreover and furthermore, as I've told you, an' ye were Emmerhard's son-in-law, he'd use his influence to get you your spurs. Here ye be, a strapping youth of three-and-twenty, not yet knighted. 'Tis a disgrace to our lineage."

"There are no wars toward, to afford opportunity for deeds of knightly dought," said Eudoric.

"Aye, 'tis true. Certes, we all hail the blessings of peace, which the wise governance of our sovran emperor hath given us for lo these thirteen years. Howsomever, to perform a knightly deed, our young men must needs waylay banditti, disperse rioters, and do suchlike fribbling feats."

As Sir Dambert paused, Eudoric interjected, "Sir, that problem now seems on its way to solution."

"How meanest thou?"

"If you'll but hear me, Father! Doctor Baldonius has set me a task, ere he'll bestow Lusina on me, which should fit me for knighthood in any jurisdiction."

"And that is?"

"He's fain to have two square yards of dragon hide. Says he needs 'em for his magical mummeries."

"But there have been no dragons in these parts for a century or more!"

"True; but, quoth Baldonius, the monstrous reptiles still abound far to eastward, in the lands of Pathenia and Pantorozia. Forsooth, he's given me a letter of introduction to his colleague, Doctor Raspiudus, in Pathenia."

"What?" cried the Lady Aniset. "Thou, to set forth on some year-long journey to parts unknown, where, 'tis said, men hop on a single leg or have faces in their bellies? I'll not have it! Besides, Baldonius may be privy wizard to Baron Emmerhard, but 'tis not to be denied that he is of no gentle blood."

"Well," said Eudoric, "so who was gentle when the Divine Pair created the world?"

"Our forebears were, I'm sure, whate'er were the case with those of the learned Doctor Baldonius. You young people are always full of idealistic notions. Belike thou'lt fall into heretical delusions, for I hear that the Easterlings have not the true religion. They falsely believe that God is one, instead of two as we truly understand."

"Let's not wander into the mazes of theology," said Sir Dambert, his chin in his fist. "To be sure, the paynim Southrons believe that God is three, an even more pernicious notion than that of the Easterlings."

"An' I meet God in my travels, I'll ask him the truth o't," said Eudoric.

"Be not sacrilegious, thou impertinent whelp! Still and all and notwithstanding, Doctor Baldonius were a man of influence to have in the family, be his origin never so humble. Methinks I could prevail upon him to utter spells to cause my crops, my neat, and my villeins to thrive, whilst casting poxes and murrains on my enemies. Like that caitiff Rainmar, eh? What of the bad seasons we've had? The God and Goddess know we need all the supernatural help we can get to keep us from penury. Else we may some fine day awaken to find that we've lost the holding to some greasy tradesman with a purchased title, with pen for lance and tally sheet for shield."

"Then I have your leave, sire?" cried Eudoric, a broad grin splitting his square, bronzed young face.

The Lady Aniset still objected, and the argument raged for another hour. Eudoric pointed out that it was not as if he were an only child, having two younger brothers and a sister. In the end, Sir Dambert and his lady agreed to Eudoric's quest, provided he return in time to help with the harvest, and take a manservant of their choice.

"Whom have you in mind?" asked Eudoric.

"I fancy Jillo the trainer," said Sir Dambert.

Eudoric groaned. "That old mossback, ever canting and haranguing me on the duties and dignities of my station?"

"He's but a decade older than ye," said Sir Dambert. "Moreover and furthermore, ye'll need an older man, with a sense of order and propriety, to keep you on the path of a gentleman. Class loyalty above all, my boy! Young men are wont to swallow every new idea that flits past, like a frog snapping at flies. Betimes they find they've engulfed a wasp, to their scathe and dolor."

"He's an awkward wight, Father, and not overbrained."

"Aye, but he's honest and true, no small virtues in our degenerate days. In my sire's time there was none of this newfangled saying the courteous 'ye' and 'you' even to mere churls and scullions. 'Twas always 'thou' and 'thee.' ''

"How you do go on, Dambert dear," said the Lady Aniset.

"Aye, I ramble. 'Tis the penalty of age. At least, Eudoric, the faithful Jillo knows horses and will keep your beasts in prime fettle." Sir Dambert smiled. "Moreover and furthermore, if I know Jillo Godmarson, he'll be glad to get away from his nagging wife for a spell."

So Eudoric and Jillo set forth to eastward, from the knight's holding of Arduen, in the barony of Zurgau, in the county of Treveria, in the kingdom of Locania, in the New Napolitanian Empire. Eudoric—of medium height, powerful build, dark, with square-jawed but otherwise undistinguished features—rode his palfrey and led his mighty destrier Morgrim. The lank, lean Jillo bestrode another palfrey and led a sumpter mule. Morgrim was piled with Eudoric's panoply of plate, carefully nested into a compact bundle and lashed down under a canvas cover. The mule bore the rest of their supplies.

For a fortnight they wended uneventfully through the duchies and counties of the Empire. When they reached lands where they could no longer understand the local dialects, they made shift with Helladic; the tongue of the Old Napolitanian Empire, which lettered men spoke everywhere.

They stopped at inns where inns were to be had. For the first fortnight, Eudoric was too preoccupied with dreams of his beloved Lusina to notice the tavern wenches. After that, his urges began to fever him, and he bedded one in Zerbstat, to their mutual satisfaction. Thereafter, however, he forebore, not as a matter of sexual morals but as a matter of thrift.

When benighted on the road, they slept under the stars—or, as befell them on the marches of Avaria, under a rain-dripping canopy of clouds. As they bedded down in the wet, Eudoric asked his companion:

"Jillo, why did you not remind me to bring a tent?"

Jillo sneezed. "Why, sir, come rain, come snow, I never thought that so sturdy a springald as ye be would ever need one. The heroes in the romances never travel with tents."

"To the nethermost hell with heroes of the romances! They go clattering around on their destriers for a thousand cantos. Weather is ever fine. Food, shelter, and a change of clothing appear, as by magic, whenever desired. Their armor never rusts. They suffer no tisics and fluxes. They pick up no fleas or lice at the inns. They're never swindled by merchants, for none does aught so vulgar as buying and selling."

"If ye'll pardon me, sir," said Jillo, "that were no knightly way to speak. It becomes not your station."

"Well, to the nethermost hells with my station, too! Wherever these paladins go, they find damsels in distress to rescue, or have other agreeable, thrilling and sanitary adventures. What adventures have we had? The time we fled from robbers in the Turonian Forest. The time I fished you out of the Albis half drowned. The time we ran out of food in the Asciburgi Mountains and had to plod fodderless over those hair-raising peaks for three days on empty stomachs."

"The Divine Pair do but seek to try the mettle of a valorous aspirant knight, sir. Ye should welcome these petty adversities as a chance to prove your manhood."

Eudoric made a rude noise with his mouth. "That for my manhood! Right now, I'd fainer have a stout roof overhead, a warm fire before me, and a hot repast in my belly. An' ever I go on such a silly jaunt again, I'll find one of those versemongers—like that troubadour, Landwin of Kromnitch, that visited us yesteryear—and drag him along, to show him how little real adventures are like those of the romances. And if he fall into the Albis, he may drown, for all of me. Were it not for my darling Lusina—"

Eudoric lapsed into gloomy silence, punctuated by sneezes.

They plodded on until they came to the village of Liptai, on the border of Pathenia. After the border guards had questioned and passed them, they walked their animals down the deep mud of the main street. Most of the slatternly houses were of logs or of crudely hewn planks, innocent of paint.

"Heaven above!" said Jillo. "Look at that, sir!"

"That" was a gigantic snail shell, converted into a small house.

"Knew you not of the giant snails of Pathenia?" asked Eudoric. "I've read of them in Doctor Baldonius' encyclopedia. When full grown, they—or rather their shells—are ofttimes used for dwellings i this land."

Jillo shook his head. " 'Twere better had ye spent more of you time on your knightly exercises and less on reading. Your sire hath never learnt his letters, yet he doth his duties well enow."

"Times change, Jillo. I may not clang rhymes so featly as Doctor Baldonius, or that ass Landwin of Kromnitch; but in these days a stroke of the pen were oft more fell than the slash of a sword. Here's a hostelry that looks not too slummocky. Do you dismount and inquire within as to their tallage."

"Why, sir?"

"Because I am fain to know, ere we put our necks in the noose! Go ahead. An' I go in, they'll double the scot at sight of me."

When Jillo came out and quote prices, Eudoric said, "Too dear. We'll try the other."

"But, Master! Mean ye to put us in some flea-bitten hovel, like that which we suffered in Bitava?"

"Aye. Didst not prate to me on the virtues of petty adversity in strengthening one's knightly mettle?"

" 'Tis not that, sir."

"What, then?"

"Why, when better quarters are to be had, to make do with the worse were an insult to your rank and station. No gentleman—"

"Ah, here we are!" said Eudoric. "Suitably squalid, too! You see, good Jillo, I did but yester'een count our money, and lo! more than half is gone, and our journey not yet half completed."

"But, noble Master, no man of knightly mettle would so debase himself as to tally his silver, like some base-born commercial—"

"Then I must needs lack true knightly mettle. Here we be!"

For a dozen leagues beyond Liptai rose the great, dense Motolian Forest. Beyond the forest lay the provincial capital of Velitchovo. Beyond Velitchovo, the forest thinned out *gradatim* to the great grassy plains of Pathenia. Beyond Pathenia, Eudoric had been told, stretched the boundless deserts of Pantorozia, over which a man might ride for months without seeing a city.

Yes, the innkeeper told them, there were plenty of dragons in the Motolian Forest. "But fear them not," said Kasmar in broken Helladic. "From being hunted, they have become wary and even timid. An' ye stick to the road and move yarely, they'll pester you not unless ye surprise or corner one."

"Have any dragons been devouring maidens fair lately?" asked Eudoric.

Kasmar laughed. "Nay, good Master. What were maidens fair doing, traipsing round the woods to stir up the beasties? Leave them be, I say, and they'll do the same by you."

A cautious instinct warned Eudoric not to speak of his quest. After he and Jillo had rested and had renewed their equipment, they set out, two days later, into the Motolian Forest. They rode for a league along the Velitchovo road. Then Eudoric, accoutered in full plate and riding Morgrim, led his companion off the road into the woods to southward. They threaded their way among the trees, ducking branches, in a wide sweep around. Steering by the sun, Eudoric brought them back to the road near Liptai.

The next day they did the same, except that their circuit was to the north of the highway.

After three more days of this exploration, Jillo became restless. "Good Master, what do we, circling round and about so bootlessly? The dragons dwell farther east, away from the haunts of men, they say."

"Having once been lost in the woods," said Eudoric, "I would not repeat the experience. Therefore do we scout our field of action, like a general scouting a future battlefield."

" 'Tis an arid business," said Jillo with a shrug. "But then, ye were always one to see further into a millstone than most."

At last, having thoroughly committed the byways of the nearer forest to memory, Eudoric led Jillo farther east. After casting about, they came at last upon the unmistakable tracks of a dragon. The animal had beaten a path through the brush, along which they could ride almost as well as on the road. When they had followed this track for above an hour, Eudoric became aware of a strong, musky stench.

"My lance, Jillo!" said Eudoric, trying to keep his voice from rising with nervousness.

The next bend in the path brought them into full view of the dragon, a thirty-footer facing them on the trail.

"Ha!" said Eudoric. "Meseems 'tis a mere cockadrill, albeit longer of neck and of limb than those that dwell in the rivers of Agisymba—if the pictures in Doctor Baldonius' books lie not. Have at thee, vile worm!"

Eudoric couched his lance and put spurs to Morgrim. The destrier bounded forward.

The dragon raised its head and peered this way and that, as if it could not see well. As the hoofbeats drew nearer, the dragon opened its jaws and uttered a loud, hoarse, groaning bellow.

At that, Morgrim checked his rush with stiffened forelegs, spun ponderously on his haunches, and veered off the trail into the woods. Jillo's palfrey bolted likewise, but in another direction. The dragon set out after Eudoric at a shambling trot.

Eudoric had not gone fifty yards when Morgrim passed close aboard a massive old oak, a thick limb of which jutted into their path. The horse ducked beneath the bough. The branch caught Eudoric across the breastplate, flipped him backward over the high cantle of his saddle, and swept him to earth with a great clatter.

Half stunned, he saw the dragon trot closer and closer—and then lumber past him, almost within arm's length, and disappear on the trail of the fleeing horse. The next that Eudoric knew, Jillo was bending over him, crying:

"Alas, my poor heroic Master! Be any bones broke, sir?"

"All of them, methinks," groaned Eudoric. "What's befallen Morgrim?"

"That I know not. And look at this dreadful dent in your beauteous cuirass!"

"Help me out of the thing. The dent pokes most sorely into my ribs. The misadventures I suffer for my dear Lusina!"

"We must get your breastplate to a smith to have it hammered out and filed smooth again."

"Fiends take the smiths! They'd charge half the cost of a new one. I'll fix it myself, if I can find a flat rock to set it on and a big stone wherewith to pound it."

"Well, sir," said Jillo, "ye were always a good man of your hands. But the mar will show, and that were not suitable for one of your quality."

"Thou mayst take my quality and stuff it!" cried Eudoric. "Canst speak of nought else? Help me up, pray." He got slowly to his feet, wincing, and limped a few steps.

"At least," he said, "nought seems fractured. But I misdoubt I can walk back to Liptai."

"Oh, sir, that were not to be thought of! Me allow you to wend afoot whilst I ride? Fiends take the thought!" Jillo unhitched the palfrey from the tree to which he had tethered it and led it to Eudoric.

"I accept your courtesy, good Jillo, only because I must. To plod the distance afoot were but a condign punishment for so bungling my charge. Give me a boost, will you?" Eudoric grunted as Jillo helped him into the saddle.

"Tell me, sir," said Jillo, "why did the beast ramp on past you without stopping to devour you as ye lay helpless? Was't that Morgrim promised a more bounteous repast? Or that the monster feared that your plate would give him a disorder of the bowels?"

"Meseems 'twas neither. Marked you how gray and milky appeared its eyes? According to Doctor Baldonius' book, dragons shed their skins from time to time, like serpents. This one neared the time of its skin change, wherefore the skin over its eyeballs had become thickened and opaque, like glass of poor quality. Therefore it could not plainly discern objects lying still, and pursued only those that moved."

They got back to Liptai after dark. Both were barely able to stagger, Eudoric from his sprains and bruises and Jillo footsore from the unaccustomed three-league hike.

Two days later, when they had recovered, they set out on the two palfreys to hunt for Morgrim. "For," Eudoric said, "that nag is worth more in solid money than all the rest of my possessions together."

Eudoric rode unarmored save for a shirt of light mesh mail, since the palfrey could not carry the extra weight of the plate all day at a brisk pace. He bore his lance and sword, however, in case they should again encounter a dragon.

The found the site of the previous encounter, but no sign either of the dragon or of the destrier. Eudoric and Jillo tracked the horse by its prints in the soft mold for a few bowshots, but then the slot faded out on harder ground.

"Still, I misdoubt Morgrim fell victim to the beast," said Eudoric. "He could show clean heels to many a steed of lighter build, and from its looks the dragon was no courser."

After hours of fruitless searching, whistling, and calling, they returned to Liptai. For a small fee, Eudoric was allowed to post a notice in Helladic on the town notice board, offering a reward for the return of his horse.

No words, however, came of the sighting of Morgrim. For all that Eudoric could tell, the destrier might have run clear to Velitchovo.

"You are free with advice, good Jillo," said Eudoric. "Well, rede me this riddle. We've established that our steeds will bolt from the sight and smell of dragon, for which I blame them little. Had we all the time in the world, we could doubtless train them to face the monsters, beginning with a stuffed dragon, and then, perchance, one in a cage in some monarch's menagerie. But our lucre dwindles like the snow in spring. What's to do?"

"Well, if the nags won't stand, needs we must face the worms on foot," said Jillo.

"That seems to me to throw away our lives to no good purpose, for these vasty lizards can outrun and outturn us and are well harnessed to boot. Barring the luckiest of lucky thrusts with the spear—as, say, into the eye or down the gullet—that fellow we erst encountered could make one mouthful of my lance and another of me."

"Your knightly courage were sufficient defense, sir. The Divine Pair would surely grant victory to the right."

"From all I've read of battles and feuds," said Eudoric, "methinks the Holy Couple's attention oft strays elsewhither when they should be deciding the outcome of some mundane fray."

"That is the trouble with reading; it undermines one's faith in the True Religion. But ye could be at least as well armored as the dragon, in your panoply of plate."

"Aye, but then poor Daisy could not bear so much weight to the site—or, at least, bear it thither and have breath left for a charge. We must be as chary of our beasts' welfare as of our own, for without them 'tis a long walk back to Trevaria. Nor do I deem that we should like to pass our lives in Liptai."

"Then, sir, we could pack the armor on the mule, for you to do on in dragon country."

"I like it not," said Eudoric. "Afoot, weighted down by that lobster's habit, I could move no more spryly than a tortoise. 'Twere small comfort to know that if the dragon ate me, he'd suffer indigestion afterward."

Jillo sighed. "Not the knightly attitude, sir, if ye'll pardon my saying so."

"Say what you please, but I'll follow the course of what meseems were common sense. What we need is a brace of those heavy steel crossbows for sieges. At close range, they'll punch a hole in a breastplate as 'twere a sheet of papyrus."

"They take too long to crank up," said Jillo. "By the time ye've readied your second shot, the battle's over."

"Oh, it would behoove us to shoot straight the first time; but better one shot that pierces the monster's scales than a score that bounce off. Howsomever, we have these fell little hand catapults not, and they don't make them in this barbarous land."

A few days later, while Eudoric still fretted over the lack of means to his goal, he heard a sudden sound like a single thunderclap from close at hand. Hastening out from Kasmar's Inn, Eudoric and Jillo found a crowd of Pathenians around the border guard's barracks.

In the drill yard, the guard was drawn up to watch a man demonstrate a weapon. Eudoric, whose few words of Pathenian were not up to conversation, asked among the crowd for somebody who could speak Helladic. When he found one, he learned that the demonstrator was a Pantorozian. The man was a stocky, snub-nosed fellow in a bulbous fur hat, a jacket of coarse undyed wool, and baggy trousers tucked into soft boots.

"He says the device was invented by the Sericans," said the villager. "They live half a world away, across the Pantorozian deserts. He puts some powder into that thing, touches a flame to it, and *boom!* it spits a leaden ball through the target as neatly as you please."

The Pantorozian demonstrated again, pouring black powder from the small end of a horn down his brass barrel. He placed a wad of rag over the mouth of the tube, then a leaden ball, and pushed both ball and wad down the tube with a rod. He poured a pinch of powder into a hole on the upper side of the tube near its rear, closed end.

Then he set a forked rest in the ground before him, rested the barrel in the fork, and took a small torch that a guardsman handed him. He pressed the wooden stock of the device against his shoulder, sighted along the tube, and with his free hand touched the torch to the touchhole. Ffft, *bang!* A cloud of smoke, and another hole appeared in the target.

The Pantorozian spoke with the captain of the guard, but they were too far for Eudoric to hear, even if he could have understood their Pathenian. After a while, the Pantorozian picked up his tube and rest, slung his bag of powder over his shoulder, and walked with downcast air to a cart hitched to a shade tree.

Eudoric approached the man, who was climbing into his cart. "God den, fair sir!" began Eudoric, but the Pantorozian spread his hands with a smile of incomprehension.

"Kasmar!" cried Eudoric, sighting the innkeeper in the crowd. "Will you have the goodness to interpret for me and this fellow?"

"He says," said Kasmar, "that he started out with a wainload of these devices and has sold all but one. He hoped to dispose of his last one in Liptai, but our gallant Captain Boriswaf will have nought to do with it."

"Why?" asked Eudoric. "Meseems 'twere a fell weapon in practiced hands."

"That is the trouble, quoth Master Vlek. Boriswaf says that should so fiendish a weapon come into use, 'twill utterly extinguish the noble art of war, for all men will down weapons and refuse to fight rather than face so devilish a device. Then what should he, a lifelong soldier, do for his bread? Beg?"

"Ask Master Vlek where he thinks to pass the night."

"I have already persuaded him to lodge with us, Master Eudoric."

"Good, for I would fain have further converse with him."

Over dinner, Eudoric sounded out the Pantorozian on the price he asked for his device. Acting as translator, Kasmar said, "If ye strike a bargain on this, I should get ten per centum as a broker's commission, for ye were helpless without me."

Eudoric got the gun, with thirty pounds of powder and a bag of leaden balls and wadding, for less than half of what Vlek had asked of Captain Boriswaf. As Vlek explained, he had not done badly on this peddling trip and was eager to get home to his wives and children.

"Only remember," he said through Kasmar, "overcharge it not, lest it blow apart and take your head off. Press the stock firmly against your shoulder, lest it knock you on your arse like a mule's kick. And keep fire away from the spare powder, lest it explode all at once and blast you to gobbets."

Later, Eudoric told Jillo, "That deal all but wiped out our funds."

"After the tradesmanlike way ye chaffered that barbarian down?"

"Aye. The scheme had better work, or we shall find ourselves choosing betwixt starving and seeking employment as collectors of offal or diggers of ditches. Assuming, that is, that in this reeky place they even bother to collect offal."

"Master Eudoric!" said Jillo. "Ye would not really lower yourself to accept menial wage labor?"

"Sooner than starve, aye. As Helvolius the philosopher said, no rider wears sharper spurs than Necessity."

"But if 'twere known at home, they'd hack off your gilded spurs, break your sword over your head, and degrade you to base varlet!"

"Well, till now I've had no knightly spurs to hack off, but only the plain silvered ones of an esquire. For the rest, I count on you to see that they don't find out. Now go to sleep and cease your grumbling."

The next day found Eudoric and Jillo deep into the Motolian Forest. At the noonday halt, Jillo kindled a fire. Eudoric made a small torch of a stick whose end was wound with a rag soaked in bacon fat. Then he loaded the device as he had been shown how to do and fired three balls at a mark on a tree. The third time, he hit the mark squarely, although the noise caused the palfreys frantically to tug and rear.

They remounted and went on to where they had met the dragon. Jillo rekindled the torch, and they cast up and down the beast's trail.

For two hours they saw no wildlife save a fleeing sow with a farrow of piglets and several huge snails with boulder-sized shells.

Then the horses became unruly. "Methinks they scent our quarry," said Eudoric.

When the riders themselves could detect the odor and the horses became almost unmanageable, Eudoric and Jillo dismounted.

"Tie the nags securely," said Eudoric. " 'Twould never do to slay our beast and then find that our horses had fled, leaving us to drag this land cockadrill home afoot."

As if in answer, a deep grunt came from ahead. While Jillo secured the horses, Eudoric laid out his new equipment and methodically loaded his piece.

"Here it comes," said Eudoric. "Stand by with that torch. Apply it not ere I give the word!"

The dragon came in sight, plodding along the trail and swinging its head from side to side. Having just shed its skin, the dragon gleamed in a reticular pattern of green and black, as if it had been freshly painted. Its great, golden, slit-pupiled eyes were now keen.

The horses screamed, causing the dragon to look up and speed its approach.

"Ready?" said Eudoric, setting the device in its rest.

"Aye, sir. Here goeth!" Without awaiting further command, Jillo applied the torch to the touchhole.

With a great boom and a cloud of smoke, the device discharged, rocking Eudoric back a pace. When the smoke cleared, the dragon was still rushing upon them, unharmed.

"Thou idiot!" screamed Eudoric. "I told thee not to give fire until I commanded! Thou has made me miss it clean!"

"I'm s-sorry, sir. I was palsied with fear. What shall we do now?"

"Run, fool!" Dropping the device, Eudoric turned and fled.

Jillo also ran. Eudoric tripped over a root and fell sprawling. Jillo stopped to guard his fallen master and turned to face the dragon. As Eudoric scrambled up, Jillo hurled the torch at the dragon's open maw.

The throw fell just short of its target. It happened, however, that the dragon was just passing over the bag of black powder in its charge.

The whirling torch, descending in its flight beneath the monster's head, struck this sack.

BOOM!

When the dragon hunters returned, they found the dragon writhing in its death throes. Its whole underside had been blown open, and blood and guts spilled out.

"Well!" said Eudoric, drawing a long breath. "That is enough knightly adventure to last me for many a year. Fall to; we must flay the creature. Belike we can sell that part of the hide that we take not home ourselves."

"How do ye propose to get it back to Liptai? Its hide alone must weigh in the hundreds."

"We shall hitch the dragon's tail to our two nags and lead them, dragging it behind. 'Twill be a weary swink, but we must needs recover as much as we can to recoup our losses."

An hour later, blood-splattered from head to foot, they were still struggling with the vast hide. Then, a man in forester's garb, with a large gilt medallion on his breast, rode up and dismounted. He was a big, rugged-looking man with a rattrap mouth.

"Who slew this beast, good my sirs?" he inquired.

Jillo spoke: "My noble master, the squire Eudoric Dambertson here. He is the hero who hath brought this accursed beast to book."

"Be that sooth?" said the man to Eudoric.

"Well, ah," said Eudoric, "I must not claim much credit for the deed." .

"But ye were the slayer, yea? Then, sir, ye are under arrest."

"What? But wherefore?"

"Ye shall see." From his garments, the stranger produced a length of cord with knots at intervals. With this he measured the dragon from nose to tail. Then the man stood up again.

"To answer your question, on three grounds: *imprimis*, for slaying a dragon out of lawful season; *secundus*, for slaying a dragon below the minimum size permitted; and *tertius*, for slaying a female dragon, which is protected the year round."

"You say this is a female?"

"Aye, 'tis as plain as the nose on your face."

"How does one tell with dragons?"

"Know, knave, that the male hath small horns behind the eyes, the which this specimen patently lacks."

"Who are you anyway?" demanded Eudoric.

"Senior game warden Voytsik of Prath, at your service. My credentials." The man fingered his medallion. "Now, show me your licenses, pray!"

"Licenses?" said Eudoric blankly.

"Hunting licenses, oaf!"

"None told us that such were required, sir," said Jillo.

"Ignorance of the law is no pretext; ye should have asked. That makes four counts of illegality."

Eudoric said, "But why—why in the name of the God and Goddess—"

"Pray, swear not by your false, heretical deities."

"Well, why should you Pathenians wish to preserve these monstrous reptiles?"

"*Imprimis*, because their hides and other parts have commercial value, which would perish were the whole race extirpated. *Secundus*, because they help to maintain the balance of nature by devouring the giant snails, which otherwise would issue forth nightly from the forest in such numbers as to strip bare our crops, orchards, and gardens and reduce our folk to hunger. And *tertius*, because they add a picturesque element to the landscape, thus luring foreigners to visit our land and spend their gold therein. Doth that explanation satisfy you?"

Eudoric had a fleeting thought of assaulting the stranger and either killing him or rendering him helpless while Eudoric and Jillo salvaged their prize. Even as he thought, three more tough-looking fellows, clad like Voytsik and armed with crossbows, rode out of the trees and formed up behind their leader.

"Now come along, ye two," said Voytsik.

"Whither?" asked Eudoric.

"Back to Liptai. On the morrow, we take the stage to Velitchovo, where your case will be tried."

"Your pardon, sir; we take the what?"

"The stagecoach."

"What's that, good my sir?"

"By the only God, ye must come from a barbarous land indeed! Ye shall see. Now come along, lest we be benighted in the woods."

The stagecoach made a regular round trip between Liptai and Velitchovo thrice a sennight. Jillo made the journey sunk in gloom, Eudoric kept busy viewing the passing countryside and, when opportunity offered, asking the driver about his occupation: pay, hours, fares, the cost of the vehicle, and so forth. By the time the prisoners reached their destination, both stank mightily because they had had no chance to wash the dragon's blood from their blood-soaked garments.

As they neared the capital, the driver whipped up his team to a gallop. They rattled along the road beside the muddy river Pshora until the river made a bend. Then they thundered across the planks of a bridge.

Velitchovo was a real city, with a roughly paved main street and an onion-domed, brightly colored cathedral of the One God. In a massively timbered municipal palace, a bewhiskered magistrate asked, "Which of you two aliens truly slew the beast?"

"The younger, hight Eudoric," said Voytsik.

"Nay, Your Honor, 'twas I!" said Jillo.

"That is not what he said when we came upon them red-handed from their crime," said Voytsik. "This lean fellow plainly averred that his companion had done the deed, and the other denied it not."

"I can explain that," said Jillo. "I am the servant of the most worshipful squire Eudoric Dambertson of Arduen. We set forth to slay the creature, thinking this a noble and heroic deed that should redound to our glory on earth and our credit in Heaven. Whereas we both had a part in the act, the fatal stroke was delivered by your humble servant here. Howsomever, wishing like a good servant for all the glory to go to my master, I gave him the full credit, not knowing that this credit should be counted as blame."

"What say ye to that, Master Eudoric?" asked the judge.

"Jillo's account is essentially true," said Eudoric. "I must, however, confess that my failure to slay the beast was due to mischance and not want of intent."

"Methinks they utter a pack of lies to confuse the court," said Voytsik. "I have told Your Honor of the circumstances of their arrest, whence ye may judge how matters stand."

The judge put his fingertips together. "Master Eudoric," he said, "ye may plead innocent, or as incurring sole guilt, or as guilty in company with your servant. I do not think that you can escape some guilt, since Master Jillo, being your servant, acted under your orders. Ye be therefore responsible for his acts and at the very least a factor of dragocide."

"What happens if I plead innocent?" said Eudoric.

"Why, in that case, an' ye can find an attorney, ye shall be tried in due course. Bail can plainly not be allowed to foreign travelers, who can so easily slip through the law's fingers."

"In other words, I needs must stay in jail until my case comes up. How long will that take?"

"Since our calendar be crowded, 'twill be at least a year and a half. Whereas, an' ye plead guilty, all is settled in a trice."

"The I plead sole guilt," said Eudoric.

"But, dear Master—" wailed Jillo.

"Hold thy tongue, Jillo. I know what I do."

The judge chuckled. "An old head on young shoulders, I perceive. Well, Master Eudoric. I find you guilty on all four counts and amerce you the wonted fine, which is one hundred marks on each count."

"Four hundred marks!" exclaimed Eudoric. "Our total combined wealth at this moment amounts to fourteen marks and thirty-seven pence, plus some items of property left with Master Kasmar in Liptai."

"So, ye'll have to serve out the corresponding prison term, which comes to one mark a day—unless ye can find someone to pay the balance of the fine for you. Take him away, jailer."

"But, Your Honor!" cried Jillo, "what shall I do without my noble master? When shall I see him again?"

"Ye may visit him any day during the regular visiting hours. It were well if ye brought him somewhat to eat, for our prison fare is not of the daintiest."

At the first visiting hour, when Jillo pleaded to be allowed to share Eudoric's sentence, Eudoric said, "Be not a bigger fool than thou

canst help! I took sole blame so that ye should be free to run mine errands; whereas had I shared my guilt with you, we had both been
mewed up here. Here, take this letter to Doctor Raspiudus; seek him
out and acquaint him with our plight. If he be in sooth a true friend of
our own Doctor Baldonius, belike he'll come to our rescue."

Doctor Raspiudus was short and fat, with a bushy white beard to
his waist. "Ah, dear old Baldonius!" he cried in good Helladic. "I mind
me of when we were lads together at the Arcane College of Saalingen
University! Doth he still string verses together?"

"Aye, that he does," said Eudoric.

"Now, young man, I daresay that your chiefest desire is to get out
of this foul hole, is't not?"

"That, *and* to recover our three remaining animals and other possessions left behind in Liptai, *and* to depart with the two square yards of
dragon hide that I've promised to Doctor Baldonius, with enough
money to see us home."

"Methinks all these matters were easily arranged, young sir. I need
only your power of attorney to enable me to go to Liptai, recover the
objects in question and return hither to pay your fine and release you.
Your firearm is, I fear, lost to you, having been confiscated by the law."

" 'Twere of little use without a new supply of the magical powder,"
said Eudoric. "Your plan sounds splendid. But, sir, what do you get out
of this?"

The enchanter rubbed his hands together. "Why, the pleasure of
favoring an old friend—and also the chance to acquire a complete
dragon hide for my own purposes. I know somewhat of Baldonius' ex-
periments. As he can do thus and so with two yards of dragon, I can
surely do more with a score."

"How will you obtain this dragon hide?"

"By now the foresters will have skinned the beast and salvaged
the other parts of monetary worth, all of which will be put up at auc-
tion for the benefit of the kingdom. And I shall bid them in." Raspiudus chuckled. "When the other bidders know against whom they bid,
I think not that they'll force the price up very far."

"Why can't you get me out of here now and then go to Liptai?"

Another chuckle. "My dear boy, first I must see that all is as ye say in Liptai. After all, I have only your word that ye be in sooth the Eudoric Dambertson of whom Baldonius writes. So bide ye in patience a few days more. I'll see that ye be sent better aliment than the slop they serve here. And now, pray, your authorization. Here are pen and ink."

To keep from starvation, Jillo got a job as a paver's helper and worked in hasty visits to the jail during his lunch hour. When a fortnight had passed without word from Doctor Raspiudus, Eudoric told Jillo to go to the wizard's home for an explanation.

"They turned me away at the door," reported Jillo. "They told me that the learned doctor had never heard of us."

As the import of this news sank in, Eudoric cursed and beat the wall in his rage. "That filthy, treacherous he-witch! He gets me to sign that power of attorney; then, when he has my property in his grubby paws, he conveniently forgets about us! By the God and Goddess, if ever I catch him—"

"Here, here, what's all this noise?" said the jailer. "Ye disturb the other prisoners."

When Jillo explained the cause of his master's outrage, the jailer laughed. "Why, everyone knows that Raspiudus is the worst skinflint and treacher in Velitchovo! Had ye asked me, I'd have warned you."

"Why has none of his victims slain him?" asked Eudoric.

"We are a law-abiding folk, sir. We do not permit private persons to indulge their feuds on their own, and we have some *most* ingenious penalties for homicide."

"Mean ye," said Jillo, "that amongst you Pathenians a gentleman may not avenge an insult by the gage of battle?"

"Of course not! We are not bloodthirsty barbarians."

"Ye mean there are no true gentlemen amongst you," sniffed Jillo.

"Then, Master Tiolkhof," said Eudoric, calming himself by force of will, "am I stuck here for a year or more?"

"Aye, but ye may get time off for good behavior at the end—three or four days, belike."

When the jailer had gone, Jillo said, "When ye get out, Master, ye must needs uphold your honor by challenging this runagate to the trial of battle, to the death."

Eudoric shook his head. "Heard you not what Tiolkhof said? They deem dueling barbarous and boil the duelists in oil, or something equally entertaining. Anyway, Raspiudus could beg off on grounds of age. We must, instead, use what wits the Holy Couple gave us. I wish now that I'd sent you back to Liptai to fetch our belongings and never meddled with his rolypoly sorcerer."

"True, but how could ye know, dear Master? I should probably have bungled the task in any case, what with my ignorance of the tongue and all."

After another fortnight, King Vladmor of Pathenia died. When his son Yogor ascended the throne, he declared a general amnesty for all crimes less than murder. Thus Eudoric found himself out in the street again, but without horse, armor, weapons, or money beyond a few marks.

"Jillo," he said that night in their mean little cubicle, "we must needs get into Raspiudus' house somehow. As we saw this afternoon, 'tis a big place with a stout, high wall around it."

"An' ye could get a supply of that black powder, we could blast a breach in the wall."

"But we have no such stuff, nor means of getting it, unless we raid the royal armory, which I do not think we can do."

"Then how about climbing a tree near the wall and letting ourselves down by ropes inside the wall from a convenient branch?"

"A promising plan, if there were such an overhanging tree. But there isn't, as you saw as well as I when we scouted the place. Let me think. Raspiudus must have supplies borne into his stronghold from time to time. I misdoubt his wizardry is potent enough to conjure foodstuffs out of air."

"Mean ye that we should gain entrance as, say, a brace of chicken farmers with eggs to sell?"

"Just so. But nay, that won't do. Raspiudus is no fool. Knowing of this amnesty that enlarged me, he'll be on the watch for such a trick. At least, so should I be, in his room, and I credit him with no less wit than mine own. . . . I have it! What visitor would logically be likely to call upon him now, whom he will not have seen for many a year and whom he would hasten to welcome?"

"That I know not, sir."

"Who would wonder what had become of us and, detecting our troubles in his magical scryglass, would follow upon our track by uncanny means?"

"Oh, ye mean Doctor Baldonius!"

"Aye. My whiskers have grown nigh as long as his since last I shaved. And we're much of a size."

"But I never heard that your old tutor could fly about on an enchanted broomstick, as some of the mightiest magicians are said to do."

"Belike he can't, but Doctor Raspiudus wouldn't know that."

"Mean ye," said Jillo, "that ye've a mind to play Doctor Baldonius? Or to have me play him? The latter would never do."

"I know it wouldn't, good my Jillo. You know not the learned patter proper to wizards and other philosophers."

"Won't Raspiudus know you, sir? As ye say he's a shrewd old villain."

"He's seen me but once, in that dark, dank cell, and that for a mere quarter hour. You he's never seen at all. Methinks I can disguise myself well enough to befool him—unless you have a better notion."

"Alack, I have none! Then what part shall I play?"

"I had thought of going in alone."

"Nay, sir, dismiss the thought! Me let my master risk his mortal body and immortal soul in a witch's lair without my being there to help him!"

"If you help me the way you did by touching off that firearm whilst our dragon was out of range—"

"Ah, but who threw the torch and saved us in the end? What disguise shall I wear?"

"Since Raspiudus knows you not, there's no need for any. You shall be Baldonius' servant, as you are mine."

"Ye forget, sir, that if Raspiudus knows me not, his gatekeepers might. Forsooth, they're likely to recall me because of the noisy protests I made when they barred me out."

"Hm. Well, you're too old for a page, too lank for a bodyguard, and too unlearned for a wizard's assistant. I have it! You shall go as my concubine!"

"Oh, Heaven above, sir, not that! I am a normal man! I should never live it down!"

To the massive gate before Raspiudus' house came Eudoric, with a patch over one eye, and his beard, uncut for a month, dyed white. A white wig cascaded down from under his hat. He presented a note, in a plausible imitation of Baldonius' hand, to the gatekeeper:

> Doctor Baldonius of Treveria presents his compliments to his old friend and colleague Doctor Raspiudus of Velitchovo, and begs the favor of an audience to discuss the apparent disappearance of two young protégés of his.

A pace behind, stooping to disguise his stature, slouched a rouged and powdered Jillo in woman's dress. If Jillo was a homely man, he made a hideous woman, least as far as his face could be seen under the headcloth. Nor was his beauty enhanced by the dress, which Eudoric had stitched together out of cheap cloth. The garment looked like what it was: the work of a rank amateur at dressmaking.

"My master begs you to enter," said the gatekeeper.

"Why, dear old Baldonius!" cried Raspiudus, rubbing his hands together. "Ye've not changed a mite since those glad, mad days at Saalingen! Do ye still string verses?"

"Ye've withstood the ravages of time well yourself, Raspiudus," said Eudoric, in an imitation of Baldonius' voice.

" 'As fly the years, the geese fly north in spring; Ah, would the years, like geese, return awing!'"

Raspiudus roared with laughter, patting his paunch. "The same old Baldonius! Made ye that one up?"

Eudoric made a deprecatory motion. "I am a mere poetaster; but had not the higher wisdom claimed my allegiance, I might have made my mark in poesy."

"What befell your poor eye?"

"My own carelessness in leaving a corner of a pentacle open. The demon got in a swipe of his claws ere I could banish him. But now, good Raspiudus, I have a matter to discuss whereof I told you in my note."

"Yea, yea, time enow for that. Be ye weary from the road? Need ye baths? Aliment? Drink?"

"Not yet, old friend. We have but now come from Velitchovo's best hostelry."

"Then let me show you my house and grounds. Your lady . . . ?"

"She'll stay with me. She speaks nought but Treverian and fears being separated from me among strangers. A mere swineherd's chick, but a faithful creature. At my age, that is of more moment than a pretty face."

Presently, Eudoric was looking at his and Jillo's palfreys and their sumpter mule in Raspiudus' stables. Eudoric made a few hesitant efforts, as if he were Baldonius seeking his young friends, to inquire after their disappearance. Each time Raspiudus smoothly turned the question aside, promising enlightenment later.

An hour later, Raspiudus was showing off his magical sanctum. With obvious interest, Eudoric examined a number of squares of dragon hide spread out on a workbench. He asked:

"Be this the integument of one of those Pathenian dragons, whereof I have heard?"

"Certes, good Baldonius. Are they extinct in your part of the world?"

"Aye. 'Twas for that reason that I sent my young friend and former pupil, of whom I'm waiting to tell you, eastward to fetch me some of this hide for use in my work. How does one cure this hide?"

"With salt, and—*unh!*"

Raspiudus collapsed, Eudoric having just struck him on the head with a short bludgeon that he whisked out of his voluminous sleeves.

"Bind and gag him and roll him behind the bench!" said Eudoric.

"Were it not better to cut his throat, sir?" said Jillo.

"Nay. The jailor told us that they have ingenious ways of punishing homicide, and I have no wish to prove them by experiment."

While Jillo bound the unconscious Raspiudus, Eudoric chose two pieces of dragon hide, each about a yard square. He rolled them together into a bundle and lashed them with a length of rope from inside his robe. As an afterthought, he helped himself to the contents of Raspiudus' purse. Then he hoisted the roll of hide to his shoulder and issued from the laboratory. He called to the nearest stableboy.

"Doctor Raspiudus," he said, "asks that ye saddle up those two nags." He pointed. "Good saddles, mind you! Are the animals well shod?"

"Hasten, sir," muttered Jillo. "Every instant we hang about here—"

"Hold thy peace! The appearance of haste were the surest way to arouse suspicion." Eudoric raised his voice. "Another heave on that girth, fellow! I am not minded to have my aged bones shattered by a tumble into the roadway."

Jillo whispered, "Can't we recover the mule and your armor, to boot?"

Eudoric shook his head. "Too risky," he murmured. "Be glad if we get away with whole skins."

When the horses had been saddled to his satisfaction, he said, "Lend me some of your strength in mounting, youngster." He groaned as he swung awkwardly into the saddle. "A murrain on thy master, to send us off on this footling errand—me that hasn't sat a horse in years! Now hand me that accursed roll of hide. I thank thee, youth; here's a little for thy trouble. Run ahead and tell the gatekeeper to have his portal well opened. I fear that if this beast pulls up of a sudden, I shall go flying over its head!"

A few minutes later, when they had turned a corner and were out of sight of Raspiudus' house, Eudoric said, "Now, trot!"

"If I could but get out of this damned gown," muttered Jillo. "I can't ride decently in it."

"Wait till we're out of the city gate."

When Jillo had shed the offending garment, Eudoric said, "Now ride, man, as never before in your life!"

They pounded off on the Liptai road. Looking back, Jillo gave a screech. "There's a thing flying after us! It looks like a giant bat!"

"One of Raspiudus' sendings," said Eudoric. "I knew he'd get loose. Use your spurs! Can we but gain the bridge . . ."

They fled at a mad gallop. The sending came closer and closer, until Eudoric thought he could feel the wind of its wings.

Then their hooves thundered across the bridge over the Pshora.

"Those things will not cross running water," said Eudoric, looking back. "Slow down, Jillo. These nags must bear us many leagues, and we must not founder them at the start."

". . . so here we are," Eudoric told Doctor Baldonius.

"Ye've seen your family, lad?"

"Certes. They thrive, praise to the Divine Pair. Where's Lusina?"

"Well—ah—ahem—the fact is, she is not here."

"Oh? Then where?"

"Ye put me to shame, Eudoric. I promised you her hand in return for the two yards of dragon hide. Well, ye've fetched me the hide, at no small effort and risk, but I cannot fulfill my side of the bargain."

"Wherefore?"

"Alas! My undutiful daughter ran off with a strolling player last summer, whilst ye were chasing dragons—or perchance 'twas the other way round. I'm right truly sorry. . . ."

Eudoric frowned silently for an instant, then said, "Fret not, esteemed Doctor. I shall recover from the wound—provided, that is, that you salve it by making up my losses in more materialistic fashion."

Baldonius raised bushy gray brows. "So? Ye seem not so grief-stricken as I should have expected, to judge from the lover's sighs and tears wherewith ye parted from the jade last spring. Now ye'll accept money instead?"

"Aye, sir. I admit that my passion had somewhat cooled during our long separation. Was it likewise with her? What said she of me?"

"Aye, her sentiments did indeed change. She said you were too much an opportunist altogether to please her. I would not wound your feelings. . . ."

Eudoric waved a deprecatory hand. "Continue, pray. I have been somewhat toughened by my months in the rude, rough world, and I am interested."

"Well, I told her she was being foolish; that ye were a shrewd lad who, an' ye survived the dragon hunt, would go far. But her words were: 'That is just the trouble, Father. He is too shrewd to be very lovable.' "

"Hmph," grunted Eudoric. "As one might say: I am a man of enterprise, thou art an opportunist, he is a conniving scoundrel. 'Tis all in the point of view. Well, if she prefers the fools of this world, I wish her joy of them. As a man of honor, I would have wedded Lusina had she wished. As things stand, trouble is saved all around."

"To you, belike, though I misdoubt my headstrong lass'll find the life of an actor's wife a bed of violets:

> Who'd wed on a whim is soon filled to the brim
> Of worry and doubt, till he longs for an out.
> So if ye would wive, beware of the gyve
> Of an ill-chosen mate; 'tis a harrowing fate.

But enough of that. What sum had ye in mind?"

"Enough to cover the cost of my good destrier Morgrim and my panoply of plate, together with lance and sword, plus a few other chattels and incidental expenses of travel. Fifteen hundred marks should cover the lot."

"Fif-teen *hundred*! Whew! I could ne'er afford—nor are these moldy patches of dragon hide worth a fraction of the sum."

Eudoric sighed and rose. "You know what you can afford, good my sage." He picked up the roll of dragon hide. "Your colleague Doctor Calporio, wizard to the Count of Treveria, expressed a keen interest in this material. In fact, he offered me more than I have asked of you, but I thought it only honorable to give you the first chance."

"What!" cried Baldonius. "That mountebank, charlatan, that faker? Misusing the hide and not deriving a tenth of the magical benefits from it that I should? Sit down, Eudoric; we will discuss these things."

An hour's haggling got Eudoric his fifteen hundred marks. Baldonius said, "Well, praise the Divine Couple that's over. And now, beloved pupil, what are your plans?"

"Would ye believe it, Doctor Baldonius," said Jillo, "that my poor, deluded master is about to disgrace his lineage and betray his class by a base commercial enterprise?"

"Forsooth, Jillo? What's this?"

"He means my proposed coach line," said Eudoric.

"Good Heaven, what's that?"

"My plan to run a carriage on a weekly schedule from Zurgau to Kromnitch, taking all who can pay the fare, as they do in Pathenia. We can't let the heathen Easterlings get ahead of us."

"What an extraordinary idea! Need ye a partner?"

"Thanks, but nay. Baron Emmerhard has already thrown in with me. He's promised me my knighthood in exchange for the partnership."

"There is no nobility anymore," said Jillo.

Eudoric grinned. "Emmerhard said much the same sort of thing, but I convinced him that anything to do with horses is a proper pursuit for a gentleman. Jillo, you can spell me at driving the coach, which will make you a gentleman, too!"

Jillo sighed. "Alas! The true spirit of knighthood is dying in this degenerate age. Woe is me that I should live to see the end of chivalry! How much did ye think of paying me, sir?"

Saint Willibald's Dragon

Esther M. Friesner

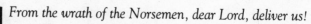

From the wrath of the Norsemen, dear Lord, deliver us!

I, Brother Theobald, write this. It is not an original thought, but it is an immediate one. Indeed, inescapable as the singular love of God and the several weaknesses of Man. Heaven be my witness, I would escape it if I might.

From the wrath of the Norsemen, dear Lord, deliver us!

So rings the cry through the halls of this, our humble monastery. Sane men are driven mad by force of having to bear this constant pummeling of the auditory sense, and madmen wish the heathen fiends would come at last to put an end to such unseemly caterwauling. Dragon-prowed ships have been sighted off the coast; there is no doubt who comes.

Why must they always favor Ireland? Is not the world wide enough? I wish I might shout in their hairy faces, *Invade some other land for a change! Hispania, Italia, Arabia Deserta! The weather is reputed to be better there.* But there is no reasoning with Vikings.

Like as not the holy places will be their first targets; not out of any conscious wish to desecrate the cross, but because they know that our churches are rich in silver, gold, and jewels. A wooden cup was good enough for Christ, but for us who serve Him . . . ? At times I think our Lord is trying to tell us something.

I wish Him luck trying to make Himself heard over the to-do going on here. A man can scarcely think on Heaven—which no doubt awaits us all instantly, the key a Viking sword—what with all this yammering.

At least I am not guilty of adding to the row. My lord abbot would tell me that it is a mark of my fallen nature that I spend these, my last moments, here in the scriptorium. And I would be sinful enough to tell him in turn that if a martyr's death guarantees us Paradise, why are my brothers weeping over the summary prospect of their faith's reward? Saint Willibald would think them loons, and his judgment in such matters must be accepted as expert. As for what he'd make of me . . . Ah, well, saints understand much and forgive more! I scribble, my brethren pray, but in the end it will all be the same: what's a little spilled ink amid so much imminently spilled blood?

Besides, I have already made petition of individual salvation to Saint Willibald.

Will that help me? I doubt it. God Himself may have to ask, "Saint *who?*" when my prayers reach the Throne. I am the only human soul on earth who knows enough to pray to such a saint, and even I would not be wise enough to do so if he were not my cousin; many generations removed, to be sure. The diligent scholar will find no mention of him in any churchly calendar, wherefore it behooves me now to write his story while yet I may. I am the last of his legitimate line, and with me dies the tale; dies soon, by the feel of the wind and the look of those longships.

(There is the chance that some few of Saint Willibald's bastard offshoots might know the legend too, and preserve it, but one should never depend on the priorities of the illegitimate.)

So:

In the reign of the emperor Marcus Aurelius Antoninus, wrongly called the Divine, the True Faith was persecuted with severity. Gone was the monster Nero, with his quaint methods of martyrdom, but only the uneducated believe that the early Church had a holiday after his death. Nero fancied himself a musician, while Aurelius was a self-declared philosopher. Of the two, I prefer the honest sadism of the former. Philosophers are always finding excuse for being just as loathsome as the rest of us, but for better reasons.

Aurelius was a sober, austere man. His wife despised and dominated him. He was a Stoic, which school of thought preached submission to all things the Divine Will might visit upon Man, pain included. This is an especially easy tenet to follow when the pain is another's. True, he never ordered Christians strapped to poles, soaked in pitch, and set alight to illuminate his banquets. That was Nero's style. Perhaps Aurelius had a delicate digestion or viewed meals as a time for nourishment without the frivolity of human converse, even if that converse be only shrieks.

On the other hand, he was the first to throw our martyrs to the lions, a triply pragmatic means of disposal that must have appealed to Aurelius' frugal heart. He rid Rome of religious dissidents, entertained the mob, and kept the arena beasts sleek, all for the same outlay. Scratch a philosopher, find a skinflint.

The times of Aurelius were the times of easy martyrdom. Not so now. Word from our brothers in Christ on the mainland often treats with the complaint that it has become nearly impossible to die for the Faith these days. When a church is despoiled, a convent ravished, a monastery sacked, nine times out of ten it is other Christians doing it, they say, and for political or economic reasons. *Lucky the abbot who can perish by the pagan's sword, a martyr,* they cry! They should be here this day if they want some luck of that sort. We will have plenty for ourselves and more to spare.

Saint Willibald was more fortunate than we. Things were different in the olden days. The martyr's crown lay well within the reach of all. How many young converts, full of adolescent zeal, pictured themselves torn to pieces by the beasts while a swarm of admiring angels descended from on high to welcome them into the Kingdom of Heaven with songs of praise? How many more spat on Jupiter's pediment solely to invoke the imperial displeasure and make their parents sorry *ex post facto* for some domestic slight? And wouldn't they feel full of holy righteousness afterward, when they gazed down from the celestial mansions and saw scornful sweethearts and unappreciative friends weeping copiously over their well-gnawed remains and wishing aloud that they had been nicer to poor Saint Gaius when the chance afforded!

The martyrdom of Saint Willibald did not spring from any such venial motivation. The young Willibald—often called Willi—was a stripling from the Germanic tribes north of the Danube. Rome was pleased to call these wild folk her subjects, under the equivocal term *foederati*, but no one asked the Germans. Truly has Honorius Hibernicus written that subjugation is a sometime thing.

At the time that young Willi was growing up, his particular tribe had decided to go along with the Romans for a spell. Goods, money, culture, philosophy, religion, and slaves were exchanged. One of these slaves, bought by Willi's father, happened to be a Christian. He had converted on the ox-cart ride over the Alps, at a point when frequent avalanches convinced him that he had nothing further to lose. Once a member of the Faith, he proceeded to spread the good word with a vengeance. He was whipped to death for it—proselytizing when he should have been slopping the pigs—but not before his zeal infected Willibald.

Faith is frightening in the young. I have seen it often enough within these walls to testify to that. Even as I write, I hear a measured chant coming from the chapel. Our younger brethren and our novices have all gotten together to welcome the swords of the rampaging Norsemen into Christ's bosom with music. It would sound better with some mature baritone and bass voices, but those are all busy praying at the top of their lungs for someone to save us. What makes these young men so eagerly expectant, while their elders quiver and quake? What great truth do they anticipate discovering at the moment of death that we greyer heads prefer to put off yet a while? This I do not know, but I have seen enough dead men to say that the startled look in their staring eyes has nothing to do with a pleasant surprise.

Willibald must have known similarly perfect faith and perfect ignorance. He embraced Christianity with a whole heart. During the secret meetings of the faithful he was one who shuddered most deliciously when news from Rome of further fatalities in Christ's name reached the congregation. He wept for the dead bodies, joyed for the freed souls, and prayed for the day when he might share their fate.

He was a long time praying. Nothing ever happened to the faithful in Germany. To begin with, there were too few of them to notice. Unless one was a slave, and using the Faith as an excuse to slough off work, martyrdom was only a wild dream of glory. The worst that Willi had to endure for his Lord was his mother's constant inquiries as to when he was going to give up all that foolishness and take a wife. He was seventeen and not getting any younger, as she once observed in a fit of philosophy to rival the *Meditations* of Aurelius himself.

Willi ignored her. He knew that he was meant for better things. So do we all, at seventeen. When I was that tender, foolheaded, wondrous age, I thought I was going to be a great scholar of the Church whose works would bring me to the notice of Rome. I was supposed to be Pope by now, not meat for a northern blade. What went wrong?

If Willibald did not ask himself that same question, I know nothing of human nature. Clearly the fault was not his, but in his situation. If martyrdom would not find him, he would seek it out. He would go to Rome and preach in the emperor's teeth! He would be bold, fearless, unafraid of death or torture! He stole from his father's house in the dead of the night and took the southward road. He also stole three loaves of bread, a handful of coppers, and his brother's best cloak to get him started on his journey.

Willibald performed his first miracle simply by not getting himself killed on the road to Rome. He was a fine figure of a lad—big-boned, blond, husky, broad at the shoulders and narrow at the hips—but even the tale that has come down through his descendants admits that there was very little insight or cunning behind those big blue eyes. Fools are the fodder of all the predators who stalk the highways of the world, yet Willi came on foot to Rome with little worse than a Cisalpine tavern wench who had conceived a passion for him that would not die or detach. Her name was Julia, and she was his first convert.

Having made a convert so easily, Willi arrived in the Holy City quite sanguine about his chances for winning the blood-stained palm of martyrdom. Julia was privy to his plans, of course. By the time they reached the outskirts of Rome there was little of his thoughts to which she was not privy. The tale recounts how she used every art of rhetoric—including a few overlooked by Aristotle—in trying to convince her soul's savior that he should not race to meet his fate.

"There is a fine line between love sacred and love profane," she is reputed to have said. "The flesh is weak, yet we may worship God while we are still confined to earthly bodies just as readily as the angels do, whose substance is pure spirit. If we use well and wisely the vessels God Himself has given us and praise His name for many, many years from these poor shells of clay, He is pleased. But if we flee the body too eagerly, does that not indicate a certain scorn for what is our Creator's very image?"

It is further related that her lengthy arguments convinced Willibald of the tenuous border between willing martyrdom and plain suicide. He promised her that he would retire into the more rustic areas surrounding the great city, there to ponder her words, "which were marvelously wise and reasoned for one of her previous calling," as my dear mother used to recite.

My mother was a sensible woman, with a pleasant's concise way of putting things. While she was proud enough to number a saint among our antecedents, and also had a horror of tampering with the family's prized oral tradition, her marginal comments at this point in the relation of Saint Willibald's history are perhaps too earthy to be included in my text. Let it suffice that she—and I—reserved some doubt as to Julia's choice of words and method of convincing Willibald to depart from Rome.

Julia herself remained in the Eternal City, where she founded both a successful business establishment and the left-hand shoot of Willibald's line.

Whatever the lady's arguments, they were effective. Willibald left Rome and did not stop running until he was well beyond the city precincts, in the farmlands. It was a journey of many days, Rome being as great a metropolis as it was.

My revered ancestor's supplies were meager. A saint requires little to keep body and soul together, but Willi was a big lad and not yet a saint. He relied on the charity of others to sustain him. When they seemed reluctant to part with any of their worldly goods, he performed that office for them, unwilling to see his fellow man condemned to eternal torment over the matter of a crust of bread, a scrap of meat, or a few coins.

Somewhere along the road, he acquired a sword. Being German, he knew how to use it. Being Christian, he never used it on his enemies. Being a saint in the making, he regarded no man as his foe.

By the time Willi reached the outlying districts, somewhat of his holy fame had preceded him. Thanks for this lay as much with the many farmers' wives and daughters he converted in passing as with those men to whom he taught the precepts of charity. It became more and more difficult for the lad to encounter generosity, either spontaneous or otherwise. He could scarcely find any people on his route at all. Therefore, it was with great joy and satisfaction that Saint Willibald came at last to the accursed villa of Lucrecia Posthuma Sabinus.

It was deep night. The lights of the villa beckoned the weary traveler to approach and take his ease, or whatever fate might present. The porter at the villa gates was old and singularly decrepit. He sized up the late caller and snickered, but did nothing else to deter Willi from going in. Between the gate and the villa proper was a garden. Though it was high summer, the air was full of the rustle of dead leaves. Pitted statues of the lesser gods showed in snowy slivers through the overhanging tangle of branches and creepers. The empty skins of locusts crackled underfoot along the weed-grown paths, but there was no other sound, not even the whir of insect wings or the cricket's scraping song.

Here would be a good place to interpolate a comparison between the villa's sinister garden and the state of an unsaved soul, but I think my ancestor will forgive me for declining the opportunity in favor of the unadorned tale.

Equally unadorned was the lady Lucrecia. When Willibald at last stepped out of the clinging garden shadows, she was waiting for him on the villa porch. At first he thought her just another statue until he realized that statues do not have long red hair that ripples in the breeze, or short red hair that is so difficult to represent effectively in most sculpture. Willibald's reaction on first beholding this handsome woman—naked, unashamed, and abutting a garden—has not survived, but we may assume that his thoughts were full of Genesis.

He was bid welcome to the Villa Sabinus and asked to join its mistress at a feast already spread in the *cenaculum*.

The lady introduced herself and did not seem at all surprised or put out by the arrival of an impromptu dinner guest. She led him through the richly appointed interior of the villa.

Within, Willi saw no servants. He had seen none besides the lone porter since his arrival, and yet the sumptuous meal of which he partook that night must have required the work of many hands. Moreover, he remarked that no sooner had he and his fair host emptied one dish than it mysteriously vanished from the table and was replaced by another. The wine too was as bizarrely replenished, gurgling up in the glasses.

These prandial miracles were all it took to convince Willi that he was in the presence of an incipient saint, and he asked the lady Lucrecia how long she had been a Christian.

The lady is reputed to have come near strangling on her wine before she was able to answer her guest's honest question. When she recovered, she rose from her couch and wordlessly bid Willi follow her into the depths of the villa. I say the depths because that is precisely where she took him, down into a webwork of cellars beneath the marble floors. There were torches to see by, though oddly enough these seemed to require no more kindling than a single word spoken by the lady as they entered each new corridor. It was a word of no language Willibald could identify, but the lady Lucrecia's oral skills simply confirmed his notion that she must be one of the Faith's most holy souls.

This was further enforced when they entered the catacombs.

Willibald counted many score of skulls and unreckonable heaps of miscellaneous human bones, all sorted out in their several niches according to kind and displayed with true pride. In this, Lucrecia Posthuma's saintliness was manifest, for obviously these must be the remains of martyrs, rescued by her single-minded efforts from the charnel houses of Rome and here on her family estate given Christian burial. Why else would a gently bred lady have so many *ossa* about the house?

He gazed at the rippling rows of skulls and smiled beatifically. They smiled back.

Lucrecia was smiling too as she sank down upon a couch built entirely of the more substantial sort of bones and topped by a skillfully executed canopy of curving ribs. She beckoned for Willibald to join her on the scented cushions spread lavishly over such a grotesque and probably uncomfortable bed.

Here our family tradition states *verbatim:* "Thus was Saint Willibald convinced at length of the lady Lucrecia's scorn for the pleasures of this world. For she had surrounded herself with mementos of man's evanescence and the triumph of the grave. Beside these grim reminders, what fleshly delights however exotic will not pall? And she did repeatedly there prove to Saint Willibald that the ecstasy of the senses is fleeting, no matter how frequently renewed, but that Death waits for all."

Having looked after Saint Willibald's welfare, body and soul, the lady at last burst into tears. Willi questioned her grief. Had he somehow offended? Had he failed to learn the lesson of mortality she had striven so valiantly to teach? If so, he was yet willing to learn more.

The lady waved aside his scholarly zeal. Between sobs she confessed a fearsome thing: she was a woman doomed. Even farther down below, lower than the catacombs underlying her home, was a cave of great antiquity. In the dark and fetid depths of this cavern there lurked a most horrendous creature, a monstrous worm, a fiery serpent, an unnatural child of Sin and Satan, offspring of that Snake which first brought evil to Mankind. . . .

In brief, the lady was embarrassed of a dragon.

"He prowls beneath this villa," she is reported to have told the saint. "I hear him dragging his great, scaly belly across the rock. No one knows how old he is. My family line goes back to before the coming of Aeneas. We have always made our home here, and we have always been the warders of this fiend."

Here Willibald suggested that the lady move elsewhere, to a more salubrious neighborhood.

"Gladly!" the lady cried. "But it is impossible. Our family records tell that in ancient times we worshiped the worm and all the dark powers he represented. We were his chosen servants, who once in every seven years were charged with providing the dragon with a human sacrifice. Failing that, we had to offer up one of our own family to the beast, preferably a tender young virgin. By this means my ancestors renewed a hideous partnership with the dragon, and in exchange for human flesh they obtained dark sorcerous powers beyond imagination."

Saint Willibald remarked as gently as possible that he did not think much of the ethics or morals of Lucrecia Posthuma's ancestors.

Lucrecia covered her fair face with her hands. Her body shook with excessive sorrow. "Do you think I like having such relatives?" she wailed. "But their old wickedness had forged a chain which binds all of my family. Once in seven years the dragon hungers for human flesh. If we do not provide, he comes forth and takes! Always it is a member of my household. It does no good to run away. The beast can follow. He has eyes that pierce the darkness of Avernus itself, claws that can slash through rock, teeth that crush steel, and wings that span the heavens!" Her voice grew very small. "Tonight is the last of the seven years just past, and I am the last of my line left alive."

Willibald fell to his knees among a pile of knucklebones. He gave thanks to God for directing his steps to the Villa Sabinus, then rose and told Lucrecia to dry her eyes.

"I will deal with the dragon," he said.

"Slay him," the lady Lucrecia specified. "It is written that the hero who slays a dragon and eats the monster's heart will be given the wisdom to understand and speak the language of all beasts. Let that be your reward."

This honorarium left Willi puzzled. "Why would I want to know the language of all beasts?" he asked.

"What harm is there in knowledge?" Lucrecia replied, and set him on the route out of the catacombs, down into the realm of the dragon.

As Willi followed his way, he continued to mull over the strange position into which the Divine Hand had shoved him. He was not a fool, and he did not fancy himself a slayer of monsters. The thought of facing a dragon was formidable. Once he stopped and was on the point of going back, but he heard the faint sound of Lucrecia's voice wafting down. The lady was laughing. There was a note of nigh hysterical joy in her merriment. No doubt she was rejoicing in the Lord and giving thanks for her deliverance. Willi took a deep breath, recalled that faith makes all things possible, and went on.

He soon left the region of paved floors and man-made corridors. He walked over undressed rock, surrounded by the unseen drips and damps of the lower world. There were still a few torches made fast to the walls, and he marveled at the fact that they were all lighted, as if in miraculous anticipation of his coming. Soon, however, he passed the last of them and had to make his way by touch in the dark.

It was very cool down there. Thus my ancestor was all the more able to perceive the point at which the temperature began to rise. There was likewise a faint though sensible glow in the offing, a natural stone archway some two spearcasts ahead whose enframed blackness seemed a shade lighter than the surrounding murk. A deep grumbling sound emanated from this most unpromising gateway, and a smell which can only be described as heartsickening, being as it was a combination of smoldering fire, moldering flesh, ancient droppings, and the prickly, insinuating odor peculiar to large reptiles.

Willi's palms grew slick with sweat. He drew his sword, though he had to shift his grip on the leather-wrapped handle several times. Never had he felt so uncomfortable with a blade, not even in the days before his salvation, when he had slain a very expensive Latin tutor back home, enraged by the slave's uncalled-for emphasis on the ablative absolute and an irritating habit of snickering knowingly over Willi's fumbled gerunds.

Thoughts of that unfortunate pedagogical episode made Willi recall the lady Lucrecia's instructions: slay the dragon and eat its heart. He shuddered. If this was how the worm smelled alive, he had little desire to smell it dead. But eat its heart or not, he was still obliged to slay the beast, and the closer he came to that fateful encounter, the less Willi liked the prospect. He was no coward, he told himself at frequent intervals (while pausing to catch his breath, readjust his grip on the sword, shake pebbles from his sandals, and make sure he was going in the right direction), but he was no killer either. Not anymore.

"The Commandment teaches *Thou shalt not kill*," he said to the darkness. "If it goes on to say *except dragons*, no one ever taught it to me that way. The worms do suffer from a poor reputation, but there must be some good in them. I have heard more people complain about the ravages of mosquitoes, weevils, slugs, and fleas than about the depredations of dragons. Noah must have taken a pair along, or there would be none left alive this day. They didn't eat anyone aboard the Ark . . . I think . . . so they are reasonable creatures. Yes, and God created them just as He formed every living thing, with a divine purpose in mind. If they have fallen away from that purpose, has not Man fallen even farther? Yet Man is to be saved! Why not dragons too?"

As Paul on the road to Damascus, so Saint Willibald beneath the Villa Sabinus: light struck, divine inspiration came, and a great miracle happened there. He smiled, sheathed his sword, commended his soul to God, and sauntered on down the tunnel, whistling a hymn.

If I may be granted one last desire before I am privileged to view my entrails littering the scriptorium floor, it would be to attend that fateful meeting of Saint Willibald and the dragon of the Villa Sabinus. Oh yes, there most certainly is an account of what transpired, but . . . it is entirely based upon Saint Willibald's own testimony, there being no other witness save the worm himself.

I hesitate to call a saint's own words suspect, although I may be forgiven this. Willi was, as I said, a German tribesman, and if there was anything those wild folk liked better than doing great deeds, it was telling them afterward. And retelling them. And telling them yet again, in case their hearers had missed any part of their exploits the first time.

Howbeit, at this point the tale goes into the mouth of Willi himself, and how it emerges is a matter of record:

"And I did enter into a vast chamber which reeked of death. My fallen nature bade me flee, but I placed my faith in the Lord and went on. Now all was light, a golden glow which radiated from the massive flanks of the dragon. This monster was couched upon a hoard of treasure whose sparkling brilliance was redoubled by reflection from the creature's shining scales, each as big as a good-sized wooden dinner plate. The beast was sleeping. I reflected upon the Sin that slumbers in us all, and thus fortified, I raised my voice in holy song.

"My singing roused the dragon, as I intended it should. Its eyes were red as blood, and when it opened its black-lined jaws, I saw a flicker of fire. So shall our Sin awake to open a gateway to the everlasting fires of Hell, if given the opportunity. The dragon uttered a grating roar, no doubt desiring to drown out my song of Truth, but I sang on. In my youth, I had often been commended for my strong wind control and my endurance. Now at last I might bring back God's gift to me multiplied. I sang louder, and the echoes within that abominated cavern took up the sacred words and battered the dragon's ears therewith.

"My faith told me I would triumph. In momentary pride, I forgot to allow for a shift in key and lost the proper harmony in my hymn. At this moment, I saw the dragon cringe. Certainly it must have been that my musical presentation of Scripture was beginning to affect the worm. I sang on, louder yet, abetted by the natural resonances of the cavern, pressing the advantage. I freely admit that the tune's true melody escaped me once or twice again, at most.

"By now, the dragon was writhing on his bed of luxury. His taloned paws pressed themselves close to the sides of his huge head, and in a pathetic voice he did beg me to cease my song, no price being too great for him to pay for the Peace of God. 'Mercy!' the dragon cried. And yet again, 'Mercy!'

"I was momentarily surprised to hear the beast speak intelligibly, but what miracle lies beyond the powers of Almighty God? I took the dragon's bloodless surrender as a good sign, and used his requests for peace and mercy as the perfect point from which to address him on the nature of Eternal Peace and Divine Mercy. He showed himself to be a willing audience. There was a moment or so when a glint of the old Devil came back into his tiny eyes, but I had only to interrupt my preaching and suggest that a song might more appropriately illustrate the lesson and the dragon was all submissive eagerness. He implored me not to sing, but to speak on.

"In the end, my words moved the monster to repentance. He freely confessed his past wickednesses. These included an unreasoning hatred of all other dragons—for the worms are notoriously solitary and grow malicious therefore—and an unquenchable enmity against the whole race of unicorns. He was not too fond of Humankind either.

"When he learned that the lady Lucrecia was the one responsible for sending me into his domain, he said, 'I used to believe her family to be the only humans wise enough to be worth sparing. I see now that I was wrong.' I said that I rejoiced to hear that he now considered all of us deserving of mercy. The beast gazed at me askance, then muttered, 'Who would have thought that a booby's shell could hatch a falcon? It must be as you say: this god of yours reserves a special protection for fools and children. A sword would have been useless against me, yet . . . Faugh! What is done, is done. For sending you to me, I must thank the lady Lucrecia properly before we go.'

"I did not follow all he said, although my duty to God constrained me to commit it to memory, but I did ask where we were going. He replied, 'Why, to have you preach to all my brethren, of course. We can't have them going about unsaved, can we? Is it not blessed to share salvation? I shall take you to them. Be not afraid. Begin with a song as you did with me—*exactly* as you began with me!—and I guarantee they shall be yours for the saving.'

"I asked whether he assumed all dragons had hearts as sensitive to softening as his own. He answered, 'Let men speak of the sensitivity of the dragon's heart. All I can vouch for is the sensitivity of our ears! Or how else do you think we come to speak the languages of all beasts, little master? Mount upon my back now and let us go. I have had you all to myself for much too long.' "

So Saint Willibald and the dragon departed the treasure cave. They left by tunnels wide and high enough for the worm to pass comfortably, even with Willi on his back. Once on the surface, the dragon took to the sky. Saint Willibald was sure that they were being conveyed directly up to Heaven, after the manner of Elijah, and he cried out to be spared yet a while, that he might complete the conversion of the dragons.

The dragon is reported to have said, "Dread not. I would not let Heaven have you." With these reassurances, the beast swooped low beneath the moon and sailed on leathern wings across the entire Villa Sabinus. Fire poured from its jaws, engulfing the fair building, the withered gardens, and the lady Lucrecia, who came running from the portico, driven by an unhealthy albeit natural desire to learn what all the racket was about.

Saint Willibald voiced a wordless cry of protest to see the lady meet such an end, her whole lithe body blazing more brightly than her wonderful hair. Gazing down a second time, eyes full of pity and terror, he noted that his awful mount had showed some restraint: the dragon's fire had spared the crabbed porter. Even as man and monster sailed farther up the towers of air, the old man executed a caper of joy hard by the trinity of bonfires that had been the villa, the garden, and the lady. Something long and flexible appeared to spring from the aged servant's lower sacral region, and great black shadows in the semblance of wings unfurled themselves behind his wizened body. He reached into the smallest of the conflagrations and pulled out a small, white spark which he thrust into a leather purse at his side. The spark in question ejaculated an almost human wail of dread and despair before being plunged into that more than midnight darkness.

Saint Willibald pondered well all that he had seen, and concluded that our senses are all harlots, not to be trusted. He berated the dragon severely for the sin of Wrath and the kindling of Lucrecia Posthuma. The worm turned his huge head over one sloping shoulder, admitted that he was truly sorry for his late transgression, and asked the saint whether he had lied in the matter of Divine Mercy for sins repented? Chastened by the beast's natural theological facility, Saint Willibald granted him prompt absolution. Then the dragon wheeled off to dexter and bore the saint away.

But whither went they? That answer, no man knows, least of all myself. I venture to assume that my ancestor did take a wife of his own, at some juncture, or else how to account for my mother's insistence that we are the last of his legitimate line?

My mother is dead. The saint's legend alone survives, with about as much truth to it as we place in legends. It is said that the converted dragon did indeed carry Saint Willibald to the mountain fastness which was the ancestral home of all his race. There the saint affected the wholesale salvation of Dragonkind entire, by the same means he used on his initial reptilian convert. He likely married afterward.

The spirit of Doubting Thomas, ever among us, might raise the objection that were all this so, we should hear no further tales of cities destroyed, maidens ravished, and would-be heroes made *exempla* of "ashes to ashes" by the draconian breed. Faith must answer here that either these instances (frequent though they be) are the work of heretic worms, or else that surely the transgressing dragons are heartily penitent afterward and as entitled to absolution as the next man.

Thus ends the chronicle, may Saint Willibald intercede for me. I do not doubt that it will be his doing entirely if some day the heathen Norsemen, like the dragons, whose images grace their warships, embrace the True Faith. Who better than the patron saint of well-meaning ignorance to give mayhem, murder, destruction, and despoliation an eternal excuse and ready forgiveness? They will still be barbarians, but they will be *our* barbarians.

Alas, I shall not live to see that day. They will slay me with the others, in the wrong God's name. From the wrath of the Norsemen, dear Lord, deliver us, but from the best intentions of our fellow creatures—dear Lord, art even Thou that powerful?

I, Brother Leo, append these words in testimony to a miracle.

And it came to pass that when our abbey was in peril of the Norsemen, may God destroy them utterly, there came out of the East a great roaring sound, and a great fire, and the rushing of many wings. And lo! There were dragons.

And the worms did descend upon the ships of the Norsemen, consuming them to ash, albeit by happenstance their fires likewise devoured two thirds of the abbey lands and buildings. And the creatures did set their mighty feet upon the earth and enter into the chapel proper, from whence they did extract some portion of the alter plate and convey the same way with them across the sea to preserve it from future raiders. Let no man of faith doubt their good intentions.

Yet there shall come no more brigands to these shores, for among the ruins of our late scriptorium was found this very scroll, miraculously preserved within a clay water jug only seven strides from the charred remain of our late Brother Theobald, through whose offices we have been vouchsafed knowledge of that saint who has surely this day been our salvation.

Our abbot agrees that we shall henceforth be the Abbey of Saint Willibald. Under his especial patronage we shall be eternally protected by the power of the fiery worms whose conversion he effected. The scroll of Brother Theobald shall be our chiefest relic, as shall the saint's bones, which a planned pilgrimage to the German lands shall surely discover soon, by revelation.

It is to be hoped that Saint Willibald's bones shall not require quite so much scraping as Brother Theobald's parchment before they may be shown to the general public. There appear within his tale of the blessed Willibald's life some sentiments unsuited to a truly pious frame of mind. Praise God, these are nothing that a little judicious removal of dried ink and insertion of more appropriate phrases cannot amend.

May Saint Willibald strengthen my hand and eye for the holy labor before me.

A Drama

of Dragons

Craig Shaw Gardner

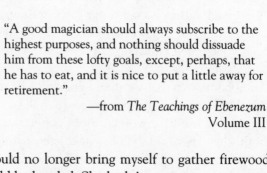

"A good magician should always subscribe to the
highest purposes, and nothing should dissuade
him from these lofty goals, except, perhaps, that
he has to eat, and it is nice to put a little away for
retirement."

—from *The Teachings of Ebenezum*
Volume III

I could no longer bring myself to gather firewood. My
world had ended. She hadn't come.

I sat for far too long in the sunlit glade where we
always met. Perhaps she didn't realize it was noon; she
had somehow been delayed; her cool blue eyes and fair blonde hair, the
way her slim young body moved, the way she laughed, how it felt when
she touched me. Surely she was on her way.

But I didn't even know her name! Only her interest in me—a magician's apprentice. She'd once called magicians the closest things to
play actors she knew in this backwater place, said she'd always admired
the stage. And then she laughed, and we kissed and—

A cold breeze sprang up behind my back. Winter was coming.

I gathered what logs and branches I could find and trudged back to my master's cottage.

In the distance I heard a sneeze. My master Ebenezum, no doubt one of the world's greatest magicians until an unfortunate occurrence involving a demon from the seventh Netherhell. My master had succeeded in banishing the foul creature, by far the most powerful he had ever faced, but his triumph was not without its costs. From that moment onward, Ebenezum found that, should he even approach something of a sorcerous nature, he would fall into an immediate and extended sneezing fit. This malady had put something of a crimp in Ebenezum's wizardly career, but my master was not one to accept defeat easily. Just this moment, he had probably made another attempt to read from one of his magic tomes. Hence the sneeze. Why else?

Unless there was something sorcerous in the air.

Perhaps there was another reason besides my mood that the world was so dark around me, another reason that she hadn't met me as we'd planned. The bushes moved on my right. Something very large flew across the sun.

I managed the front door with the firewood still in my arms. I heard the wizard sneeze. Repeatedly. My master stood in the main room, one of his great books spread on the table before him. I hurried to his aid, forgetting, in my haste, the firewood that scattered across the table as I reached for the book, a few miscellaneous pieces falling among the sneezing Ebenezum's robes.

I closed the book and glanced apprehensively at the mage. To my surprise, Ebenezum blew his nose on a gold-inlaid, dark blue sleeve and spoke to me in the calmest of tones.

"Thank you, 'prentice." He delicately removed a branch from his lap and laid it on the table. "If you would dispose of this in a more appropriate place?"

He sighed deep in his throat. "I'm afraid that my affliction is far worse than I imagined. I may even have to call on outside assistance for my cure."

I hastened to retrieve the firewood. "Outside assistance?" I inquired discreetly.

"We must seek out another magician as great as I," Ebenezum said, his every word heavy with import. "Though to do that, we might have to travel as far as the great city of Vushta."

"Vushta?" I replied. "With its pleasure gardens and forbidden palaces? The city of unknown sins that could doom a man for life? That Vushta?" All at once, I felt the lethargy lift from my shoulders. I quickly deposited the wood by the fireplace.

"That Vushta." Ebenezum nodded. "With one problem. We have not the funds for traveling, and no prospects for gaining same."

As if responding to our plight, a great gust blew against the side of the cottage. The door burst open with a swirl of dirt and leaves, and a short man wearing tattered clothes, face besmirched with grime, staggered in and slammed the door behind him.

"Flee! Flee!" the newcomer cried in a quavering voice. "Dragons! Dragons!" With that, his eyes rolled up in his head and he collapsed on the floor.

"I have found, however," Ebenezum said as he stroked his long, white beard, "in my long career as a magician, Wuntvor, if you wait around long enough, something is bound to turn up."

(2)
"Dire creatures from the Netherhells should always
be faced directly, unless it is possible to face them
some other way, say from behind a bush, in
perfect safety."
—from *The Teachings of Ebenezum*
Volume V

With some water on the head and some wine down the gullet, we managed to revive the newcomer.

"Flee!" he sputtered as he caught his breath. He glanced about wildly, his pale blue eyes darting from my master to me to floor to ceiling. He seemed close to my master in age, but there the similarity ceased. Rather than my master's mane of fine, white hair, the newcomer was balding, his hair matted and stringy. Instead of the wizard's masterful face, which could convey calm serenity or cosmic anger with the flick of an eyebrow, the other's face was evasive; small nose and chin, a very wrinkled brow, and those eyes, darting blue in his dark, mud-spattered face.

"Now, now, good sir," Ebenezum replied in his most reasonable voice, often used to charm young ladies and calm bill collectors. "Why the hurry? You mentioned—dragons?"

"Dragons!" The man stood somewhat shakily. "Well, at least dragon! One of them has captured Gurnish Keep!"

"Gurnish Keep?" I queried.

"You've seen it," Ebenezum murmured, his cold gray eyes still on our guest. " 'Tis the small castle on yonder hill at the far side of the woods." Ebenezum snorted in his beard. "Castle? 'Tis really more of a stone hut, but it's the home of our neighbor, the Duke of Gurnish. It's a very small dukedom. For that matter, he's a very small duke."

Our visitor was, if anything, more agitated than before. "I didn't run all the way through Gurnish Forest to hear a discussion of the neighborhood. We must flee!"

"Gurnish Forest?" I inquired.

"The trees right behind the hut," my master replied. "Surely the Duke's idea. Everyone else knows the area as Wizard's Woods."

"What do you mean, Wizard's Woods?" the newcomer snapped. "This area is Gurnish Forest. Officially. As Gurnish Keep is an official castle!"

" 'Tis only a matter of opinion," Ebenezum replied, a smile that could charm both barbarians and maiden aunts once again upon his face. "Haven't we met somewhere before?"

"Possibly." The newcomer, who was somewhat shorter than my master's imposing frame, shifted uneasily under the wizard's gaze. "But shouldn't we flee? Dragons, you know."

"Come now, man. I wouldn't be a full-fledged wizard if I hadn't dealt with a dragon or two." Ebenezum looked even more closely at the newcomer than he had before. "Say. Aren't you the Duke of Gurnish?"

"Me?" the smaller man said. His eyes shifted from my master to me and back again. "Well—uh—" He coughed. "I suppose I am."

"Well, why didn't you say so? I haven't seen you since you stopped trying to tax me." Ebenezum's smile went to its broadest as he signaled me to get our guest a chair. The duke obviously had money.

"Well, this whole situation's a bit awkward," our honored guest said as he stared at the floor. "I'm afraid I feel rather undukeish."

"Nonsense. A run-in with a dragon can unnerve anyone. Would you like some more wine? A nice fire to warm you?"

"No, thank you." The duke lowered his voice even more than before. "Don't you think it would be better if we fled? I mean, dragons. And I've seen other things in the forest. Perhaps if your powers were—" The duke coughed again. "You see, I've heard of your accident."

Ebenezum bristled a bit at the last reference, but the smile more or less remained on his face. "Gossip, good duke. Totally blown out of proportion. We'll deal with your dragon in no time."

"But the dragon's taken over Gurnish Keep! He's immense, bright blue and violet scales, twenty-five feet from head to tail. His wings scrape the ceiling of my great hall! And he's invincible. He's captured my castle and beautiful daughter, and defeated my retainer!"

Beautiful daughter? My thoughts turned to the girl of my dreams. Where had she gone? What had kept her away?

"Only a child!" the duke cried. "No more than seventeen. Fine blonde hair, beautiful blue eyes, a lovely, girlish figure. And the dragon will burn her to a crisp if we don't do his bidding!"

Blonde? Blue? Figure? I had a revelation.

"Come now, man," Ebenezum remarked. "Calm down. It's common knowledge that dragons tend to be overdramatic. All the beast's really done so far is to overwhelm one retainer. I assume you still only had one retainer?"

She hadn't deserted me! She was only held prisoner! All the time she and I had spent together, all those long, warm afternoons, that's why she would tell me nothing of herself! A duke's daughter!

The duke glared at my master. "It wouldn't be like that if my subjects paid their taxes!"

A duke's daughter. And I would rescue her! There'd be no need for secrecy then. How magnificent our lives would be!

A fire lit in Ebenezum's eyes. "Perhaps if certain local nobility were not so concerned with extending the borders of his tiny dukedom—" The wizard waved his hands and the fire disappeared. "But that's not important. We have a dragon to evict. As I see it, the elements here are quite ordinary. Dragon captures castle and maiden. Very little originality. We should be able to handle it tidily."

The duke began to object again, but Ebenezum would have none of it. Only one thing affected his nose more than sorcery—money— and the smell of it was obvious in the cottage. My master sent the duke outside while we gathered the paraphernalia together for dragon fighting.

When I had packed everything according to my master's instructions, Ebenezum beckoned me into his library. Once in the room, the wizard climbed a small stepladder, and, carefully holding his nose, pulled a slim volume from the uppermost shelf.

"We may have need of this." His voice sounded strangely hollow, most likely the result of thumb and forefinger pressed into his nose. "In my present condition, I can't risk using it. But it should be easy enough for you to master, Wuntvor."

He descended the ladder and placed the thin, dark volume in my hands. Embossed in gold on the cover were the words "How to Speak Dragon."

"But we must be off!" Ebenezum exclaimed, clapping my shoulder. "Musn't keep a client waiting. You may study that book on our rest stops along the way."

I stuffed the book hurriedly in the paraphernalia-filled pack and shouldered the whole thing, grabbed my walking staff and followed my master out the door. With my afternoon beauty at the end of my journey, I could manage anything.

My master had already grabbed the duke by the collar and propelled him in the proper direction. I followed at Ebenezum's heels as fast as the heavy pack would allow. The wizard, as usual, carried nothing. As he often had explained, it kept his hands free for quick conjuring and his mind free for sorcerous conjecture.

I noticed a bush move, then another. Rustling like the wind pushed through the leaves, except there was no wind. The forest was as still as when I had waited for my afternoon love. Still the bushes moved.

Just my imagination, I thought. Like the darkness of the forest. I glanced nervously at the sky, half expecting the sun to disappear again. What was so big that it blotted out the sun?

A dragon?

But my musings were cut short by a man dressed in bright orange who stood in our path. He peered through an odd instrument on the end of a pole.

I glanced at the duke, walking now at my side. He had begun to shiver.

The man in orange looked up as we approached. "Good afternoon," he said, the half frown on his face disproving the words. "Could you move a little faster? You're blocking the emperor's highway, you know."

The duke shook violently.

"Highway?" Ebenezum asked, stopping mid-path rather than hurrying by the man in orange.

"Yes, the new road that the great and good Emperor Flostok III has decreed—"

"Flee!" the duke cried. "Dragons! Dragons! Flee!" He leapt about, waving his hands before the emperor's representative.

"See here!" the orange man snapped. "I'll have none of this. I'm traveling to see the Duke of Gurnish on important business."

The duke stopped hopping. "Duke?" he said, pulling his soiled clothing back into place. "Why, I'm the Duke of Gurnish. What can I help you with, my good man?"

The man in orange frowned even deeper. "It's about the upkeep of the road . . ."

"Certainly." The duke glanced back at us. "Perhaps we should go somewhere that we can talk undisturbed." The duke led the man in orange into the underbrush.

"They deserve each other," Ebenezum muttered. "But to business." He looked at me solemnly. "A bit about dragons. Dragons are one of the magical sub-species. They exist largely between worlds, partly on Earth and partly in the Netherhells, and never truly belong to either. There are other magical sub-species—"

Ebenezum's lecture was interrupted by a commotion in the underbrush. Large arms with a thick growth of grayish-brown hair rose and fell above the bushes, accompanied by human screams.

"Another sub-species is the troll," Ebenezum remarked.

I let my pack slide from my back and firmly grasped my staff. They would eat my true love's father! I had never encountered trolls before, but this was as good a time as any to learn.

"Slobber! Slobber!" came from the bushes before us. A rough voice, the sound of a saw biting into hardwood. I assumed it was a troll.

"Wait!" another voice screamed. "You can't do this! I'm a representative of the emperor!"

"Slobber! Slobber!" answered a chorus of rough voices.

"Let's get this over with!" Anther voice, high and shaky. The duke?

Although the voices were quite close now, it was getting difficult to distinguish individual words. It just sounded like a large amount of screaming, punctuated by cries of "slobber!" I lifted my staff over my head and ran forward with a scream of my own.

I broke into a small clearing with four occupants. One was the duke. The other three were among the ugliest creatures I'd seen in my short life. Squat and covered with irregular tufts of gray-brown fur, which did nothing to hide the rippling muscles of their barrel-like arms and legs. Three pairs of very small red eyes turned to regard me. One of them swallowed something that looked a good deal like an orange-clad foot.

The sight of the three hideous creatures completely stopped my forward motion. They regarded me in silence.

"Oh, hello," I said, breaking into the sinister quiet. "I must have wandered off the path. Excuse me."

One of the trolls barrelled toward me on its immensely powerful legs. "Slobber," it remarked. It was time to leave. I turned and bumped into my master, who ignored me as he made a mystic gesture.

"No slobber! No slobber!" the trolls cried and ran back into the heart of the woods.

I picked myself up and helped the wizard regain his feet as well. Ebenezum sneezed for a full three minutes, the result of his actually employing magic. When he caught his breath at last, he wiped his nose on his robe and regarded me all too evenly.

"Wuntvor," he said quietly. "What do you mean by dropping all our valuable equipment and running off, just so you can be swallowed by—"

The duke ran between the two of us. "Flee! Flee! Dragons! Trolls! Flee!"

"Add you!" my master said, his voice rising at last. "I've had enough of your jumping about, screaming hysterical warnings! Why do you even worry? You were surrounded by trolls and they didn't touch you. You lead a charmed life!" He grabbed the duke's shoulder with one hand and mine with the other and pushed us back to the trail.

"Come," he continued. "We will reach Gurnish Keep before nightfall. There, my assistant and I will deal with this dragon, and you, good duke, will pay us handsomely for our efforts." The wizard deposited us on the trail and walked briskly toward the castle before the duke could reply.

"Look!" The duke pulled at my sleeve. There was a break in the trees ahead, affording a clear view of the hill on the wood's far side. There, atop the hill, was Gurnish Keep, a stone building not much larger than Ebenezum's cottage. Smoke poured from the Keep's lower windows, and once or twice I thought I saw the yellow-orange flicker of flame.

"Dragon," the duke whispered. I hurriedly reached into my satchel and pulled out *How to Speak Dragon*. The time to start learning was now.

I opened the book at random and scanned the page. Phrases in common speech filled one side. Opposite these were the same phrases in dragon. I started reading from the top:

"Pardon me, but could you please turn your snout?"

"Sniz me heeba-heeba szzz."

"Pardon me, but your claw is in my leg."

"Sniz mir sazza grack szzz."

"Pardon me, but your barbed tail is waving perilously close . . ."

The whole page was filled with similar phrases. I closed the book. It had done nothing to reassure me.

Ebenezum shouted at us from far up the trail. I ran to follow, dragging the Duke of Gurnish with me.

We walked through the remaining forest without further difficulty. The woods ended at the edge of a large hill called Wizard's Knoll or Mount Gurnish, depending upon whom you spoke with. From there, we could get a clear view of the castle. And the smoke. And the flames.

The duke began to jabber again about the dangers ahead, but was silenced by a single glance from my master. The wizard's cool gray eyes stared up toward the castle, but somehow beyond it. After a moment, he shook his head and flexed his shoulders beneath his robes. He turned to me.

"Wunt," he said. "More occurs here than meets the eye." He glanced again at the duke, who was nervously dancing on a pile of leaves. "Not just a dragon, but three trolls. That's a great deal of supernatural activity for a place as quiet as Wizard's Woods."

I expected the duke to object to the wizard's choice of names, but he was strangely quiet. I turned to the pile of leaves where he had hidden.

The duke was gone.

"Methinks," Ebenezum continued, "some contact has been made with the Netherhells of late. There is a certain instrument in your pack . . ."

My master went on to describe the instrument and its function. If we set it up at the base of the hill, it would tell us the exact number and variety of creatures from the Netherhells lurking about the district.

I held up the instrument. My master rubbed his nose. "Keep it at a distance. The device carries substantial residual magic."

I put the thing together according to the wizard's instructions, and, at his signal, spun the gyroscope that topped it off.

"Now, small points of light will appear." Ebenezum sniffled loudly. "You can tell by the color of—"

He sneezed mightily, again and again. I looked to the device. Should I stop it?

Ebenezum sneezed to end all sneezes, directly at the instrument. The device fell apart.

"By the Netherhells!" Ebenezum exclaimed. "Can I not perform the simplest of spells?" He looked at me, and his face looked very old. "Put away the apparatus, Wunt. We must use the direct approach. Duke?"

I explained that the duke had vanished.

"What now?" Ebenezum looked back toward the forest. His cold gray eyes went wide. He blew his nose hastily.

"Wunt! Empty the pack!"

"What?" I asked, startled by the urgency of my master's voice. Then I looked back to the woods, and saw it coming. A wall of black, like some impenetrable cloud, roiling across the forest. But this cloud extended from the sky to the forest floor, and left complete blackness behind. It sped across the woods like a living curtain that drew its darkness even closer.

"Someone plays with great forces," Ebenezum said. "Forces he doesn't understand. The pack, Wunt!"

I dumped the pack's contents on the ground. Ebenezum rifled through them, tossing various arcane tomes and irreplacable devices out of his way, until he grasped a small box painted a shiny robin's egg blue.

The magician sneezed in triumph. He tossed me the box.

"Quick, Wunt!" he called, blowing his nose. "Take the dust within that box and spread it in a line along the hill!" He waved at a rocky ridge on the forest edge as he jogged up the hill and began to sneeze again.

I did as my master bid, laying an irregular line of blue powder across the long granite slab. I looked back to the woods. The darkness was very close, engulfing all but the hill.

"Run, Wunt!"

I sprinted up the hill. The wizard cried a few ragged syllables and followed. He tripped as he reached the hilltop, and fell into an uncontrollable sneezing fit.

I turned back to look at the approaching blackness. The darkly tumbling wall covered all the forest now, and tendrils of the stuff reached out toward the hill like so many grasping hands. But the fog's forward motion had stopped just short of the ragged blue line.

There was a breeze at my back. I turned to see Ebenezum, still sneezing but somehow standing. One arm covered his nose, the other reached for the sky. His free hand moved and the breeze grew to a wind and then a gale, rushing down the hill and pushing the dark back to wherever it had come.

After a minute the wind died, but what wisps of fog remained in the forest below soon evaporated beneath the bright afternoon sun. My master sat heavily and gasped for breath as if all the air had escaped from his lungs.

"Lucky," he said after a minute. "Whoever raised the demon fog had a weak will. Otherwise . . ." The magician blew his nose, allowing the rest of the sentence to go unsaid.

A figure moved through the woods beneath us. It was the duke.

"Too exhausted to fight dragon," Ebenezum continued, still breathing far too hard. "You'll have to do it, Wunt."

I swallowed and picked up *How to Speak Dragon* from the hillside where it lay. I turned to look at Gurnish Keep, a scant hundred yards across the hilltop. Billows of smoke poured from the windows, occasionally accompanied by licks of flame. And, now that we stood so close, I could hear a low rumble, underlining all the other sounds in the field in which we stood. A rumble that occasionally grew into a roar.

This dragon was going to be everything I expected.

The duke grabbed at my coatsleeve. "Dragon!" he said. "Last chance to get out!"

"Time to go in there," Ebenezum said. "Look in the book, Wunt. Perhaps we can talk the dragon out of the castle." He shook the quivering duke from his arm. "And if you, good sir, would be quiet for a moment, we could go about saving your home and daughter. Quite honestly, I feel you have no cause for complaint with the luck you've been having. Most people would not have survived the evil spell that recently took over the woods. How you manage to bumble through the powerful forces at work around here is beyond . . ." Ebenezum's voice trailed off. He cocked an eyebrow at the duke and stroked his beard in thought.

The rumble from the castle grew louder again. I opened the thin volume I held in my sweating palms. I had to save my afternoon beauty.

I flipped frantically from page to page, finally finding a phrase I thought appropriate.

"Pardon me, but might we speak to you?"

In the loudest voice I could manage, I spat out the dragon syllables.

"Sniz grah! Subba Ubba Szzz!"

A great, deep voice reverberated from within the castle. "Speak the common tongue, would you?" it said. "Besides, I'm afraid I don't have a commode."

I closed the book with a sigh of relief. The dragon spoke human!

"Don't trust him!" the duke cried. "Dragons are deceitful!"

Ebenezum nodded his head. "Proceed with caution, Wunt. Someone *is* being deceitful." He turned to the duke. "You!"

"Me?" the Gurnish nobleman replied as he backed in my direction. Ebenezum stalked after him.

They were squabbling again. But I had no time for petty quarrels. I firmly grasped my staff, ready to confront the dragon and my afternoon beauty.

The duke was right behind me now, his courage seemingly returned. "Go forward, wizard!" he cried in a loud voice. "Defeat the dragon! Banish him forever!"

"Oh, not a wizard, too!" cried the voice from within the castle. "First I get cooped up in Gurnish Keep, then I have to capture your beautiful daughter, and now a wizard! How dull! Doesn't anyone have any imagination around here?"

I came to a great oak door. I nudged it with my foot. It opened easily and I stepped inside to confront the dragon.

It stood on its haunches, regarding me in turn. It was everything the duke had mentioned, and more. Blue and violet scales, twenty-five feet in length, wings that brushed the ceiling. The one oversight in the duke's description appeared to be the large green top hat on the dragon's head.

I saw her a second later.

She stood in front and slightly to one side of the giant reptile. She was as beautiful as I'd ever seen her.

"Why, Wuntvor," she said. "What are you doing here?"

I cleared my throat and pounded my staff on the worn stone pavement. "I've come to rescue you."

"Rescue?" She looked up at the dragon. The dragon rumbled. "So father's gotten to you, too?"

The duke's voice screamed behind me. "I warned you! Now the dragon will burn you all to cinders!"

The dragon snorted good naturedly and turned to regard the ceiling.

"The game is up, duke!" Ebenezum called from the doorway, far enough away so that the dragon's magical odor would not provoke another attack. "Your sorcerous schemes are at an end!"

"Yes, father," my afternoon beauty said. "Don't you think you've gone far enough?" She looked at my master. "Father so wanted control of the new Trans-Empire Highway, to put toll stations throughout the woods below, that he traded in his best retainer for the services of certain creatures from the Netherhells, which he'd use to frighten off anyone who stood in the way of his plans."

She turned and looked at the dragon. "Luckily, one of those creatures was Hubert."

"Betrayed!" The duke clutched at his heart. "My own daughter!"

"Come, father. What you're doing is dangerous and wrong. Your greed will make a monster of you. I've been worrying what my future was with you and the castle. But now I know." She glanced happily back to the dragon. "Hubert and I have decided to go on the stage."

The duke was taken aback.

"What?"

"Yes, good sir," Hubert the dragon remarked. "I have some small experience in the field, and, on talking with your daughter, have found that she is just the partner I have been looking for."

"Yes, father. A life on the stage. How much better than sitting around a tiny castle, waiting to be rescued by a clumsy young man."

Clumsy? My world reeled around me. Not wishing to be rescued was one thing, considering the situation. But to call me clumsy? I lowered my staff and walked toward the door.

"Wait!" my afternoon beauty cried. I turned quickly. Perhaps she had reconsidered her harsh words. Our long afternoons together still meant something!

"You haven't seen our act!" she exclaimed. "Hit it, dragon!"

She danced back and forth across the castle floor, the dragon beating time with its tail. They sang together.

"Let's raise a flagon
For damsel and dragon,
The best song and dance team in the whole, wide world.
Our audience is clapping,
And their toes are tapping,
For a handsome reptile and a pretty girl!"

The dragon blew smoke rings at the end of a line and breathed a bit of fire at the end of a verse. Six more verses followed, more or less the same. Then they stopped singing and began to shuffle back and forth.

They talked in rhythm.

"Hey, dragon. It's good to have an audience again."

"I'll say, damsel. I'm all fired up!"

They paused.

"How beautiful it is in Gurnish Keep! What more could you ask for, damsel, than this kind of sunny day?"

"I don't know, dragon. I *could* do with a shining knight!"

They paused again.

"Romance among reptiles can be a weighty problem!"

"Why's that, dragon?"

"When I see a pretty dragoness, it tips my scales!"

They launched into song immediately.

"Let's raise a flagon
For damsel and dragon—"

"I can't stand it any more!" the Duke of Gurnish cried. "Slabyach! Grimace! Trolls, get them all!"

A trapdoor opened in the corner of the castle floor. The trolls popped out.

"Quick, Wunt!" Ebenezum cried. "Out of the way!" But before he could even begin to gesture, he was caught in a sneezing fit.

The trolls sauntered toward us. I bopped one on the head with my staff. The staff broke.

"Slobber!" exclaimed the troll.

"Roohhaarrr!" came from across the room. The dragon stood as well as it was able in the confines of the castle's great hall. It carefully directed a thin lance of flame toward each troll's posterior.

"No slobber! No slobber!" the trolls exclaimed, escaping back through the trapdoor.

"Thank you," Ebenezum said after blowing his nose. "That was quite nice of you."

"Think nothing of it," the dragon replied. "I never sacrifice an audience."

(3)
"The best spells are those that right wrongs, bring happiness, return the world to peace and cause a large quantity of the coin of the realm to pass into the wizard's possession."
—from *The Teachings of Ebenezum*
Volume IXX

"I finally got our good Lord of Gurnish to listen to reason," my master said when we returned to our cottage. "When I mentioned how close to the palace I might be soon, and that I might find myself discussing the region, the duke saw his way to hire me as a consultant." Ebenezum pulled a jangling pouch from his belt. "The duke will now most likely receive clearance to build his toll booths. Pity he no longer has the money for their construction."

"And what of his daughter and the dragon?" I asked.

"Hubert is flying to Vushta with her this very instant. I gave them a letter of introduction to certain acquaintances I have there, and they should find a ready audience."

"So you think they're that good?"

Ebenezum shook his head vigorously. "They're terrible. But the stage is a funny thing. I expect Vushta will love them.

"But enough of this." The wizard drew another, smaller pouch from his bag. "Hubert was kind enough to lend me some ground dragon's egg. Seems it's a folk remedy among his species; gives quick, temporary relief. I've never found this particular use for it in any of my tomes, but I've tried everything else. What do I have to lose?"

He ground the contents of the pouch into a powder and dropped it in a flagon of wine.

"This might even save us a trip to Vushta." He held his nose and lifted the concoction to his lips. My hopes sank as he drank it down. With the duke's daughter gone, a trip to Vushta was the only thing I had to look forward to.

The wizard opened a magical tome and breathed deeply. He smiled.

"It works! No more sneezing!"

His stomach growled.

"It couldn't be." A strange look stole over the wizard's face. He burped.

"It is! No wonder I couldn't find this in any of my tomes! I should have checked the *Netherhell Index*! It's fine for dragons, but for humans—" He paused to pull a book from the shelf and leaf rapidly through it. He burped again. His face looked very strained as he turned to me.

"Neebekenezer's Syndrome of Universal Flatulence!" he whispered. A high, whining sound emerged from his robes.

"Quick, Wunt!" he cried. "Remove yourself, if you value your sanity!"

I did as I was told. Even from my bed beneath the trees, I could hear the whistles, groans and muffled explosions all night long.

We would be traveling to Vushta after all.

THE GEORGE BUSINESS

Roger Zelazny

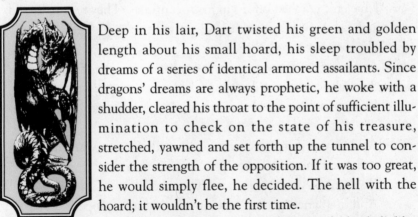

Deep in his lair, Dart twisted his green and golden length about his small hoard, his sleep troubled by dreams of a series of identical armored assailants. Since dragons' dreams are always prophetic, he woke with a shudder, cleared his throat to the point of sufficient illumination to check on the state of his treasure, stretched, yawned and set forth up the tunnel to consider the strength of the opposition. If it was too great, he would simply flee, he decided. The hell with the hoard; it wouldn't be the first time.

As he peered from the cave mouth, he beheld a single knight in mismatched armor atop a tired-looking gray horse, just rounding the bend. His lance was not even couched, but still pointing skyward.

Assuring himself that the man was unaccompanied, he roared and slithered forth.

"Halt," he bellowed, "you who are about to fry!"

The knight obliged.

"You're the one I came to see," the man said. "I have—"

"Why," Dart asked, "do you wish to start this business up again? Do you realize how long it has been since a knight and dragon have done battle?"

"Yes, I do. Quite a while. But I—"

"It is almost invariably fatal to one of the parties concerned. Usually your side."

"Don't I know it. Look, you've got me wrong—"

"I dreamt a dragon dream of a young man named George with whom I must do battle. You bear him an extremely close resemblance."

"I can explain. It's not as bad as it looks. You see—"

"*Is* your name George?"

"Well, yes. But don't let that bother you—"

"It *does* bother me. You want my pitiful hoard? It wouldn't keep you in beer money for the season. Hardly worth the risk."

"I'm not after your hoard—"

"I haven't grabbed off a virgin in centuries. They're usually old and tough, anyhow, not to mention hard to find."

"No one's accusing—"

"As for cattle, I always go a great distance. I've gone out of my way, you might say, to avoid getting a bad name in my own territory."

"I know you're no real threat here. I've researched it quite carefully—"

"And do you think that armor will really protect you when I exhale my deepest, hottest flames?"

"Hell, no! So don't do it, huh? If you'd please—"

"And that lance . . . You're not even holding it properly."

George lowered the lance.

"On that you are correct," he said, "but it happens to be tipped with one of the deadliest poisons known to Herman the Apothecary."

"I say! That's hardly sporting!"

"I know. But even if you incinerate me, I'll bet I can scratch you before I go."

"Now that would be rather silly—both of us dying like that—

wouldn't it?" Dart observed edging away. "It would serve no useful purpose that I can see."

"I feel precisely the same way about it."

"Then why are we getting ready to fight?"

"I have no desire whatsoever to fight with you!"

"I'm afraid I don't understand. You said your name is George, and I had this dream—"

"I can explain it."

"But the poisoned lance—"

"Self-protection, to hold you off long enough to put a proposition to you."

Dart's eyelids lowered slightly.

"What sort of proposition?"

"I want to hire you."

"Hire me? Whatever for? And what are you paying?"

"Mind if I rest this lance a minute? No tricks?"

"Go ahead. If you're talking gold your life is safe."

George rested his lance and undid a pouch at his belt. He dipped his hand into it and withdrew a fistful of shining coins. He tossed them gently, so that they clinked and shone in the morning light.

"You have my full attention. That's a good piece of change there."

"My life's savings. All yours—in return for a bit of business."

"What's the deal?"

George replaced the coins in his pouch and gestured.

"See that castle in the distance—two hills away?"

"I've flown over it many times."

"In the tower to the west are the chambers of Rosalind, daughter of the Baron Maurice. She is very dear to his heart, and I wish to wed her."

"There's a problem?"

"Yes. She's attracted to big, brawny barbarian types, into which category I, alas, do not fall. In short, she doesn't like me."

"That *is* a problem."

"So, if I could pay you to crash in there and abduct her, to bear her off to some convenient and isolated place and wait for me, I'll come along, we'll fake a battle, I'll vanquish you, you'll fly away and I'll take her home. I am certain I will then appear sufficiently heroic in her eyes to rise from sixth to first position on her list of suitors. How does that sound to you?"

Dart sighed a long column of smoke.

"Human, I bear your kind no special fondness—particularly the armored variety with lances—so I don't know why I'm telling you this. . . . Well, I do know, actually. . . . But never mind. I could manage it, all right. But, if you win the hand of that maid, do you know what's going to happen? The novelty of your deed will wear off after a time—and you know that there will be no encore. Give her a year, I'd say, and you'll catch her fooling around with one of those brawny barbarians she finds so attractive. Then you must either fight him and be slaughtered or wear horns, as they say."

George laughed.

"It's nothing to me how she spends her spare time. I've a girlfriend in town myself."

Dart's eyes widened.

"I'm afraid I don't understand. . . ."

"She's the old baron's only offspring, and he's on his last legs. Why else do you think an uncomely wench like that would have six suitors? Why else would I gamble my life's savings to win her?"

"I see," said Dart. "Yes, I can understand greed."

"I call it a desire for security."

"Quite. In that case, forget my simple-minded advice. All right, give me the gold and I'll do it." Dart gestured with one gleaming vane. "The first valley in those western mountains seems far enough from my home for our confrontation."

"I'll pay you half now and half on delivery."

"Agreed. Be sure to have the balance with you, though, and drop it during the scuffle. I'll return for it after you two have departed. Cheat me and I'll repeat the performance, with a different ending."

"The thought had already occurred to me.—Now, we'd better practice a bit, to make it look realistic. I'll rush at you with the lance, and whatever side she's standing on I'll aim for it to pass you on the other. You raise that wing, grab the lance and scream like hell. Blow a few flames around, too."

"I'm going to see you scour the tip of that lance before we rehearse this."

"Right.—I'll release the lance while you're holding it next to you and rolling around. Then I'll dismount and rush toward you with my blade. I'll whack you with the flat of it—again, on the far side—a few times. Then you bellow again and fly away."

"Just how sharp is that thing, anyway?"

"Damned dull. It was my grandfather's. Hasn't been honed since he was a boy."

"And you drop the money during the fight?"

"Certainly.—How does that sound?"

"Not bad. I can have a few clusters of red berries under my wing, too. I'll squash them once the action gets going."

"Nice touch. Yes, do that. Let's give it a quick rehearsal now and then get on with the real thing."

"And don't whack too hard. . . ."

That afternoon, Rosalind of Maurice Manor was abducted by a green-and-gold dragon who crashed through the wall of her chamber and bore her off in the direction of the western mountains.

"Never fear!" shouted her sixth-ranked suitor—who just happened to be riding by—to her aged father who stood wringing his hands on a nearby balcony. "I'll rescue her!" and he rode off to the west.

Coming into the valley where Rosalind stood backed into a rocky cleft, guarded by the fuming beast of gold and green, George couched his lance.

"Release that maiden and face your doom!" he cried.

Dart bellowed, George rushed. The lance fell from his hands and the dragon rolled upon the ground, spewing gouts of fire into the air. A red substance dribbled from beneath the thundering creature's left wing. Before Rosalind's wide eyes, George advanced and swung his blade several times.

". . . and that!" he cried, as the monster stumbled to its feet and sprang into the air, dripping more red.

It circled once and beat its way off toward the top of the mountain, then over it and away.

"Oh George!" Rosalind cried, and she was in his arms. "Oh, George . . ."

He pressed her to him for a moment.

"I'll take you home now," he said.

That evening as he was counting his gold, Dart heard the sound of two horses approaching his cave. He rushed up the tunnel and peered out.

George, now mounted on a proud white stallion and leading the gray, wore a matched suit of bright armor. He was not smiling, however.

"Good evening," he said.

"Good evening. What brings you back so soon?"

"Things didn't turn out exactly as I'd anticipated."

"You seem far better accoutered. I'd say your fortunes had taken a turn."

"Oh, I recovered my expenses and came out a bit ahead. But that's all. I'm on my way out of town. Thought I'd stop by and tell you the end of the story.—Good show you put on, by the way. It probably would have done the trick—"

"But—?"

"She was married to one of the brawny barbarians this morning, in their family chapel. They were just getting ready for a wedding trip when you happened by."

"I'm awfully sorry."

"Well, it's the breaks. To add insult, though, her father dropped dead during your performance. My former competitor is now the new baron. He rewarded me with a new horse and armor, a gratuity and a scroll from the local scribe lauding me as a dragon slayer. Then he hinted rather strongly that the horse and my new reputation could take me far. Didn't like the way Rosalind was looking at me now I'm a hero."

"That is a shame. Well, we tried."

"Yes. So I just stopped by to thank you and let you know how it all turned out. It would have been a good idea—if it had worked."

"You could hardly have foreseen such abrupt nuptials.—You

know, I've spent the entire day thinking about the affair. We *did* manage it awfully well."

"Oh, no doubt about that. It went beautifully."

"I was thinking . . . How'd you like a chance to get your money back?"

"What have you got in mind?"

"Uh—When I was advising you earlier that you might not be happy with the lady, I was trying to think about the situation in human terms. Your desire was entirely understandable to me otherwise. In fact, you think quite a bit like a dragon."

"Really?"

"Yes. It's rather amazing, actually. Now—realizing that it only failed because of a fluke, your idea still has considerable merit."

"I'm afraid I don't follow you."

"There is—ah—a lovely lady of my own species whom I have been singularly unsuccessful in impressing for a long while now. Actually, there are an unusual number of parallels in our situations."

"She has a large hoard, huh?"

"Extremely so."

"Older woman?"

"Among dragons, a few centuries this way or that are not so important. But she, too, has other admirers and seems attracted by the more brash variety."

"Uh-huh. I begin to get the drift. You gave me some advice once. I'll return the favor. Some things are more important than hoards."

"Name one."

"My life. If I were to threaten her she might do me in all by herself, before you could come to her rescue."

"No, she's a demure little thing. Anyway, it's all a matter of timing. I'll perch on a hilltop nearby—I'll show you where—and signal you when to begin your approach. Now, this time I have to win, of course. Here's how we'll work it. . . ."

George sat on the white charger and divided his attention between the distant cave mouth and the crest of a high hill off to his left.

After a time, a shining winged form flashed through the air and settled upon the hill. Moments later, it raised one bright wing.

He lowered his visor, couched his lance and started forward. When he came within hailing distance of the cave he cried out:

"I know you're in there, Megtag! I've come to destroy you and make off with your hoard! You godless beast! Eater of children! This is your last day on earth!"

An enormous burnished head with cold green eyes emerged from the cave. Twenty feet of flame shot from its huge mouth and scorched the rock before it. George halted hastily. The beast looked twice the size of Dart and did not seem in the least retiring. Its scales rattled like metal as it began to move forward.

"Perhaps I exaggerated. . . ." George began, and he heard the frantic flapping of giant vanes overhead.

As the creature advanced, he felt himself seized by the shoulders. He was borne aloft so rapidly that the scene below dwindled to toy size in a matter of moments. He saw his new steed bolt and flee rapidly back along the route they had followed.

"What the hell happened?" he cried.

"I hadn't been around for a while," Dart replied. "Didn't know one of the others had moved in with her. You're lucky I'm fast. That's Pelladon. He's a mean one."

"Great. Don't you think you should have checked first?"

"Sorry. I thought she'd take decades to make up her mind—without prompting. Oh, what a hoard! You should have seen it!"

"Follow that horse. I want him back."

They sat before Dart's cave, drinking.

"Where'd you ever get a whole barrel of wine?"

"Lifted it from a barge, up the river. I do that every now and then. I keep a pretty good cellar, if I do say so."

"Indeed. Well, we're none the poorer, really. We can drink to that."

"True, but I've been thinking again. You know, you're a very good actor."

"Thanks. You're not so bad yourself."

"Now supposing—just supposing—you were to travel about. Good distances from here each time. Scout out villages, on the continent and in the isles. Find out which ones are well off and lacking in local heroes. . . ."

"Yes?"

". . . And let them see that dragon-slaying certificate of yours. Brag a bit. Then come back with a list of towns. Maps, too."

"Go ahead."

"Find the best spots for a little harmless predation and choose a good battle site—"

"Refill?"

"Please."

"Here."

"Thanks. Then you show up, and for a fee—"

"Sixty-forty."

"That's what I was thinking, but I'll bet you've got the figures transposed."

"Maybe fifty-five and forty-five then."

"Down the middle, and let's drink on it."

"Fair enough. Why haggle?"

"Now I know why I dreamed of fighting a great number of knights, all of them looking like you. You're going to make a name for yourself, George."

THE DRAGONBONE FLUTE

Lois Tilton

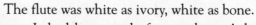

The flute was white as ivory, white as bone.

It had been made from a dragon's hollow wing-bone, found one day by a shepherd in a mountainside cave. The bones had lain gleaming in the darkness, the high-arched ribs, the skull with its deep hollow sockets, the razor-edged teeth. Yet it was only one delicate wingtip that he took home to the sod-roofed hut where he lived on the mountain, to spend the long summer evenings patiently boring the fingerholes.

When it was finished he took it outside and blew the first tentative note. The sound was thrillingly clear, high and light. Soon, if he shut his eyes while he played, it almost seemed that he could see dragons soaring, their eyes like jewels, vast wings extended to catch the updraft from the sunwarmed valleys far below.

Summer ended, and when the sky turned gray and the cold wind began to blow down from the peak, the shepherd gathered his animals and went down into the valley. Within days the trails were blocked by snow, and now was the time to sit by the fire in the company of other men. From time to time, when the tavern in the village was full of laughter and dancing, the shepherd would take out his flute and join in with the viol and recorder while the villagers skipped and rollicked to the well-known country tunes. It was a good way to pass the winter evenings and earn a tankard or two of thick brown ale.

But when the snow melted and the new grass came green on the mountain, he gathered up his newly shorn flock to drive it back up to the summer pasture. Now, once again, his songs were of dragons and flight. They seemed to come from the heart of the flute itself, as if the hollow bone retained an echo of the dragon's own voice.

So he sat and played on the mountainside one day when suddenly a black shadow seemed to blot out the sun. As his sheep ran bleating in mindless panic, he looked up to see the vast shape of a dragon plunging down at him, talons extended, tail lashing the sky in a frenzy of rage. Then he heard its voice in his mind, even as he dropped to the ground in a futile effort to evade those claws: *Mlakazar! My mate! Death! Death! Who killed him? Who has his bones?*

The shepherd in his desperate terror cried aloud, "No!" and felt the wind of the dragon's passage engulfing him in its hot, sulphurous scent as he awaited the piercing agony of the talons seizing his flesh. But instead he rolled free, cowering on the ground as the dragon hovered directly overhead, the beating of its wings battering him like a gale. *My mate! I heard the voice of his bones!*

The shepherd in his fear got to his knees, stammering, "I . . . found the bones in a cave. I took only one—this one—to make a flute. I never killed . . . never . . ."

Slowly the dragon lowered itself to the ground, transfixing the trembling man with its gaze, red tongue licking in and out of its mouth. *Yes, this is his, this is his voice. Show me. Show me the rest of the bones.*

He led, the dragon followed, claws scoring the earth of the mountainside to bare stone. The cave was above the grass line, a place the shepherd had found the year before while climbing up to retrieve a strayed lamb. It was then he had spotted the break in the rock and the dim gleam of fleshless bone inside.

The dragon was only barely able to squeeze its bulk through the opening of the cave. The bones lay as the shepherd had found them, as they must have lain for tens of years to be stripped and worn so white. The shepherd felt the cry of the dragon's grief: *Mlakazar!*

He began to plead for his life, "You càn see how long ago it must have been. I swear! I meant no harm! I never touched—never took but the one bone. Oh, forgive!"

The dragon lowered its head in sorrow. The shepherd could see now that it was old and a female, her blue-green hide and scales worn. Her eyes were pallid opals, red-veined with age. *Let me hear,* she said at last. *Let me hear the voice of my mate.*

So the shepherd took his flute from his belt and with shaking hands began to play. He played the song of flight, the song of freedom in the air, glorying in the strength of his wings. He played from the flute's heart, not knowing how he did, and beside him the dragon wept huge golden tears.

His voice lives again, she said at last.

"I meant no harm," the shepherd said again, uncertainly. "I was alone up here on the mountain. I thought, a little music, a song or two . . ."

Yes, said the dragon. *I know what it is to be alone.* And after a moment she spread her wings and beat her way into the sky.

The shepherd immediately put down the flute and began to search the mountainside anxiously for his flock, hoping they had not all plunged to their deaths in their panicked rush from descending death. He glanced nervously up at the dragon, soaring about a distant peak, well aware that she could easily swallow a sheep with a single snap of her jaws.

It took three days to gather in the flock, scattered as they had been. And for days after that he did not dare touch the flute for fear of the dragon, that it might return and devour them. Yet from time to time he could see her far-off shape wheeling above him in the sky, bringing back memories of the song of flight, and finally he realized that nothing he did could endanger his sheep or protect them if the dragon wished him harm. So he let the dead dragon's voice live again, and he was no longer alone on the mountain.

But as the summer days grew longer, the presence of the dragon had other consequences. One day an armed man rode up to the high pasture. A squire rode with him, leading a much larger stallion bearing weapons and armor, most conspicuously a lance fully twelve feet long.

The shepherd pulled off his cap as the knight beckoned him over. "Herdsman! Here! What do you know of the drake?"

"Sir?"

"The dragon, lout! I've had word there's a dragon been spotted up in these mountains. Prime trophy! Looking for his lair. Well?"

The shepherd glanced nervously up into the empty sky, then shook his head. "No, Sir. No dragon up here, Sir." As the knight scowled, he added, "I couldn't stay up here with my sheep if there was a dragon on the mountain, Sir. Not with my sheep."

The horseman cursed and turned his glare onto his squire, dismounting. "It's getting late. I'll stay here the night. Go fetch one of those lambs."

The shepherd protested in vain as his lamb was slaughtered and spitted over his own fire. The knight only threw him a coin and ordered him to stop his complaints. In the morning the unwelcome visitors rode on, but the shepherd knew they would not be the last.

That winter, when he led his flock down from the mountain, the villagers pressed him with questions of their own, for they had seen the far-off shape of the dragon soaring high among the peaks. But the shepherd would admit nothing. Only, at last, that nothing had been at the sheep, no dragon, no eagle, no stray pack of wolves. And as they could see for themselves that the flock had not noticeably diminished, the villagers could only shake their heads.

But the shepherd kept mostly to himself throughout that winter, nursing a solitary ale at the side of the fire, and when the patrons of the tavern called for a song from his flute, he shook his head, saying he had lost it on the mountain.

In the spring, he drove his flock out almost before the snow had cleared the trails. Never had the mountain air seemed so fresh and clean, the sunshine so bright. And in the far, far-off distance, a speck of dark flew against the glistening snowcaps, a dragon soaring on outspread wings. His heart lifted at the sight.

She descended almost as soon as he had reached his pasture, with a stiff rustle of leathery wings. *Play, shepherd, play. Let me hear his voice again.* And the shepherd put the flute of bone to his mouth and let the song of flight spill out.

"He was your only mate?" he asked her once.

The dragon shook her scarred, blue-scaled head. *A mate is for life.*

"For life," the shepherd said sadly, thinking of the churchyard where he had buried his wife so many years ago, before he went up onto the mountain. "Yes, it is the same with some of us."

The dragon was ancient, even for one of her kind. Her leathery wings were scarred, her scales broken and cracked. The shepherd was concerned, for all her immense size, thinking of errant knights and the cruel steel heads of their lances. "This place is dangerous for you," he urged her, but again and again the dragon would return. *Play, shepherd. Let his voice live again.*

Then indeed rumors spread that a dragon had returned to the mountain. Knights and other adventurers would make their way to the high pasture in search of the great head for a trophy, the fabled gold of the hoard. Always the shepherd would show them the flock grazing placidly and unmolested on the tender grass. "I've been grazing this flock up here for half a man's lifetime. Think you that I'd bring my sheep to a dragon's lair?"

So the season passed and the one after. Each spring the shepherd climbed the mountain trails more slowly. The dragon's eyes grew more dim.

Then one spring the sky was empty when the shepherd arrived at the high pasture with his flock. He went to bed that night with a heavy heart, and his flute was silent. But in the morning when he opened the door of his hut she was waiting for him, steaming in the mists. The huge head hung low, and her wings were tattered. *Play, shepherd. Let me hear him one last time.*

He played, and the music of the flute soared higher and lighter than ever. He played until his breath was exhausted, while the dragon's golden tears ran silently from the faded veined opal of her eyes.

When he was finished, she began to creep away with painful slowness, dragging her ruined wings. The shepherd knew her destination. He followed until she came to the cave where her mate's bones lay. Before she crawled inside, squeezing her bulk through the narrow opening, she turned one last time to face the shepherd. *He was black! Bright black! Mlakazar!*

He waited until sunset colored the mountaintops, but she never emerged again.

The shepherd returned to his solitary existence on the mountain, to his sheep and their new lambs. From time to time he would take out the dragonbone flute and play a few notes, but the sky remained empty.

Then one day in late summer he felt a strange stirring in his heart. He put the flute to his mouth and played the old song of flight, the song of the dragon in his youth and power, soaring on the highest currents of the wind.

At first the shepherd thought he must be dreaming. The sky was full of dragons, wings outstretched, their jewel-tone scales glinting in the sunlight. He blinked, and the flute almost fell from his hands, but the dragons were still there and he could hear their voices in his mind, crying, *Flight! Flight!*

Then, as they dove closer, he saw that these dragons were each no larger than a swan, and he realized they must be newly hatched. *Flight!* they called. *Flight! Flight!* And he played for them again, watching with renewed joy as they swooped and plunged and tumbled in the air. Though he spoke to them, they made no answer, only repeating the same cry.

The next morning, the shepherd once again made the climb to the cave near the mountain's peak. His steps were slower than they had been when he first made this ascent and found a cave full of dry white bones. But this time dragons played above his head.

The immense bulk of a dragon does not decay quickly, even in the summer heat, and the shepherd had to tie a scarf over his face before he could enter the dark, narrow space of the cave. But as soon as his eyes grew accustomed to the light, he was able to make out what he had sought—the precious broken, gold-veined shards of the dragons' eggs, incubated long months in the decomposing warmth of their mother's remains. His heart raced at the first sight of so much wealth, but at last he left the cave as empty-handed as he had come. How could he sell them, even downriver in the marketplace? How could he let the world know of their existence?

Dragons flew over his head as he climbed slowly back down the mountain.

There were twelve of them—gold and green and russet and blue and a solitary jet-brilliant black. Their eyes were bright, their wings supple and unscarred. They grew rapidly in the waning summer days, preying on the smaller beasts of the mountainside. As their wings became stronger they went farther and farther from the cave, until they were flying from peak to peak, higher and higher, until they soared above the most lofty snowcaps.

Yet always they returned to the mountain where they had been born, to the sound of the shepherd's dragonbone flute.

But there came a day in autumn, when the grass was turning coarse and yellow, when the shepherd came upon the carcass of one of his yearling lambs on an outcrop of rock, torn open and half-devoured. The marks of a dragon's talons were clearly visible on the remains.

Despite the shepherd's increased vigilance, several days later another lamb was missing. He grieved, knowing that by the next spring the dragons would be grown strong enough to carry off a mature ram. Now at last he felt the bitter truth of the answer he had always made to the questing knights, that he would not be able to pasture his flock on the mountain if there were dragons laired nearby.

That fall he drove his sheep down to the valley before the first snowflakes flew in the sky. Some of the villagers shook their heads and wondered aloud how many more years the old shepherd would be able to spend all alone up on the mountainside. A few of them suggested that he ought to hire a boy to run after the sheep. To all of them the shepherd made scant response. He sat alone through the winter evenings by the fireside of the tavern, and when people spoke of dancing, none of them seemed to remember the sweet, lively music of the bone flute, lost so many years ago.

Then one evening, as night was coming on, there was a commotion outside the tavern: the stamping of horses and the ring of steel. The innkeeper bustled, shouting for his sons to tend the beasts, his maids to look lively in the kitchen and make up the best bed for the noble knight and his servant.

The customers nearest the door hurried outside, followed quickly by the rest. The shepherd left his seat last of all, dread in his heart. The crowd had gathered thickly around the horses, hindering the tavern's boy in his efforts to lead them into the stable. It was only at the last moment that the shepherd caught a glimpse of what was tied across the largest mount's back, a dragon as large as the horse itself, wings trussed up so they would not drag on the ground, the jewel-tones of its eyes gone dull and its scales still lustrous, gleaming black, the rarest of dragon-colors.

Never again would his wings bear him up into the sky, never again would he experience the pure joy of flight or ever know the long, loyal happiness of a mate.

Soon the knight came into the tavern, followed by the admiring company, where the landlord himself served him his ale. He was a young fellow, fair and flushed with pride, not at all reluctant to boast of his deed in slaying the drake.

"He flew at me with his claws all extended, mouth wide open, hissing—"

"Breathing fire?" one of the serving maids asked eagerly.

"Well," the knight admitted, reluctantly compelled to honesty, "not exactly." He took a deep swallow of his ale. "I couched my lance. The drake came at me, and I spitted him like a charging boar. The point of my lance ran in below his ribs and out between his wings. The force drove my mount to his knees." The knight was on his feet with the excitement of his own ale. "I jumped clear, pulled my sword—"

The crowd exclaimed at the bright ring of steel, stepping back as he pulled his blade free, reenacting the epic battle. "But the drake was already dead. Killed with one blow!"

The shepherd at the back of the room shook his head in sorrow. "Young and foolish, young and foolish," he thought. What had the black dragon known in his short life of knights or lances or swords?

He realized suddenly that a question was being addressed to him. "You, shepherd! You graze your flock on the mountains, is that right?"

the knight was asking. "Did you ever see any dragonsign up there? Any sign of a lair?"

The shepherd shook his head again. "Knights came here before, asking me. No, no dragonsign on my mountain. Couldn't bring my sheep up there if there was dragons, now, could I?"

As always, the crowd nodded in acknowledgment of this obvious truth. The shepherd added, "Now, that one I saw tied on the horse. I don't think that one looked the size to take a sheep. Lamb, maybe. Young lamb. Not a sheep, though."

The young knight scowled at this belittling of his deed and shouted loudly to the innkeeper for more ale. In the morning he would be gone with his trophy, but others of his kind would come when they heard of his deed, eager for dragonslaying. One by one the dragons would fall to the lance, the gold and green and russet and blue.

It was a harsh winter that came to the valley that year, filling the passes with snow, so that the village was cut off for weeks from the rest of the world. By the time the snow began to melt, the shepherd had sold his flock, telling the buyer, "Getting too much for me, climbing up the mountain every year. Slowing down. Ache in my joints these days."

He pocketed the gold, little as there was. He might have gotten a better price at the spring fair downriver at the market town, but there wasn't time for that.

He made one last stop before he left the village, at the graveside of his wife. He knelt for a moment on the damp, cold ground, but after so long he hardly knew what to say. "Not like a dragon," he thought, getting stiffly back to his feet. "We forget."

Without his flock, he was only three days climbing up to the hidden cave, even with the half-melted banks of snow blocking his way. From time to time he glanced up, and at last he saw them, the faraway specks that were dragons circling overhead.

At the very back of the fissure in the rock, beyond the carcass of the blue-green dragon, the precious gold-veined broken shells were still untouched. Carefully, he picked them up, the green, the red, the jet, and put them away in his pack. Then, using his knife, he began to cut away a single hollow wingtip bone from the dried and leathery remains.

It was different working this half-raw bone, scraping away the adhering hide, carving out the holes for his mouth and fingers. When it was finished, the flute had a shrill, harsh tone, with a melancholy pitch that hinted of pain and bereavement.

The shepherd put down his tools and stepped outside his hut. Lifting his head to the sky, he put the flute to his mouth and began to play. It was a song of peril and death. Dragons writhed on sharp lances tearing through their vitals. Swords hacked at broken scales, at the delicate bones of their wings, breaking, crippling. No longer able to fly, the dragons twisted, turning in vain on their tormentors, helpless against the steel of their weapons.

Dragons died. Their blood poured out onto the green grass, singeing it brown. Their sightless skulls were impaled on spears as trophies. Their mates circled in the sky, bereft, keening their grief, while their bones slowly bleached and bare and white, to crumble at last into powder and dust.

And constantly as a counterpoint to the song, repeated again and again: Flee! Far away! Far away!

The shepherd played until his lips could not shape another note, until his fingers, with their aching joints, could barely move. When he put down the flute at last, the sky was empty.

Alone, he waited on the mountain, but the dragons did not return.

And when several days had passed and he was sure, he took both flutes and snapped them in half and laid them in the cave with the rest of the dragons' bones.

The path he took down from the mountain led not to the village of his birth but farther downriver to the market town and its spring fair. And beyond to the cities of the plains, where no man could see the snowcapped mountains and the glint of dragons flying against the sun.

THE ICE DRAGON

George R.R. Martin

Adara liked the winter best of all, for when the world grew cold the ice dragon came.

She was never quite sure whether it was the cold that brought the ice dragon or the ice dragon that brought the cold. That was the sort of question that often troubled her brother Geoff, who was two years older than her and insatiably curious, but Adara did not care about such things. So long as the cold and the snow and the ice dragon all arrived on schedule, she was happy.

She always knew when they were due because of her birthday. Adara was a winter child, born during the worst freeze that anyone could remember, even Old Laura, who lived on the next farm and remembered things that had happened before anyone else was born. People still talked about that freeze. Adara often heard them.

They talked about other things as well. They said it was the chill of that terrible freeze that had killed her mother, stealing in during her long night of labor past the great fire that Adara's father had built, and creeping under the layers of blankets that covered the birthing bed. And they said that the cold had entered Adara in the womb, that her skin had been pale blue and icy to the touch when she came forth, and that she had never warmed in all the years since. The winter had touched her, left its mark upon her, and made her its own.

It was true that Adara was always a child apart. She was a very serious little girl who seldom cared to play with the others. She was beautiful, people said, but in a strange, distant sort of way, with her pale skin and blond hair and wide clear blue eyes. She smiled, but not often. No one had ever seen her cry. Once when she was five she had stepped upon a nail imbedded in a board that lay concealed beneath a snowbank, and it had gone clear through her foot, but Adara had not wept or screamed even then. She had pulled her foot loose and walked back to the house, leaving a trail of blood in the snow, and when she had gotten there she had said only, "Father, I hurt myself." The sulks and tempers and tears of ordinary childhood were not for her.

Even her family knew that Adara was different. Her father was a huge, gruff bear of a man who had little use for people in general, but a smile always broke across his face when Geoff pestered him with questions, and he was full of hugs and laughter for Teri, Adara's older sister, who was golden and freckled, and flirted shamelessly with all the local boys. Every so often he would hug Adara as well, especially when he was drunk, which was frequent during the long winters. But there would be no smiles then. He would only wrap his arms around her, and pull her small body tight against him with all his massive strength, sob deep in his chest, and fat wet tears would run down his ruddy cheeks. He never hugged her at all during the summers. During the summers he was too busy.

Everyone was busy during the summers except for Adara. Geoff would work with his father in the fields and ask endless questions about this and that, learning everything a farmer had to know. When he was not working he would run with his friends to the river, and have adventures. Teri ran the house and did the cooking, and worked a bit at the inn by the crossroads during the busy season. The innkeeper's daughter was her friend, and his youngest son was more than a friend, and she would always come back giggly and full of gossip and news from travellers and soldiers and king's messengers. For Teri and Geoff the summers were the best time, and both of them were too busy for Adara.

Their father was the busiest of all. A thousand things needed to be done each day, and he did them, and found a thousand more. He worked from dawn to dusk. His muscles grew hard and lean in summer, and he stank from sweat each night when he came in from the fields, but he always came in smiling. After supper he would sit with Geoff and tell him stories and answer his questions, or teach Teri things she did not know about cooking, or stroll down to the inn. He was a summer man, truly.

He never drank in summer, except for a cup of wine now and again to celebrate his brother's visits.

That was another reason why Teri and Geoff loved the summers, when the world was green and hot and bursting with life. It was only in summer that Uncle Hal, their father's younger brother, came to call. Hal was a dragonrider in service to the king, a tall slender man with a face like a noble. Dragons cannot stand the cold, so when winter fell Hal and his wing would fly south. But each summer he returned, brilliant in the king's green-and-gold uniform, en route to the battlegrounds to the north and west of them. The war had been going on for all of Adara's life.

Whenever Hal came north, he would bring presents; toys from the king's city, crystal and gold jewelry, candies, and always a bottle of some expensive wine that he and his brother could share. He would grin at Teri and make her blush with his compliments, and entertain Geoff with tales of war and castles and dragons. As for Adara, he often tried to coax a smile out of her, with gifts and jests and hugs. He seldom succeeded.

For all his good nature, Adara did not like Hal; when Hal was there, it meant that winter was far away.

Besides, there had been a night when she was only four, and they thought her long asleep, that she overheard them talking over wine. "A solemn little thing," Hal said. "You ought to be kinder to her, John. You cannot blame *her* for what happened."

"Can't I?" her father replied, his voice thick with wine. "No, I suppose not. But it is hard. She looks like Beth, but she has none of Beth's warmth. The winter is in her, you know. Whenever I touch her I feel the chill, and I remember that it was for her that Beth had to die."

"You are cold to her. You do not love her as you do the others."

Adara remembered the way her father laughed then. "Love her? Ah, Hal. I loved her best of all, my little winter child. But she has never loved back. There is nothing in her for me, or you, any of us. She is such a cold little girl." And then he began to weep, even though it was summer and Hal was with him. In her bed, Adara listened and wished that Hal would fly away. She did not quite understand all that she had heard, not then, but she remembered it, and the understanding came later.

She did not cry; not at four, when she heard, or six, when she finally understood. Hal left a few days later, and Geoff and Teri waved to him excitedly when his wing passed overhead, thirty great dragons in proud formation against the summer sky. Adara watched with her small hands by her sides.

There were other visits in other summers, but Hal never made her smile, no matter what he brought her.

Adara's smiles were a secret store, and she spent of them only in winter. She could hardly wait for her birthday to come, and with it the cold. For in winter she was a special child.

She had known it since she was very little, playing with the others in the snow. The cold had never bothered her the way it did Geoff and Teri and their friends. Often Adara stayed outside alone for hours after the others had fled in search of warmth, or run off to Old Laura's to eat the hot vegetable soup she liked to make for the children. Adara would find a secret place in the far corner of the fields, a different place each winter, and there she would build a tall white castle, patting the snow in place with small bare hands, shaping it into towers and battlements like those Hal often talked about on the king's castle in the city. She would snap icicles off from the lower branches of trees, and use them for spires and spikes and guardposts, ranging them all about her castle. And often in the dead of winter would come a brief thaw and a sudden freeze, and overnight her snow castle would turn to ice, as hard and strong as she imagined real castles to be. All through the winters she would build on her castle, and no one ever knew. But always the spring would come, and a thaw not followed by a freeze; then all the ramparts and walls would melt away, and Adara would begin to count the days until her birthday came again.

Her winter castles were seldom empty. At the first frost each year, the ice lizards would come wriggling out of their burrows, and the fields would be overrun with the tiny blue creatures, darting this way and that, hardly seeming to touch the snow as they skimmed across it. All the children played with the ice lizards. But the others were clumsy and cruel, and they would snap the fragile little animals in two, breaking them between their fingers as they might break an icicle hanging from a roof. Even Geoff, who was too kind ever to do something like that, sometimes grew curious, and held the lizards too long in his efforts to examine them, and the heat of his hands would make them melt and burn and finally die.

Adara's hands were cool and gentle, and she could hold the lizards as long as she liked without harming them, which always made Geoff pout and ask angry questions. Sometimes she would lie in the cold, damp snow and let the lizards crawl all over her, delighting in the light touch of their feet as they skittered across her face. Sometimes she would wear ice lizards hidden in her hair as she went about her chores, though she took care never to take them inside where the heat of the fire would kill them. Always she would gather up scraps after the family ate, and bring them to the secret place where her castle was a-building, and there she would scatter them. So the castles she erected were full of kings and courtiers every winter; small furry creatures that snuck out from the woods, winter birds with pale white plumage, and hundreds and hundreds of squirming, struggling ice lizards, cold and quick and fat. Adara liked the ice lizards better than any of the pets the family had kept over the years.

But it was the ice dragon that she loved.

She did not know when she had first seen it. It seemed to her that it had always been a part of her life, a vision glimpsed during the deep of winter, sweeping across the frigid sky on wings serene and blue. Ice dragons were rare, even in those days, and whenever it was seen the children would all point and wonder, while the old folks muttered and shook their heads. It was a sign of a long and bitter winter when ice dragons were abroad in the land. An ice dragon had been seen flying across the face of the moon on the night Adara had been born, people said, and each winter since it had been seen again, and those winters had been very bad indeed, the spring coming later each year. So the people would set fires and pray and hope to keep the ice dragon away, and Adara would fill with fear.

But it never worked. Every year the ice dragon returned. Adara knew it came for her.

The ice dragon was large, half again the size of the scaled green war dragons that Hal and his fellows flew. Adara had heard legends of wild dragons larger than mountains, but she had never seen any. Hal's dragon was big enough, to be sure, five times the size of a horse, but it was small compared to the ice dragon, and ugly besides.

The ice dragon was a crystalline white, that shade of white that is so hard and cold that it is almost blue. It was covered with hoarfrost, so when it moved its skin broke and crackled as the crust on the snow crackles beneath a man's boots, and flakes of rime fell off.

Its eyes were clear and deep and icy.

Its wings were vast and batlike, colored all a faint translucent blue. Adara could see the clouds through them, and oftentimes the moon and stars, when the beast wheeled in frozen circles through the skies.

Its teeth were icicles, a triple row of them, jagged spears of un-equal length, white against its deep blue maw.

When the ice dragon beat its wings, the cold winds blew and the snow swirled and scurried and the world seemed to shrink and shiver. Sometimes when a door flew open in the cold of winter, driven by a sudden gust of wind, the householder would run to bolt it and say, "An ice dragon flies nearby."

And when the ice dragon opened its great mouth, and exhaled, it was not fire that came streaming out, the burning sulfurous stink of lesser dragons.

The ice dragon breathed *cold*.

Ice formed when it breathed. Warmth fled. Fires guttered and went out, shriven by the chill. Trees froze through to their slow secret souls, and their limbs turned brittle and cracked from their own weight. Animals turned blue and whimpered and died, their eyes bulging and their skin covered over with frost.

The ice dragon breathed death into the world; death and quiet and *cold*. But Adara was not afraid. She was a winter child, and the ice dragon was her secret.

She had seen it in the sky a thousand times. When she was four, she saw it on the ground.

She was out building on her snow castle, and it came and landed close to her, in the emptiness of the snow-covered fields. All the ice lizards ran away. Adara simply stood. The ice dragon looked at her for ten long heartbeats, before it took to the air again. The wind shrieked around her and through her as it beat its wings to rise, but Adara felt strangely exalted.

Later that winter it returned, and Adara touched it. Its skin was very cold. She took off her glove nonetheless. It would not be right otherwise. She was half afraid it would burn and melt at her touch, but it did not. It was much more sensitive to heat than even the ice lizards, Adara knew somehow. But she was special, the winter child, cool. She stroked it, and finally gave its wing a kiss that hurt her lips. That was the winter of her fourth birthday, the year she touched the ice dragon.

The winter of her fifth birthday was the year she rode upon it for the first time.

It found her again, working on a different castle at a different place in the fields, alone as ever. She watched it come, and ran to it when it landed, and pressed herself against it. That had been the summer when she had heard her father talking to Hal.

They stood together for long minutes until finally Adara, remembering Hal, reached out and tugged at the dragon's wing with a small hand. And the dragon beat its great wings once, and then extended them flat against the snow, and Adara scrambled up to wrap her arms about its cold white neck.

Together, for the first time, they flew.

She had no harness or whip, as the king's dragonriders use. At times the beating of the wings threatened to shake her loose from where she clung, and the coldness of the dragon's flesh crept through her clothing and bit and numbed her child's flesh. But Adara was not afraid.

They flew over her father's farm, and she saw Geoff looking very small below, startled and afraid, and knew he could not see her. It made her laugh an icy, tinkling laugh, a laugh as bright and crisp as the winter air.

They flew over the crossroads inn, where crowds of people came out to watch them pass.

They flew above the forest, all white and green and silent.

They flew high into the sky, so high that Adara could not even see the ground below, and she thought she glimpsed another ice dragon, way off in the distance, but it was not half so grand as *hers*.

They flew for most of the day, and finally the dragon swept around in a great circle, and spiraled down, gliding on its stiff and glittering wings. It let her off in the field where it had found her, just after dusk.

Her father found her there, and wept to see her, and hugged her savagely. Adara did not understand that, nor why he beat her after he had gotten her back to the house. But when she and Geoff had been put to sleep, she heard him slide out of his own bed and come padding over to hers. "You missed it all," he said. "There was an ice dragon, and it scared everybody. Father was afraid it had eaten you."

Adara smiled to herself in the darkness, but said nothing.

She flew on the ice dragon four more times that winter, and every winter after that. Each year she flew farther and more often than the year before, and the ice dragon was seen more frequently in the skies above their farm.

Each winter was longer and colder than the one before.

Each year the thaw came later.

And sometimes there were patches of land, where the ice dragon had lain to rest, that never seemed to thaw properly at all.

There was much talk in the village during her sixth year, and a message was sent to the king. No answer ever came.

"A bad business, ice dragons," Hal said that summer when he visited the farm. "They're not like real dragons, you know. You can't break them or train them. We have tales of those that tried, found frozen with their whip and harness in hand. I've heard about people that have lost hands or fingers just by touching one of them. Frostbite. Yes, a bad business."

"Then why doesn't the king do something?" her father demanded. "We sent a message. Unless we can kill the beast or drive it away, in a year or two we won't have any planting season at all."

Hal smiled grimly. "The king has other concerns. The war is going badly, you know. They advance every summer, and they have twice as many dragonriders as we do. I tell you, John, it's hell up there. Some year I'm not going to come back. The king can hardly spare men to go chasing an ice dragon." He laughed. "Besides, I don't think anybody's ever killed one of the things. Maybe we should just let the enemy take this whole province. Then it'd be *his* ice dragon."

But it wouldn't be, Adara thought as she listened. No matter what king ruled the land, it would always be *her* ice dragon.

Hal departed and summer waxed and waned. Adara counted the days until her birthday. Hal passed through again before the first chill, taking his ugly dragon south for the winter. His wing seemed smaller when it came flying over the forest that fall, though, and his visit was briefer than usual, and ended with a loud quarrel between him and her father.

"They won't move during the winter," Hal said. "The winter terrain is too treacherous, and they won't risk an advance without dragonriders to cover them from above. But come spring, we aren't going to be able to hold them. The king may not even try. Sell the farm now, while you can still get a good price. You can buy another piece of land in the south."

"*This* is my land," her father said. "I was born here. You too, though you seem to have forgotten it. Our parents are buried here. And Beth too. I want to lie beside her when I go."

"You'll go a lot sooner than you'd like if you don't listen to me," Hal said angrily. "Don't be stupid, John. I know what the land means to you, but it isn't worth your life." He went on and on, but her father would not be moved. They ended the evening swearing at each other, and Hal left in the dead of the night, slamming the door behind him as he went.

Adara, listening, had made a decision. It did not matter what her father did or did not do. She would stay. If she moved, the ice dragon would not know where to find her when winter came, and if she went too far south it would never be able to come to her at all.

It did come to her, though, just after her seventh birthday. That winter was the coldest one of all. She flew so often and so far that she scarcely had time to work on her ice castle.

Hal came again in the spring. There were only a dozen dragons in his wing, and he brought no presents that year. He and her father argued once again. Hal raged and pleaded and threatened, but her father was stone. Finally Hal left, off to the battlefields.

That was the year the king's line broke, up north near some town with a long name that Adara could not pronounce.

Teri heard about it first. She returned from the inn one night flushed and excited. "A messenger came through, on his way to the king," she told them. "The enemy won some big battle, and he's to ask for reinforcements. He said our army is retreating."

Their father frowned, and worry lines creased his brow. "Did he say anything of the king's dragonriders?" Arguments or no, Hal was family.

"I asked," Teri said. "He said the dragonriders are the rear guard. They're supposed to raid and burn, delay the enemy while our army pulls back safely. Oh, I hope Uncle Hal is safe!"

"Hal will show them," Geoff said. "Him and Brimstone will burn 'em up."

Their father smiled. "Hal could always take care of himself. At any rate, there is nothing we can do. Teri, if any more messengers come through, ask them how it goes."

She nodded, her concern not quite covering her excitement. It was all quite thrilling.

In the weeks that followed, the thrill wore off, as the people of the area began to comprehend the magnitude of the disaster. The king's highway grew busier and busier, and all the traffic flowed from north to south, and all the travellers wore green-and-gold. At first the soldiers marched in disciplined columns, led by officers wearing plumed golden helmets, but even then they were less than stirring. The columns marched wearily, and the uniforms were filthy and torn, and the swords and pikes and axes the soldiers carried were nicked and ofttimes stained. Some men had lost their weapons; they limped along blindly, empty-handed. And the trains of wounded that followed the columns were often longer than the columns themselves. Adara stood in the grass by the side of the road and watched them pass. She saw a man with no eyes supporting a man with only one leg, as the two of them walked together. She saw men with no legs, or no arms, or both. She saw a man with his head split open by an axe, and many men covered with caked blood and filth, men who moaned low in their throats as they walked. She *smelled* men with bodies that were horribly greenish and puffed-up. One of them died and was left abandoned by the side of the road. Adara told her father and he and some of the men from the village came out and buried him.

Most of all, Adara saw the burned men. There were dozens of them in every column that passed, men whose skin was black and seared and falling off, who had lost an arm or a leg or half of a face to the hot breath of a dragon. Teri told them what the officers said, when they stopped at the inn to drink or rest; the enemy had many, many dragons.

For almost a month the columns flowed past, more every day. Even Old Laura admitted that she had never seen so much traffic on the road. From time to time a lone messenger on horseback rode against the tide, galloping toward the north, but always alone. After a time everyone knew there would be no reinforcements.

An officer in one of the last columns advised the people of the area to pack up whatever they could carry, and move south. "They are coming," he warned. A few listened to him, and indeed for a week the road was full of refugees from towns farther north. Some of them told frightful stories. When they left, more of the local people went with them.

But most stayed. They were people like her father, and the land was in their blood.

The last organized force to come down the road was a ragged

troop of cavalry, men as gaunt as skeletons riding horses with skin pulled tight around their ribs. They thundered past in the night, their mounts heaving and foaming, and the only one to pause was a pale young officer, who reigned his mount up briefly and shouted, "Go, go. They are burning everything!" Then he was off after his men.

The few soldiers who came after were alone or in small groups. They did not always use the road, and they did not pay for the things they took. One swordsman killed a farmer on the other side of town, raped his wife, stole his money, and ran. His rags were green-and-gold.

Then no one came at all. The road was deserted.

The innkeeper claimed he could smell ashes when the wind blew from the north. He packed up his family and went south. Teri was distraught. Geoff was wide-eyed and anxious and only a bit frightened. He asked a thousand questions about the enemy, and practiced at being a warrior. Their father went about his labors, busy as ever. War or no war, he had crops in the field. He smiled less than usual, however, and he began to drink, and Adara often saw him glancing up at the sky while he worked.

Adara wandered the fields alone, played by herself in the damp summer heat, and tried to think of where she would hide if her father tried to take them away.

Last of all, the king's dragonriders came, and with them Hal.

There were only four of them. Adara saw the first one, and went and told her father, and he put his hand on her shoulder and together they watched it pass, a solitary green dragon with a vaguely tattered look. It did not pause for them.

Two days later, three dragons flying together came into view, and one of them detached itself from the others and circled down to their farm while the other two headed south.

Uncle Hal was thin and grim and sallow-looking. His dragon looked sick. Its eyes ran, and one of its wings had been partially burned, so it flew in an awkward, heavy manner, with much difficulty. "Now will you go?" Hal said to his brother, in front of all the children.

"No. Nothing has changed."

Hal swore. "They will be here within three days," he said. "Their dragonriders may be here even sooner."

"Father, I am scared," Teri said.

He looked at her, saw her fear, hesitated, and finally turned back to his brother. "I am staying. But if you would, I would have you take the children."

Now it was Hal's turn to pause. He thought for a moment, and finally shook his head. "I can't, John. I would, willingly, joyfully, if it were possible. But it isn't. Brimstone is wounded. He can barely carry me. If I took on any extra weight, we might never make it."

Teri began to weep.

"I'm sorry, love," Hal said to her. "Truly I am." His fists clenched helplessly.

"Teri is almost full-grown," their father said. "If her weight is too much, then take one of the others."

Brother looked at brother, with despair in their eyes. Hal trembled. "Adara," he said finally. "She's small and light." He forced a laugh. "She hardly weighs anything at all. I'll take Adara. The rest of you take horses, or a wagon, or go on foot. But go, damn you, *go*."

"We will see," their father said noncommittally. "You take Adara, and keep her safe for us."

"Yes," Hal agreed. He turned and smiled at her. "Come, child. Uncle Hal is going to take you for a ride on Brimstone."

Adara looked at him very seriously. "No," she said. She turned and slipped through the door and began to run.

They came after her, of course, Hal and her father and even Geoff. But her father wasted time standing in the door, shouting at her to come back, and when he began to run he was ponderous and clumsy, while Adara was indeed small and light and fleet of foot. Hal and Geoff stayed with her longer, but Hal was weak, and Geoff soon winded himself, though he sprinted hard at her heels for a few moments. By the time Adara reached the nearest wheat field, the three of them were well behind her. She quickly lost herself amid the grain, and they searched for hours in vain while she made her way carefully toward the woods.

When dusk fell, they brought out lanterns and torches and continued their search. From time to time she heard her father swearing, or Hal calling out her name. She stayed high in the branches of the oak she had climbed, and smiled down at their lights as they combed back and forth through the fields. Finally she drifted off to sleep, dreaming about the coming of winter and wondering how she would live until her birthday. It was still a long time away.

Dawn woke her; dawn and a noise in the sky.

Adara yawned and blinked, and heard it again. She shinnied to the uppermost limb of the tree, as high as it would bear her, and pushed aside the leaves.

There were dragons in the sky.

She had never seen beasts quite like these. Their scales were dark and sooty, not green like the dragon Hal rode. One was a rust color and one was the shade of dried blood and one was black as coal. All of them had eyes like glowing embers, and steam rose from their nostrils, and their tails flicked back and forth as their dark, leathery wings beat the air. The rust-colored one opened its mouth and roared, and the forest shook to its challenge, and even the branch that held Adara trembled just a little. The black one made a noise too, and when it opened its maw a spear of flame lanced out, all orange and blue, and touched the trees below. Leaves withered and blackened, and smoke began to rise from where the dragon's breath had fallen. The one the color of blood flew close overhead, its wings creaking and straining, its mouth half-open. Between its yellowed teeth Adara saw soot and cinders, and the wind stirred by its passage was fire and sandpaper, raw and chafing against her skin. She cringed.

On the backs of the dragons rode men with whip and lance, in uniforms of black-and-orange, their faces hidden behind dark helmets. The one on the rust dragon gestured with his lance, pointing at the farm buildings across the fields. Adara looked.

Hal came up to meet them.

His green dragon was as large as their own, but somehow it seemed small to Adara as she watched it climb upward from the farm. With its wings fully extended, it was plain to see how badly injured it was; the right wing tip was charred, and it leaned heavily to one side as it flew. On its back, Hal looked like one of the tiny toy soldiers he had brought them as a present years before.

The enemy dragonriders split up and came at him from three

sides. Hal saw what they were doing. He tried to turn, to throw himself at the black dragon head-on, and flee the other two. His whip flailed angrily, desperately. His green dragon opened its mouth, and roared a weak challenge, but its flame was pale and short and did not reach the oncoming enemy.

The others held their fire. Then, on a signal, their dragons all breathed as one. Hal was wreathed in flames.

His dragon made a high wailing noise, and Adara saw that it was burning, *he* was burning, they were all burning, beast and master both. They fell heavily to the ground, and lay smoking amidst her father's wheat.

The air was full of ashes.

Adara craned her head around in the other direction, and saw a column of smoke rising from beyond the forest and the river. That was the farm where Old Laura lived with her grandchildren and *their* children.

When she looked back, the three dark dragons were circling lower and lower above her own farm. One by one they landed. She watched the first of the riders dismount and saunter toward their door.

She was frightened and confused and only seven, after all. And the heavy air of summer was a weight upon her, and it filled her with a helplessness and thickened all her fears. So Adara did the only thing she knew, without thinking, a thing that came naturally to her. She climbed down from her tree and ran. She ran across the fields and through the woods, away from the farm and her family and the dragons, away from all of it. She ran until her legs throbbed with pain, down in the direction of the river. She ran to the coldest place she knew, to the deep caves underneath the river bluffs, to chill shelter and darkness and safety.

And there in the cold she hid. Adara was a winter child, and cold did not bother her. But still, as she hid, she trembled.

Day turned into night. Adara did not leave her cave.

She tried to sleep, but her dreams were full of burning dragons.

She made herself very small as she lay in the darkness, and tried to count how many days remained until her birthday. The caves were nicely cool; Adara could almost imagine that it was not summer after all, that it was winter, or near to winter. Soon her ice dragon would come for her, and she would ride on its back to the land of always-winter, where great ice castles and cathedrals of snow stood eternally in endless fields of white, and the stillness and silence were all.

It almost felt like winter as she lay there. The cave grew colder and colder, it seemed. It made her feel safe. She napped briefly. When she woke, it was colder still. A white coating of frost covered the cave walls, and she was sitting on a bed of ice. Adara jumped to her feet and looked up toward the mouth of the cave, filled with a wan dawn light. A cold wind caressed her. But it was coming from outside, from the world of summer, not from the depths of the cave at all.

She gave a small shout of joy, and climbed and scrambled up the ice-covered rocks.

Outside, the ice dragon was waiting for her.

It had breathed upon the water, and now the river was frozen, or at least a part of it was, although she could see that the ice was fast melting as the summer sun rose. It had breathed upon the green grass that grew along the banks, grass as high as Adara, and now the tall blades were white and brittle, and when the ice dragon moved its wings the grass cracked in half and tumbled, sheared as clean as if it had been cut down with a scythe.

The dragon's icy eyes met Adara's, and she ran to it and up its wing, and threw her arms about it. She knew she had to hurry. The ice dragon looked smaller than she had ever seen it, and she understood what the heat of summer was doing to it.

"Hurry, dragon," she whispered. "Take me away, take me to the land of always-winter. We'll never come back here, never. I'll build you the best castle of all, and take care of you, and ride you every day. Just take me away, dragon, take me home with you."

The ice dragon heard and understood. Its wide translucent wings unfolded and beat the air, and bitter arctic winds howled through the fields of summer. They rose. Away from the cave. Away from the river. Above the forest. Up and up. The ice dragon swung around to the north. Adara caught a glimpse of her father's farm, but it was very small and growing smaller. They turned their back to it, and soared.

Then a sound came to Adara's ears. An impossible sound, a sound that was too small and too far away for her to ever have heard it, especially above the beating of the ice dragon's wings. But she heard it nonetheless. She heard her father scream.

Hot tears ran down her cheeks, and where they fell upon the ice dragon's back they burned small pockmarks in the frost. Suddenly the cold beneath her hands was biting, and when she pulled one hand away Adara saw the mark that it had made upon the dragon's neck. She was scared, but still she clung. "Turn back," she whispered. "Oh, *please*, dragon. Take me back."

She could not see the ice dragon's eyes, but she knew what they would look like. Its mouth opened and a blue-white plume issued, a long cold streamer that hung in the air. It made no noise; ice dragons are silent. But in her mind Adara heard the wild keening of its grief.

"Please," she whispered once again. "Help me." Her voice was thin and small.

The ice dragon turned.

The three dragons were outside of the barn when Adara returned, feasting on the burned and blackened carcasses of her father's stock. One of the dragonriders was standing near them, leaning on his lance and prodding his dragon from time to time.

He looked up when the cold gust of wind came shrieking across the fields, and shouted something, and sprinted for the black dragon. The beast tore a last hunk of meat from her father's horse, swallowed, and rose reluctantly into the air. The rider flailed his whip.

Adara saw the door of the farmhouse burst open. The other two riders rushed out, and ran for their dragons. One of them was struggling into his pants as he ran. He was barechested.

The black dragon roared, and its fire came blazing up at them. Adara felt the searing blast of heat, and a shudder went through the ice dragon as the flame played along its belly. Then it craned its long neck around, and fixed its baleful empty eyes upon the enemy, and opened its frost-rimed jaws. Out from among its icy teeth its breath came streaming, and that breath was pale and cold.

It touched the left wing of the coal-black dragon beneath them, and the dark beast gave a shrill cry of pain, and when it beat its wings again, the frost-covered wing broke in two. Dragon and dragonrider began to fall.

The ice dragon breathed again.

They were frozen and dead before they hit the ground.

The rust-colored dragon was flying at them, and the dragon the color of blood with its barechested rider. Adara's ears were filled with their angry roaring, and she could feel their hot breath around her, and see the air shimmering with heat, and smell the stink of sulfur.

Two long swords of fire crossed in midair, but neither touched the ice dragon, though it shriveled in the heat, and water flew from it like rain whenever it beat its wings.

The blood-colored dragon flew too close, and the breath of the ice dragon blasted the rider. His bare chest turned blue before Adara's eyes, and moisture condensed on him in an instant, covering him with frost. He screamed, and died, and fell from his mount, though his harness hand remained behind, frozen to the neck of his dragon. The ice dragon closed on it, wings screaming the secret song of winter, and a blast of flame met a blast of cold. The ice dragon shuddered once again, and twisted away, dripping. The other dragon died.

But the last dragonrider was behind them now, the enemy in full armor on the dragon whose scales were the brown of rust. Adara screamed, and even as she did the fire enveloped the ice dragon's wing. It was gone in less than an instant, but the wing was gone with it, melted, destroyed.

The ice dragon's remaining wing beat wildly to slow its plunge, but it came to earth with an awful crash. Its legs shattered beneath it, and its wing snapped in two places, and the impact of the landing threw Adara from its back. She tumbled to the soft earth of the field, and rolled, and struggled up, bruised but whole.

The ice dragon seemed very small now, and very broken. Its long neck sank wearily to the ground, and its head rested amid the wheat.

The enemy dragonrider came swooping in, roaring with triumph. The dragon's eyes burned. The man flourished his lance and shouted.

The ice dragon painfully raised its head once more, and made the only sound that Adara ever heard it make: a terrible thin cry full of melancholy, like the sound the north wind makes when it moves around the towers and battlements of the white castles that stand empty in the land of always-winter.

When the cry had faded, the ice dragon sent cold into the world one final time: a long smoking blue-white stream of cold that was full of snow and stillness and the end of all living things. The dragonrider flew right into it, still brandishing whip and lance. Adara watched him crash.

Then she was running, away from the fields, back to the house and her family within, running as fast as she could, running and panting and crying all the while like a seven year old.

Her father had been nailed to the bedroom wall. They had wanted him to watch while they took their turns with Teri. Adara did not know what to do, but she untied Teri, whose tears had dried by then, and they freed Geoff, and then they got their father down. Teri nursed him and cleaned out his wounds. When his eyes opened and he saw Adara, he smiled. She hugged him very hard, and cried for him.

By night he said he was fit enough to travel. They crept away under cover of darkness, and took the king's road south.

Her family asked no questions then, in those hours of darkness and fear. But later, when they were safe in the south, there were questions endlessly. Adara gave them the best answers she could. But none of them ever believed her, except for Geoff, and he grew out of it when he got older. She was only seven, after all, and she did not understand that ice dragons are never seen in summer, and cannot be tamed nor ridden.

Besides, when they left the house that night, there was no ice dragon to be seen. Only the huge corpses of three war dragons, and the smaller bodies of three dragonriders in black-and-orange. And a pond that had never been there before, a small quiet pool where the water was very cold. They had walked around it carefully, headed toward the road.

Their father worked for another farmer for three years in the south. His hands were never as strong as they had been, before the nails had been pounded through them, but he made up for that with the strength of his back and his arms, and his determination. He saved whatever he could, and he seemed happy. "Hal is gone, and my land," he would tell Adara, "and I am sad for that. But it is all right. I have my daughter back." For the winter was gone from her now, and she smiled and laughed and even wept like other little girls.

Three years after they had fled, the king's army routed the enemy in a great battle, and the king's dragons burned the foreign capital. In the peace that followed, the northern provinces changed hands once more. Teri had recaptured her spirit and married a young trader, and she remained in the south. Geoff and Adara returned with their father to the farm.

When the first frost came, all the ice lizards came out, just as they had always done. Adara watched them with a smile on her face, remembering the way it had been. But she did not try to touch them. They were cold and fragile little things, and the warmth of her hands would hurt them.

THE HIDDEN DRAGON

Barbara Delaplace

Sarah remembered exactly when she first saw the dragon. It was just a glimpse out of the corner of her eye, and vanished as soon as she turned her head to look directly at it, but she was sure of what she saw all the same: a flash of rust-colored scales on a snaky, spike-fringed tail that disappeared amongst the shrubbery.

It was a mistake turning her head. James was in the middle of one of his lectures and immediately noticed her inattention. "I expect you to listen to me when I'm talking to you, Sarah. It's not time for another lesson in courteous behavior, is it?"

She instantly focused on him again, the all-too-familiar chill running down her back. "I'm sorry, James. I shouldn't have let myself be distracted. It's just something I saw out in the yard. It was so odd—" She bit her lip and stopped. Better not to have said anything at all. James was a practical man, as he often said. He had no time for fantasy or metaphysical mumbo jumbo.

241

"What do you think you saw?" His tone was reasonable, controlled, and her anxiety began to grow.

"Nothing, James, really."

"You must have seen *something*, Sarah. You turned away from me. It must have been something very unusual for you to suddenly ignore me like that." His voice was becoming harder.

"I thought I saw a deer." She didn't dare mention what she *really* thought she'd seen. "It must have been my imagination. I'm sorry, I won't let it happen again."

"A deer is hardly odd out here, Sarah. Our home is isolated and we see them fairly frequently. I think you're lying to me." His eyes were cold as he looked at her. "I won't stand for that."

The sessions in the bedroom were always worse if he accused her of lying. Better to tell the truth.

"It was just out of the corner of my eye. For a moment . . ." she paused.

"Yes?" His patience was an ominous presence.

"For a moment it looked like . . . like the tail of a dragon. But it couldn't have been." It *couldn't* have been. "It had to have been a deer, and I just imagined the rest. I know better."

She'd appeased him, slightly. His face wasn't as terrifyingly frozen. "You have an overactive imagination, Sarah. We both know that. It's something we have to work on together. Might-be's and what-if's are simply a waste of time. I think we'd better discuss it in the bedroom." He turned away.

"Yes, James." He was right; he always was. It must have been her overactive imagination. She steeled herself and followed him.

Her back was too painful to let her sleep. So she waited until the sound of James' breathing became slow and even—he always slept deeply after an evening session spent correcting her—then slipped quietly from the bedroom.

Once she reached the living room Sarah relaxed, alone and safe. For now, at least. The armchair was out of the question because of her back, so she settled cross-legged on the floor in front of the huge picture window overlooking the flower beds and the stream. The scene was so peaceful in the moonlight, as always. She sighed with pleasure. When she was alone and it was quiet and she could sit undisturbed—that was the best time of all.

She glanced across the lawn to the vegetable garden. She loved watching the deer that came to the brook to drink, but they were a constant threat to her salad greens and she kept a watchful eye on—

The dragon was there. Crouched quietly on the smooth lawn, neck gathered into a compact sinous curve, tail looping away in a graceful arc past the garden.

"No," she whispered. There weren't any such things as dragons. Maybe she was dreaming? But she could feel the shaggy texture of the rug under her hands, smell the cool freshness of the night air whispering in through the half-open window, hear the breeze rustling the leaves just outside. Her dreams never had this sharp reality of the senses.

The dragon uncoiled its neck and stretched out its head, seeming to test the air for some exotic scent. Moonlight shimmered off its scales, stealing away their daytime hues. Sarah watched the creature's supple movements, her startled fear briefly forgotten as the massive head quested to and fro, then swung back toward the garden. It nosed gently among the herbs bordering the garden's edges. She had an absurd impulse to shout at it to leave her favorite lavender alone, when it came out of its crouch and moved toward the house.

Sarah scrambled to her feet as her fear rushed back over her. She *had* to be imagining this! She backed away from the window, ready to run—where? part of her mind laughed hysterically. What protection was a window or a wall against a thing the size of a dragon? *But it wasn't real,* another part of her mind shouted. She backed into the coffee table and lost her balance, reached out a steadying hand—

—and when she looked up the dragon had disappeared. The lawn was empty. Somehow that was even more discomfitting. She knew she should go to the window—that's what James would do. No, he'd go outside, flashlight in hand, firmly resolved to show her the reality of the situation. There would be no dragon if James was here.

But she wasn't James, and it was very late. She was tired and confused; her back throbbed dully. There were painkillers and sleeping pills in the bathroom. She decided to make use of them to get some sleep—then she wouldn't have any more visions of mythical beasts in her yard.

The next morning James remarked solicitously on her wan appearance. "You should look after yourself better, Sarah—you're not getting enough rest."

"I feel fine, James."

"All right, then. I'll see you tonight." He gave her an abstracted kiss, his mind already on the demands of his job in the city, and was out the door.

She heard the car drive off as she finished her coffee and sighed. She'd slept, but the dragon seemed to lurk in one corner of her mind, and her slumber was restless. Somehow she got the impression it was a sentinal, watching for something. . . . Enough of this! she thought briskly. It was only a dream. Or hallucination. Or something. What she needed was a friend to talk to.

James didn't seem to appreciate how lonely she was out here. The place had been a good buy and was a good investment. But there were no neighbors, and she had no car to enable her to visit the city. ("After all, we really only need one car and I have to use it to get to work. Besides, you have lots to do, keeping the house and the garden shipshape. You don't have time to waste gossiping with idle women.") And somehow since their marriage, she'd lost track of her old friends, until now all she had, really, was her husband.

Oh, but this was self-indulgent nonsense, as James always said. He was right—she did have lots to do. And it wasn't going to get done if she just sat here drinking coffee. She picked up the dishes, and headed for the sink. Time to get started on the "lots to do."

She'd fully intended to start in on the dishes and the other housework, but when she glanced out the window and saw the dewy freshness of the morning, she couldn't resist the temptation. She could do the housework later—now was the time to enjoy the garden.

Sarah loved growing things. Fortunately, James felt a well-kept garden added to the value of their home, so she could indulge in her love with a clear conscience. The warmth of the sun, the droning of the bees, the green and the fragrant scents, all combined to soothe her spirit and leave her in a tranquil frame of mind. She knelt to inspect some lambs' ears. They were coming along nicely, and she stroked the soft furry leaves with pleasure.

She stood up and was about to go to the vegetable garden when she noticed a depression in the smooth expanse of grassy lawn. And there was another, some feet away from it. Muttering "moles" to herself, Sarah went over to inspect them. Each had several gouges in front of it, and there were a few dead leaves scattered about, their rusty-red color standing out sharply against the green background. She bent over to sweep them into her hand and realized she'd never seen any quite like these: long narrow ovals which gleamed dully, like leather. They were leathery in texture, too. Now what sort of plant would have leaves like that? A cactus, maybe? But cactus didn't grow around here; there was too much rain. And conifers simply didn't have needles like this. . . .

Then Sarah stopped deceiving herself and knew the depressions were footprints. And the leaves were scales.

So the dragon was real. Here's the evidence I can hold in my hand. She felt a strange sense of relief. *I'm not out of my mind, thank God!* she thought. *I really did see it.* But of course that led to the next questions: *Where did it come from? And why is it here?*

Though she pondered all morning as she watered and weeded and pruned, she couldn't seem to make sense of it. One thing she *did* know—there was no question of telling James about this, even though she had solid, tangible evidence of the dragon's reality. She *couldn't*; she didn't know why. But something within her rose so strongly in protest that she didn't dare even question the assumption.

By noon Sarah was finished in the garden. Her muscles ached; she was more than ready for a break. And the gurgling of the stream was a seductive reminder of how good the water would feel. Taking her cap off and wiping her perspiring face, she walked down the slope of the lawn to the brook. At the edge, she sat down and removed her sneakers.

"Ahhhhhh," she sighed as she dabbled her bare feet into the cool water. "Just what the doctor ordered." She leaned back but decided she'd be more comfortable on her stomach; the bruises on her back were still too sensitive. She rolled over and rested her chin on her forearms. It was so relaxing just listening to the sounds of the stream, not having to worry about anything. *Not even James' demands*, said a tiny voice within.

The fugitive thought made her start guiltily. Why, James didn't demand much. And it wasn't as if she had anyone else to worry about, what with no children. Compared to the workload so many women carried these days, she was fortunate indeed that all she had to worry about was James.

She realized she was hearing more than just the sounds of the stream—there was also a sound of crunching or snapping, as if something was being broken in half. And it seemed to be coming from James' workshop.

The workshop was some yards away from the house and shaded by several towering evergreens; an insulated line was strung from the house to provide electricity. Squirrels lived in the evergreens and had made both the workshop roof and the power line part of their personal elevated highway. Probably one of them was simply working its way through a lunchtime pinecone, but Sarah thought she'd better check just in case it had decided to gnaw through the power line instead—a couple of the trees' inhabitants had developed a regrettable taste for electrician's tape. She got to her feet and picked up her abandoned sneakers, then walked back up the slope.

She was halfway up the hill when she realized the sound wasn't coming from the roof of the workshop but rather midway between the two buildings. And it was too loud to be made by a snacking squirrel. Squirrels didn't hiss to themselves either. Tension tightened her stomach as she reached the top. She had an uneasy feeling she knew what might be making the sounds.

Her premonition was right. The dragon had returned.

Its head lifted and turned sharply toward her as she appeared, and Sarah stepped back nervously. But it made no move toward her and simply regarded her calmly. As in her dreams, it gave a sense of purpose, of watching for something.

She noticed the creature seemed to have brightened in color

since that first glimpse yesterday. Its body glowed a rich mahogany red, while the crest of spikes that ran the length of its neck and back were copper-colored in the sunlight. So were the powerful claws on each foot.

Sarah gasped in dismay when she realized what was between those front feet: one of James' fly fishing rods, now a splintered ruin. Obviously that was the source of the snapping noises that had first attracted her attention. But how had the dragon gotten hold of it? Her glance darted to the workshop, where James kept his fishing tackle. Several rods leaned against the wall, while others were scattered about in the grass. Now she remembered; he'd been working on them yesterday evening. Keeping a watchful eye on the dragon, she went over and restored them to order.

But she wouldn't be able to explain the broken rod to James. What could she do? Fear welled up inside her as she thought of what *he* might do. The only thing she could think of was to hide the remains of the rod in the garbage, and pretend—convincingly, she desperately hoped—that she had no idea what happened to it when he noticed it was gone. She knew he'd notice; by malicious chance the dragon had destroyed the one rod he'd be sure to miss, his favorite black graphite.

This was assuming the dragon would move away from what was left of the fishing rod, of course. Something that large moved when *it* wanted to, she thought wryly. But to her amazement, the great beast backed carefully away from the splintered bits, then turned and moved away into the trees.

Sarah didn't wait to question her good luck. She swiftly gathered up the broken pieces and took them into the house. There, she wrapped them up in old newspapers before disposing of them in the trash can.

She was on tenterhooks when James came home, but this time chance was with her. He'd brought home work from the office, and immediately after dinner he became immersed in it, only emerging when it was time for bed. Sarah breathed a grateful prayer for escaping—thus far—and went to bed herself. But she didn't sleep well.

* * *

For several days James continued to be occupied by work. But one evening he came home early. She was in the kitchen, busy with a new pastry recipe, when he swept in, caught her up in a hug, and announced, "All finished up! And I'm taking a few well-earned days off."

She hugged him back. "That's wonderful, James. You've been working so hard."

"That's what Peter said when he told me to take the time. And I know just what I'm going to do—a little fishing."

Somehow she kept the smile fixed on her face, even though her stomach tightened. "Just what you need, some time to outwit a few trout."

He didn't seem to notice her tension. "I'm going to change and go out to the workshop to get my gear ready. Pine Lake, here I come!" He released her and went into the bedroom to change out of his suit.

She was glad her voice sounded so natural. "I'll call you when dinner's ready."

"Fine!" A minute later, he came through the kitchen and headed out the back door toward the workshop.

Anxiety gnawed at her while she finished the pastry and prepared the salad and vegetables for the meal. But there was no sound of the workshop door slamming, no outburst of cursing. She started the meat cooking, then went out onto the front porch. Perhaps looking out over the stream would calm her down.

It didn't. The dragon was coiled up on the front lawn. Her fear increased sharply. James mustn't see it! *Why not?* an inner voice asked. *Just* what *would he do about it? What* could *he do about it?* But it didn't help her unreasoning certainty that she couldn't let him see the dragon. It *had* to go away. *So what are you going to do? Shoo it away with the broom? Get the Dragonsbane from the medicine cabinet?*

Without stopping to think how bizarre—or dangerous—her behavior appeared, she stepped off the porch and walked toward the beast. It watched her approach with unblinking eyes. Her steps slowed as she got nearer, until she stopped a few yards away.

She hadn't really realized how big the dragon was, until now. With the body curled up, it was difficult to tell its length, but its head alone was as big as her torso. And she noted with surprise that it had blue eyes. *I never heard of a dragon with blue eyes*, she thought. Of course, now that she thought of it, none of the stories she'd read about dragons mentioned their eye color at all. And there was something else about its eyes. Something about them was strangely familiar. . . .

With a start, she remembered why she was out here: to somehow get the dragon to go away. As if it heard her unspoken thought, it uncoiled its body, and she backed hastily away. It paused for a moment to yawn, and Sarah felt her blood go cold at the glimpse of the daggerlike teeth lining upper and lower jaw. Then the vast mouth closed again. The creature regarded her steadily for another moment, then glided away into the trees. She watched it go with enormous relief, then returned to the kitchen and dinner.

James came into the house just as she was about to call him, his face puzzled. "Sarah, have you seen my graphite rod?" he asked.

Her anxiety returned in a sudden rush, but she kept her voice steady. "Why, no. I haven't been inside the workshop for a long time, you know."

"Yes, yes, I know that. You haven't run into it anywhere else, by any chance?"

Her heart in her mouth, she replied, "No, I haven't."

"Neither have I. It must have been one of the ones I loaned to Peter. It figures, now that I want to use it. I'll have to ask him about it Monday. You can serve now." And with that, he sat down at the table. To her relief, there was no further mention of the missing fishing rod.

Sarah didn't sleep well again that night. Between worrying about whether James would discover she was lying and wondering about the dragon's continued presence, she tossed and turned through the dark hours.

In the morning James noted her pale, tired face. "You've been looking run-down the last few days, Sarah."

"I haven't been getting much sleep lately, that's all."

"I think you should take it easy today while I'm gone. It'll do you good."

"Well, perhaps after I get the housework done."

"That'll be fine." And giving her a peck on the cheek, he hurried out the door to finish loading the car for his fishing trip.

After he left, she'd intended to start in on the housework, but the singing of the birds in the morning air lured her outside and down to the brook. The grassy bank, warmed and fragrant, invited her to lie back and bask in the sunlight. And she was so tired. She'd just close her eyes for a moment. . . .

"Sarah!" James' angry voice snapped her awake. He was standing above her, furious. She blinked, glancing about hastily, and realized from the angle of the sun how late it was. Why, she had been so weary she must have slept all day! "Sarah! You're not listening to me!" She realized James was still talking to her and scrambled to her feet. "I come home and what do I find? The breakfast dishes still undone! Dinner not started!"

It must have been because she wasn't fully awake that she was so reckless. "But James, it's not as if the dishes *had* to be done. I'll do them tonight. And I'll start dinner right away and we can eat in half an hour."

"I don't expect to have to wait for my dinner because my wife has been wasting the day sleeping!"

"But you said I should take it easy today, that I wasn't getting enough rest. . . ." Her voice trailed away as she saw his face.

"Are you contradicting me, Sarah?"

She lowered her eyes and replied in a low voice, "No, James."

"It certainly sounded to me like you were. No wife of mine contradicts me. I'm going to have to correct you for this."

Fear, her familiar friend, returned. "I'm sorry, James."

"That's too bad, Sarah. Apologies aren't enough. You seem to delight in thwarting me, and I'm going to punish you for it. Come along." He turned and started up the sloping lawn to the house.

And once again, out of the corner of her eye, she saw the dragon. It seemed to shine red-gold in the rays of the late afternoon sun. She hastily focused her attention on James' back. Right now she had more important things to worry about. Dutifully she followed him.

Once they were inside the house, she turned toward the bedroom, but his voice stopped her. "Where do you think you're going, Sarah?"

Timidly, she answered "I thought you wanted to . . ."

"I want you to fix my dinner first. We'll deal with your laziness and insubordination later."

Dread ran through her. But what could she do? "Yes, James, of course. I'll start it right away."

And as she drearily started her preparations, she could hear James in the bedroom making his preparations for after the meal: the sound of a limber rod whipping through the air and smashing down on the pillow. The sound sickened her.

The next morning she hurt so much she didn't want to move; her back, buttocks and thighs throbbed with pain. But James, as usual, behaved as if nothing at all had happened the night before. "Good morning, Sarah. It's a beautiful day. Why don't you get up and we'll have breakfast together out on the lawn?"

Her voice was muffled. "I'm afraid I don't feel very well, James. Thank you all the same, but I think I'll stay in bed for a while."

"Can I bring you something to eat? Or some juice or coffee?"

"No, thank you. I'll just rest for a while."

"Whatever you wish." He finished dressing and left the room. Once alone, she managed to roll out of bed and moved unsteadily into the bathroom. She opened the cabinet and took out a bottle of pain-killing tablets. It was safe to take them now—James didn't like to see the damage he caused during the sessions in the bedroom. Then she walked stiffly back into the bedroom and lay down again in her customary position, on her stomach, waiting for the pills to ease the pain and make her drowsy. She was dimly aware of James coming in to brush his teeth, telling her he'd be out in his workshop. Then she drifted away into the arms of sleep. And seemed to feel the presence of the dragon at the edge of her mind, watching, waiting.

By the following day, she didn't hurt so much and was able to move around fairly easily. James was still asleep when she stepped into the bathroom and shut the door, so the sound of the water filling the bathtub wouldn't wake him. She stripped off her robe and turned so she could inspect the back of her body in the mirror. Well, at least it no longer looked quite so raw. With resignation, she poured baking soda into the lukewarm water, turning it into a soothing bath. She glanced at the mirror again, and the sight of the wounds striping her body suddenly enraged her. *What* right *had he to do this to her?* But just as quickly she pushed the mutinous thought down. James was her husband; she'd married him for better or worse, till death parted them. She took those vows very seriously.

She turned to face the mirror. *Count your blessings,* she told herself wryly. *At least he doesn't hit you in the face. No black eyes for Sarah.* Her eyes were one of her best features. She played up their blueness with . . . her thoughts stopped abruptly as she stared at her reflected face. The dragon had eyes exactly the shade of her eyes—*that's* why they looked familiar! That would give anyone a shock—seeing a part of themselves transformed into a monster like that.

Seeing a part of themself transformed. Suddenly she remembered how the dragon had twice done what she wished it to. How it had nosed at the lavender, her favorite of all the plants in the garden. How it had known which fishing rod was James' particular pet rod. How it appeared whenever she was particularly upset and frightened, when James . . . no! *No!* Coincidence. It *had* to be. *It* had *to be!* Such a monster couldn't have *anything* to do with her! She was a gentle woman, a dutiful and loving wife. James once told her it was her gentleness that had attracted him most of all. Something that powerful and dangerous couldn't be *any* part of her! *It wasn't her!* There was a startling clash of breaking glass. She realized she'd smashed her clenched fist against the mirror, sobbing aloud.

"Sarah! Are you all right?" James pulled the bathroom door open, shock in his face as he surveyed her tear-stained face, the broken mirror, her bleeding hand.

"No! Get away from me!" she sobbed, throwing on her robe and brushing past him.

"Sarah! Come back here! Sarah!" He was coming after her, and she couldn't bear to face him, not right now.

"Leave me alone!" She ran into the kitchen, then the living room, her heart racing.

"Sarah, come here! Now!" He was getting closer.

"Go away!" she cried.

"Are you defying me, missy?" His voice was loud and angry, and as he entered the living room, she saw he was infuriated with her.

She ran out onto the porch, down the steps, to the lawn. If she could only get away— She stumbled over the edge of a flower bed and fell to the ground. She could hear his footsteps, his harsh breathing, and rolled over to face him, ignoring the fierce ache in her back and buttocks. His face was flushed and he reached down to grab her arm, jerking her up to her feet—

—there was a roar behind them. James turned, disbelief and fear on his face when he saw the dragon, glowing fiery red, rearing above him. It roared again, mouth gaping wide, those vicious teeth gleaming in the morning light. The great head snaked down and the jaws closed around his torso. He screamed in terror and agony as the monster effortlessly lifted him high in the air. Sarah watched in horror as he struggled feebly in the dragon's grip, screaming again and again until the jaws crunched closed, cutting the awful sounds off. Then with terrible ease, the neck corkscrewed sideways as the dragon flung the body away.

Sarah sank to the ground, shaking. It seemed deathly quiet now. The dragon curled up, watching her quietly. It no longer glowed red but was its original rusty color.

She sat there for a long time, until the dragon had gone and the shaking stopped.

She'd have to call the police. She'd tell them she'd heard the sounds of a bear, a grizzly, that it attacked her husband, that she'd heard the screams. She—they—didn't own a gun, so the police wouldn't expect her to be able to rush to James' defense. "No, we didn't hunt, officer," she could hear herself saying. "My husband enjoyed fishing, but—" she could hear the break in her voice that would come there.

They'd believe her. Really, there was no other possible explanation, was there? And they'd be nice to her. A new widow who had just lost her husband thanks to the attack of a wild beast? They'd treat her gently. That would be a nice change after the way James treated her.

They'd *better* be nice to her. After all, if they weren't, the dragon would come back. . . .

$\mathcal{L}$AST DRAGON

Steve Rasnic Tem

Alec thrashed in bed. His muscles cramped. His right arm flapped and struck his chest. He had been dreaming that his wife's tongue was scraping at his eyes, his son's fingers clawing his shoulders. So real that his night's sweat was irritating the wounds.

His left fist tightened reflexively and made a painful knot under his lower back.

His body felt huge and unmanageable. It rocked and shook out of control.

His eyes sprang open and tried to focus. He coughed into his sheets and, terrified of choking, managed to turn his mouth to the side.

On Sunday mornings, he used to hide in bed until noon. His mother warned him about what happened to lazy boys who didn't go to church.

His father used to toss him into the air, too high. He'd kept his arms rigid and immobile at his sides in fright. This one thing had frightened him, this one thing. He'd never flown before, and it had scared him. No logical power could hold him up. It was magic.

"Daddy! Stop!"

"Fly, Alec! Fly! I won't drop you!"

Then one day his father did drop him. Alec had fallen slowly, trying to push his arms out to break the fall. But he had been immobile. For just a few moments, he had been paralyzed.

Alec was fully awake now. The room was dark; heavy curtains covered most of the walls. "Light," he whispered. Nothing. Someday, as the sclerosis increasingly affected his throat, the house's computer would have to be reprogrammed to allow for a wider range in interpreting vocal commands. But this morning he knew it was just fatigue, just a lack of focus. He concentrated, and after a time again said, "Light." Curtains pulled back; ceiling panels began to glow dimly. "Light light light," he said, and the brightness increased almost to daytime intensity. He could feel Earth's sun beyond the sheer yellow gauze that covered the windows, and soothing familiarity chased away the night's last alien dreams.

Earth's sun. He had to remind himself. He saw so little of the outside world that he could have just as easily been on Bennett, sleeping in the corporate headquarters there.

His throat burned from getting the lights on. And there was always this additional strain, not knowing if it was going to work anymore, if he was going to be left whispering in the dark, his throat aching, a headache blossoming from his attempts. He could have used the timer and saved his voice, but he never did. Each morning he wanted to make sure his larynx still worked.

Rick should have been up by now. Alec hated waiting; it made him feel helpless. But if he complained, the man might quit, and Alec wasn't up for another change.

The entire house could be equipped with personal-care robotic handlers and controllers. It wouldn't cost him much; a few technicians from one of his plants could install the whole works. But he wanted humans around him, touching him, not a house full of metal arms. And robotic amplification wasn't anything like doing it on his own, anyway. At least he did have the choice. He was Alec Bennett. That name had control over people and things, even if the man behind the name did not.

Today, his wife and children were moving out of the house. He hadn't had the power to hold them, the words to convince them to stay. Most of the arguments had stopped this past year—he'd felt relieved. He'd thought things were going to be okay now. But they'd all just been avoiding him, not saying what they felt, not wanting to provoke an argument. They were hiding from him.

The last big argument had been a year ago with his older son, Gene, fifteen at the time. It had been typical—unproductive, frustrating. And frightening, because now Gene was old enough to really hurt him if the argument went too far, if the volatile teenager were to lose control. That had become the peak of Alec's feelings of helplessness: to be frightened of his own son. It made him ashamed, and yet now he missed all the arguing—at least then his son was talking to him.

"You can't tell me what to do!" Gene had looked almost crazy in his anger, and as the boy continued to shout, Alec found himself wondering at what terrible thing he had brought home to them all.

"The aide quit, Gene. And my tube's popped. See, it runs down through the bedding and attaches to the pumps under the floor—"

"Jesus! You're messin' yourself, Dad!"

"Please, just get the tube back in."

But his son had just backed away from him, looking at the body of his origin wasted by the disease. His son's face was full of fear and loathing for the disease. Alec had spent hours explaining the nature of the disease, how no one was going to "catch" it. But now he could see that little of that must have sunk in. His son was seeing his own body lying there on the bed, spent and wasted.

"You're always asking me to touch you like that, and there's machines, Jesus. I mean, you can afford it."

"Gene, the tube!"

But Gene had already left the room. Alec could hear him debating with his brother and sister about whose turn it was to help, and arguing over the personal-care machinery again. They hated him, or maybe they hated the disease, not that there was much difference anymore. And Marie was off at some club meeting again, so she couldn't talk to them.

"Get in here, *all* of you!" No one answered. He'd shouted for several minutes before giving it up. He'd lost them. He couldn't even tell them to do something as simple as throwing an empty milk carton away, and be sure they'd do it.

A hand was rocking his shoulder. His eyes blurred. Sometimes it seemed that, when he wasn't remembering the bad times, he couldn't recall their faces at all. The hand touched him again. "Rick?" he whispered.

"Yes, Mr. Bennett. Want a bath today?"

Alec looked down. Rick's arms were protected by membranous gloves, a little paler than white flesh, more the color of cotton after it's been boiled. He'd thought the man had finally gotten over the fear of infection. "Afraid of catching a cold?" Rick didn't respond. "Talk to me, Rick."

Rick busied himself with the covers. "Just trying to be sanitary, Mr. Bennett. Now, how about that bath?"

Actually, Rick was braver than most; money could buy a little courage now and then when he really needed it. But it was getting harder every year, and Alec wondered how long Rick was going to last. They all thought they were going to catch the disease, and he honestly couldn't reassure them completely; no one knew enough about Bennett's Sclerosis.

Sometimes Alec imagined tiny cracks appearing in his skin. Sometimes he could swear he could see them, and they would spread onto Rick's arm, flaking the flesh away.

That first year after Alec came back from Bennett the media had been in a state of excitement that was almost sexual. The Bennett story had encompassed a number of topics sure to tantalize and entertain the public. The corporation-owned planet. The father's questionable business deals. And the rich, pampered son who was the first and only known victim of an extraterrestrial disease. Payoffs to regulating agencies. Aggressive exploitation of the strange new landscape. Rumors of safety violations. Rumors of dragons.

An insistent touch at his shoulder. "Mr. Bennett? Your bath?"

"No," he said, staring at the gloves covering Rick's arms and hands. "No, no thanks."

Rick didn't seem surprised. In the best of times Alec had an intense fear of the water. Even taking a bath, Alec would picture himself sinking beneath the surface, unable, even unwilling, to raise his arms to save himself. Whenever he and his assistants drove or flew over rivers or lakes, he'd have to turn from the window.

"Messages this morning?"

Rick pulled the recorder out of his back pocket and pushed the red button. After a squawk of interference Alec could hear the voice of Malcolm, nominal head of Bennett Corp. ". . . everything's ready. Not much chance of anybody catching on. Needless to say, I would still like to talk you out of this. We have an entire squadron of pilots ready to send up after this thing. . . ."

"Shut it off," Alec said.

"There's more."

"I don't need any more."

Alec looked at the wall. The polished mahogany beyond his feet stretched a good twenty feet left of his bed, another twenty feet right. Patterns of light and shade moved across the segments of bone that had been set into the wood planks.

The enormous skull had been taken apart; the three plates that had formed the cap of the skull had been spread and mounted here into a broad arch. A six-foot nasal ridge hung from the center. Below these pieces, bolted to the wall a few inches from the floor, were the numerous broken sections of a long, thin jawbone. Alec could slice his hand open with just a careless touch along that bone, but he was far removed from that kind of danger.

Rick followed his gaze. "I don't know how you can stand to look at that thing. Makes my skin crawl just to be in the room with it."

"In fact, I don't think it's that skull making your skin crawl." It was hardly a skull, more like a collection of armored plate, what had been left once the skin had burned away. Alec could picture where the creature's gas sacs had been—in both cheeks and temples, and suspended under the jaw. The eyes had been deeply set on either side of the nasal ridge. Dark red, glowing like the mahogany. The mouth so wide. That last time on Bennett he'd peered directly into that hunger, the jaws steadily expanding until he'd thought the mouth might swallow the ship whole.

It had been night, and his father had insisted that the pilot shield the exhaust so the creature's infrared wouldn't pick them up. His father had wanted to *show* Alec. He was always showing him things. The crash had been sudden, unexpected. An accident. No one had thought the dragon intended to attack. When the mouth had dropped open and they had stared at the night inside, it had seemed that the beast was showing surprise rather than hunger or rage.

Alec had been thrown out before the explosion. Soaked in the creature's vital fluids, he'd escaped with just a broken leg and a few scrapes. Or so they had all thought.

Watching the shadowed mahogany for movement, for the faintest flicker of light, he heard Rick say, "So they think that's the carrier. That *thing*."

The fire had been nightmarish in its speed and volume. With three to four percent more oxygen than Earth, the planet was a firetrap. The creature's sacs had exploded. It had roared, its head blazing, wings shrinking in the heat.

Rick's voice continued to intrude into Alec's thoughts. "Why don't you let them take care of it? You've got lots of pilots, and most of them better than you."

Either he had been delirious or the creature had turned its burning skull his way, looked at him, before falling ponderously into the flames.

"You're a rich man, but you're *ill*."

Alec willed himself to move, but could not. He felt huge, impossibly heavy. He felt his skin burning, imagined catching the sheets on fire. Rick started to move toward him. "Don't . . ." Alec gasped. "Let it be."

Rick stepped away from the bed and stared out the open window. "Just tell me when you're ready, Mr. Bennett." A tiredness was evident in the young healthy voice.

Standing by that window, Alec had first felt the symptoms of Bennett's Sclerosis. He'd had his father buried on the planet.

Rick was pulling nervously at the arm coverings he wore, as if trying to protect a larger portion of his body. As if the sclerosis might reach out and penetrate his skin. As if Alec had brought back from Bennett something more than a viral disease—a native of that planet, an alien that thrived within the house of his body.

"My best people don't think it's contagious, Rick. I've told you that before." That was true—his top researchers thought there had to be actual contact of body fluids—but all the same Alec felt like a liar.

Rick just stood there, his back to Alec, watching the sun through the window. "Just being careful, Mr. Bennett." Rick scratched at his sleeves.

"I pay you enough, don't I?"

"You do that. And I have a family to support. But that's not the only reason I stay." He said the last part almost angrily.

"I had a family. . . ." Alec stopped, embarrassed.

Alec had been back on Earth a month when he had felt the first signs of his illness. He'd been standing in this bedroom he'd shared with Marie and watching nothing in particular, still feeling a little disoriented because Bennett's sun was the same size and color as Sol and because this time of year the climate was similar.

His arms and legs had begun to tingle, a low-grade burn deep under his skin that had made him think at first that he must have stepped onto an exposed wire. No matter where he had moved, the strange, vaguely disturbing sensation continued. He had begun to feel dizzy and had sat back down on the bed for a time.

When after an hour the sensation had passed, he had gone in to work. He'd thought it was odd, but since it went away, he'd chalked it up to a sleep disturbance, the flu, maybe something he'd eaten. Then a month later his vision had begun to blur. A month after that, he had lost control forever. The illness progressed like a brush fire.

The disease made him feel, simply, *other*. It resembled multiple sclerosis in many ways, but MS had been cured over fifty years before. And Bennett's Sclerosis, as it was soon to be labeled, worked more quickly, scar tissue grew more rapidly—like a fungus, some said—and there appeared to be no periods of remission. People wouldn't touch him, as if afraid something might burst through his skin.

It had been like a machine running down. The immune system backfiring. The alien virus replicating the body's nerve tissue. So his body had become alien to itself, the body had become a dragon, attacking itself. It couldn't help itself—the invader had to be repelled. Scavengers in the immune system ate away at the myelin. First, its layers were pried apart, then nerve transmission began to short-circuit, then the myelin simply disappeared so that Alec became all exposed wires and loose electrical impulses. Scare tissue had crept over the nervous system the way ice sheathed the skeletal branches of a tree in winter.

His brain had been less seriously affected, his thoughts intact. Except sometimes thoughts arose that he did not recognize as his own.

"We're running a little late," Rick was saying, moving toward him. "Let me help you."

He tried to turn himself in bed. His arms flopped uselessly; he couldn't even feel them. He had the sudden, nonsensical fear that someone had cut them off when he wasn't looking.

A tremor began in his right leg. He tried to shut it off, but the mental plea had no effect.

"When are you leaving?" Rick asked.

"Next week."

"You know, I don't understand you. What if this just makes it worse?"

"I made *intimate* contact with the dragon. I was drenched in it. They think that's where the disease might have come from. Somebody has to get one of those things, dead or alive, so they can study it. Maybe they can find a cure."

"Let them send a *professional* pilot. Or a full-time hero."

"I have to see one again, myself. There may not be any more. My people have sighted only one the past four years. They think it's the last dragon. I just can't risk waiting."

Rick kept his eyes on Alec. When he walked around the room, he moved awkwardly, his head turned toward the bed. It was obvious to Alec that he was trying to avoid looking at the dragon skull.

"Want to get ready for the day, now?"

"Sure, why not?"

Alec dozed as Rick began rubbing him down with a damp cloth. Rick used to carry him into the bathroom for this. Not anymore. Alec had felt too vulnerable, sitting slumped over the toilet. He used to fantasize Marie coming to him, taking off her clothes. They hadn't made love in a very long time.

Someone stepped into the bedroom. He could sense someone by the door, just beyond the limits of his vision. He saw Rick turn around.

"Machines and some special clothes can do this, too, you know," Marie said. Alec felt momentarily disoriented. Rick turned back toward the bed, looking irritated. He bent over, grunted, and pulled up Alec's pants a little too roughly.

Alec tried to clear his eyes. He felt on the verge of tears. "Rick, my eyes . . ." Rick dabbed at his eyes and cheeks with a towel. Marie swam suddenly into focus. Dark-haired, doe-eyed, beautiful. "Machines have their place. But not here, not like this." Rick was wiping at the metallic caps set into the back of Alec's skull. "Careful, there. I'm going to be needing those soon." He looked up at his wife. "So . . . when are you leaving?"

"An hour, maybe two. You forgot to give me the key to storage."

Alec found himself chuckling mirthlessly. "I haven't been too good with details of late."

"Well, that makes you the perfect pilot, now doesn't it?"

Rick sighed. "He's a good pilot, actually. Or so I hear." He worked so furiously at the clothes that Alec was afraid they were going to rip.

"It's not safe!" Marie snapped.

"I *have* to do this. If you really still cared, you'd know that."

"They're really going to let you do this, huh? Go back there, find the thing?"

"*They're* not going to *let* me do anything."

"Chasing dragons, like some kid."

"There are dragons everywhere, Marie." Alec chuckled again. "It's a dirty job, but somebody has to do it."

Marie's voice broke. "Stay here, Alec. We'll stay. I don't really want to leave—you must know that. But I can't sit still while you do this stupid thing. It's bad enough watching you die from something you can't help. But you don't *have* to go back to Bennett. Stay, Alec. I'll talk to the kids."

Alec tried to control his trembling, but could not. He was broken meat, flopping, ugly. "No."

Alec heard the sound of ripping cloth. Rick cursed and began removing the shirt.

The bedroom door slammed. Alec felt a need to say something, but the silence was suddenly intimidating.

"Mr. Bennett?"

"Yeah?"

"Good luck." Rick gripped his hand, tightly enough that he eventually felt it.

Again he was seven years old. Again his father tossed him into the air. Again his father did not catch him. But he wasn't so afraid this time—he felt himself flying, despite his weight, despite his awkwardness, despite his doubt.

Alec dropped rapidly toward the enormous canyon bisecting the northern hemisphere of Bennett. He was fully plugged—adjusting the intensity of his more private thoughts against the almost subliminal babble of the computer medium. At last achieving some sort of balance, he felt the mental underpinnings of his ghostlike arms and legs reach out gradually and drift into the composite wings and weave-layered hull of his craft.

The illusion was that these actions were all conscious and deliberate on his part. In fact, the computer's controls had taken over and were leading him gently into the system, allowing him to become part of the machinery with the least possible discomfort and disorientation. Before most of his impulses to act had even reached the conscious level, they had been recognized, evaluated, then accepted or rejected by the computer. Reaction times were crucial on Bennett—with a gravity slightly higher than Earth's, even a short fall could be fatal. The dragon had evolved under those conditions; no human could beat that.

Here, he was as light as a dream.

The compound's staff was down eighty percent since his father died, for Alec no longer saw the need for personnel largely involved in resource exploitation. They had been all set up for him, the plane fueled, checked and ready, and everyone seemed remarkably compliant to his wishes. Malcolm must have already explained to them that their novice employer was stubborn. But when they first carried him in, Alec did notice a few disgruntled-looking pilots standing around.

He spun the plane upside down, then dropped and rolled to the left. Up here, it was as if his muscles could do anything. The computerized controls made each arm seem to have numerous independently moving joints. At times he was afraid of folding up like a suitcase and plummeting to the ground.

The predominant colors on Bennett were gray, gray-green, and red. Some of the red came from rock formations in and around the numerous canyons and short mountains. Earthquakes brought bits of red up into the gray rock fields.

The other red came from a short, thick plant—a strange amalgam of moss, fern, and shrub—with a brilliant crimson center. It grew everywhere on the planet. Many of these plants were spoiled by spots of black char.

A third of the plain south of Bennett Compound was now on fire, filling the thick air with carbon dioxide and tiny particles of black ash that attacked his windscreen like hyperactive gnats. Periodically, a cleansing spray washed through the microscopic V-grooves which tattooed the hull. Alec was aware of this spray as a vague, ghostlike dampness somewhere in his skin.

But even with the spray, particles occasionally burst into flame along the ship's fuselage. A sudden nimbus of white light or a rainbow blazed off the forward canard.

The constant fires were a nuisance, but they destroyed enough plants to keep the oxygen level down. A couple of percentage points more, and Bennett could have been an inferno.

Every few minutes the computer cycled through a systems check. He could eavesdrop when he was in the right state of mind. Electrical schematics overlapped microhydraulic graphic simulations on the undersides of his eyelids. Weaponry alignments multiplied across the mindscreen, then suddenly burst like bright, incendiary bombs.

He could visualize the wide telemetry shield, fielding impulses from his skull plugs and transmitting them to the computer controls, then feeding it all back through his ethereal, yet perfect-looking arms and legs and the parts of the plane his arms and legs had become.

The plane dropped past red-brown walls dirty with gray-green and crimson growth. He didn't see any fires in the immediate vicinity, but they were raging only a few miles away, and he appeared to be dragging the ash down with him. It swarmed over him so thickly that at first he thought his eyes had suddenly grown worse.

Broad plateaus and massive chimney formations rose from a valley floor still miles below him. At times they came close enough together to form their own narrow passages. He was afraid to drop much farther. It would be like a labyrinth down there. And he would need the height when the dragon ventured out, if it did.

The bodies of the mountains were ponderous, spotted with red and green disease. Enormous, infested mounds of alien flesh. He felt sure that, if he broke into them, there'd be alien maggots: blue and green and brilliant silver, star- and cone-shaped heads.

The forward canard helped pull him out of the drop. The sides of the fuselage, his sides, rippled once, then set for better air flow.

Now he had another vista on the canyon: a series of flat places along an ever-broadening series of cliffsides, arranged like enormous steps, rich with the crimson-hearted plants. On some of these steps he could see short, broad grazers, a smaller and slightly hairy version of the hippopotamus. One looked up in a kind of slow-motion startle, then lowered its head again. In the shadowed rock behind it, there appeared to be a wide tunnel opening.

Puff birds, their cheek sacs bloated comically, floated around the plane. If Alec looked carefully enough, he could see blotches of lizard colonies on the canyon walls, their jaws long and broad, crocodile-like. Hand-length insects with bloated wings and clawlike feet landed on the hull of his craft and were immediately washed away.

Wing, fin, and hull surfaces changed shape sixty times a second in a graceful, coordinated ballet.

He felt, to the core, lighter than air, with no care that his arms and legs were dead because he didn't need them any more. He felt the rockets within his dead fingers, the fire inside his eyes straining behind the goggles. Darkness filled his chest.

Then he saw the dragon. At first it was a bit of black ash, turning the corner of the rock tower far below him. Fluttering and twisting in the wind, it seemed the remnant of some scorched field of alien, vegetable life. It changed shape as it rose, from time to time sending out projections first one way, then another, so that at times it resembled a black, funereal pinwheel.

Then it was a bat, flapping slowly upward out of the shadowed valley toward the heat-baked peaks and plateaus at the top.

Then it was a small black sail boat, floating unsupported in the valley air. A ghost ship. A Flying Dutchman.

And then it was a dragon, resembling everything and nothing.

It was hard to see the thing's wings clearly. They were three times the length of his plane. Vaguely batlike, but with gas sacs lining the top and a doubling of the black-gray mottled skin where more gas might be trapped. The wing span appeared to be about eight times the height.

The dragon wrapped itself in its wings, then unwrapped, furled and unfurled, a dark lady teasing with her lingerie.

A wing dropped down, and Alec could see the dragon's head. The top of the skull was broad and pale, and Alec thought of the extinct condor. The eyes were large and opaque, seemingly without centers. The huge mouth dropped open, loose on its hinges, gulping air, as if hungry for anything that might cross it. He assumed that the large areas surrounding eyes and nose and mouth were gas-filled as well, since they appeared to change shape now and then, going from flat planes to gnarled ridges and swirls, giving the face as a whole an almost limitless expression.

The body was as dark as the wings, dull, and largely hidden.

The dragon lost altitude suddenly. For a moment it wrapped itself tightly for the drop, then unfurled its wings and let them drift up behind it. Alec watched as the dragon rapidly closed on one of the grazers on the steps below. Its wings spread, covering the step from view. Then it was rising rapidly, the grazer struggling in the dragon's jaws, a thin ribbon of yellow fluid trailing from a neck wound. When the dragon let go, the grazer smashed back onto the step and was still. The dragon settled slowly over it and began to gnaw.

The sheer physicality of the dragon was enough to take Alec's breath away. The plane rocked back and forth anxiously. Alec tried to stretch himself, but the wings would not budge. A warning light went off. He felt small and vulnerable, yet drawn to this physical massiveness, this beast of ancient health. Without thinking much about it, he felt the plane drifting down, the altitude readout racing past his eyes, blurring in a way that was almost soothing.

He was at nearly the same level as the dragon. It had finished its meal and winged itself gently off the cliffside. It hung in midair, watching the ship, watching Alec.

The creature's cheeks and neck billowed. Dust and ash shot up from it, as if caught in a thermal.

Alec let the plane ease closer, rocking slightly in the canyon updrafts.

The roaring thunder suddenly filled him, almost shaking the plane out of sync with him, a sensation he thought must be akin to out-of-body travel. A black cloud filled his field of vision at the same time that electrical charges worked at loosening his scalp.

The cloud fluttered and beat at his windscreen. Huge wing edges curled down at their tips. Then he was rocketing sideways, wings shifting, the rear thrust nozzles swiveling rapidly to direct him away from the looming blood-red rock walls.

Now the dragon was beneath him, massive devil's head coming up in front of the plane. The thing was flying upside down, blank eyes watching him, and Alec was suddenly bucking the plane ever so slightly, jabbing his belly fin at the dragon's exposed torso, then rolling out, climbing, banking, and settling back into his altitude once he saw that the dragon hadn't followed this time.

The dragon rose to a point distant and slightly beneath him, allowing him to circle. Its wings shuddered and rippled like a black paper kite. Only the head was immobile, held rigid in the turbulent air like an African mask. It drifted in the currents, watching.

Watching. One night when Marie had stood over him, thinking he was asleep, she'd lifted the covers, touching him hesitantly.

"Alec?" she'd whispered. "I'm . . . sorry. I just can't."

He had been surprised, and oddly touched.

The dragon revolved in midair, wings rising, dropping, paddling forward and back, darkness caught on a wheel.

The dragon was blowing air, or gas, out of cheeks, mouth, neck sacs. It began rising toward him. The instruments were in Alec's head, his eyes. The electronic goggles came up. Air speed, wind speed, and a half-dozen other functions read out along a muted silver band that ran across the bottom of the lens. Prepared to meet the dark, he aimed with the goggles and fired.

A cliff off to the dragon's left exploded into red debris. Alec trembled. A light flashed on his display. He looked out. The dragon was climbing above him.

From underneath, the creature's body blended in with its wings. Then the wings began to rotate, the head turned down, the dark mass hesitated, and the dragon was suddenly dropping. In seconds the mouth gaped grotesquely, the jaws unhinged, the gas sacs receding, expanding.

Alec pulled away and began to spin in an evasive maneuver. His sensation that the dragon was with him was confirmed by a ballet of graphic stick figures spinning at the bottom of his goggles. Black flaps slapped at his windscreen. He closed his eyes, felt his stomach drop as he cut the thrusters, tensed his shoulders, and prepared the surfaces for the drop. Swiveling the thrusters and cutting them back in, he roared toward the valley floor until he'd left the dragon behind him, then let his canards and altered surfaces bring him back up.

He stared at the dragon, feeling fire at the edge of his lips and at the tips of his fingers. The dragon stared down at him. It was terrible in its huge, limp fleshiness, but somehow Alec could not bring himself to imagine its destruction.

He saw the disease moving through his body, growing, reaching out to embrace his beautiful children and his wife. He saw their faces dissolve in slow motion, in blues and greens and reds.

Then he realized the dragon was descending farther toward the canyon floor, going away. And he was doing nothing to pursue it.

Alec watched until the dragon shrank back to a twist of black ash, then he dropped quickly, following the dragon around several twists in the narrowing canyon, past towers, chimneys, and spires. The surrounding cliffs loomed progressively closer, and at times Alec felt compelled to bring the wings in to reduce their span. Vegetation became sparser this far down, the lizards were in more abundance, and the grazers were nowhere to be seen.

Alec maneuvered through a series of swirled rock formations, following the rocketing dragon that now looked eagle-sized as it threaded the bull's-eyes, into dragon country.

Part of the wall began to curl overhead, and Alec could see that the canyon here was narrowing, gaining a partial roof. He hesitated, and the plane slowed down, but as the dragon drew farther away from him, escaping, he was seized by a sudden desperation and felt the plane shoot forward.

The wall curled more as he flew its length, forming more than a complete roof over him now, beginning to drop on the other side like a frozen wave. The space here was still hardly confined—a hundred such planes could have flown wingtip to wingtip and could still have room to spare. The walls danced with broken light.

He was enclosed in an almost seamless tunnel.

Alec suddenly experienced vertigo, imagined himself falling through miles of earth with no one there to catch him. He was too heavy, too awkward. Too ugly. He could not fly.

Bright warning lights tattooed his eyelids. He wondered that the plane had let him go this far, but knew proceeding was better than stalling out.

A message was up on his windscreen: THIS IS A HAZARDOUS FLIGHT AREA. ADVISE AGAINST PROCEEDING.

Alec wondered how long it had been there.

Amazingly, the plane flew on, faster and faster. He wished his wife and children could have seen it. Flying through the dark with no hands to hold him.

But it wasn't at all dark in the tunnel. He looked around. A yellowish growth covered the walls, broken here and there by a grayish, tendriled vegetation. But it was all blurred, blending together.

Up ahead the dragon revolved as if in slow motion, though Alec knew it was traveling faster than he was. Its wings were glistening panels of silver light that, when looked at, almost hurt the eyes. Rainbow light flowed over its head and down its back, trailed off into a tail of fiery dust, and traveled over the dark form, like hordes of migrating, fluorescent parasites in the dragon's skin.

The tunnel opened up periodically into a necklace of enormous chambers. The dragon slowed down, seeming to float, maneuvering coyly behind occasional spires and hanging lobes of stone. Coquettish.

Alec burned his thrusters lightly, wings tilted upward and the jets along his wing edges straining. So although there was forward progression, it was, like the dragon's, just short of a stall. An encounter between two winged insects.

Dark, concave ridges with sharp rock dividers, like the body impressions of a huge snake, ringed the chambers. Ribbed stone grew along the walls like roots or stiffened entrails.

His instruments detected activity in the recessed galleries, dark patterns of movement. Vague impressions of limbs and wings and unclassifiable appendages, nothing more.

The walls seemed closer, fecund and teeming. He suddenly imagined he could smell the stone.

Minute bits of material were bouncing off the skin of the plane, some of it darting off before it could be misted away.

Occasionally, something raked lightly along the underside of the ship, too close and too softly for stone.

Ahead of him the tunnel split, both branches far narrower than the one he had been in. The dragon floated at the juncture, its glowing wings and face drifting through highly stylized patterns of light, like a woman dancing in a kimono, her face painted a brilliant white.

He stared for what seemed to be a long time before following the dragon into the starboard tunnel.

The bright kimono began to wrap him. The plane revolved once rapidly on its axis, freeing itself. Alec imagined being wrapped within his own sheets, unable to get loose, paralyzed.

Ahead of him the dragon was imitating, making huge loops out of its pliant wings, twirling itself like a pinwheel.

Another tunnel was opening, even narrower. The dragon straightened and dove through it. Alec hesitated, the plane slowed, but there was nowhere else to go. He had to trust the dragon's expertise. He dropped his nose and entered.

The tunnel widened, then began to curve steadily upward, narrowing again. Tilting farther up, Alec could feel the strain. Soon they were almost vertical, facing a dimness ahead. Alec could now guess.

The dragon was racing up the hollow insides of a chimney formation. Alec shifted focus, gritted his teeth, and allowed his ship to follow as if towed. He felt sick to his stomach.

The ship gave him something for the nausea—he could feel the change beginning back in his throat. The center of the chimney was a seamless gray, speckled in red. The warning lights cooled, just in time for Alec to burst out of the chimney and into the dazzling sunlight.

As the plane floated out over the valley again, Alec scanned the sky frantically for some sign of the dragon. Nothing. He could see the gleam off the domes of Bennett Compound on the lip of the distant canyon wall. He'd come back to the departure point. Ground vehicles waited along the edge. He soared closer, into gathering shadow.

The shadow wrapped him up with a roar. Dark sheets wound around his chest until he couldn't breathe. A cry caught in his throat, his goggles blazed red, and with a high-pitched whine he pitched over, dragging his mind screaming behind him.

He fired again and again, turning dirt and rock and sky into flame.

His eyes came open with the sense that the plane was folding back its wings. He looked out, straight down, at a fast-approaching ribbon of blue. He was a child falling out of bed, the bedclothes around him so tightly he could not move. He was a child tossed and dropped by his father. He was a dragon too large and much too dark to fly.

The water rose. The aide had left him in his bath too long. He could not move his arms. His legs were gone. And he was slipping fast beneath the waves.

Alec screamed as muscles seemed to tear from bone, as bones bent and snapped. But he was rising, pulling out of the dive, and the disfigurement was only illusory, he reminded himself, no matter how terrible.

He strained for the canyon rim, dragging the plane up behind him. Enough. He had no business here.

And then he slammed into darkness, and the darkness gave way around him, then came back fighting, eating his windscreen, folding wing and fuselage, crushing him.

The devil's head roared above him, blank eyes blazing. Flames coruscated down wings shrinking, turning to silver.

Crazily, the ship's computers began cycling through a systems check. Alec watched microhydraulics multiply and disappear, electrical systems blossom. His perfect cobalt-and-lime legs and arms jumbled, doubled, then faded away.

And on the top edge of the telemetry shield, the dragon's severed muscles and nerves danced madly. He'd speared it, pinned it. He could almost imagine reaching out and grasping it in his hand. It wasn't going to get away.

He could see the edge of the cliff only a few yards above him, in one unobscured corner of his windscreen. Personnel in red suits lined the lip. He'd never make it; he could feel the plane falling.

He reached with his mind, and the thrusters pushed.

He felt his stomach rise, the leap in his thighs.

And suddenly he was lifting both plane and shield-pinioned dragon up over the edge of the cliff to solid ground. Plane and dragon skidded over broken rock, crimson-hearted scrub, and cinnamon-colored soil to a shuddering stop.

Alec thought of his body breaking, the disease spilling out, the disease murdering everyone around him, his beautiful, sleeping children, his wife. He heaved his useless body. He thrashed, palsied, cramping.

"Get him out of there!"

Technicians in black masks were pulling Alec out of his harness and trying to slip a mask over his face. He fought them. Smoke haloed their bulbous heads. He smelled something sharp. Ash began to fill his mouth.

He tried to turn. The dragon roared.

"Get him out!"

His head fell back when they lifted him. He could see the dragon rolling on its side, creasing a cindered wing. Huge blank eyes settled, stared.

Alec was exhilarated. It was like wrestling and pinning the nightmare, even as he was dreaming it.

Great cheeks blew clouds of gas that exploded into flame. Sacs ruptured, flames shot up, dark flesh blistered.

"Tether it!"

The techs carried metal claws to the dragon's trembling, black-gray mottled sides. The devil's head fell forward.

And Alec felt his own head fall forward. He looked down at his feet, caught by the twisted hull. His withered feet. Once grounded, he wasn't much of a bird, or dragon. His people were still trying to pull him out from under the telemetry shield. The dragon sprawled over the rest of the plane and beyond, sides heaving. Yellow liquid bubbled around the wound where the dragon had crashed into the plane, where the telemetry shield entered muscle and nerve, short-circuiting the dragon, becoming a part of the dragon. The dragon was part of his plane.

The dragon tried to rise, but kept jamming the plane wreckage farther into its wound as it struggled. The huge head faced Alec, still terrible, still beautifully dark.

This is wrong, he thought.

Alec was still in range of the telemetry shield—he could still control it, but his people almost had him loose, and then it would be too late.

Alec thought to lift his head. The dragon's head stirred.

Alec imagined his arms raised. Burnt wings fluttered.

Alec visualized the telemetry shield, the dragon pinned there. He tried to make the dragon rise, but it fell back, the wings flapping involuntarily, muscles cramped, its body huge, unmanageable, useless, alien.

What am I doing? he thought.

The dragon might contain his cure. He just needed to allow his people to drag it away.

The dragon thrashed, wings and muscles powerless. Its huge head turned. Alec stared into dark and found something familiar there.

They might be able to reverse the sclerosis. He'd walk. Marie and the children would come back. They'd all welcome him because he'd be clean again.

Who needs it? He'd changed, and if they'd loved him, they'd have accepted his changing.

The dragon's body flapped and rolled. Oddly lovely, mothlike. The last of its kind, tossed high and dropped, helpless. But still so strong; if it got back to its lair, it might be able to pick the pieces out. It might be able to heal. Again the eyes enveloped Alec, so dark they left him gasping.

He watched as the technicians struggled to attack the grappling claws. The thing bellowed hideously, leathery skin flapping. The beast had poisoned him, changed his life, infected him with its darkness.

The beast had changed him. The beast had brought out a life different from the one Alec had intended.

A darkness ran in his own veins, dragon's breath in his lungs. Another world lay under the bridges between neural synapses, a place where dreamers and their nightmares were the same, where only dragons and their hunters might fly.

The dragon had made him fly through the dark.

I have a choice, he thought.

Alec pushed with his mind just as his people pulled him loose of the plane, almost out of range of the telemetry link with the dragon. And the dragon rose with the crumpled plane clinging to its belly.

It staggered to the cliff's edge and went over while Alec watched, the technicians holding him back from the lip.

And under the shouts, the frantic scramble, Alec had a brief moment inside the dragon's head as it slipped over the cliff's edge, the wind filling broken wings, the darkness filling enormous eyes, heedless of the fire crisping its back as it dived once more into its alien world.

THE WIZARD'S BOY

Nancy Varian Berberick

The Venerable Alan is dead. In the Halls of the King they have summoned the bards to sing the lay of life, to tell the tales of his many long years. What tales they will tell, I can guess. There is one, however, which they will tell, and tell with only part of the truth. And that is the founding tale. We have become a revered Order, now. We have become wise men, counselors, respected lords. There was a time when the title "wizard" was not applied to our kind. There was a time when we were labeled conjurers, fortune-tellers, sorcerers, and worse. We were held in little respect, and much fear. It was not then as it is now. I have seen the lifetime of two kings. We are a long-lived Order. The Venerable Alan had seen the reign of two more kings than I. They love him now, and they mourn him.

Come to me, and sit close. Draw up your stools and benches. Heat your ale, and find a place of comfort. The tale I would tell you is one that I know you have not heard. The tale I would tell you is one the bards chose long ago to embroider and make more suitable to these times.

Are you comfortable? Is your ale warm? Listen, then, and I will tell you the tale of The Venerable Alan and The Wizard's Boy.

I did not become a wizard in the usual way. There was, in the time of my own youth, no Seeking, no itinerant wizard sweeping through the villages and castles in great pomp and mystery to choose among the young children for those who might be considered for wizard's teaching. Things, in my youth, were very much different. There was no Order. There were, at that time, but few wizards, and they were named sorcerers, and spoken of with fear and scorn.

First I was a thief. I was the son of a thief, and had to my credit the teachings of a father who ended his own long career upon the gibbet. I was privileged to attend that death. It was not I who considered it a privilege, but the folk of the town who finally caught and hanged him. It was in their minds, I think, to draw for me a lesson in the ending of a thief's life. It was a harsh lesson, and one which stayed with me ever.

That is not to say that I never stole again. Indeed, upon leaving behind that wretched town I had nothing but the clothes upon my back, the fraying boots upon my feet, and the admonitions of the townsfolk to go and steal no more.

But I tried. I journeyed ever with the sight of my father, hanging lifeless and ruined upon the gibbet. I knew that I wanted to face no such fate. I wanted no crossroads grave for myself. I knew, as well, that I was poorly equipped for any other career than thievery. We are fatalists as children. We understand the reality of life in a world where power is held by those older and larger than we. I do not wonder that I viewed my prospects with a large degree of cynicism.

Still, the degree and reason for my thievery changed. I stole now only what I must. I stole when I could find no work, when I could not beg for my needs. There is no place for a homeless boy of ten years in a world which views strangers with suspicion and mislike. I made attempts at respectability. I would stop in every good-sized town or village, petition innkeepers, stablemen, shopkeepers, for the work which would keep me clothed and housed and fed. I was not often successful, but I was persistent. It was not until I was certain that there would be no work for me that I stole what I needed. It was in such a village that I met Alan.

My boots, which had been frayed and wearing thin at the time of my father's death, had worn through and finally become useless. A morning and an afternoon of seeking employment had served to show me that there was no one in the village who would risk the presence of an unknown boy in his shop or inn. I had begged a few scraps of food and a sip of ale from the baker's wife at the nooning, but it was nearing night now, and my belly was making known to me its need for more. And my feet were sore and gritty with the dust and pebbles which had worked their way through the holes in the soles of my boots. As the sun bled in setting across the western sky, I sneaked, carefully, I thought, into the back of a tanner's shop. There were a pair of soft leather boots there which would nicely fit me. The shop was closed for the evening meal, and I did not think that the tanner would soon return.

I was wrong. I had the boots in my hand, not stopping to put them on, and was making my way back out through the rear of the shop when I was caught.

The tanner, a big, burly man, grabbed for me, missed, and sent up a shout which fair roused the whole of the small village. I ran, pelting through the narrow streets, the tanner and several others who had answered his cry giving chase. I tore past the baker's shop, down an alley, and through the courtyard of the village inn.

Dashing here and there, I made my way toward the inn, thinking to hide myself among the crowd which was surely within. There, I ran up against someone and I was caught.

I thought of nothing for a moment, for I was panicked. I heard my heart pounding in my ears, and surely I wheezed like a bellows for all to hear, for it had been a long run. Big hands grasped my arms. I staggered, for my knees were weak with the effort of the run and with fear. There would be a beating next, and I hoped nothing more.

He shook me, not hard, and not unkindly, but more to get my attention. He had it.

I looked up. Behind me the angry sounds of my pursuit faded. I knew that the tanner and his friends were there, clamoring for me to be turned over to them. I had no thought for them. There was no room for thought of anything but the man who held me.

He was tall, and not so young, but not so old. His robes were an indistinct brown color. Over these he wore a hooded cloak of fine burgundy wool. The hood was thrown back, revealing hair of darkest black, touched in places with grey and long enough to nearly touch his shoulders. His beard was thick and glossy, with more grey in it than his hair. His face, weather worn and craggy, spoke of travel. All this I saw, while trapped by the grip of his eyes. They kept me with a hold far surer than the grip his hands still had upon my arms. They were black, if they could be given any color, and they were as deep as cavern pools, running still and quiet. I looked into them, and I was lost to all around me.

I felt every secret being plumbed from me. I was convinced that this man was able to see into my most inner places and that nothing could be hidden from that dark regard. For myself, I learned nothing. That gaze which took and inspected every part of me gave nothing back. I might well have sought to use the night sky for a window. And then he spoke.

"Who are you, boy?"

There was gentleness in his voice. His eyes, then, revealed something a little like wonder and more like recognition.

I could do nothing but answer. I told him my name, and he nodded as though I had confirmed information which had already come to him from some other source.

"He stole the boots!" And with the tanner's aggrieved and belligerent cry, I was suddenly back in the real world.

The stranger looked past me then, and regarded those in the courtyard who muttered with uneasy agreement. He reached down, taking the boots which were still clutched in my hand. "These?"

"Aye." The tanner's tone was changing. There was a subtle undertone of fear beneath his word of agreement.

He tossed them to the tanner, who was too startled to catch them and let them fall to the cobbles at his feet. "They are returned."

The tanner grumbled behind me and muttered of punishment.

The hand still upon my shoulder turned me, and I faced my accusers. I thought then that he would turn me over to them, and I began to tremble, for I had no love of beatings. But he did not. He extended his arm so that I was enfolded in the burgundy cloak. I felt the cold nudge of the sword which was sheathed at his side. I knew then that there would be no beating.

The tanner looked about him for the support of his friends. There was none, for they were fading away, looking uncomfortable and making it clear that they would not press the matter. After all, the boots were returned, and they had business to which they should attend.

Alone, the tanner stood his ground a moment longer. His eyes went from the stranger to me, and widened suddenly with something like fear or perhaps understanding. He picked up his boots and hastily left.

"Why did you steal the boots?"

I looked up at him from the haven of his cloak and shrugged. "Mine are worn to useless, m'lord." I did not know that he could rightly claim the title, but I sensed that if he could not claim it by birth, I might so name him and not be far wrong.

He smiled. "So you steal?"

"It was the only way at the time."

"Ah. A pragmatist."

I did not know what that meant, but it did not sound insulting, so I only nodded. He laughed.

"Where do you live, boy?"

"Nowhere, m'lord."

"Your parents?"

"My father is dead this past year. My mother ten years ago."

"I see."

He seemed to consider something, and then nodded as though he had come to a decision. He regarded me closely again, and again I felt that I was swimming in waters too deep for my skill. I began to shake, and tried to stop it. I had little success. When he saw this, his smile deepened.

"I need a servant. But not one who will steal from me."

I lifted my chin at that, and answered far more arrogantly than I would have had I known who he was. "I do not steal if my belly is full, m'lord."

"Or if there are boots upon your feet?" He was amused.

"Aye."

He loosed me then, and I stepped away, but not far. He reached into the pouch which hung at his belt and took out several coins. "Go buy the boots, boy."

I took the coins and stared. They were twice what the boots were worth, and far more riches than I had ever held. Even so, I do not believe that I would have taken them and run. "All of this, m'lord?"

"The tanner will feel well paid for his trouble tonight. Buy them and return to me here."

"Aye, m'lord."

I found the tanner in his shop, alone at his workbench. He was not working, but sitting silently. I paid him with all the coins I had been given, yet he tried to return them, saying that the boots were not for sale.

"But, sir," I said, puzzled by the refusal to sell his wares and by the long, suspicious looks he was giving me from the corners of his eyes. His looks made me shiver. "I offer you twice what the boots are worth."

"Aye, and what do you offer me but conjurer's gild?"

"Conjurer's gild? These?" I held out the coins. There was nothing wrong with them that I could see. They were the small square coin of the realm, marked on both sides with the sheaf of wheat which stamped them as good king's coin.

"No, sir, these are good."

"You had them of the —" He stopped, shook his head once, and picked one of the coins from my hand, examining it closely. "You had them of the man in the stable yard?"

"Aye."

He peered more closely at the coin. "Well, it seems sound enough." Squaring his shoulders, he took the rest of the coins. "Very well, then, boy. Take the boots. And take something else."

"What then?" I asked, my hands already stroking the fine, soft leather of the boots which were now mine.

"Take heed, boy. You throw your lot in with a conjurer."

Again I shivered. "How do you know that? My lord seems a right enough man." Still, there was doubt in my mind, cast there by the certainty in his own expression.

"He is a conjurer. We know his kind here. We know his tricks and schemes." The tanner's smile was sour.

"You name him conjurer . . ." I whispered.

"Aye, and that he is. Have a care, boy, that you sell your soul for more than a pair of boots for your feet."

My soul! The boots grew heavy in my hand. Was that the price of footwear? I remembered his clear dark eyes, the firm, kindly way in which the stranger, now named conjurer, had stood for me against the tanner and his fellows. My soul? I did not think that he was bargaining for my soul. I did not think, then, that he was what the tanner named him. Shrugging and tucking the boots under my arm, I left the tanner to his profit.

Still, the tanner's words were much with me as we began our journeys. Alan did not try to hide his identity from me. Neither did he at once disclose it. It came soon enough. As he wished, I acted as his servant. He did not have a horse, so we traveled on foot. It was not long before I discovered that the tanner's warning held truth: I had fallen in with a conjurer.

There was a night, not long after our association began, when we were camping in the depth of the forest. I had trapped two rabbits for our dinner. The night was chill and wet. It had been raining since the dawn of that cold, grey day, and while Alan skinned my catch, I tried to light a fire from the best of the wet wood that I had gathered.

I had no success with the kindling. The sparks from my flint would leap, arc, and fall to their deaths upon the wet twigs and leaves. After many attempts, my hands stiff and awkward with chill, I cursed roundly.

Alan laid the meat aside, glanced up at me, and smiled from the shadows of the hood which he had drawn over his head against the drizzle. "A strong oath for a lad so young," he said softly.

"Aye, but not strong enough to light a fire," I grumbled.

"It is a wet night. It might be that you ask too much of your flint and tinder, boy."

"I ask it to do only what it should."

"Aye, but not what it can."

I sat back on my heels and tossed the flint aside with an expression of disgust. My anger was, I thought, a good covering for the disappointment which I felt at the prospect of a cold camp and no dinner.

Again Alan smiled. "Let me see if I can help."

I wished him luck, hunkered upon the damp ground, and watched with little hope for a fire this night.

He moved closer to the ring of stones I had fashioned to contain the fire. He rearranged the kindling only a little, then took a small breath.

"A fire," he said softly, and I knew that he was not speaking to me. Neither, I thought, was he speaking to himself, as a man does when reviewing the tasks at hand. "A fire. To warm our meal, to warm our night. A fire for kindly purposes only."

It was as though he asked a boon of someone. I shivered, and the shivering had little to do with the cold or the damp. The warning words of the tanner came into my mind, and I hugged myself against the chill and the advance of fear.

"A fire, bright and hot. A fire for comfort." He lifted his eyes, his gaze passing over me as though I were not there. It traveled high, and I could not but follow where it went, past the heights of the trees, up to the grey and starless sky. The forest became still around us. The drip and sigh of the drizzle seemed to fade to nothing. The soft rustle of forest creatures, hunting in the night, vanished.

His voice was a sigh. "A fire." My eyes came back to him, and I was not able to see his face now. Shadows had drifted across it, shadows which did not touch his shoulders or the rest of him. And through the shadows I could see the light of his eyes.

Words fell from his lips, now, and they were words which I had never heard before, but which were, in some frightening way, familiar to me.

"*Fūrr haētu flamma cuman hēr for thes tīma ti wearm! Fūrr! Cuman hūr!*"

The words spilled from him like silver water. It seemed to me, crouched before the lifeless fire ring, that I could see the words, feel them. I was too frightened now to even shiver. I would make no move at all which might call his attention to me.

"Fūrr haētu flamma cuman . . ." His voice rose, loud and strong, and then fell fully away. There was no echo of his words among the forest trees. He lifted his hands then, and placed them above my little pile of kindling. He left them there, only a scant inch above the wet wood, for a long moment.

Then he moved. Only his hands, but the motion caught my attention and held it. He lifted his hands slowly, as though pulling with them a great weight. His fingers curled, gripping something I could not see.

"Fūrr!" he said again, his voice a whisper now, and strained. "Furr, cuman her!"

And it came. It came first as soft, thin tendrils of smoke. But soon the tendrils thickened, became darker, and at their roots, far down among the larger pieces of wood which I had laid as a base for the fire, flame licked. He raised his hands higher, straining now, and the flame became two, and three, and leaped triumphantly into the night.

There was fire.

Slowly I got to my feet, keeping my eyes ever upon the enchanted flame. I thought of flight, I thought of bolting through the wet forest, running until I became lost, running until he could no longer find me or my soul.

But I did not run. I did not run because he fell back upon his heels, bringing his hands, the hands which had only seconds ago worked sorcery, up to cover his face.

"Sorcerer," I whispered. It was not an accusation, and I was sorry that it sounded like one once spoken.

He dropped his hands and lifted his eyes to mine. "Aye."

I shivered. Not from cold, but from fear. I was well traveled for my ten years. For that I may thank my former career. I had the common knowledge of conjurers, tricksters, dabblers in the unknown, therefore the forbidden. My mind told me that I was in danger. *The first thing a conjurer will take*, the common knowledge said, *is the soul. So fine is his skill that you will not realize your loss until it is too long gone.*

And yet I could see nothing evil, nothing fell, in the dark, tired eyes of the man who revealed himself as part of that suspect brotherhood. There was only Alan, tired, and yet very much the same man who had defended me from the grim harvest of my thievery.

I listened not to my mind but to my heart. In the light of his fire I could see that he was breathing differently, much like a man who has expended a great deal of effort.

"M'lord," I asked softly, going to his side. "Are you unwell?"

He raised his hand and waved my question gently away.

"M'lord, can I get you anything? Water—?"

"Hush, boy," he said at last. His voice was weary, but patient. He placed a hand upon my shoulder and got slowly to his feet. "Ah. That is better."

"Are you ill?"

This seemed to amuse him, for he smiled. "Not at all, boy. Only used."

"Used?"

"Aye. Used. Magic is not free for the taking, boy. One must give something in return." He raised his arm, stretching muscles which were cramped and stiff.

"What—what do you give, m'lord?"

He paused in his stretch, abandoned it, and came to stand beside me. His hand moved down, lifted my face up to his own. I felt again that sense of falling into the depths of his gaze. I was, again, held by the dark eyes which had only moments ago glowed with sorcerous power.

"Do—do you seek my soul, m'lord?" I whispered.

He did not speak for a moment, but seemed to be considering my words. When he did speak, his voice was colored with amusement. "No, boy. Or, perhaps, yes."

I trembled now, and moved away from his hand. He shook his head, his eyes softening. "No, boy. I do not seek your soul to take and keep. It is only that if I seek it, I seek it to show to you."

"M'lord?"

"Enough of this now." He shrugged his shoulders as though throwing off a burden. He took up the skinned rabbits and the sticks I had found to spit them. "Are you not hungry? Our dinner has been delayed a little, but it is more than enough time to make my belly impatient. Come, spit the rabbits, and we will eat."

I took the meat from him, and the spits. The tanner's words seemed of no more importance to me.

He was not flagrant with his skills, or prodigal of them. I well knew the effort it cost him to use his magic now. *Magic is not for free . . . one must give something in return.* I wondered, as I traveled with him, what it was that Alan gave. But I never asked. I had lost the first layers of my fear. I was no longer afraid of him. But I was not comfortable with the idea of magic. I had been too well versed in the common knowledge to lose that fear very soon.

He asked me once, if I would like to learn his skills.

"No, m'lord. These skills are beyond me." I smiled and shook my head. "I can steal a pair of boots—"

"Sometimes," he said with wry amusement.

"Aye. Most times. But I would not try to steal the fire."

"Is that what you think I do? Steal the fire?"

I shrugged.

"Well, well. It might be an answer. From whom do you think I steal it?

The gods?"

"The gods? Aye, maybe."

He smiled at that. "There are no gods, boy, but those of our own making."

I did not argue with him. I had little truck with gods in my short life. Were there gods, indeed? I did not know, and cared less. There was a body of gods commonly worshiped, but they had few of my petitions, and had answered even less.

"Whatever, m'lord. No, I have no wish to learn your skills."

"A pity."

"Could you teach me?" The contrary question came, almost unbidden, to my lips. I would not wish to learn, I assured myself, but I was only curious to know if the power could be learned.

But Alan shrugged. "It does not matter, does it? You would not learn."

"Well, aye." He could not have failed to hear the disappointment in my voice. It was obvious even to me.

His careful gaze held me for a long time. He is seeking something, I thought. What does he seek when he watches me like that?

Our travels took us from town to village to town, stopping at the inns and staying a few days. At night Alan would join the folk gathered at the landlord's hearth and exchange the news of the day. He was a great gossip and loved to hear the tales and legends of the area. He had not told me what task engaged him, and I could not see that any did, except the gathering of tales and the exchange of news.

Sometimes I asked him where we were going, and he always answered the same.

"We are looking for the dragon, boy."

I would laugh and tell him that everyone knew there were no such creatures as dragons. They inhabited the nursery tales which women told to keep young children behaved and certainly not the real world.

He would laugh, too, and say that perhaps I was right.

And so we visited the towns, and he would sit and gossip the nights away. He made no use of his magic, and he maintained, as best he could, the persona of a simple traveler. But at night, by the fading light of an inn's hearth or over the embers of a dying campfire, he would watch me. I would catch, at times, the light of hope in his eyes, and a careful speculation.

Winter had come. I had been with Alan for more than a year, and our journeying took us less and less to the villages and towns. In the autumn he had purchased two horses, and this surprised me, although I was not unhappy to finally ride. By the time the first snow had fallen, we were in the foothills of the northern mountains, and we had not entered a town for nearly a month. We had actually passed two by, and as I saw the last one disappear behind the rocky bend of a river, I asked him again where we were bound.

"Seeking the dragon, boy."

The same answer. I began to wonder if he was serious.

We traveled ever upward, farther and farther, until we lost the beeches and birch trees and were surrounded by the hoary eaves of evergreens. The thin skin of the earth gave way in many places now to rocky bone, thrusting upward in boulders through the soil. We traveled above the tree line, and there were places where all the majesty of mountain and forest was revealed to us.

After a time we came to places ravaged by fire. Trees were stripped and blackened. Few creatures ran to hide from us, and dinner was difficult to find. What I was able to catch was hoarded and made to last for many days.

Wrapped in my cloak one night, finishing our scant meal, I asked him what he thought must have caused the fire.

"Lightning, perhaps?" I asked, for it had been known to happen that a bolt would strike a tree and the fire would spread, unchecked, killing thousands of acres, hundreds of miles of trees.

Alan shook his head. "The dragon."

I looked at him long and saw that he was in earnest. "There are no dragons," I said, more to quiet my awakening fear than to refute his statement. I did not laugh this time.

Neither did he. "There is one. And that one guards what I seek."

I looked around me at the blackened forest, thinking that in the nursery tales they told you that dragons breathed fire. I huddled deeper into my cloak. I was afraid.

He saw that and smiled. "You need not fear, boy, for we will part company before I meet the dragon."

That gave me even greater fear. "Never, m'lord."

"I am afraid so, boy. You can be of little use to me then, and perhaps a hindrance. I would ask you to wait for me, though, for it may be, I hope it will be, that I will return and we can continue together."

I was frightened, there was no covering it, and I made no attempt to hide it. I was coming to love him. It was, perhaps, that he was good to me, or because a boy at that age easily loves the one who acts as a father to him. Whatever it was, I was not going to leave him. I told him this, but he would have none of it.

"You can journey with me a little farther. Then we will part company. Wait, if you will, or leave. That is your choice, boy."

There was no appeal to that calm decision, and I did not speak further. But I resolved in my heart not to leave him.

He told me then the purpose of his visits to the towns. He did not love the local gossip for its own sake, he said, but it was the surest way to learn the tales and legends of an area. The farther north we had come, the more often did he hear the tales of the dragon.

It guarded something, he did not say what, but it was something he was willing to throw his life away for; therefore, I judged it to be of great value. A treasure, perhaps, or a talisman. I did not ask, for I reasoned that it must be a fearful treasure if it was worth his life to gain.

We traveled for two more days at the timberline, he silent and I inwardly stiffening my resolve not to leave him no matter how he commanded me. And then we came to the peak.

It was a huge bare place, a giant rocky prominence pocked with the mouths of caves, covered with scree and boulders. Not a living thing grew upon its barren sides. It loomed above us like an angry skull. It made me afraid.

We were silent for a long time, he watching the peak, I watching him. I knew that he was going to dismiss me. I had my arguments, weak as even I thought they were, prepared.

He looked away from the peak. "It is time, boy."

"No, m'lord. I will not leave now."

"You do not have a choice."

"Will you tie me here, then, or take my horse?"

He smiled. "I do not think that will be necessary. You will do as you are bid, as you always have. It has been one of your chief virtues." Here he smiled again, for we both knew that my virtues were few.

"How can you ask this of me? We have traveled together for more than a year, m'lord. I thought I had earned your trust."

If I had thought that last would be a telling shot, I was mistaken. Alan merely nodded. "You have, over and over again, boy. And now I would entrust you with one more thing."

"To abandon you when you need me!"

"No. You are to wait here." He reached beneath his cloak and took out the dagger which was sheathed there. In the sunlight I could see a glimmer of light along the hilt of the sword he always wore.

He is mad, I thought then, and going against a dragon with only a sword. I said nothing, but took the dagger he held out to me. It was a beautiful thing, slim and sharp. The grip was chased silver and bore a single pale green jewel.

"Keep it in your boot, boy. You may need it."

"I want to help you!" It came out more as a wail than an insistence, and I was ashamed to hear the crack in my voice.

"You cannot help, and would only hinder."

"You are going after a dragon with a sword. Where will that get you?" I was angry and my voice mocked. "He will melt your sword, m'lord, and then where will you be?"

It surprises me now, looking back, that he was so patient with me. But he was, perhaps because he understood something of my feelings. He spoke softly, his voice even and reasonable. "I have more than my sword, boy. I have the magic."

"But I want to help."

That caused him to laugh. He did not laugh unkindly, but he was surely amused. I was wounded.

"I am pleased that even now I can provide amusement, m'lord."

"Do not be hurt, boy. But you cannot help. You cannot go against a dragon." He paused then, but went on. "And you have no magic."

I was chastened. He was right. I had no magic, and I was, after all, only a small boy, a hindrance. Should I not have turned away the opportunity to learn of his magic? In my mind I knew that I could not have learned enough to be able to help him now. It must take many years of study, I reasoned. Still, in my heart I felt the sharp fang of regret.

"What would you have me do?"

"Ah. Now that is better. Wait here. Wait as long as you can or dare. You will know if I am able to return. When you decide that I cannot, you must run for your life. Run as hard as you have ever run before, for if I fail, the dragon will be out and his fury will seek victims. Run back the way we came, boy, and make your way to the King."

I stared at him. "To the King, m'lord? It is a month's ride to the King. And once there, how will I gain entrance to see him?"

He nodded to the dagger he had given me. "That will be your pass to the King. He will know it well, for it was his until he gifted me with it."

"The King gave you this?" I could not reconcile my picture of Alan the conjurer with this Alan who was now telling me that the King himself had gifted him with a jeweled dagger.

"When you see him, tell him you have come from me. And tell him that I have failed."

"Failed in what, m'lord?"

"He will know. If he wishes you to know, he will tell you."

"But—"

"You butt more than a ram sensing a ewe in heat, boy!" Alan's dark eyes flared with a sudden anger. "It is enough that you do as you are bid. Will you?"

"Aye, m'lord. I will."

His expression grew kinder. He reached across the horses and dropped a hand upon my arm. "You have been a good servant. I hope that we will leave here together. But if we do not, I know that you will do as I bid."

I loved him then. Tears sprang to my eyes, and I dashed them angrily away with the back of my hand. "Aye, m'lord, I will." And truly I thought that I would.

He was satisfied. "Tell the King, then, that you have studied with me. He will find a place for you."

"Studied with you? I have not studied with you, m'lord."

"Think you not? Aye, well, the King may find differently." He left me then with no further word, and I watched him go. He took his horse as far up the scree as he could and then left it. I saw him drop his hand beneath his cloak to loose his sword. Poor sword, and what good would it be against dragons?

I had truly intended to obey his instruction, partly through fear and mostly through love. But I did not. When he was far from me, nearly halfway up the peak, I started to move forward. I thought I was only going for a better look, for I was loathe to stay back when I could see.

I walked my horse up the scree, guiding him carefully at first, and then giving him his head, leaving him alone to pick his own way. We drew even with the place where Alan had left his own mount and passed it. But soon the way was too hard and I stopped. On foot I crept farther up the rocky slope. The scree had given way to hard rock, but the path, such as it was, led straight up now.

I was an active boy, and found little difficulty scrambling for a hand- and foothold where necessary. I still think that I had thought only to see. He was out of my sight now, too far up for me to catch even a glimpse of him.

I balanced where I was, hands clinging to a ledge above my head, feet braced against a jutting rock below. There I stood when the sound came.

It was a horrible noise, a trumpeting, a bugling, and a hissing all at once. The air was filled with sulfurous stink, my breath caught in my throat, gagging me with fear. I trembled in every limb and would have run back the way I came, heedless of caution, but for the sound of his cry.

It was not a cry of pain or fear, but the bellowed sound of Alan's magic words, commands in that almost-familiar language of power. The shrieking increased. The air about me throbbed with stench and power. I clutched my handhold and squeezed my eyes shut.

I heard his voice again, and this time it was a cry of pain. I did not think, for if I had, I surely would not have done what I did. I scrambled upward again, my mind a grey blank wall, not admitting fear or pain or hope. I simply responded to Alan's cry.

The way twisted. There was no longer a path. I scrambled and climbed, clinging to rocks I never would have chosen for holds if I had been able to think.

And then I saw the dragon.

It was horrible. It was huge, and it stank like sulfur and cesspits. In the fading afternoon light, the scales of its armor reflected the golden sunlight. At its feet, small and to my eyes vulnerable, lay Alan. He did not move. Is he dead, I thought. The pain of loss ran through me.

My eyes ran with tears and stung. I could not put up a hand to wipe them, for I was clinging with precarious balance to the edge of the long drop from the dragon's cave.

Venom ran from the dragon's jaws. It dropped, hissing and steaming to the ground where Alan lay. "Oh move, my lord!" And he did, but barely and only slowly.

The beast rose above him. It was larger than my eyes could see in one terrified glance. There are words bards use to describe dragons. There are phrases they call upon time after time. They tell of wide reaches of leathery wings, arched and clawed. They tell of a head larger than the body of a horse, of a neck muscled and scaled, thicker around than the largest tree in the forest. They tell of the stink of the flames which issue from the maw of such a beast. They have not seen a dragon.

Had they, had they once come within sighting distance of a dragon, they would not tell of these things. They would tell, instead, in words which stuttered with fear, of the soul-chilling terror of the beast. They would tell of the stone to which their limbs turned, while their hearts and minds screamed for flight. They would tell how every pur-pose, good and ill, fled their hearts, blotted out by the immense shadow of a beast which should have lived only in legend.

I did not flee. I pretend to no nobility of heart. I would have fled had I the power to move, had I been able to get my paralyzed limbs to take me back down the mountain. But I could not. So I hung, shaking and weeping in my terror.

Alan moved again, hunching his shoulders, gathering his breath to speak. I could barely hear his words about the dragon's steaming pant.

"Poeir ti cloake, poeir for strengthū; ti ban faer!"

His words were soft, quiet, but bore, even to my untutored ears, a power. Through the sting of my tears, through the darkness of my fear, I could see that his sword arm was bent under him in a way that no arm should bend.

"Poeir ti cloake." I barely saw his lips move, his eyes were squeezed tightly shut, whether to lock out the sight of the dragon or to lock in his concentration, I did not know.

"Poeir for strengthū."

He asks for strength, I thought, and wondered how I knew. It was the language of magic which he spoke, a language foreign to me, and yet so haunting and familiar. I listened to Alan's words, repeated them in my heart, and took faint strength from them.

"Poeir ti ban faer . . ." His voice was ragged and stumbling now.

Power to banish fear . . . There was no lessening of the fear in my heart. *Poeir ti ban faer*, I repeated silently. And there was, faintly, a soft-ening of the terror which had turned my limbs to stone.

The beast turned its head as I watched, and the flame of its breath passed above us, close enough to scorch.

"*Poeir*," I whispered. "*Poeir for strengthu!*" Not for me, I begged silently, not for me! For Alan! Not breathing, not thinking of anything but Alan who lay at the feet of Death, I clambered upward, forcing my hands to grasp the crumbly shale, forcing my feet to find grips and hold them. I could barely control my limbs. Fear might have been lessened, but it was not banished. I stood upon the ledge and stumbled toward Alan.

"*Poeir*," I said, hearing my own voice as a weak croaking. *Poeir ti ban faer, for strengthu!*" The dragon reared back again, beat its wings against the sky, and darted suddenly downward, fangs gleaming in the sharp light of day.

"Dragon! No! Dragon!" I screamed. I dropped to my knees beside Alan, and he twisted toward me, his face shaped by pain to one I hardly knew.

"What word, m'lord? What word?"

"Yield!" he gasped. "*Gielden.*"

"*Gielden!*" I screamed. "*Gielden!*"

The dragon paused, its eyes gleaming with dark hatred. Alan grasped my wrist. "A spell, boy. A spell."

A spell? I knew no spell! But the words I had heard him use, those which I had repeated, might be shaped into a spell, might they not? I took a long breath. "*Bi min poeir*, Dragon, *gielden!*"

It did not yield, but it drew back. The words arrested its dripping fangs, stilled, for a precious moment, that downward swoop which would have ended Alan's life. I leaped to my feet, scrambling in and under the enormous foreleg of the beast, running for Alan's sword. The stench of the dragon rose up and staggered me.

"*Poeir ti ban faer.*" This time my chant was supported by Alan's voice. The ground beneath my feet seemed suddenly less solid, my breath was light in my chest. My head seemed filled with a tightening kind of light and fire. I darted beneath the dragon's leg, my arm brushing against scales which felt like armor. I snatched up the sword which lay behind the leg of the beast, just below the enormous sweep of its chest. Whirling, I tossed it to Alan who caught it, fumbling, in his left hand.

Spade-shaped and huge, the dragon's scaled head lowered, darting in and down toward where I cowered beneath it. Venom and flame dripped from its fangs, huge black eyes glittered and whirled as it sought me.

"Run, boy!" Alan cried. His voice was cracked with his pain, breaking up. There was an edge of desperate fear there. "Run, boy!"

But I could not run. Run to where? A dash forward or to either side would bring the dragon's huge head sweeping after me, fangs bared and seeking the taste of my blood. Where could I run?

"*Poeir ti ban faer,*" I whispered. I was light with fear, and frozen with it. But as I spoke the words, I felt a part of me leaving, withdrawing from my body. Even as I realized this, I felt something new enter me, a power and a strange kind of strength which had nothing to do with strength of limb. It was a kind of strength of heart.

I took the deepest breath I could in the dragon-reek, glanced at Alan who was climbing slowly to his feet. His face was white and strained with fear and pain. He hefted the sword in his left hand, not his sword hand for that arm was broken and dangling at a sickening angle.

"*Poeir,*" he gasped.

"*Poeir,*" I said after him. "*Poeir for strengthū!*" The dragon's head was snaking closer, weaving back and forth now, seeking me and the best way to snatch at me.

I am too near his leg, I realized, for him to risk a clear attack. Aye, and if I was behind the leg . . . I did not waste time on the thought, but darted behind the huge trunk of the foreleg. In the shadow of his leg and chest, I could hear the rumble of the bellow of rage which was working its way from the cavern of its throat. "Strike, m'lord! Strike now!"

He did not need me to direct his stroke. There is a place just under the jaw, a tender and vulnerable place where the scales of a dragon's armor do not quite overlap. It was that place Alan struck, thrusting his sword in with all the strength his left arm possessed.

He cried aloud, whether from pain or triumph, I could not tell. The stink around us grew and doubled. Black blood, hissing and steaming as it felt the cool touch of the air, ran down the dragon's neck.

"Get out, boy!" And as he needed no instruction from me to strike, I needed no warning from him to flee. The air was filled with the death screams, screams which rose higher and louder, filling the air until they were not so much sounds as feelings, not so much heard with the ears but felt in every part of my body and mind.

Out from under the bulk of the monster, crouching as close to the ledge of the cliff as I dared, I watched Alan follow up his advantage and strike again and again until the thing, its throat torn, its jugular in bloody shreds, reared a last time, blotting out the sun with the immensity of its bulk, and fell.

That fall, that crashing weight, sent me sprawling face downward, retching from the death-stench. I looked up, wiped dirt and sickness from my mouth, and saw Alan wiping his sword upon his cloak.

He stood, weaving upon legs which seemed about to fail him, caught his balance and looked back at me.

"*Heorte-cild*," he said, his eyes bright in his pain-drawn face. "*Heorte-cild*."

Heart's child. The word's were soft upon my heart. He staggered, stumbled once, and went into the dragon's cave. Heart's child. I do not know how long he was there, or what he did, for the thing that I called strength of heart had left me. My legs gave out and my sight grew dark. I fainted.

He told me he was angry, over and over, as he wiped my face clean. He told me he would dismiss me, for he had no need of a servant who could not follow orders. I knew he did not mean it, for his ministrations were tender and his eyes belied all of his words. I helped him down the mountain when we were both steadier, leaving behind us the reek and stink of the dead monster.

We did not find our horses until we were nearly a mile from the dragon's mount. When we did, I tore the spare shirt in my pack into strips to bind Alan's arm and form a rude sling. I helped him to mount carefully and led his horse while riding my own.

I told him that it was a miracle that the animals had not died from fear. He told me it was a miracle that I had not died from my own stupidity—and what did I think I was about disobeying his explicit orders? Had we both been killed, who would have gone to the King?

Alan looked at me then, and shook his head. "You do not understand."

"That is certain, m'lord. What did you seek in the dragon's lair?"

He smiled then and reached inside his cloak. He withdrew a small object, no larger than an egg. From what I could see of it, it was a jewel, blue in color, and brilliant. But it did not seem valuable enough, as lovely as it was, to risk his life in the taking. He saw my judgment in my eyes.

"No, it does not look like much, does it?"

"It is beautiful. But no, I cannot think it worth your life, m'lord."

Alan laughed. "I assure you, boy, it is. I assure you that it would be worth the lives of a regiment to recover."

"But what is it, m'lord?"

"What?" He tucked the jewel back inside his cloak and pretended surprise at my question. "Could you, the great sorcerer that you are, not be aware of what I carry?"

"I am no sorcerer, m'lord," I answered, knowing even then that my words could not be true. "I only tried to help."

He softened, then. "Aye, you are boy. And help you did."

I caught his meaning and shook my head again. Hope was balanced against fear. I could feel in memory the terrible feeling of draining and filling, that feeling that something I knew nothing about was lending strength to me. I shivered and told him that I only provided the distraction that he needed to kill the beast. But he did not agree.

"There is power in you, boy. The discovery was painful. Aye, I know that. But by its discovery, you have saved others such pain."

Alan reached out his good hand and lifted my chin, his eyes finding mine and holding them. There was, in his own eyes, a light of satisfaction. But when he spoke his words were wry and amused. "I recognized you, boy, when I first saw you. It took time, though, for you to recognize yourself."

"And the jewel, m'lord?" I turned the subject purposely, not wanting to dwell upon the power and the things it took in exchange.

His hand dropped to the place where the jewel lay within his cloak. "A key, boy. A simple key."

"To what, m'lord?"

"Why to a treasure, of course."

I shook my head again. "It seems part of a treasure, not a key."

"Still, it is a key. It lay in legend as long as it lay in that dragon's hoard. Some said it was real, some said it was a fable."

"What does it do?"

He laughed aloud at that. Silently, he removed the jewel from its place of safety. "Put out your hand, boy."

Slowly I did. He dropped the jewel into my palm. It was cool and hard. But even as I thought it so, it began to gleam and grow warm. It took, quickly, the warmth of a living thing, and I knew that it should not have garnered the warmth of my own body that fast. Startled, I looked up.

"It is warm, m'lord. And see how it glows!"

Alan smiled, but it was not a smile of amusement, more one of gratification. He reached for the jewel again and let it sit, for a moment, in his own hand. It lost none of its glow.

"This might have told you something many months ago, boy, had we had it then."

"What, m'lord?"

"That you have the power. That you will make a good student."

"Student. What will I study?"

"Much. And it may be that you will teach us, as well. We are a much-maligned brotherhood, those of us with the power. Tricksters, conjurers, dabblers in evil they call us." He laughed and it was a bitter sound. "But that will change."

"How?"

"With the help of the King. We will found an Order, an Order not of sorcerers and tricksters, but of men skilled in magic and of men who would seek the power to be found in truth."

"It is the King's will?"

"Aye, so it is. It is his mission you have saved, boy, as well as my own life. You will find us both grateful. They will call us tricksters no more, boy. They will call us wise men. Wizards."

Alan shifted uncomfortably in his saddle, and I knew that his arm pained him despite the bandage and sling that I had rigged. He gestured with his good hand and we stopped. He reached across the necks of our horses and placed his hand upon my shoulder. "You will be welcomed, boy, by the King."

"M'lord?"

"Aye, you will be. You will study hard, and you will someday make a fine wizard, boy."

I stared at him. There was weariness in his voice and no prophecy. He spoke his words not in faith but from some sure knowledge. I, a wizard? I, part of a respected Order? I wondered what lay ahead to transform a thief and a servant into a wizard. But if he did not speak in faith, it was I who accepted in faith and in love.

That day I was content to simply travel with him. It took us more than a month of journeying to reach the court of the King. During that time we stopped in the villages and towns, listened to the gossip, and he healed. His great treasure he kept ever close to him, never letting it go from the safety of its place in his cloak.

It was upon that stone that our Order was founded. But it was not upon that stone that my own faith was founded. The base of my faith was Alan. I saw not, in those days, the founding of Orders. I saw only the beginning of a new place for me. And glimmering and new to me, I caught, through his eyes, and soon through my own, glimpses of my own soul: the soul I had feared he would take, the soul he had given me.

Many have come after me, many have loved him as I did, for ever did he inspire the love of those souls he sought to uncover. I have watched, in wonder and joy, as he brought, one by one, slowly and carefully, the many boys into our Order who gave to it its strength and respected status. For me, however, those who came later were merely repetitions of the miracle that visited me that long-ago day.

For I, once a thief, lately a servant, was, that day, a Wizard's Boy.

A Hiss of Dragon

Gregory Benford & Marc Laidlaw

"Incoming dragon!" Leopold yelled, and ducked to the left. I went right.

Dragons come in slow and easy. A blimp with wings, this one settled down like a wrinkled brown sky falling. I scrambled over boulders, trying to be inconspicuous and fast at the same time. It didn't seem like a promising beginning for a new job.

Leopold and I had been working on the ledge in front of the Dragon's Lair, stacking berry pods. This Dragon must have flown toward its Lair from the other side of the mountain spire, so our radio tag on him didn't transmit through all the rock. Usually they're not so direct. Most Dragons circle their Lairs a few times, checking for scavengers and egg stealers. If they don't circle, they're usually too tired. And when they're tired, they're irritable. Something told me I didn't want to be within reach of this one's throat flame.

I dropped my berrybag rig and went down the rocks feet first. The boulders were slippery with green moss for about 20 meters below the ledge, so I slid down on them. I tried to keep the falls to under four meters and banged my butt when I missed. I could hear Leopold knocking loose rocks on the other side, moving down toward where our skimmer was parked.

A shadow fell over me, blotting out Beta's big yellow disk. The brown bag above thrashed its wings and gave a trumpeting shriek. It had caught sight of the berry bags and knew something was up. Most likely, with its weak eyes, the Dragon thought the bags were eggers—off season, but what do Dragons know about seasons?—and would attack them. That was the optimistic theory. The pessimistic one was that the Dragon had seen one of us. I smacked painfully into a splintered boulder and glanced up. Its underbelly was heaving, turning purple: anger. Not a reassuring sign. Eggers don't bother Dragons that much.

Then its wings fanned the air, backward. It drifted off the ledge, hovering. The long neck snaked around, and two nearsighted eyes sought mine. The nose expanded, catching my scent. The Dragon hissed triumphantly.

Our skimmer was set for a fast takeoff. But it was 200 meters down, on the only wide spot we could find. I made a megaphone of my hands and shouted into the thin mountain mist, "Leopold! Grab air!"

I jumped down to a long boulder that jutted into space. Below and a little to the left I could make out the skimmer's shiny wings through the shifting green fog. I sucked in a breath and ran off the end of the boulder.

Dragons are clumsy at level flight, but they can drop like a brick. The only way to beat this one down to the skimmer was by falling most of the way.

I banked down, arms out. Our gravity is only a third of Earth normal. Even when falling, you have time to think things over. I can do the calculations fast enough—it came out to nine seconds—but getting the count right with a Dragon on your tail is another matter. I ticked the seconds off and then popped the chute. It fanned and filled. The skimmer came rushing up, wind whipped my face. Then my harness jerked me to a halt. I drifted down. I thumped the release and fell

free. Above me, a trumpeting bellow. Something was coming in at four
o'clock and I turned, snatching for my blaser. Could it be that fast? But
it was Leopold, on chute. I sprinted for the skimmer. It was pointed
along the best outbound wind, flaps already down, a standard precaution. I belted in, sliding my feet into the pedals. I caught a dank, foul
reek of Dragon. More high shrieking, closer. Leopold came running up,
panting. He wriggled into the rear seat. A thumping of wings. A ceiling of wrinkled leather. Something hissing overhead.

Dragons don't fly, they float. They have a big green hydrogen-
filled dome on their backs to give them lift. They make the hydrogen
in their stomachs and can dive quickly by venting it out the ass. This
one was farting and falling as we zoomed away. I banked, turned to get
a look at the huffing brown mountain hooting its anger at us, and
grinned.

"I take back what I said this morning," Leopold gasped. "You'll
draw full wages *and* commissions, from the start."

I didn't say anything. I'd just noticed that somewhere back there I
had pissed my boots full.

I covered it pretty well back at the strip. I twisted out of the skimmer and slipped into the maintenance bay. I had extra clothes in my
bag, so I slipped on some fresh socks and thongs.

When I was sure I smelled approximately human, I tromped back
out to Leopold. I was damned if I would let my morning's success be
blotted out by an embarrassing accident. It was a hirer's market these
days. My training at crop dusting out in the flat farmlands had given
me an edge over the other guys who had applied. I was determined to
hang on to this job.

Leopold was the guy who "invented" the Dragons, five years ago.
He took a life form native to Lex, the bloats, and tinkered with their
DNA. Bloats are balloonlike and nasty. Leopold made them bigger,
tougher, and spliced in a lust for thistleberries that makes Dragons
hoard them compulsively. It had been a brilliant job of bioengineering.
The Dragons gathered thistleberries, and Leopold stole them from the
Lairs.

Thistleberries are a luxury good, high in protein, and delicious.

The market for them might collapse if Lex's economy got worse—the copper seams over in Bahinin had run out last month. This was nearly the only good flying job left. More than anything else, I wanted to keep flying. And *not* as a crop duster. Clod-grubber work is a pain.

Leopold was leaning against his skimmer, a little pale, watching his men husk thistleberries. His thigh muscles were still thick; he was clearly an airman by ancestry, but he looked tired.

"Goddamn," he said. "I can't figure it out, kid. The Dragons are hauling in more berries than normal. We can't get into the Lairs, though. You'd think it was mating season around here, the way they're attacking my men."

"Mating season? When's that?"

"Oh, in about another six months, when the puffbushes bloom in the treetops. The pollen sets off the mating urges in Dragons—steps up their harvest, but it also makes 'em meaner."

"Great," I said. "I'm allergic to puffbush pollen. I'll have to fight off Dragons with running eyes and a stuffy nose."

Leopold shook his head absently; he hadn't heard me. "I can't understand it—there's nothing wrong with my Dragon designs."

"Seems to me you could have toned down the behavior plexes," I said. "Calm them down a bit—I mean, they've outgrown their competition to the point that they don't even *need* to be mean anymore. They don't browse much as it is . . . nobody's going to bother them."

"No way—there's just not the money for it, Drake. Look, I'm operating on the margin here. My five-year rights to the genetic patents just ran out, and now I'm in competition with Kwalan Rhiang, who owns the other half of the forest. Besides, you think gene splicing is easy?"

"Still, if they can bioengineer *humans* . . . I mean, we were beefed up for strength and oxy burning nearly a thousand years ago."

"But we weren't blown up to five times the size of our progenitors, Drake. I made those Dragons out of mean sons of bitches—blimps with teeth is what they were. It gets tricky when you mess with the life cycles of something that's already that unstable. You just don't understand what's involved here."

I nodded. "I'm no bioengineer—granted."

He looked at me and grinned, a spreading warm grin on his deeply lined face. "Yeah, Drake, but you're good at what you do—really good. What happened today, well, I'm getting too old for that sort of thing, and it's happening more and more often. If you hadn't been there I'd probably be stewing in that Dragon's stomach right now—skimmer and all."

I shrugged. That gave me a chance to roll the slabs of muscle in my shoulders, neck, and pectorals—a subtle advertisement that I had enough to keep a skimmer aloft for hours.

"So," he continued, "I'm giving you full pilot rank. The skimmer's yours. You can fly it home tonight, on the condition that you meet me at the Angis Tavern for a drink later on. And bring your girl Evelaine, too, if you want."

"It's a deal, Leopold. See you there."

I whistled like a dungwarbler all the way home, pedaling my new skimmer over the treetops toward the city. I nearly wrapped myself in a floating thicket of windbrambles, but not even this could destroy my good mood.

I didn't notice any Dragons roaming around, though I saw that the treetops had been plucked of their berries and then scorched. Leopold had at least had the foresight, when he was gene tinkering, to provide for the thistleberries' constant replenishment. He gave the Dragons a throat flame to singe the treetops with, which makes the berries regrow quickly. A nice touch.

It would have been simpler, of course, to have men harvest the thistleberries themselves, but that never worked out, economically. Thistleberries grow on top of virtually unclimbable thorntrees, where you can't even maneuver a skimmer without great difficulty. And if a man fell to the ground . . . well, if it's on the ground, it has spines, that's the rule on Lex. There's nothing soft to fall on down there. Sky life is more complex than ground life. You can actually do something useful with sky life—namely, bioengineering. Lex may be a low-metal world—which means low-technology—but our bioengineers are the best.

A clapping sound, to the left. I stopped whistling. Down through the greenish haze I could see a dark form coming in over the treetops, its wide rubbery wings slapping together at the top of each stroke. A smackwing. Good meat, spicy and moist. But hard to catch. Evelaine and I had good news to celebrate tonight; I decided to bring her home smackwing for dinner. I took the skimmer down in the path of the smackwing, meanwhile slipping my blaser from its holster.

The trick to hunting in the air is to get beneath your prey so that you can grab it while it falls, but this smackwing was flying too low. I headed in fast, hoping to frighten it into rising above me, but it was no use. The smackwing saw me, red eyes rolling. It missed a beat in its flapping and dived toward the treetops. At that instant a snagger shot into view from the topmost branches, rising with a low farting sound. The smackwing spotted this blimplike thing that had leaped into its path but apparently didn't think it too threatening. It swerved about a meter under the bobbing creature—

And stopped flat, in midair.

I laughed aloud, sheathing my blaser. The snagger had won his meal like a real hunter.

Beneath the snagger's wide blimplike body was a dangling sheet of transparent sticky material. The smackwing struggled in the moist folds as the snagger drew the sheet upward. To the unwary smackwing that clear sheet must have been invisible until the instant he flew into it.

Within another minute, as I pedaled past the spot, the snagger had entirely engulfed the smackwing, and was unrolling its sticky sheet as it drifted back into the treetops. Pale yellow eyes considered me and rejected the notion of me as food. A ponderous predator, wise with years.

I flew into the spired city: Kalatin.

I parked on the deck of our apartment building, high above the jumbled wooden buildings of the city. Now that my interview had been successful, we'd be able to stay in Kalatin, though I hoped we could find a better apartment. This one was as old as the city—which in turn had been around for a great deal of the 1,200 years humans had been on Lex. As the wood of the lower stories rotted, and as the building crumbled away, new quarters were just built on top of it and settled into place. Someday this city would be an archaeologist's dream. In the meantime, it was an inhabitant's nightmare.

Five minutes later, having negotiated several treacherous ladders and a splintering shinny pole into the depths of the old building, I crept quietly to the wooden door of my apartment and let myself in, clutching the mudskater steaks that I'd picked up on the way home. It was dark and cramped inside, the smell of rubbed wood strong. I could hear Evelaine moving around in the kitchen, so I sneaked to the doorway and looked in. She was turned away, chopping thistleberries with a thorn-knife.

I grabbed her, throwing the steaks into the kitchen, and kissed her.

"Got the job, Evey!" I said. "Leopold took me out himself and I ended up saving his—"

"It *is* you!" She covered her nose, squirming away from me. "What is that smell, Drake?"

"Smell?"

"Like something died. It's all over you."

I remembered the afternoon's events. It was either the smell of Dragon, which I'd got from scrambling around in a Lair, or that of urine. I played it safe and said, "I think it's Dragon."

"Well take it somewhere else. I'm cooking dinner."

"I'll hop in the cycler. You can cook up the steaks I brought, then we're going out to celebrate."

The Angis Tavern is no skiff joint, good for a stale senso on the way home from work. It's the best. The Angis is a vast old place, perched on a pyramid of rock. Orange fog nestles at the base, a misty collar separating it from the jumble of the city below.

Evelaine pedaled the skimmer with me, having trouble in her gown. We made a wobbly landing on the rickety side deck. It would've been easier to coast down to the city, where there was more room for a glide approach, but that's pointless. There are thick cactus and thorn-bushes around the Angis base, hard to negotiate at night. In the old days it kept away predators; now it keeps away the riffraff.

But not completely: two beggars accosted us as we dismounted, offering to shine up the skimmer's aluminum skin. I growled convincingly at them, and they skittered away. The Angis is so big, so full of crannies to hide out in, they can't keep it clear of beggars, I guess.

We went in a balcony entrance. Fat balloons nudged against the ceiling, ten meters overhead, dangling their cords. I snagged one and stepped off into space. Evelaine hooked it as I fell. We rode it down, past alcoves set in the rock walls. Well-dressed patrons nodded as we eased down, the balloon following. The Angis is a spire, broadening gradually as we descended. Phosphors cast creamy glows on the tables set into the walls. I spotted Leopold sprawled in a webbing, two empty tankards lying discarded underneath.

"You're late," he called. We stepped off onto his ledge. Our balloons, released, shot back to the roof.

"You didn't set a time. Evelaine, Leopold." Nods, introductory phrases.

"It seems quite crowded here tonight," Evelaine murmured. A plausible social remark, except she'd never been to an inn of this class before.

Leopold shrugged. "Hard times mean full taverns. Booze or sensos or tinglers—pick your poison."

Evelaine has the directness of a country girl and knows her own limitations; she stuck to a mild tingler. Service was running slow, so I went to log our orders. I slid down a shinny pole to the first bar level. Mice zipped by me, eating up tablescraps left by the patrons; it saves on labor. Amid the jam and babble I placed our order with a steward and turned to go back.

"You looking for work?" a thick voice said.

I glanced at its owner. "No." The man was big, swarthy, and sure of himself.

"Thought you wanted Dragon work." His eyes had a look of distant amusement.

"How'd you know that?" I wasn't known in the city.

"Friends told me."

"Leopold hired me today."

"So I hear. I'll top whatever he's paying."

"I didn't think business was that good."

"It's going to get better. Much better, once Leopold's out of the action. A monopoly can always sell goods at a higher price. You can start tomorrow."

So this was Kwalan Rhiang. "No thanks. I'm signed up." Actually, I hadn't signed anything, but there was something about this man I didn't like. Maybe the way he was so sure I'd work for him.

"Flying for Leopold is dangerous. He doesn't know what he's doing."

"See you around," I said. A senso was starting in a nearby booth. I took advantage of it to step into the expanding blue cloud, so Rhiang couldn't follow and see where we were sitting. I got a lifting, bright sensation of pleasure, and then I was out of the misty confusion, moving away among the packed crowd.

I saw them on the stairway. They were picking their way down it delicately. I thought they were deformed, but the funny tight clothes gave them away. Offworlders, here for the flying. That was the only reason anybody came to Lex. We're still the only place men can seriously fly longer than a few minutes. Even so, our lack of machines keeps most offworlders away; they like it easy, everything done for them. I watched them pick their way down the stairs, thinking that if the depression got worse, offworlders would be able to hire servants here, even though it was illegal. It could come to that.

They were short as children but heavyset, with narrow chests and skinny limbs. Spindly people, unaugmented for Lex oxy levels. But men like that had colonized here long ago, paying for it in reduced lifetimes. I felt as though I was watching my own ancestors.

Lex shouldn't have any oxy at all, by the usual rules of planetary evolution. It's a small planet, 0.21 Earth masses, a third gee of gravity. Rules of thumb say we shouldn't have any atmosphere to speak of. But our sun, Beta, is a K-type star, redder than Sol. Beta doesn't heat our upper atmosphere very much with ultraviolet, so we retain gases. Even then, Lex would be airless except for accidents of birth. It started out with a dense cloak of gas, just as Earth did. But dim old Beta didn't blow the atmosphere away, and there wasn't enough compressional heating by Lex itself to boil away the gases. So they stuck around, shrouding the planet, causing faster erosion than on Earth. The winds moved dust horizontally, exposing crustal rock. That upset the isostatic balance in the surface, and split open faults. Volcanoes poked up. They belched water and gas onto the surface, keeping the atmosphere dense. So Lex ended up with low gravity and a thick atmosphere. Fine, except that Beta's wan light also never pushed many heavy elements out this far, so Lex is metal-poor. Without iron and the rest you can't build machines, and without technology you're a backwater. You sell your tourist attraction—flying—and hope for the best.

One of the offworlders came up to me and said, "You got any sparkers in this place?"

I shook my head. Maybe he didn't know that getting a sendup by tying your frontal lobes into an animal's is illegal here. Maybe he didn't care. Ancestor or not, he just looked like a misshapen dwarf to me, and I walked away.

Evelaine was describing life in the flatlands when I got back. Leopold was rapt, the worry lines in his face nearly gone. Evelaine does that to people. She's natural and straightforward, so she was telling him right out that she wasn't much impressed with city life. "Farmlands are quiet and restful. Everybody has a job," she murmured. "You're right that getting around is harder—but we can glide in the updrafts, in summer. It's heaven."

"Speaking of the farmlands," I said, "an old friend of mine came out here five years ago. He wanted in on your operations."

"I was hiring like crazy five years ago. What was his name?"

"Lorn Kramer. Great pilot."

Leopold shook his head. "Can't remember. He's not with me now, anyway. Maybe Rhiang got him."

Our drinks arrived. The steward was bribable, though—Rhiang was right behind him.

"You haven't answered my 'gram," Rhiang said directly to Leopold, ignoring us. I guess he didn't figure I was worth any more time.

"Didn't need to," Leopold said tersely.

"Sell out. I'll give you a good price." Rhiang casually sank his massive flank on our table edge. "You're getting too old."

Something flickered in Leopold's eyes; he said nothing.

"Talk is," Rhiang went on mildly, "market's falling."

"Maybe," Leopold said. "What you been getting for a kilo?"

"Not saying."

"Tight lips and narrow minds go together."

Rhiang stood, his barrel chest bulging. "You could use a little instruction in politeness."

"From you?" Leopold chuckled. "You paid off that patent clerk to release my gene configs early. Was that polite?"

Rhiang shrugged, "That's the past. The present reality is that there may be an oversupply of thistleberries. Market isn't big enough for two big operations like ours. There's too much—"

"Too much of you, that's my problem. Lift off, Rhiang."

To my surprise, he did. He nodded to me, ignored Evelaine, and gave Leopold a look of contempt. Then he was gone.

I heard them first. We were taking one of the outside walks that corkscrew around the Angis spire, gawking at the phosphored streets below. A stone slide clattered behind us. I saw two men duck behind a jutting ledge. One of them had something in his hand that glittered.

"You're jumpy, Drake," Evelaine said.

"Maybe." It occurred to me that if we went over the edge of this spire, hundreds of meters into the thorn scrabble below, it would be very convenient for Rhiang. "Let's move on."

Leopold glanced at me, then back at the inky shadows. We strolled along the trail of volcanic rock, part of the natural formation that made the spire. Rough black pebbles slipped underfoot. In the distant star-flecked night, skylight called and boomed.

We passed under a phosphor. At the next turn Leopold looked back and said, "I saw one of them. Rhiang's right-hand man."

We hurried away. I wished for a pair of wings to get us off this place. Evelaine understood instantly that this was serious. "There's a split in the trail ahead," Leopold said. "If they follow, we'll know . . ." He didn't finish.

We turned. They followed. "I think I know a way to slow them down," I said. Leopold looked at me. We were trying to avoid slipping in the darkness and yet make good time. "Collect some of these obsidian frags," I said.

We got a bundle of them together. "Go on up ahead," I said. We were on a narrow ledge. I sank back into the shadows and waited. The two men appeared. Before they noticed me I threw the obsidian high into the air. In low gravity it takes a long time for them to come back down. In the darkness the two men couldn't see them coming.

I stepped out into the wan light. "Hey!" I yelled to them. They stopped, precisely where I thought they would. "What's going on?" I said, to stall.

The biggest one produced a knife. "This."

The first rock hit, coming down from over a hundred meters above. It slammed into the boulder next to him. Then three more crashed down, striking the big one in the shoulder, braining the second. They both crumpled.

I turned and hurried along the path. If they'd seen me throw they'd have had time to dodge. It was an old schoolboy trick, but it worked.

The implications, though, were sobering. If Rhiang felt this way, my new job might not last long.

I was bagging berries in the cavernous Paramount Lair when the warning buzzer in my pocket went off. A Dragon was coming in. I still had time, but not much. I decided to finish this particular bag rather than abandon the bagging-pistol. The last bit of fluid sprayed over the heap of berries and began to congeal instantly, its tremendously high surface tension drawing it around the irregular pile and sealing perfectly. I holstered the gun, leaving the bag for later. I turned—

A slow flapping boom. Outside, a wrinkled brown wall.

Well, I'd fooled around long enough—now I dived for safety. The Dragon's Lair was carpeted with a thick collection of nesting materials. None were very pleasant to burrow through, but I didn't have any choice. Behind me I could hear the Dragon moving around; if I didn't move out of his way in a hurry I might get stepped on. The emergency chute on my back tangled in a branch, just as the stench in the Lair intensified. I hurried out of it and went on. I'd just have to be sure not to fall from any great heights. I didn't worry about it, because my skimmer was parked on the ledge just outside the Lair.

I stuck my head up through the nest to judge my position. The bulk of the Dragon was silhouetted against the glare of the sky, which was clear of fog today. The beast seemed to be preening itself. That was something I never thought they did outside of the mating season—which was six months away.

I scrambled backward into the nest. The buzzer in my pocket went off again, though it was supposed to signal just once, for ten seconds. I figured the thing must have broken. It quieted and I moved on, thinking. For one thing, the Dragon that occupied this Lair was supposed to have been far from home right now—which meant that my guest didn't really belong here. Dragons never used the wrong Lair unless it was the mating season.

I frowned. Why did that keep coming up?

Suddenly there was a rush of wind and a low, thrumming sound. The light from outside was cut off. I poked my head into the open.

Another Dragon was lumbering into the Lair. *This* was really impossible. Two Dragons sharing a Lair—and the wrong one at that! Whatever their reasons for being here, I was sure they were going to start fighting pretty soon, so I burrowed deeper, moving toward the nearest wall.

My elbow caught on something. Cloth. I brushed it away, then looked again. A Dragonrobber uniform like my own. It was directly beneath me, half-buried in the nesting material. I caught my breath, then poked at the uniform. Something glittered near one empty sleeve: an identification bracelet. I picked it up, shifted it in the light, and read the name on it: *Lorn Kramer.*

Lorn Kramer! So he had been in Leopold's group after all. But that still didn't explain why he'd left his clothes here.

I tugged at the uniform, dragging it toward me. It was limp, but tangled in the nest. I jerked harder and some long, pale things rattled out of the sleeve.

Bones.

I winced. I was suddenly aware that my present situation must be somewhat like the one that had brought him here.

I looked into the Lair again. One of the Dragons was prodding its snout at the other, making low, whuffling sounds. It didn't look like a hostile gesture to me. In fact, it looked like they were playing. The other Dragon wheeled about and headed for the entrance. The first one followed, and in a minute both of them had left the Lair again—as abruptly and inexplicably as they had entered it.

I saw my chance. I ran across the Lair, grabbed my skimmer, and took off. I moved out, pedaling furiously away from the Dragons, and glanced down.

For a minute I thought I was seeing things. The landscape below me was blurred, though the day had been clear and crisp when I'd flown into the Lair. I blinked. It didn't go away, but got clearer. There was a cloud of yellowish dust spreading high above the forest, billowing up and around the Lairs I could see. Where had it come from?

I sneezed, passing through a high plume of the dust. Then my eyes began to sting and I sneezed again. I brought the skimmer out of the cloud, but by this time my vision was distorted with tears. I began to cough and choke all at once, until the skimmer faltered as I fought to stay in control, my eyes streaming.

I knew what that dust was.

Nothing affected me as fiercely as puffbush pollen: it was the only thing I was really allergic to.

I stopped pedaling.

It affected Dragons, too. It set off their mating urges.

But where was the damned stuff coming from? It was six months out of season. I started pedaling again, legs straining. I turned to get a better view.

A flash of light needled past my head, and I knew. Three skimmers shot into view from around the spire of Paramount Lair. The tip of one of my wings was seared away by a blaser. My skimmer lurched wildly, but I held on and brought it up just as the fist skimmer came toward me. Its pilot was wearing a filtermask. Attached to the skimmer were some empty bags that must have held the puffbush pollen. But what I was looking at was the guy's blaser. It was aimed at me.

I reeled into an updraft, pulling over my attacker, grabbing for my own blaser. The skimmer soared beneath me, then careened into a sharp turn. It was too sharp. The guy turned straight into the path of his companion. The two skimmers crashed together with a satisfying sound, then the scattered parts and pilots fell slowly toward the tree-tops. Seconds later, the forest swallowed them up.

I looked for the third man, just as he came up beside me. The bas-tard was grinning, and I recognized that grin. It was Kwalan Rhiang's.

He nodded once, affably, and before I could remember to use my blaser, Rhiang took a single, precise shot at the chainguard of my skim-mer. The pedals rolled uselessly. I was out of control. Rhiang lifted away and cruised out of sight, leaving me flailing at the air in a ruined skimmer.

I had exactly one chance, and this was to get back to the Lair I'd just abandoned. I was slightly higher than the opening, so I glided in, backpedaled for the drop—and crashed straight into the wall, thanks to my ruined pedals. But I made it in alive, still able to stand up and brush the dirt from my uniform. I stood at the mouth of the Lair, star-ing out over the forest, considering the long climb that lay below me.

And just then the Dragons returned.

Not one, this time—not even two. *Five* shadows wheeled over-head; five huge beasts headed toward the Lair where I was standing. And finally, five Dragons dropped right on top of me.

I leaped back just in time, scrambling into the blue shadows as the first Dragon thumped to the ledge. It waddled inside, reeking. I moved back farther. Its four friends were right behind. I kept moving back.

Well, at least now I knew *why* they were doing this. Kwalan Rhiang had been setting off their mating urges by dusting the Dragons with puffbush pollen, messing up their whole life cycle, fooling with their already nasty tempers. It made sense. Anything less subtle might have gotten Rhiang into a lot of trouble. As it was, he'd doubtless fly safely home, waiting for Leopold's Dragons to kill off Leopold's men.

Out in the cavernous Lair, the Dragons began to move around, prodding at each other like scramblemice, hooting their airy courting sounds. The ground shook with their movement. Two seemed to be fe-males, which suggested that I might look forward to some fighting be-tween the other three. Great.

I fumbled at my pockets for something that might be of help. My warning buzzer had shattered in my rough landing; I threw it away. I still had my bagging-gun, but it wouldn't do me a lot of good. My blaser seemed okay. I unholstered it and began to move along the wall. If I went carefully, I might be able to get onto the outer ledge.

Two of the males were fighting now, lunging, the sounds of their efforts thundering around me. I made a short run and gained a bit of ground. One of the Dragons retreated from the battle—apparently the loser. I groaned. He had moved directly into my path.

A huge tail pounded at the ground near me and a female started backing my way, not looking at me. There was no place to go. And I was getting tired of this. I decided to warn her off. I made a quick shot at her back, nipping her in the hydrogen dome. She squawked and shuffled away, confused. I went on.

I stopped. There was a hissing sound behind me. Turning, I could see nothing but the Dragon I'd just shot. She didn't appear to be making the sound, but it was coming from her direction. I peered closer, through the blue gloom, and then saw where the noise was coming from.

Her hydrogen dome was deflating.

I nearly laughed aloud. Here was the answer to my problem. I could deflate the Dragons, leaving them stranded, unable to fly, while I climbed down this spire without fear of pursuit. I lifted my blaser and aimed at the male nearest the rear of the Lair. A near miss, then a hit. Hydrogen hissed out of his dome as well. Then I got the second female, and another male who was directly across from me.

One Dragon to go. The others were roaring and waddling. The Lair was full of the hissing sound.

I turned to my last opponent. He wasn't looking my way, but he was blocking my exit. I moved in closer and lifted my blaser.

Then he saw me.

I flung myself aside just as he bellowed and pounded forward, filling the entrance to the Lair, blocking out the sunlight. I rolled into the thorny nest. I fired once, hitting him in the snout. He swung his head toward me, pushing me around toward the outer ledge, bellowing. I fired again, and once more missed his hydrogen dome. I made a dash around his rump just as he spun my way, tail lashing against me. His dark little eyes narrowed as he sighted me, and his throat began to ripple.

My time was up. He was about to blast me with his throat flame.

The Dragon opened his mouth, belched hydrogen, and ignited it by striking a spark from his molars—

That was the wrong thing to do.

I saw it coming and ducked.

The cavern shuddered and blew up. The orange explosion rumbled out, catching the Dragons in a huge rolling flame. I buried myself in the nesting strands and grabbed onto the lashing tail of my attacker. Terrified by the blast, he took off. My eyebrows were singed, my wrists burned.

The world spun beneath me. A tendril of smoke drifted into view just below, mingled with flaming bits of nesting material and the leathery hide of Dragons. Then my view spun again and I was looking at the sky. It gradually dawned on me that I was clinging to a Dragon's tail.

It occurred to the Dragon at the same time. I saw his head swing toward me, snapping angrily. His belly was flashing purple. Every now and then he let out a tongue of flame, but he couldn't quite get at me. Meanwhile, I held on for my life.

The Dragon flew on, but my weight seemed to be too much for it. We were dropping slowly toward the trees, as easily as if I'd punctured his bony dome with my blaser. But it would be a rough landing. And I'd have to deal with the Dragon afterward.

I spied something rising from the trees below us. It shot swiftly into the air after a high-flying bulletbird, its transparent sheet rippling beneath its blimplike body. It was a huge snagger—as big as my own skimmer. I kicked on the Dragon's tail, dragging it sideways. The Dragon lurched and spun and then we were directly over the snagger.

I let go of the tail and dropped, my eyes closed.

In a second, something soft rumpled beneath me. I had landed safely atop the snagger. I opened my eyes as the Dragon—having lost my weight—shot suddenly upward. I watched it glide away, then looked down at the snagger, my savior. I patted its wide, rubbery body. My weight was pushing it slowly down, as if I were riding the balloons in the Angis Tavern. I looked forward to a comfortable trip to the ground.

"I like your style, kid."

I jumped, nearly losing my place on the snagger. The voice had come out of midair. Literally.

"You," I said. No more was necessary. He was banking around behind me.

Kwalan Rhiang had returned in his skimmer. He circled easily about me as I fell toward the treetops. He came in close, smiling, his huge legs pedaling him on a gentle course. I had to turn my head to keep an eye on him.

"I said before I'd top what Leopold was paying you," he shouted, his thick voice cutting the high air. "After today, I think I'd pay *double*. I could use someone like you."

I felt my face harden. "You bastard. You're responsible for what just happened. Why would I work for someone who's tried to kill me?"

He shrugged. "Gave you a chance to prove yourself. Come on, you're wasting your time with Leopold."

"And you're wasting your time with me."

He shrugged again, utterly sure of himself. "As you wish. I gave you a chance."

I nodded. "Now just go away."

"And leave you to tell Leopold about all'this? You don't think I'm going to let you back alive, do you?"

I froze. Rhiang slid a blaser from its holster at his waist and aimed it at my head. His grin widened. The muzzle dropped a fraction, and I breathed a little easier.

"No," he said distantly, "why kill you straight off? Slow deaths are more interesting, I think. And harder to trace."

He aimed at the snagger. If he punctured it I'd drop into the trees. It was a long fall. I wouldn't make it.

I growled and grabbed for the gun at my waist, bringing it up before Rhiang could move. He stared at me for a moment, then started laughing. I looked at what I was holding.

"What're you going to do with that?" he said. "Bag me?"

It was my bagging-pistol, all right. I'd dropped the blaser back in the Lair. But it would still serve a purpose.

"Exactly," I said, and fired.

The gray fluid squirted across the narrow gap between us, sealing instantly over Rhiang's hands. He fired the blaser but succeeded only in melting the bag enough to let the weapon break away. It fell out of sight.

His eyes were wide. He was considering death by suffocation.

"No," he choked.

But I didn't fire at his head. I put the next bag right over his feet, sealing the pedal mechanism tight. His legs jerked convulsively. They slowed. Rhiang began to whimper, and then he was out of control. His skimmer turned and glided away as he hurried to catch any updraft he could. He vanished behind Paramount Lair, and was gone.

I turned back to observe the treetops. Rhiang might be back, but I doubted it. First he'd have a long walk ahead of him, over unpleasant terrain, back to his base . . . *if* he could maneuver his skimmer well enough to land in the treetops, and make the long, painful climb down.

But I didn't worry about it. I watched the thorntrees rise about me, and presently the snagger brought me gently to the ground. I dismounted, leaving the snagger to bob back into the air, and began to walk gingerly across the inhospitable ground, avoiding the spines. A daggerbush snapped at me. I danced away. It was going to be a rough walk out. Somewhere behind me, Rhiang might be facing the same problem. And he wanted me dead.

But I didn't have as far to go.

A Plague of Butterflies

Orson Scott Card

The butterflies awoke him. Amasa felt them before he
saw them, the faint pressure of hundreds of half-dozens
of feet, weighting his rough wool sheet so that he
dreamed of a shower of warm snow. Then he opened his
eyes and there they were, in the shaft of sunlight like a
hundred stained-glass windows, on the floor like a carpet woven by an inspired lunatic, delicately in the air
like leaves falling upward in a wind.

At last, he said silently.

He watched them awhile, then gently lifted his
covers. The butterflies arose with the blanket. Carefully
he swung his feet to the floor; they eddied away from his
footfall, then swarmed back to cover him. He waded through them like
the shallow water on the edge of the sea, endlessly charging and then
retreating quickly. He who fights and runs away, lives to fight another
day. You have come to me at last, he said, and then he shuddered, for
this was the change in his life that he had waited for, and now he
wasn't sure he wanted it after all.

318

They swarmed around him all morning as he prepared for his journey. His last journey, he knew, the last of many. He had begun his life in wealth, on the verge of power, in Sennabris, the greatest of the oil-burning cities of the coast. He had grown up watching the vast ships slide into and out of the quays to void their bowels into the sink of the city. When his first journey began, he did not follow the tankers out to sea. Instead, he took what seemed the cleaner way, inland.

He lived in splendor in the hanging city of Besara on the cliffs of Carmel; he worked for a time as a governor in Kafr Katnei on the plain of Esdraelon until the Megiddo War; he built the Ladder of Ekdippa through solid rock, where a thousand men died in the building and it was considered a cheap price.

And in every journey he mislaid something. His taste for luxury stayed in Besara; his love of power was sated and forgotten in Kafr Katnei; his desire to build for the ages was shed like a cloak in Ekdippa; and at last he had found himself here, in a desperately poor dirt farm on the edge of the Desert of Machaerus, with a tractor that had to be bribed to work and harvests barely large enough to pay for food for himself and petrol for the machines. He hadn't even enough to pay for light in the darkness, and sunset ended every day with imperturbable night. Yet even here, he knew that there was one more journey, for he had not yet lost everything: still when he worked in the fields he would reach down and press his fingers into the soil; still he would bathe his feet in the rush of water from the muddy ditch; still he would sit for hours in the heat of the afternoon and watch the grain standing bright gold and motionless as rock, drinking sun and expelling it as dry, hard grain. This last love, the love of life itself—it, too, would have to leave, Amasa knew, before his life would have completed its course and he would have consent to die.

The butterflies, they called him.

He carefully oiled the tractor and put it into its shed.

He closed the headgate of the ditch and shoveled earth into place behind it, so that in the spring the water would not flow onto his fallow fields and be wasted.

He filled a bottle with water and put it into his scrip, which he slung over his shoulder. This is all I take, he said. And even that felt like more of a burden than he wanted to bear.

The butterflies swarmed around him, and tried to draw him off toward the road into the desert, but he did not go at once. He looked at his fields, stubbled after the harvest. Just beyond them was the tumble of weeds that throve in the dregs of water that his grain had not used. And beyond the weeds was the Desert of Machaerus, the place where those who love water die. The ground was stone: rocky outcroppings, gravel; even the soil was sand. And yet there were ruins there. Wooden skeletons of buildings that had once housed farmers. Some people thought that this was a sign that the desert was growing, pushing in to take over formerly habitable land, but Amasa knew better. Rather the wooden ruins were the last remnants of the woeful Sebasti, those wandering people who, like the weeds at the end of the field, lived on the dregs of life. Once there had been a slight surplus of water flowing down the canals. The Sebasti heard about it in hours; in days they had come in their ramshackle trucks; in weeks they had built their scrappy buildings and plowed their stony fields, and for that year they had a harvest because that year the ditches ran a few inches deeper than usual. The next year the ditches were back to normal, and in a few hours one night the houses were stripped, the trucks were loaded, and the Sebasti were gone.

I am a Sebastit, too, Amasa thought. I have taken my life from an unwilling desert; I give it back to the sand when I am through.

Come, said the butterflies alighting on his face. Come, they said, fanning him and fluttering off toward the Hierusalem road.

Don't get pushy, Amasa answered, feeling stubborn. But all the same he surrendered, and followed them out into the land of the dead.

The only breeze was the wind on his face as he walked, and the heat drew water from him as if from a copious well. He took water from his bottle only a mouthful at a time, but it was going too quickly even at that rate.

Worse, though: his guides were leaving him. Now that he was on the road to Hierusalem, they apparently had other errands to run. He first noticed their numbers diminishing about noon, and by three there were only a few hundred butterflies left. As long as he watched a particular butterfly, it stayed; but when he looked away for a moment, it was gone. At last he set his gaze on one butterfly and did not look away at all, just watched and watched. Soon it was the last one left, and he knew that it, too, wanted to leave. But Amasa would have none of that. If I can come at your bidding, he said silently, you can stay at mine. And so he walked until the sun was ruddy in the west. He did not drink; he did not study his road; and the butterfly stayed. It was a little victory. I rule you with my eyes.

"You might as well stop here, friend."

Startled to hear a human voice on this desolate road, Amasa looked up, knowing in that moment that his last butterfly was lost. He was ready to hate the man who spoke.

"I say, friend, since you're going nowhere anyway, you might as well stop."

It was an old-looking man, black from sunlight and naked. He sat in the lee of a large stone, where the sun's northern tilt would keep him in shadow all day.

"If I wanted conversation," Amasa said, "I would have brought a friend."

"If you think those butterflies are your friends, you're an ass."

Amasa was surprised that the man knew about the butterflies.

"Oh, I know more than you think," said the man. "I lived at Hierusalem, you know. And now I'm the sentinel of the Hierusalem Road."

"No one leaves Hierusalem," said Amasa.

"I did," the old man said. "And now I sit on the road and teach travelers the keys that will let them in. Few of them pay me much attention, but if you don't do as I say, you'll never reach Hierusalem, and your bones will join a very large collection that the sun and wind gradually turn back into sand."

"I'll follow the road where it leads," Amasa said. "I don't need any directions."

"Oh, yes, you'd rather follow the dead guidance of the makers of the road than trust a living man."

Amasa regarded him for a moment. "Tell me, then."

"Give me all your water."

Amasa laughed—a feeble enough sound, coming through splitting lips that he dared not move more than necessary.

"It's the first key to entering Hierusalem." The old man shrugged. "I see that you don't believe me. But it's true. A man with water or food can't get into the city. You see, the city is hidden. If you had miraculous eyes, stranger, you could see the city even now. It's not far off. But the city is forever hidden from a man who is not desperate. The city can only be found by those who are very near to death. Unfortunately, if you once pass the entrance to the city without seeing it because you had water with you, then you can wander on as long as you like, you can run out of water and cry out in a whisper for the city to unveil itself to you, but it will avail you nothing. The entrance, once passed, can never be found again. You see, you have to know the taste of death in your mouth before Hierusalem will open to you."

"It sounds," Amasa said, "like religion. I've done religion."

"Religion? What is religion in a world with a dragon at its heart?"

Amasa hesitated. A part of him, the rational part, told him to ignore the man and pass on. But the rational part of him had long since become weak. In his definition of man, "featherless biped" held more truth than "rational animal." Besides, his head ached, his feet throbbed, his lips stung. He handed his bottle of water to the old man, and then for good measure gave him his scrip as well.

"Nothing in there you want to keep?" asked the old man, surprised.

"I'll spend the night."

The old man nodded.

They slept in the darkness until the moon rose in the east, bright with its thin promise of a sunrise only a few hours away. It was Amasa who awoke. His stirring roused the old man.

"Already?" he asked. "In such a hurry?"

"Tell me about Hierusalem."

"What do you want, friend? History? Myth? Current events? The price of public transportation?"

"Why is the city hidden?"

"So it can't be found."

"Then why is there a key for some to enter?"

"So it *can* be found. Must you ask such puerile questions?"

"Who built the city?"

"Men."

"Why did they build it?"

"To keep man alive on this world."

Amasa nodded at the first answer that hinted at significance. "And what enemy is it, then, that Hierusalem means to keep out?"

"Oh, my friend, you don't understand. Hierusalem was built to keep the enemy in. The old Hierusalem, the new Hierusalem, built to contain the dragon at the heart of the world."

A story-telling voice was on the old man now, and Amasa lay back on the sand and listened as the moon rose higher at his left hand.

"Men came here in ships across the void of the night," the old man said.

Amasa sighed.

"Oh, you know all that?"

"Don't be an ass. Tell me about Hierusalem."

"Did your books or your teachers tell you that this world was not unpopulated when our forefathers came?"

"Tell me your story, old man, but tell it plain. No myth, no magic. The truth."

"What a simple faith you have," the old man said. "The truth. Here's the truth, much good may it do you. This world was filled with forest, and in the forest were beings who mated with the trees, and drew their strength from the trees. They became very treelike."

"One would suppose."

"Our forefathers came, and the beings who dwelt among the trees smelt death in the fires of the ships. They did things—things that looked like magic to our ancestors, things that looked like miracles. These beings, these dragons who hid among the leaves of the trees, they had science we know little of. But one science we had that they had never learned, for they had no use for it. We knew how to defoliate a forest."

"So the trees were killed."

"All the forests of the world now have grown up since that time.

Some places, where the forest had not been lush, were able to recover, and we live in those lands now. But here, in the Desert of Machaera— this was climax forest, trees so tall and dense that no underbrush could grow at all. When the leaves died, there was nothing to hold the soil, and it was washed onto the plain of Esdraelon. Which is why that plain is so fertile, and why nothing but sand survives here."

"Hierusalem."

"At first Hierusalem was built as an outpost for students to learn about the dragons, pathetic little brown woody creatures who knew death when they saw it, and died of despair by the thousands. Only a few survived among the rocks, where we couldn't reach them. Then Hierusalem became a city of pleasure, far from any other place, where sins could be committed that God could not see."

"I said truth."

"I say listen. One day the few remaining students of the science of the dragons wandered among the rocks, and there found that the dragons were not all dead. One was left, a tough little creature that lived among the grey rocks. But it had changed. It was not woody brown now. It was grey as stone, with stony outcroppings. They brought it back to study it. And in only a few hours it escaped. They never recaptured it. But the murders began, every night a murder. And every murder was of a couple who were coupling, neatly vivisected in the act. Within a year the pleasure seekers were gone, and Hierusalem had changed again."

"To what it is now."

"What little of the science of the dragons they had learned, they used to seal the city as it is now sealed. They devoted it to holiness, to beauty, to faith—and the murders stopped. Yet the dragon was not gone. It was glimpsed now and then, grey on the stone buildings of the city, like a moving gargoyle. So they kept their city closed to keep the dragon from escaping to the rest of the world, where men were not holy and would compel the dragon to kill again."

"So Hierusalem is dedicated to keeping the world safe for sin."

"Safe from retribution. Giving the world time to repent."

"The world is doing little in that direction."

"But some are. And the butterflies are calling the repentant out of the world, and bringing them to me."

Amasa sat in silence as the sun rose behind his back. It had not fully passed the mountains of the east before it started to burn him.

"Here," said the old man, "are the laws of Hierusalem:

"Once you see the city, don't step back or you will lose it.

"Don't look down into holes that glow red in the streets, or your eyes will fall out and your skin will slide off you as you walk along, and your bones will crumble into dust before you fully die.

"The man who breaks a butterfly will live forever.

"Do not stare at a small grey shadow that moves along the granite walls of the palace of the King and Queen, or he will learn the way to your bed.

"The Road to Dalmanutha leads to the sign you seek. Never find it."

Then the old man smiled.

"Why are you smiling?" asked Amasa.

"Because you're such a holy man, Saint Amasa, and Hierusalem is waiting for you to come."

"What's your name, old man?"

The old man cocked his head. "Contemplation."

"That's not a name."

He smiled again. "I'm not a man."

For a moment Amasa believed him, and reached out to see if he was real. But his finger met the old man's flesh, and it did not crumble.

"You have so much faith," said the old man again. "You cast away your scrip because you valued nothing that it contained. What *do* you value?"

In answer, Amasa removed all his clothing and cast it at the old man's feet.

He remembers that once he had another name, but he cannot remember what it was. His name now is Gray, and he lives among the stones, which are also grey. Sometimes he forgets where stone leaves off and he begins. Sometimes, when he has been motionless for hours, he has to search for his toes that spread in a fan, each holding to stone so firmly that when at last he moves them, he is surprised at where they were. Gray is motionless all day, and motionless all night. But in the hours before and after the sun, then he moves, skittering sure and rapid as a spider among the hewn stones of the palace walls, stopping only to drink in the fly-strewn standing water that remains from the last storm.

These days, however, he must move more slowly, more clumsily than he used to, for his stamen has at last grown huge, and it drags painfully along the vertical stones, and now and then he steps on it. It has been this way for weeks. Worse every day, and Gray feels it as a constant pain that he must ease, must ease, must ease; but in his small mind he does not know what easement there might be. So far as he knows, there are no others of his kind; in all his life he has met no other climber of walls, no other hanger from stone ceilings. He remembers that once he sought out couplers in the night, but he cannot remember what he did with them. Now he again finds himself drawn to windows, searching for easement, though not sure at all, holding in his mind no image of what he hopes to see in the dark rooms within the palace. It is dusk, and Gray is hunting, and is not sure whether he will find mate or prey.

I have passed the gate of Hierusalem, thought Amasa, and I was not near enough to death. Or worse, sometimes he thought, there is no Hierusalem, and I have come this way in vain. Yet this last fear was not a fear at all, for he did not think of it with despair. He thought of it with hope, and looked for death as the welcome end of his journey, looked for death which comes with its tongue thick in its mouth, death which waits in caves during the cool of the day and hunts for prey in the last and first light, death which is made of dust. Amasa watched for death to come in a wind that would carry him away, in a stone that would catch his foot in midstep and crumble him into a pile of bone on the road.

And then in a single footfall Amasa saw it all. The sun was framed, not by a haze of white light, but by thick and heavy clouds. The orchards were also heavy, and dripped with recent rain. Bees hummed around his head. And now he could see the city rising, green and grey and monumental just beyond the trees; all around him was the sound of running water. Not the tentative water that struggled to stay alive in the thirsty dirt of the irrigation ditch, but the lusty sound of water that is superfluous, water that can be tossed in the air as fountains and no one thinks to gather up the drops.

For a moment he was so surprised that he thought he must step backward, just one step, and see if it wouldn't all disappear, for Amasa did not come upon this gradually, and he doubted that it was real. But he remembered the first warning of the old man, and he didn't take that backward step. Hierusalem was a miracle, and in this place he would test no miracles.

The ground was resilient under his feet, mossy where the path ran over stone, grassy where the stones made way for earth. He drank at an untended stream that ran pure and overhung with flowers. And then he passed through a small gate in a terraced wall, climbed stairs, found another gate, and another, each more graceful than the last. The first gate was rusty and hard to open; the second was overgrown with climbing roses. But each gate was better tended than the last, and he kept expecting to find someone working a garden or picnicking, for surely someone must be passing often through the better-kept gates. Finally he reached to open a gate and it opened before he could touch it.

It was a man in the dirty brown robe of a pilgrim. He seemed startled to see Amasa. He immediately enfolded his arms around something and turned away. Amasa tried to see—yes, it was a baby. But the infant's hands dripped with fresh blood, it was obviously blood, and Amasa looked back at the pilgrim to see if this was a murderer who had opened the gate for him.

"It's not what you think," the palmer said quickly. "I found the babe, and he has no one to take care of him."

"But the blood."

"He was the child of pleasure seekers, and the prophecy was fulfilled, for he was washing his hands in the blood of his father's belly." Then the pilgrim got a hopeful look. "There is an enemy who must be fought. You wouldn't—"

A passing butterfly caught the pilgrim's eye. The fluttering wings circled Amasa's head only once, but that was sign enough.

"It is you," the pilgrim said.

"Do I know you?"

"To think that it will be in my time."

"*What* will be?"

"The slaying of the dragon." The pilgrim ducked his head and, freeing one arm by perching the child precariously on the other, he held the gate open for Amasa to enter. "God has surely called you."

Amasa stepped inside, puzzled at what the pilgrim thought he was, and what his coming portended. Behind him he could hear the pilgrim mutter, "It is time. It is time."

It was the last gate. He was in the city, passing between the walled gardens of monasteries and nunneries, down streets lined with shrines and shops, temples and houses, gardens and dunghills. It was green to the point of blindness, alive and holy and smelly and choked with business wherever it wasn't thick with meditation. What am I here for? Amasa wondered. Why did the butterflies call?

He did not look down into the red-glowing holes in the middles of streets. And when he passed the grey labyrinth of the palace, he did not look up to try to find a shadow sliding by. He would live by the laws of the place, and perhaps his journey would end here.

The Queen of Hierusalem was lonely. For a month she had been lost in the palace. She had strayed into a never-used portion of the labyrinth, where no one had lived for generations, and now, search as she might, she could find only rooms that were deeper and deeper in dust.

The servants, of course, knew exactly where she was, and some of them grumbled at having to come into a place of such filth, full of such unstylish old furniture, in order to care for her. It did not occur to *them* that she was lost—they only thought she was exploring. It would never do for her to admit her perplexity to them. It was the Queen's business to know what she was doing. She couldn't very well ask a servant, "Oh, by the way, while you're fetching my supper, would you mind mentioning to me where I *am*?" So she remained lost, and the perpetual dust irritated all her allergies.

The Queen was immensely fat, too, which complicated things. Walking was a great labor for her, so that once she found a room with a bed that looked sturdy enough to hold her for a few nights, she stayed until the bed threatened to give way. Her progress through the unused rooms, then, was not in a great expedition, but rather in fits and starts. On one morning she would arise miserable from the bed's increasing incapacity to hold her, eat her vast breakfast while the servants looked on to catch the dribbles, and then, instead of calling for singers or someone to read, she would order four servants to stand her up, point her in the direction she chose, and taxi her to a good, running start.

"That door," she cried again and again, and the servants would propel her in that direction, while her legs trotted underneath her, trying to keep up with her body. And in the new room she could not stop to contemplate: she must take it all in on the run, with just a few mad glances, then decide whether to try to stay or go on. "On," she usually cried, and the servants took her through the gradual curves and maneuvers necessary to reach whatever door was most capacious.

On the day that Amasa arrived in Hierusalem, the Queen found a room with a vast bed, once used by some ancient rake of a prince to hold a dozen paramours at once, and the Queen cried out, "This is it, this is the right place, stop, we'll stay!" and the servants sighed in relief and began to sweep, to clean, and to make the place livable.

Her steward unctuously asked her, "What do you want to wear to the King's Invocation?"

"I will not go," she said. How could she? She did not know how to get to the hall where the ritual would be held. "I choose to be absent this once. There'll be another one in seven years." The steward bowed and left on his errand, while the Queen envied him his sense of direction and miserably wished that she could go home to her own rooms. She hadn't been to a party in a month, and now that she was so far from the kitchens the food was almost cold by the time she was served the private dinners she had to be content with. Damn her husband's ancestors for building all these rooms anyway.

Amasa slept by a dunghill because it was warmer there, naked as he was; and in the morning, without leaving the dunghill, he found work. He was wakened by the servants of a great Bishop, stablemen who had the week's manure to leave for the farmers to collect. They said nothing to him, except to look with disapproval at his nakedness, but set to work, emptying small wheelbarrows, then raking up the dung to make a neater pile. Amasa saw how fastidiously they avoided touching the dung; he had no such scruples. He took an idle rake, stepped into the midst of the manure, and raked the hill higher and faster than the delicate stablemen could manage on their own. He worked with such a will that the Stablemaster took him aside at the end of the task.

"Want work?"

"Why not?" Amasa answered.

The Stablemaster glanced pointedly at Amasa's unclothed body. "Are you fasting?"

Amasa shook his head. "I just left my clothing on the road."

"You should be more careful with your belongings. I can give you livery, but it comes out of your wages for a year."

Amasa shrugged. He had no use for wages.

The work was mindless and hard, but Amasa delighted in it. The variety was endless. Because he didn't mind it, they kept him shoveling more manure than his fair share, but the shoveling of manure was like a drone, a background for bright rhinestones of childish delight: morning prayers, when the Bishop in his silver gown intoned the powerful words while the servants stood in the courtyard clumsily aping his signs; running through the street behind the Bishop's carriage shouting "Huzzah, huzzah!" while the Bishop scattered coins for the pedestrians; standing watch over the carriage, which meant drinking and hearing stories and songs with the other servants; or going inside to do attendance on the Bishop at the great occasions of this or that church or embassy or noble house, delighting in the elaborate costumes that so cleverly managed to adhere to the sumptuary laws while being as ostentatious and lewd as possible. It was grand, God approved of it all, and even discreet prurience and titillation were a face of the coin of worship and ecstasy.

But years at the desert's edge had taught Amasa to value things that the other servants never noticed. He did not have to measure his drinking water. The servants splashed each other in the bathhouse. He could piss on the ground and no little animals came to sniff at the puddle, no dying insects lit on it to drink.

They call Hierusalem a city of stone and fire, but Amasa knew it was a city of life and water, worth more than all the gold that was forever changing hands.

The other stablemen accepted Amasa well enough, but a distance always remained. He had come naked, from outside; he had no fear of uncleanliness before the Lord; and something else: Amasa had known the taste of death in his mouth and it had not been unwelcome. Now he accepted as they came the pleasures of a stableman's life. But he did not need them, and knew he could not hide that from his fellows.

One day the Prior told the Steward, and the Steward the Stablemaster, and the Stablemaster told Amasa and the other stablemen to wash carefully three times, each time with soap. The old-timers knew what it meant, and told them all: It was the King's Invocation that came but once in seven years, and the Bishop would bring them all to stand in attendance, clean and fine in their livery, while he took part in the solemn ordinances. They would have perfume in their hair. And they would see the King and Queen.

"Is she beautiful?" Amasa asked, surprised at the awe in the voices of these irreverent men when they spoke of her.

And they laughed and compared the Queen to a mountain, to a planet, to a moon.

But then a butterfly alighted on the head of an old woman, and suddenly all laughter stopped. "The butterfly," they all whispered. The woman's eyes went blank, and she began to speak:

"The Queen is beautiful, Saint Amasa, to those who have the eyes to see it."

The servants whispered: See, the butterfly speaks to the new one, who came naked.

"Of all the holy men to come out of the world, Saint Amasa, of all the wise and weary souls, you are wisest, you are weariest, you are most holy."

Amasa trembled at the voice of the butterfly. In memory he suddenly loomed over the crevice of Ekdippa, and it was leaping up to take him.

"We brought you here to save her, save her, save her," said the old woman, looking straight into Amasa's eyes.

Amasa shook his head. "I'm through with quests," he said.

And foam came to the old woman's mouth, wax oozed from her ears, her nose ran with mucus, her eyes overflowed with sparkling tears.

Amasa reached out to the butterfly perched on her head, the fragile butterfly that was wracking the old woman so, and he took it in his hand. Took it in his right hand, folded the wings closed with his left, and then broke the butterfly as crisply as a stick. The sound of it rang metallically in the air. There was no ichor from the butterfly, for it was made of something tough as metal, brittle as plastic, and electricity danced between the halves of the butterfly for a moment and then was still.

The old woman fell to the ground. Carefully the other servants cleaned her face and carried her away to sleep until she awakened. They did not speak to Amasa, except the Stablemaster, who looked at him oddly and asked, "Why would you want to live forever?"

Amasa shrugged. There was no use explaining that he wanted to ease the old woman's agony, and so killed it at its cause. Besides, Amasa was distracted, for now there was something buzzing in the base of his brain. The whirr of switches, infinitely small, going left or right; gates going open and closed; poles going positive and negative. Now and then a vision would flash into his mind, so quickly that he could not frame or recognize it. Now I see the world through butterfly's eyes. Now the vast mind of Hierusalem's machinery sees the world through mine.

Gray waits by this window: it is the one. He does not wonder how he knows. He only knows that he was made for this moment, that his life's need is all within this window, he must not stray to hunt for food because his great stamen is dewing with desire and in the night it will be satisfied.

So he waits by the window, and the sun is going; the sky is grey, but still he waits, and at last the lights have gone from the sky and all is silent within. He moves in the darkness until his long fingers find the edge of the stone. Then he pulls himself inside, and when his stamen scrapes painfully against the stone, immense between his legs, he only thinks: ease for you, ease for you.

His object is a great mountain that lies breathing upon a sea of sheets. She breathes in quick gasps, for her chest is large and heavy and hard to lift. He thinks nothing of that, but only creeps along the wall until he is above her head. He stares quizzically at the fat face; but it holds no interest for him. What interests Gray is the space at her shoulders where the sheets and blankets and quilts fall open like a tent door. For some reason it looks like the leaves of a tree to him, and he drops onto the bed and scurries into the shelter.

Ah, it is not stone! He can hardly move for the bouncing, his fingers and toes find no certain purchase, yet there is this that forces him on: his stamen tingles with extruding pollen, and he knows he cannot pause just because the ground is uncertain.

He proceeds along the tunnel, the sweating body to one side, the tent of sheets above and to the other side. He explores; he crawls clumsily over a vast branch; and at last he knows what he has been looking for. It is time, oh, time, for here is the blossom of a great flower, pistil lush for him. He leaps. He fastens to her body as he has always fastened to the limbs of the great wife trees, to the stone. He plunges stamen into pistil and dusts the walls with pollen. It is all he lived for, and when it is done, in only moments when the pollen is shed at last, he dies and drops to the sheets.

The Queen's dreams were frenzied. Because her waking life was wrapped and closed, because her bulk forced an economy of movement, in her sleep she was bold, untiring. Sometimes she dreamed of great chases on a horse across broken country. Sometimes she dreamed of flying. Tonight she dreamed of love, and it was also athletic and unbound. Yet in the moment of ecstasy there was a face that peered at her, and hands that tore her lover away from her, and she was afraid of the man who stared at the end of her dream.

Still, she woke trembling from the memory of love, only wistfully allowing herself to recall, bit by bit, where she really was. That she was lost in the palace, that she was as ungainly as a diseased tree with boles and knots of fat, that she was profoundly unhappy, that a strange man disturbed her dreams.

And then, as she moved slightly, she felt something cold and faintly dry between her legs. She dared not move again, for fear of what is was.

Seeing that she was awake, a servant bowed beside her. "Would you like your breakfast?"

"Help me," she whispered. "I want to get up."

The servant was surprised, but summoned the others. As they rolled her from the bed, she felt it again, and as soon as she was erect she ordered them to throw back the sheets.

And there he lay, flaccid, empty, grey as a deflated stone. The servants gasped, but they did not understand what the Queen instantly understood. Her dreams were too real last night, and the great appendage on the dead body fit too well the memory of her phantom lover. This small monster did not come as a parasite, to drain her; it came to give, not to receive.

She did not scream. She only knew that she had to run from there, had to escape. So she began to move, unsupported, and to her own surprise she did not fall. Her legs, propelled and strengthened by her revulsion, stayed under her, held her up. She did not know where she was going, only that she must go. She ran. And it was not until she had passed through a dozen rooms, a trail of servants chasing after her, that she realized it was not the corpse of her monstrous paramour she fled from, but rather what he left in her, for even as she ran she could feel something move within her womb, could feel something writhing, and she must, she must be rid of it.

As she ran, she felt herself grow lighter, felt her body melting under the flesh, felt her heaps and mounds erode away in an inward storm, sculpting her into a woman's shape again. The vast skin that had contained her belly began to slap awkwardly, loosely against her thighs as she ran. The servants caught up with her, reached out to support her, and plunged their hands into a body that was melting away. They said nothing; it was not for them to say. They only took hold of the loosening folds and held and ran.

And suddenly through her fear the Queen saw a pattern of furniture, a lintel, a carpet, a window, and she knew where she was. She had accidently stumbled upon a familiar wing of the palace, and now she had purpose, she had direction, she would go where help and strength were waiting. To the throne room, to her husband, where the king was surely holding his Invocation. The servants caught up with her at last; now they bore her up. "To my husband," she said, and they assured her and petted her and carried her. The thing within her leaped for joy: its time was coming quickly.

Amasa could not watch the ceremonies. From the moment he entered the Hall of Heaven all he could see were the butterflies. They hovered in the dome that was painted like the midsummer-night sky, blotting out the tiny stars with their wings; they rested high on painted pillars; camouflaged except when they fanned their graceful wings. He saw them where to others they were far too peripheral to be seen, for in the base of his brain the gates opened and closed, the poles reversed, always in the same rhythm that drove the butterflies' flight and rest. Save the Queen, they said. We brought you here to save the Queen. It throbbed behind his eyes, and he could hardly see.

Could hardly see, until the Queen came into the room, and then he could see all too clearly. There was a hush, the ceremonies stopped, and all gazes were drawn to the door where she stood, an undulant mass of flesh with a woman's face, her eyes vulnerable and wide with fright and trust. The servants' arms reached far into the folds of skin, finding God-knew-what grip there: Amasa only knew that her face was exquisite. Hers was the face of all women, the hope in her eyes the answer to the hope of all men. "My husband!" she cried out, but at the moment she called she was not looking at the King. She was looking at Amasa.

She is looking at me, he thought in horror. She is all the beauty of Besara, she is the power of Kafr Katnei, she is the abyss of Ekdippa, she is all that I have loved and left behind. I do not want to desire them again.

The King cried out impatiently, "Good God, woman!"

And the Queen reached out her arms toward the man on the throne, gurgled in agony and surprise, and then shuddered like a wood fence in a wind.

What is it, asked a thousand whispers. What's wrong with the Queen?

She stepped backward.

There on the floor lay a baby, a little grey girlchild, naked and wrinkled and spotted with blood. Her eyes were open. She sat up and looked around, reached down and took the placenta in her hands and bit the cord, severing it.

The butterflies swarmed around her, and Amasa knew what he was meant to do. As you snapped the butterfly, they said to him, you must break this child. We are Hierusalem, and we were built for this epiphany, to greet this child and slay her at her birth. For this we found the man most holy in the world, for this we brought him here, for you alone have power over her.

I cannot kill a child, Amasa thought. Or did not think, for it was not said in words but in a shudder of revulsion in him, a resistance at the core of what in him was most himself.

This *is* no child, the city said. Do you think the dragons have surrendered just because we stole their trees? The dragons have simply changed to fit a new mate; they mean to rule the world again. And the gates and poles of the city impelled him, and Amasa decided a thousand times to obey, to step a dozen paces forward and take the child in his arms and break it. And as many times he heard himself cry out, I cannot kill a child! And the cry was echoed by his voice as he whispered, "No."

Why am I standing in the middle of the Hall of Heaven, he asked himself. Why is the Queen staring at me with horror in her eyes? Does she recognize me? Yes, she does, and she is afraid of me. Because I mean to kill her child. Because I cannot kill her child.

As Amasa hesitated, tearing himself, the grey infant looked at the King. "Daddy," she said, and then she stood and walked with gathering certainty toward the throne. With such dexterous fingers the child picked at her ear. Now. Now, said the butterflies.

Yes, said Amasa. No.

"My daughter!" the King cried out. "At last an heir! The answer to my Invocation before the prayer was done—and such a brilliant child!"

The King stepped down from his throne, reached to the child and tossed her high into the air. The girl laughed and tumbled down again.

Once more the King tossed her in delight. This time, however, she did not come down.

She hovered in the air over the King's head, and everyone gasped. The child fixed her gaze on her mother, the mountainous body from which she had been disgorged, and she spat. The spittle shone in the air like a diamond, then sailed across the room and struck the Queen on her breast, where it sizzled. The butterflies suddenly turned black in midair, shriveled, dropped to the ground with infinitesimal thumps that only Amasa could hear. The gates all closed within his mind, and he was all himself again; but too late, the moment was passed, the child had come into her power, and the Queen could not be saved.

The King shouted, "Kill the monster!" But the words still hung in the air when the child urinated on the King from above. He erupted in flame, and there was no doubt now who ruled in the palace. The grey shadow had come in from the walls.

She looked at Amasa, and smiled. "Because you were the holiest," she said, "I brought you here."

Amasa tried to flee the city. He did not know the way. He passed a palmer who knelt at a fountain that flowed from virgin stone, and asked, "How can I leave Hierusalem?"

"No one leaves," the palmer said in surprise. As Amasa went on, he saw the palmer bend to continue scrubbing at a baby's hands. Amasa tried to steer by the patterns of the stars, but no matter which direction he ran, the roads all bent toward one road, and that road led to a single gate. And in the gate the child waited for him. Only she was no longer a child. Her slate-grey body was heavy-breasted now, and she smiled at Amasa and took him in her arms, refused to be denied. "I am Dalmanutha," she whispered, "and you are following my road. I am Acrasia, and I will teach you joy."

She took him to a bower on the palace grounds, and taught him the agony of bliss. Every time she mated with him, she conceived, and in hours a child was born. He watched each one come to adulthood in hours, watched them go out into the city and affix themselves each to a human, some man, some woman, or some child. "Where one forest is gone," Dalmanutha whispered to him, "another will rise to take its place."

In vain he looked for butterflies.

"Gone, all gone, Amasa," Acrasia said. "They were all the wisdom that you learned from my ancestors, but they were not enough, for you hadn't the heart to kill a dragon that was as beautiful as man." And she *was* beautiful, and every day and every night she came to him and conceived again and again, telling him of the day not long from now when she would unlock the seals of the gates of Hierusalem and send her bright angels out into the forest of man to dwell in the trees and mate with them again.

More than once he tried to kill himself. But she only laughed at him as he lay with bloodless gashes in his neck, with lungs collapsed, with poison foul-tasting in his mouth. "You can't die, my Saint Amasa," she said. "Father of Angels, you can't die. For you broke a wise, a cruel, a kind and gentle butterfly."

THE EVER-AFTER

eluki bes shahar

Ruana Rulane was a hero. Practically speaking, in terms of semantics and sex, she should have been a heroine, but heroines are rather more associated with the staunch maintenance of husbands, children, and the gentler arts of domestic order.

But Ruana Rulane was a hero—which is to say, vastly inconvenient except in time of war. And this was peacetime.

This was not to say she wasn't a well-tried and acceptable hero, as self-willed anarchic moralists go. She had slain giants, faced down bandits, meddled where she wasn't wanted for the sheer joy of it, gotten brief glory and a little legend and would have had more if she'd stopped in any of the places willing to take in a hero and a sword.

But she didn't. Like most heroes, she was on a quest. Like some heroes, she was pretty sure she'd thrown over her every happiness in favor of having her own way. She'd listened too hard one day to an inner voice that told her she was special, and after a solid young life-time of backing and forthing, missed opportunities and bad choices, she'd followed her convictions to the point where she was sitting in a worn saddle on an indifferent horse on a muddy road, hearing the carved bone rings in her hair go rattle-click and watching someone else's destiny make a royal nuisance of itself in front of her.

Destiny blocked the road, spilled into the rut-wet, half-plowed spring fields, and squandered itself joyously on the land around. Destiny was two dozen of the Grey Duke's soldiers and a jagranatha more glorious than anything found outside a festival procession in the war-duke's capital. The only trouble with the jagranatha was that it was not in the city. It was in the country, and so it was in a ditch. And the four-teen milk-white oxen with gilded horns and golden nose-rings who drew it went with such commendable gravity and unstoppable deliber-ation that the jagranatha was now wedged eternally into the sloppy space between the fields and the road.

This was a grave misfortune for the Grey Duke and whatever pos-session of his needed to travel with such pomp. But it did not seem to contain, as a situation, the seeds of any wrong whatsoever that needed to be righted, and Ruana did not intend to let her horse stand and ac-quire whatever Crownking-forgotten ailments an overheated nag left standing in cold mud could catch. So she turned her beast aside for a politic detour over the half-plowed fields, and with inevitability was hailed back by the soldiers to help pull the sacred cart out of the ditch.

One more horse and one more body wasn't going to make any dif-ference. Ruana knew it. The soldiers knew it. But they were all of them, including the oxen, snabbled by destiny, sorcery, or the perver-sity of human nature, and so the soldiers called to her, and she came, and the jibes started out "boy" and went on "woman" and then some-body knew her story.

Ruana Rulane, the Twiceborn. Genuine hero, certified oddity, ripe with triumph and tragedy and perils surmounted. They were disap-pointed that she didn't look more like a glittering ale-house legend, though the Grey Duke's men of all people should have known better. They began jostling one another as men do, badgering their disap-pointment into contempt, angry and somehow cheated that they couldn't claim the pleasant conquests and certifications of grace that she could and didn't. And then it came, as it had to. The sword, the tale, and the challenge, and Ruana stood in the cold mud to hear it.

Half a year, a year ago (tales varied), it came to the Grey Duke's attention that there was something new in his domain, and he wanted it. This much was fact. The lightning, firedrakes, visions, and intimations godly and demonic varied from man to man. Ruana did her best, in kindness, to believe all of them. In the end the Duke, well and truly impressed by something, had sent one of the wide carts that conveyed idols through his city into the dispirited mud of the northwest to claim his prize.

They'd found it. They were bringing it back. And possibly by autumn the Grey Duke's soldiers escorting the jagranatha would have covered the one-week-on-horseback's distance to the city.

It was a sword, they said, that killed anyone who touched it except a true hero. And then they laughed and let the matter lie for a moment, and one of them cuffed the drover back to his place at the head of the first yoke of oxen.

The oxen heaved, the jagranatha tipped, and there was a forerunnering sound of sliding. Then Ruana saw the sword. It was the dreaming, lit-seawater green of meteoric glass, shimmering wicked, wide-bladed and translucent.

Love me, it said, and Ruana's spirit lived in her eyes to answer.

Then there was a winking flame of rubies caught cloudy candyfire in the blade, and Ruana looked away, heartsick. A mock blade. A ritual blade. Nobody jewelled a sword-blade he meant to use.

But there was more noisy fuss as the Grey Duke's magic sword slid into the mud and lay glinting on its jellied surface, and gradually Ruana, standing flatfoot and perilous with the mud sliding intimate into her boots, realized none of the Grey Duke's swordsmen dared touch it. Priests had loaded it with chants and wooden tongs, priests who were now fat and warm and fuddled with wine at the best inn to be reached in a day's journey.

Just before the moment when twenty cold and irritated soldiers doing a job both dangerous and ridiculous decided to prove to a traveller with a legend that she could be miserable too, Ruana walked out from among them and picked up the sword that killed with a touch.

She knew priests and didn't like them. Most of them lied.

It was a two-handed sword—had to be, with that size—but the black-bone hilt was grooved to make it possible to lift one-handed. There was a ruby round as an egg and clear as water in the pommel, and the weapon rallied sweetly, with lightsome balance.

She did not die.

"Happen it be I'll take this toy off to yon grey fat chanters for you, and spare you each the trouble of being where the other is." Her voice was husky, having been forced to loudness on a number of battlefields.

They wouldn't come near her. They didn't stop her. She could have taken the sword anywhere she chose. But Ruana knew the name of the inn the priests would be at and had every intention of going only there. She saw no point in stealing useless enchanted swords and less point in being hunted out of the Grey Duke's holdings before time.

She would be, eventually. It was inevitable. Heroes don't compromise and dukes don't reason. He'd send people to chase her off or summon her and offer her gold to do something she didn't want. And then . . . Well, there were always more lands to the south.

But that was for later. The mud dried on her boots as her horse jogged down the road.

Love me, said the sword, seductive in her hand as she rode, and made her dream of triumph. Of finding the mythic Starharp and playing it to wake the sleeping Crownking. Of doing deeds to draw the singers from their patrons' praises to make a song of her and her alone.

Lost, glittered the sword. *Lost, forsaken, betrayed* . . . The sky grew dark. Ruana frowned, and spurred her horse, and remembered.

Once, a long time ago in the far north country, there was an eclipse, and in its shadow a woman was brought to bed of her firstborn in the same hour its father died. She lost husband and daughter in that hour, and then her name, because to baffle the vengeance of the cheated child-ghost it was decreed by the elders of that small village that Ruana should become a man. The bone ornaments were quickly brought, and the drums and herbs, and when the dance was over there was no grief spent on husband and girlchild, for Rulane Twiceborn had none.

And when Rulane had been schooled to an honorable man's estate, skilled with sword and bow and sling, Ruana left. Sword and horse and ivory dice were all the patrimony and dowry of Ruana Rulane.

Hero, hero, hero, sang the drumsong of the horse's hooves. The sword she carried for another was light and glowing in her hands. Never a moment to weep for the daughter died borning, no tears to give for her lover, her husband, dead under the ice. They had taken everything from her—her name, her family, her past, her future.

Lost. Lost, forsaken, betrayed . . . The sword danced in her hand, instinct with violence.

With such a sword as this she could return to the place where she had been born, and with its blade of liquid light school priest-elders to sorrow. She could make the stars weep for the day that had birthed such a glorious abomination—not man, not woman, not mother nor yet the child of any mother. Twiceborn. Ruana Rulane, the Twiceborn.

The ghosts of future glory gathered around her. They would pay; oh, how they would pay.

Ruana checked the horse and gazed down at the sharp-wild sword with dreaming eyes. *Shadowkiss,* she named it, and touched the heart's-blood crystal of the gems in the blade.

But why would I want to go back north? Her mouth stretched wry with puzzlement. Her past was a story, and a pretty story for a singer's tongue, but it was over and done. If she could even find the village where she had been born it would be nothing like she remembered. And though she might kill the villagers every one, she could not make them sorry that they had protected themselves from evil times.

The lure of her past drew back. *Sword, what are you?*

Lover.

Ruana picked up the reins again and urged the horse onward.

The river bridge was out, and her horse didn't like the water. She couldn't blame the beast, with the river running spring-flood high, but the ferryman who should have been there was nowhere to be seen. He might be off drinking Duke's gold, or dead, or as little fond of a river in spate as Ruana's horse was. At any rate, he wasn't there.

She swung west, following the riverbank. The sword lay across her thighs, hot and living. A spare league south was the inn full of priests whose charge she had carried off. Soon enough (she would do it, in their place) a rider would come from the soldiers to dress her abduction of the sword in fantastic language. She made no doubt he'd find a way across the river. Trouble always did, and then it would be the priests who decided how much more trouble to make.

Still, likely they wouldn't make a decision before tomorrow dawn. She could ride all night if she had to, providing she could ford the river by the end of the day.

And give the sword back. Her hand tightened on the rough bone of the hilt. If she could.

Shadowkiss.

The edge of the river became sheer-cut mud cliffs and brambles, narrow enough to jump on a better horse. Ruana followed the river road as it swung inland, and the dripping trees opened to fields again.

Burned fields.

Here there had been no spring plowing. Last year's weed and stubble were seared to black, gone liquid with the rain, and her horse shied at the stink.

Then she came to the freehold.

She had seen a number like it here in the south. A fine big house with barns and stables, and lesser houses for carle and carline in a ring just inside the ditches that could hold palisades in time of war.

No more. The cottages were smoke and ash. The barn door hung half off its hinges, displaying emptiness, and the stable was charcoal bones. If the palisades had ever been erected, there was no sign of them now.

She wasn't an utter fool. A magic sword and a duke's displeasure were trouble enough. If she wanted more she could come back here later to find what had blighted the crops and burned the buildings. Later. Half of being a live hero was the timing. She clucked to her horse and turned its head to ride away.

But they came out of the house to her and stood starveling-gaunt in ragged gowns and tunics, survivors of a freehold that saw outsiders maybe twice in a year, and not even that now that the horses were dead.

There was no use asking them why they didn't leave, no more than asking them why they didn't fight. Either choice was suicide. The land and their labor on it were all they had.

They looked at Ruana with hungry eyes, and even her patched and worn leathers were finery to them. Hero, they said to the bone rings braided in her hair, and stretched their eyes to the luminous glass-green of her jewelled sword. Save us.

"Ah, damn the lot of you!" the hero snarled, brandishing the borrowed sword in a glittering arc. It hummed, sweet as pack-ice in deep winter, and her horse side-stepped, unimpressed. The old question rose unbidden in her mind, and there was still only one answer.

If not her, then who? If not now, when?

"Happen some one of you will know where it bides," she said resignedly. "Happen you'll show me where to go."

She'd known what it was when she saw the fields. They didn't like the warmth of a southern summer; left alone this one might sleep till autumn. But the crofters wouldn't go out to the fields while they thought it was there, and if they did, it would be roused by the scent and sound of prey and attack.

She bullied them into giving her what she needed, coaxing them with promises of victory and brave tales of heroism. With a few hours of daylight left, she loaded the casks and the torches and the firepot onto her horse and went off with the least terrified of the survivors to show her the way.

The worm had laired upland. Her horse stopped at the edge of the gummy, cast-seared earth, and would go no farther. She swore, and tied the shivering animal to a tree, blindfolding it to make it stand. The glass sword she sheathed reluctantly in the earth and drew her own familiar blade of browned iron. It would not do to injure what she was still hoping to return.

But it hurt to let it go. They were meant to be together. Together their word would shape the world.

"What do you want me to do?" The boy's voice jarred her back to herself.

In truth, she'd counted herself lucky he'd come with her this far. It was an act of bravery, and there'd be no particular virtue in being a hero if bravery was easily come by. Now she took a closer look at him and saw, if not the noble lineaments of singer's tales, at least the mark of more and better food in childhood.

"Land-holder's bairn be, hinny?" she asked kindly.

The northland dialect was unfamiliar to him, but he understood enough. "My father was freeholder here. The dragon killed him. Now I'm freeholder. I want to help you kill the dragon."

Ruana saw the stubbornness under the dirt, and the bleak knowledge that to hold the crofters to him now he must add "Dragonslayer" to his name, like it or not.

"Well then," she said, accepting. "If you're after killing worm, my callant, take up one of those casks and come along."

". . . worm-lair has two ways in. Other one'll be hidden, and likely we could spend a planter's year looking for it. But worm's a fashious hellicat, and if we block up one entrance, he'll be bound to come and see why."

She was far from being as confident as she sounded, but she had killed worms before, even with unskilled help. Fire blinded them, and at the very least the thing would lair somewhere else.

Dickon stuck the torches into the ground. Ruana lit them all from the firepot, then stove in the top of the first oil-cask.

"Mind you get ready to run."

"I'm not afraid!" But his hands were shaking as he took the open cask and headed up the side of the worm-hill.

"Hurry, damn you!" The words came out more sharply than she'd intended. They'd made enough noise to wake it; if the worm came out on top of Dickon, he wouldn't have to worry about holding his father's lands.

His feet left dusty footprints on the tarry surface of the hill. The oil slopped all around the hole in the earth as he poured it in. He threw the cask after it.

"There's something down there—I saw it!" Dickon gasped, sliding down the hill again with hasty grace.

The earth shook, and a blind white shaft of flesh burst up out of the hole. Too soon! Ruana snatched up the nearest torch and shied it past Dickon's head, praying it would stay lit, would ignite the oil, that a thousand different luck-chances would fall her way.

The cask, balanced on the worm's head, fell. The torch struck its oil-slicked side and set the creature afire in a rush of flame.

She heard the boy and the horse both scream, and perhaps the fear that she should feel would come later in dreams. For now she was here to kill the worm.

It towered up to the sky, a column as big as the body of an ox and glistening with the juices running from its split, seared flesh. Its head was ringed with ruined eyes, and clashing triangular teeth lined its mouth and throat. It smelled of rotting cheese.

Ruana Rulane ran up the side of the worm-hill, over the new wetness that made her boot soles smoke. She reached the marrow-fat translucence of the body of the worm and cut deep into the leather-over-jelly of it. Slow, grey-white gobbets of ooze began pushing through the widening rip.

The worm wailed—she felt its soundless cry as a lancing pain in her head. It tried to retreat, but even the smooth sides of its tunnel were too painful against its skin. Thrashing blindly, it searched for the source of its agony, slamming its body again and again against the ground outside its nest.

The third time it hit the ground, Ruana jumped to its back. Before it had time to throw her off, she locked her ankles together behind its head and drove her good iron sword into its skull.

The treetops flashed by below her as it reared, carrying her up into the last rays of the setting sun. The sword sank in deep and she began to saw, wondering for a brief moment if she would have done anything so foolhardy as face down a worm alone at eventide if she weren't grieving already about giving up that Duke's bawbee of a glass sword.

Then there was no time to wonder, only to curse, as the pale jelly of the worm foamed up over her gauntlets and began to burn on her skin. Black liquid sprayed out of its mouth and seeped up through the wound she had made; one of her hair-rings cut her cheek as she was whipped giddily around. And still it would not die.

"Crownking!" she cried, but the Sleeping God did not hear. Furious now, she stabbed and gouged and plunged her hand deep into the acid slime of the worm's body to find something solid to cut that would end its life. Her fingers met around a gut-slippery thickness somewhere inside—she squeezed and, madly, pulled.

Then the pain in her head was blinding, and for an instant she was free of both earth and worm.

It was still dying as she shook her hair out of her eyes—knowing enough, even now, not to touch her face. Her hands closed on emptiness; her sword was gone.

The trees had broken her fall and not her neck. She groped to her feet with a groan. Better than she deserved; how could she have been so stupid?

There were some questions better not asked. She stripped off her half-eaten gloves and looked at the raw red flesh beneath. Water, first, to wash them, then the other cask of oil to save the skin, always assuming the horse that carried it hadn't managed to bolt.

The worm was lying fully extended now, dead and already beginning to rot. Eighteen feet, maybe twenty. A prize specimen . . .

But not big enough to do the damage she'd seen at the farmstead.

She heard a scream—Dickon—and looked up.

A second worm was coming. This one flew.

And she didn't have a sword.

The Crownking, before he slept, had seen fit to put two of every kind of beast into the world, and the worm was no exception. What she was seeing now, Ruana guessed, was a she-worm, and it looked like being the last thing she was going to see. The creature's body bulged and tapered, and wings like rainbow and pond-slick made a haze over its back in the fading twilight.

Find a plan, damme—otherwise you've just wakened the thing to raze the holding again!

Things happened too fast. The buzz of the she-worm's wings filled the air, and Ruana saw the white flash of Dickon's face off to her left. He was terrified, but he was here, and then he grabbed for something and she knew what it must be. She ran toward him, shouting "No!"

The flash of blue fire made her leap back, and for a moment she saw every bone in Dickon's body illuminated like bright day. He drew the god-sword free of the earth before it killed him, and even dead staggered two steps toward her with it, wide eyes blankly white and hair dancing in a spirit-wind from hell.

Ruana Rulane was the Twiceborn, and knew to a nicety the hurt that magic could do. But whatever the sword might do to her now was nothing to what the worm would do—to her and to others. She dragged the sword from the dead child's hands and turned to face the worm.

New strength sang through her body, and she didn't grudge the blood that dript from raw hands onto the hilt of the sword. The hero with the magic sword faced the dragon, and called it in gleeful north-land accents to come and die.

But the thing danced on wingtips just out of her reach and slashed at her with its barbed tail. A circle of eyes, glass and mirrors, gave Ruana back a thousand self-images. So she did what she had to, luring it back into the darkness of the trees where it could not use its wings, where her only defense against the vague murderous paleness was Shadowkiss.

No ritual blade this, but a killing engine edged sharper than glass, lighter and stronger than any smith-forged sword. Each time the sword struck it bit ruinously deep; fast and deadly and meant for her hand alone. Ruana butchered the loathly worm in darkness so total she could not be sure when it died, only that it was dead when she staggered away from the body.

There was no moon. She followed the sound of the water to the riverbank and fainted with her hands in the stream.

In her dreams she rode the worm again, and its torso writhed and bucked between her thighs—only to change, dreamlike, to the body of a man who laughed and clasped her and held her close.

"Ruana, Ruana, Ruana Rulane—Rulane the Twiceborn!" He sang her name and shimmered away to mist before she could see his face.

"Who are you?" She knew the answer. Demon-dreams, and she too tired to wake. She reached, dreaming, for her sword.

"Name me and I'll tell you! Name me and I'll stay!"

The promise came from nowhere and everywhere. She bit her lips shut over the name.

She was standing on a misty plain. Shadowkiss was in her hand, sensuous as jade. The light from its gems stained the shrouding fog pink.

"Who am I?" mist-echo demanded.

"Where am I?" Ruana countered. *On the edge of heart's desire*, came the inward certainty. Ahead the mist thinned. Rocks appeared; a cave.

She was standing on the wet sand of ebb tide, and as she walked toward the sea-cave her boots made no sound. Once inside she heard the booming rhythm of the surf, and by the glittering salt-blue flame of torches she could see damp-rotted frescoes weeping down the curving walls: Crownking and Starharp, the lesser gods, heroes, ancient kings, and men. Battles and wars in undiscovered countries, and at their center the Starharp waited, to wake the Crownking and play to life new universes.

It glittered on its altar, recurving framework charmed golden out of starlight and strung with a silver purer than any metal. Here was the linchpin of the turning world, waiting only the mortal who would take it up and become the centerpiece of all the gods.

This was what she wanted. This was what drew her, through a life of bad inns, worse food, and no more home than blanket and saddle-tree. To take the Starharp and do a deed remembered down through the ages, to change the shape of the world.

The other entered the cave behind her. This was the truth, the answer, and the bargain. She could name the other if she chose, and gain . . .

A hero's sword for a true hero, chosen of the gods to be the herald of a new age. A lover for her love, and the promise that everything she had done to reach this place was justified and paid for, burnished right and inevitable and necessary.

She lowered the swordpoint to the sand. She did not need the outward symbol now.

"Ruana," said the other, shadow of her self. Arms embraced her from behind, and on their hands' fingers were green glass rings set with rubies.

"Name me," said her shadow, and in the words echoed every consequence of her actions. The Starharp filled her eyes with gold and silver light.

Loved. Worshiped. Glorified. Avenged.

"You killed the boy."

For a moment it seemed even the Starharp glowed less bright.

"It is my nature. Soon all will know our legend, and no one from the lowliest peasant to the highest lord will dare to lay hands on the sword of the Twiceborn. Do not set one unimportant boy against that. Do not shame me. I have waited for you since the universe was made; together we are complete. With me you take up a mad god's curse and a glorious destiny; to play the Starharp and bring order to all the worlds. Ruana. Beloved."

And all at the cost of one unimportant boy. Take the sword—or decide that some glory asked too high a price.

Ruana Rulane made her choice.

"Name me."

"Shadowkiss."

She woke in the morning to river mist that convinced her she still slept, to larksong that was no respecter of dragons, to a splitting head and blistered hands and an empty belly. Her back hurt.

She was glad to be alive.

The horse was dead. The worm and its mate were nothing now but odd bone barbs.

The boy Dickon was a featherweight in her arms. She took him back to the freehold and told the survivors the tale—that she and the freeholder's son between them had slain the dragon and its mate, and that now the woods and fields were safe. The crofters gave her bandages for her hands and a share in their breakfast. They gave the hero's sword a reverent distance, and buried the boy in the stableyard where the stones could easily be taken up. Ruana left before they were done.

Midday on foot she found a ford and then began the laborious process of finding the main road again.

Shadowkiss was wrapped in blanket scraps and slung over her shoulder. The Grey Duke had sent his men for the sword, and Ruana had told them she would take it to his priests. And so she would, but now it seemed she would take it to the duke as well—and farther. It was an inconvenient fact of life that the future seemed to hold killing and maybe imprisonment and certainly the disappointment of a powerful overlord in the matter of the god-sword Shadowkiss. The duke would certainly want what he considered his and she had no intention of giving it to him.

Her muscles protested the unaccustomed exercise, and her horseman's boots weren't meant for walking. It was something of a relief when the Grey Duke's soldiers showed up.

They surrounded her with nocked arrows and conspicuous amulets, and one or two made the sign against magic. She eased her pack and saddle to the ground while a fat priest on a fat mule blew smoke and ash toward her out of a dish. A terrified acolyte dashed up to souse her with flower water.

She shook it out of her eyes with a curse and drew the sword. It sliced through the bindings of its improvised scabbard and flashed all the colors of ocean in the sun.

She could see each move she would make in her mind. It did not matter that the soldiers were six. First the man slain to gain her a mount, then the others dead from horseback, then the priest, left gutted and handless alive for the rooks, to warn his gods their freedom's end was coming.

So simple.

"Take the sword!" The priest's voice was cross but not yet frightened.

"You!" she shouted back. "Get you down; I've no mind to walk to the city."

The duke's men stared. Shadowkiss keened its disappointment in a voice only she could hear. Ruana filled her lungs and spoke again.

"Listen, my callants. Your duke will want to know what's kept you so long on the road. Do you want him having the chanter's way of it only? You're sworn to take this sword to him and I'll not stop you—so get that useless noise off his beast and we'll be off." The soldiers looked at one another. One of them smiled and the others laughed.

"And look you mind the sword," she said, as the captain started toward the priest. "Happen it kills heroes, too."

Her feet were tied beneath the belly of the mule and the captain led it. After the first day they got her a horse.

On the third day they gave her a scabbard to fit the sword, and her feet were untied.

On the sixth day they entered Corchado.

It was not the largest city for priests, or the biggest for markets, but it was the city you must take to take the South. Somewhere farther down the road they spoke of this as the northland, and even there they spoke of Corchado. It was built on a hill made of the broken stones of enemy cities, and enemy bones were mortared into the bricks of its walls.

The soldiers brought her through the town, and she brandished what she carried for all to see. Shadowkiss urged her to find the way to Ocean, where the Starharp waited and the Crownking slept. It forgave her betrayal and loved her again, dreaming and promising her destiny. Ruana had never seen the ocean nor spoken to anyone who had. The way to Ocean would be a journey through legend.

The castle portcullis closed behind her. The sword was in its sheath, and her hand was on her sword hilt as she dismounted. There was an inevitability about the situation it was hard not to admire. The duke wanted the sword, to which he had only a tentative claim at best. Ruana had a better one, but things being what they were, the moment she enforced it people would die. She had no faith in the healing power of common sense. She had come because she was no sneak thief, and because she had said she would, but against that waited the arrogance of princes, pat and foolish as a singer's tale.

Eight men in gilded plate armor presented themselves in the courtyard. Their captain was in plumes and scarlet. Shadowkiss foretold their deaths and Ruana waited for them to demand the sword she carried.

But they didn't.

"You're to come with me, Rulane Twiceborn. The Duke will see you."

The parade-captain looked at Ruana.

Not so much older than an unimportant boy.

Ruana took her hand from the sword hilt. This time it was harder.

The captain closed the door behind her. The room held one man.

Now Ruana drew the sword. In the dim room it gathered all the light and gave back color brighter than the tapestries. The Duke looked up. He stood at the tall desk by the window, turning the pages of a book with jewelled covers.

"Is this what you sent for, my fine one?" Ruana asked.

His eyes were a little darker than amber, his hair already streaked with grey.

"Apparently," he said. "Will you give it to me?"

Begin here, and set the terms for a thousand years of war, because the sword Shadowkiss is invincible and the companion it has chosen will live until the end of the world. Ruana had carried the sword for a week and she knew. She could not give it up, or allow it to be taken from her, or destroy it, or let it be destroyed while she lived. And if somehow she were killed, the sword in fury and grief would take a new lover, and the killing would not end.

Elegant. Precise. A chain reaction begun when sword chose companion; inevitable, predictable, and infinitely repeatable as long as there were honor and glory and a desire to be . . .

A hero.

"Your soldiers did all you told them, but you should have gone yourself. The sword's not for you, nor ever will be."

The Duke closed the book and stepped forward. He wore no armor and his hands were empty.

"The sword is for no one. Do you know why I wanted it, Rulane

Twiceborn? I wanted it to bury far beneath my castle where it would never see the sun, where no man would touch it and die—or touch it and live." He took another step forward, and another, and now Ruana could smell the oils and spices of him, see the grace notes of power in the ivory fold of linen and the rich glow of the wool that he wore.

"Since before the universe was born," the Duke said slowly, "Shadowkiss has waited to take a companion. It is powerless without one; that is its nature. It was forged to fight the final battle of ancient gods, and those who made it wrought cruel as the grave and more cunning than Death. It is a living thing; the legends say it dreams. When I heard it was in the land, I sent for it—"

"To bury it. Aye, and if it's what you say, that'd solve your fine muddle—until your son's time, or your grandson's. Or did you think no one would ever know about the god-sword with Corchado sitting on it? Armies have marched for less."

Ruana lowered the sword slowly until its point touched the floor. It glowed bright enough to cast shadows on the stone and light the desperation on the face of the Duke.

"Even a lifetime is more than the world will have if you leave this room alive. Help me slay the sword. If there is any chance that I am right, will you take the chance that I am wrong?"

"I'd sooner spin flax into gold than try to find the truth in a prophecy. Or a prince. And I'm a mortal fond of taking chances."

The lines in the Duke's face were deeper now, but he smiled wearily. "I am too late, then. Whatever you've come to do, Twiceborn, try. I've had time to prepare. If you manage to get out of here alive I promise you a war such as the world has never seen. But tell me first: What has it promised you?"

A name. A song. Glory to outlast life and deeds to change the world.

"Never you mind. But I'll tell you this: your chanter's nonsense is a thought right, a grand name-calling, and proudful. You say my sword lives. You're right. But what is yon sleekit thing but a bairn, with a bairn's temper and a sharper edge? It wants its own way, that's all, and no thought to afterward or anyone else. But living things learn. There won't be war for Shadowkiss this spring or any other. I'll see to that."

She flipped the sword back into its sheath and rested her hand on the pommel. The effort it cost her was not visible for anyone to see.

"Are you saying you can control it? You're mad. It will make you serve it."

"How? Would I be here if I couldn't control the sword—or would I be off waiting for you to bring me a pretty war to pass the time, all banners and causes and bad cess to you for a fool?"

Shadowkiss whipped her blood to icefire and music, but it had lost, and now it knew it. It had bound itself to Ruana Rulane without discovering she held a child's life as important as a kingdom, and that all the glittering, well-tried gifts in its armory of illusion had no power over her.

"Make up your own mind, Duke. If you can't believe me, best try to kill me now. But I don't lie. And happen there's work for a blade like this—you've got worm on your north, did you know?"

Vengeance and power, love, glory, and renown—

"I—What did you say?"

He'd thought he had only two choices. Kill Rulane Twiceborn and hide the hellblade . . . for a time. Or failing that, plunge the country into war that spread until no one remembered why he fought.

But there was a third choice. Trust a hero.

"Worm," Ruana repeated with amused patience. "You call it dragon, but it'll blight a field just as fast whatever its name is."

The Grey Duke looked down at his hands as if he could not imagine their uses. Then he looked at the hero.

"Well. Worms. I can see that requires my immediate attention. Will you use Shadowkiss in my service, then, Rulane Twiceborn?"

She shook her head in a clatter of ornaments and smiled slightly. "Happen you might think so, but you'll be wrong. I'll use it for what's right, and kind, and mannerly. If you'll settle for that, well enough, and I'll be glad to stay."

The Duke looked at her, measuring, and slowly smiled. She did not kneel, or offer to.

"Why not? Very well. Stay with me. I'll give you anything you ask beside. Even, as they say, unto half my lands."

"Oh, aye, as to that, I'm no thief either, and it's peculiar manners you must have in the south, my hinny. A horse and a bed will do me. Kingdoms are a nuisance, and I've already got a sword." The hero smiled again with acceptance and regret. "And my destiny."

Once there were gods, and of their legacy one last touchstone remained. There was only one thing it knew how to do, and in its particular innocence it could not imagine anything beyond that.

Now it would learn.

She had wanted the Starharp, and the glory of it was within her grasp. She wanted her own way, and with Shadowkiss she would be invincible.

Heroes are inconvenient. They have no sense of proportion. Over glory or freedom Ruana Rulane chose instead the peculiar conceit that you did not have to be a hero to matter, but because she was a hero she took up the sword anyway, knowing that for the rest of her life she would have to set her will against that of Shadowkiss every waking hour.

Even though she loved it.

It was heroism, though not the sort that makes legends. In a way, Ruana had been made for one task just as the sword had.

It loved its companion. That was its nature. Even now, it would not betray her. Shadowkiss was bound. There would be world and time, and no escape. Ever.

Trapped through all the long nights and the empty days to come. Without battle, without war, without any sort or kind of glory—shackled forever to the useless hollow business of work, and duty, and responsibility.

For an unimportant boy. For the heresy that bread was preferable to destiny, and kindness to high drama. For the knowledge that childhood ends, and that in the end even gifts must be paid for.

To every seduction it could offer, Ruana Rulane the Twiceborn would ask "Why?" and proud love would compel Shadowkiss to answer, and know its answers scorned. Until in the end it had no more answers, and no more belief in the bright beauty of war.

And the sword wept.

Dragons' Teeth

David Drake

The sound of squealing axles drifted closer on the freezing wind. The watching Roman raised his eyes an inch above the rim of his brush-screened trench. A dozen Sarmatian wagons were hulking toward him into the twilight. Their wheels of uncured oak, gapped and irregular at the fellies, rumbled complainingly as they smashed stiff grass and bushes into the unyielding soil.

A smile of grim satisfaction brushed Vettius' lips as the Sarmatians approached. He did not touch the bow that lay beside him; it was still too soon.

The enormous weight of the wagons turned every finger's breadth of rise into a steep escarpment up which the oxen had to plod. They grunted out great plumes of breath as they threw their weight into the traces. Sexless, almost lifeless in their poses of stolid acceptance, the drivers hunched on the high wagon seats. Like the oxen, they had been at their killing work since dawn. The wind slashed and eddied about the canopies of aurochs hide which covered the boxes. Tendrils of smoke from heating fires within squirmed through the peaks. They hung for a moment in the sunset before scudding off invisibly.

The last of the wagons was almost within the defile, Vettius noted. It would be very soon now.

Among the Sarmatians the whole family travelled together, even to war. The children and nursing mothers huddled inside the wagons. So did the warriors; their work, like that of the horses tethered behind each wain, was yet to come. Soon the wagons would halt and laager up in the darkness. Using night as a shroud, the reivers would mount and thunder across the frozen Danube. Laughingly they would return before dawn with booty and fresh Roman ears.

The only picket Vettius could see from where he lay was a single rider slightly ahead and to the left of the wagons. Earlier in the day he might have been guide or outrider. Hours had passed. Wagons had bunched or straggled according to the strength of their teams and the temper of their drivers. Now, while the sun bled like an open wound in the western sky, the rider was almost a part of the jumbled line and no protection for it. Vettius smiled again, and his hand was on the bow.

The wind that moaned around the wagons scuffed up crystals from the snow crusts lying in undulant rills among the brush. The shaggy pony's rump and belly sparkled. The beast's torso, like its rider's, was hidden under armor of broad horn scales, each one painstakingly sewn onto a leather backing by the women of the family. Across his pommel rested a slender lance more than eighteen feet long. The Sarmatian fondled its grip as he nodded over his mount's neck, neglecting to watch the bushes that clawed spiked shadows from the sun.

A sound that trickled through the wind made him straighten; unexpected movement caught his eye. Then the Roman archer rose up from behind a bush far too small to conceal a man the way it had. The Sarmatian, spurring his horse in incredulous panic, heard the slap of the bowstring, heard the loud pop as one scale of his cuirass shattered. After the bodkin-pointed arrow ripped through his chest he heard nothing at all.

"Let's get 'em!" Vettius shouted, nocking another arrow as his first target pitched out of the saddle. The trumpeter crouching behind him set the silver-mounted warhorn to his lips and blasted out the attack. Already the shallow hillsides were spilling soldiers down on the unprepared Sarmatians.

The driver of the lead wagon stood up, screaming a warning. The nearest Roman thrust her through the body with his spear. With two slashes of his short-sword, the legionary cut open the canopy behind her and plunged inside with a howl of triumph.

Sarmatians leaped out the back of the second wagon, trying to reach their horses. Three legionaries met them instead. Vettius had set fifty men in ambush, all picked veterans in full armor. None of the others had bows—the legate had feared a crossfire in the dusk—but sword and spear did the butcher's work on the startled nomads. The Sarmatians were dressed for war in armor of boiled leather or aurochs horn, but they had no shields and their light swords were no match for the heavy Roman cut-and-thrust blades. One at a time the nomads jumped down to be stretched on the ground by a stab, a quick chop, or even the heavy smash of a shield rim. Death trebled, the legionaries stood waiting for each victim. The fading sunlight gleamed from their polished helmets and greaves and touched with fire the wheels of bronze and vermillioned leather that marked their shields.

The legate's practiced eye scanned the fighting. The wrack showed the Sarmatians had battled with futile desperation. A baby lay beside the fourth wagon. Its skull had been dashed in on the wagon box, but its nails were stained with Roman blood. The oxen bellowed, hamstrung in the yoke. One was spurting black jets through a heart-deep channel. This day was Rome's vengeance; retribution for a thousand sudden raids, a thousand comrades crumpled from a chance arrow or a dagger thrust in the night.

Only toward the rear where three wagons had bunched together was there real fighting. Vettius ran down the line of wagons though his quiver was almost emptied when he saw one of his men hurtle through the air in a lifeless somersault. The legionary crashed to the ground like a load of scrap metal. His whole chest and body armor had been caved in by an enormous blow. Measurably later the man's sword completed its own parabola and clanked thirty feet away.

"Get back!" Vettius shouted when he saw the windrow of ruined bodies strewn in front of him. "Stand clear!" Before he could say more, the killer was lumbering toward him around the back of the wagon.

The horsehair crest wobbling in the waning sunlight increased the figure's titanic height, but even bareheaded the giant would have been half again as tall as the six-foot soldier. Worse, he was much heavier built than a man, a squat dwarf taller than the wagon. He carried no shield but his whole body shone with a covering of smooth bronze plates. Both gauntleted hands gripped the haft of an iron-headed mace. The six-foot helve was as thick as a man's calf and the head could have served as an anvil.

The giant strode toward Vettius with terrifying agility.

Vettius arced his bow. The shaft of his arrow splintered on the monster's breastplate. It left only a bright scar on the metal. Vettius stepped back, nocking another missile and shifting his aim to the oddly-sloped helmet. The face was completely covered except for a T-shaped slot over the eyes and nose. The light was very dim but the narrow gap stood out dead black against the helmet's luster. As the giant started to swing his mace parallel to the ground, Vettius shot again.

The arrow glanced off the bronze and howled away into the darkness.

Vettius leaped upward and fell across the wagon seat as the giant's mace hurtled toward him. The spiked head smashed into a wheel with awesome force, scattering fragments of wood and making the whole wagon shudder. As it rocked, the driver's hacked corpse tumbled to the ground leaving the Roman alone on the seat as he sighted along his last arrow.

The giant had reversed his grip on the mace. Now he swung his weapon upward with no more apparent effort than a man with a fly-whisk. As the head came level with the giant's hips, the mace slipped from his fingers to fly forward and burst through the side of the wagon. The titan reeled backward. A small tuft of feathers was barely visible where the helmet slot crossed the bridge of his nose.

The earth trembled when he fell.

Shaking with reaction himself, Vettius dropped his now-useless bow and craned his neck to peer over the wagon's canopy at the remaining fighting. Some of the wains were already burning. Confusion or the victors had spilled the heating fires from their earthenware pots and scattered coals into the cloth and straw of the bedding.

"Save me a prisoner!" Vettius bellowed against the wind. "For Mithra's sake, save me a prisoner!"

He jumped to the ground and cautiously approached the fallen giant. The helmet came off easily when he grasped it by the crest and yanked. Beneath the bronze the face was almost human. The jaw was square and massive; death's rictus had drawn thin lips back from leonine tushes, yellowed and stark. The nose squatted centrally like a smashed toad, and from it the face rose past high flat eyesockets to enormous ridges of bone. There was virtually no forehead so that the brows sloped shallowly to a point on the back of the skull. Only their short tight coils distinguished the eyebrows from the black strands that covered the rest of the head.

No wonder the helmet looked odd, Vettius thought bleakly. He would believe in the face, in a man so large, because they were there for him to touch; but he would have called another man a liar for claiming the existence of something so impossible. Perhaps believing in the impossible was the secret of the success of the Christians whose god, dead three hundred years, was now beginning to rule the Empire.

The trumpeter approached from behind with his horn slung and a bloody sword in his right hand. The torque he now wore was of gold so pure and soft that he had spread it by hand to get it off a dead nomad and rebent it around his own neck.

"Sir!" he called, "are you all right?"

"Give me a hand here," Vettius grunted unresponsively as he tugged at the mace. Together the men pulled the weapon from the fabric of the wagon. Vettius gave a curt order and hefted it alone as his subordinate stepped back. "Ha!" he snorted in disbelief. The mace weighed at least two talents, the weight of a small man or a fair-sized woman.

He let it thud to the ground and walked away from it. "May the Bull bugger me if I don't learn more about this," he swore.

The doorkeeper had difficulty slamming the door against the gust of wind that followed Vettius into the anteroom. Moist air from the baths within condensed to bead the decorated tiles and rime the soldier's cape of black bearskin. He wore the bear's head as a cowl. The beast's glass eyes usually glared out above Vettius' own; now they too were frosted and the doorkeeper, turning, shuddered at the look of blank agony they gave him.

Vettius shrugged off the cape and stamped his muddy boots on the floor. The doorkeeper sighed inwardly and picked up his twig broom. The damned man had been stomping through the muck like a common soldier instead of riding decently in a litter as befit his rank. The slave said nothing aloud as he swept, though; the legate had a reputation for violence and he already wore a dark glower this afternoon.

Walking through the door of the changing room, Vettius tossed his cape to one of the obsequious attendants and began to unlace his boots. While he sat on a bench and stripped off his thick woolen leggings, the other attendant looked delicately at the miry leather and asked with faint disdain, "Will you have these cleaned while you bathe, sir?"

"Dis, why should I?" the soldier snarled. "I've got to wear them out of here, don't I?"

The attendant started at his tone. Vettius chuckled at the man's fear and threw the filthy leggings in his face. Laying both his tunics on the bench, he surveyed the now apprehensive slaves and asked, "Either of you know where Dama is?"

"The Legate Vettius?" called a voice from the inner hallway. A third attendant poked his head into the changing room. "Sir? If you will follow me. . . ."

The attendant's sandals slapped nervously down the hallway past steam rooms on the right and the wall of the great pool on the left. Tiles of glaucous gray covered the floors and most of the walls, set off by horizontal bands of mosaic. A craftsman of Naisso who had never been to the coast had inset octopuses and dolphins cavorting on a bright green sea. The civilization I protect, Vettius thought disgustedly. The reason I bow to fat fools.

At the corner of the hall the attendant stopped and opened one of the right-hand doors. Steam puffed out. Vettius peered in with his hand on the jamb to keep from slipping on the slick tile. Through the hot fog he could make out the figure of the small man who lay on one of the benches.

"Dama?" the soldier called uncertainly.

"Come on in, Lucius," invited the other. He rose to his elbow and the light on his head of tight blond curls identified him. "How did it go?"

"The interrogation was fine," Vettius answered; but his tone was savage, that of a man used to taking out his frustrations in slaughter and very close to the point of doing so again. "We didn't need much persuasion to get the prisoner to tell us everything he knew about the giant. It came from a tent village called Torgu, and he says the shaman running the place has ten more just like it."

"If one, why not eleven?" Dama mused. "But I didn't think the Sarmatians ever made a shaman chief."

"I didn't either," Vettius agreed darkly, "and that wasn't the last strange thing he told us about this wizard, this Hydaspes. He was at Torgu when the family we ambushed got there late in the fall, nervous as the Emperor's taster and fussing around the village to look over each new arrival. He wasn't claiming much authority, either. Then about two months ago a horseman rode in from the east. Our prisoner didn't talk with the fellow but he saw him give a package the size of his fist to Hydaspes. That was what the wizard had been waiting for. He laughed and capered all the way to his tent and didn't come out again for a week. When he did, he started giving orders like a king. Since now he had a nine-foot giant behind him, everyone obeyed. In back of Hydaspes' tent there was a long trench in the frozen ground and a lot of dirt was missing. Nobody the prisoner knew hung about behind there to see if the wizard really was digging up giants there night after night—they were all scared to death by then."

"So a one-time hedge wizard gets a giant bodyguard," the merchant said softly, "and he unites a tribe under him. If he can do that, he may just as easily become king of the whole nation. What would happen, Lucius, if the Sarmatians got a real king, a real leader who stopped their squabbling and sent them across the Danube together?"

The white fear that had been shimmering around the edges of Vettius' mind broke through again and tensed all his muscles. "A century ago the Persians unified Mesopotamia against us," he said. "Constant fighting. Some victories, more losses. But we could accept that on one frontier—it's a big empire. On two at the same time. . . . I can't say what would happen."

"We'd better deal with Hydaspes soon," Dama summarized flatly, "or Hydaspes will deal with us. Have you told Celsus?"

"Oh, I told the Count," Vettius snapped, "but he didn't believe me—and besides, he was too busy reaming me out for leading the ambush myself. It was undignified for a legate he said."

Dama crowed, trying to imagine Vettius too dignified for a fight.

"That's the sort he is," the soldier agreed with a rueful smile. "He expects me to keep my cut-throats in line without dirtying my boots. A popular attitude this side of the river, it seems."

Knuckles slammed on the steam-room door. Both men looked up sharply.

"Sirs, quickly!" the attendant hissed from outside.

Dama threw the door open for the frightened attendant. "Sirs," the slave explained, "the Count has come for the legate Vettius. I misdirected him, thinking you might want to prepare, but he'll be here any moment."

"I'll put on a tunic and meet him in the changing room," the soldier decided. "I've no desire to be arrested in the nude."

The frightened changing room attendants had disappeared into the far reaches of the building, leaving the friends to pull on their linen tunics undisturbed. Celsus burst in on them without ceremony, followed by two of his runners. He's not here to charge me after all, Vettius thought, not without at least a squad of troops. Though Mithra knew, his wishes would have supported a treason indictment.

"Where have you been?" the official stormed. His round face was almost the color of his toga's broad maroon hem.

"Right here in the bath, your excellency," Vettius replied without deference.

"Word just came by heliograph," the count sputtered. "There were ten attacks last night, ten! Impregnable monsters leading them—Punicum, Novae, Frasuli, Anarti—posts wiped out!"

"I told you there were other attacks planned," the soldier replied calmly. "None of them were in my sector. I told you why that was too."

"But you lied when you said you killed a monster, didn't you?" accused Celsus, stamping his foot. "At Novae they hit one with a catapult and the bolt only bounced off!"

"Then they didn't hit him squarely," Vettius retorted. "The armor isn't that heavy. And I told you, I shot mine through the viewslit in his helmet."

The count motioned his runners away. Noticing Dama for the first time he screamed, "Get out! Get out!"

The merchant bowed and exited behind the runners. He stood near the door.

"Listen," Celsus whispered, plucking at the soldier's sleeve to bring his ear lower, "you've got to do something about the giants. It'll look bad if these raids continue."

"Fine," Vettius said in surprise. "Give me my regiment and the Fifth Macedonian, and some cavalry—say the Old Germans. I'll level Torgu and everyone in it."

"Oh no," his pudgy superior gasped, "not so much. The Emperor will hear about it and the gods know what he'll think. Oh, no—fifty men, that was enough before."

"Are you—" Vettius began, then rephrased his thought. "This isn't an ambush for one family, your excellency. This is disposing of a powerful chief and maybe a thousand of his followers, a hundred miles into Sarmatia. I might as well go alone as with fifty men."

"Fifty men," Celsus repeated. Then, beaming as if he were making a promise, he added, "You'll manage, I'm sure."

The two riders were within a few miles of Torgu before they were noticed.

"I shouldn't have let you come," Vettius grumbled to his companion. "Either I should have gone myself or else marched my regiment in and told Celsus to bugger himself."

Dama smiled. "You don't have any curiosity, Lucius. You only see the job to be done. Myself, I want to know where a nine-foot giant comes from."

They eyed the sprawling herd of black cattle which were finding some unimaginable pasturage beneath the snow crust. Perhaps they were stripping bark from the brush that scarred the landscape with its black rigidity. A cow scented the unfamiliar horses approaching it. The animal blatted and scrambled to its feet, splashing dung behind it. When it had bustled twenty feet away, the cow regained enough composure to turn and stare at the riders, focusing the ripple of disturbance that moved sluggishly through other bovine minds. Face after drooling, vacant face rotated toward them; after long moments, even the distant herdsman looked up from where he huddled over his fire in the lee of a hill.

Dama's chest grew tight. There was still another moment's silence while the Sarmatian made up his mind that there really were Romans riding toward Torgu through his herd. When at last he grasped that fact, he leaped to his feet yipping his amazement. For an instant he crouched bowlegged, waiting for a hostile move. When the intruders ignored him, the Sarmatian scampered to his horse and lashed it into a startled gallop for home.

The merchant chewed at his cheeks, trying to work saliva into a mouth that had gone dry when he realized they would be noticed. He'd known they were going to meet Sarmatians: that was the whole purpose of what they were doing. But now it was too late to back out. "About time we got an escort," he said with false bravado. "I'm surprised the Sarmatians don't patrol more carefully."

"Why should they?" Vettius snorted. "They know they're safe over here so long as a brainless scut like Celsus is in charge of the border."

They jogged beyond the last of the cattle. Without the Sarmatian's presence the beasts were slowly drifting away from the trampled area where they had been herded. If they wandered far they would be loose at night when the wolves hunted.

"Cows," Vettius muttered. "It's getting hard to find men, my friend."

Half a mile away on the top of the next rolling hill an armored horseman reined up in a spatter of snow. He turned his head and gave a series of short yelps that carried over the plain like bugle calls. Moments later a full score of lancers topped the brow of the hill and pounded down toward the interlopers.

"I think we'll wait here," the soldier remarked.

"Sure, give them a sitting target," Dama agreed with a tense smile.

Seconds short of slaughter, the leading Sarmatian raised his lance. The rest of the troop followed his signal. The whole group swept around Vettius and Dama to halt in neighing, skidding chaos. One horse lost its footing and spilled its rider on the snow with a clatter of weapons. Cursing, the disgruntled Sarmatian lurched toward the Romans with his short, crooked sword out. From behind Dama, the leader barked a denial and laid his lance in front of the man. The merchant breathed deeply but did not relax his grip on the queerly shaped crossbow resting on his saddle until the glowering Sarmatian had remounted.

The leader rode alongside Vettius and looked up at the soldier on his taller horse. "You come with us to Torgu," he ordered in passable Greek.

"That's right," Vettius agreed in Sarmatian. "We're going to Torgu to see Hydaspes."

There was a murmur from the Sarmatians. One of them leaned forward to shake an amulet bag in the soldier's face, gabbling something too swiftly to be understood.

The leader had frowned when Vettius spoke. He snapped another order and kicked his horse forward. Romans and Sarmatians together jogged up the hill, toward the offal and frozen muck of Torgu.

On the bank of a nameless, icebound stream stood the village's central hall and only real building. Dama glanced at it as they rode past. Its roughly squared logs were gray and streaked with odd splits along the twisted grain. Any caulking there might have been in the seams had fallen out over the years. The sides rose to a flaring roof of scummed thatch, open under the eaves to emit smoke and the stink of packed bodies. The hall would have seemed crude in the most stagnant backwaters of the Empire; the merchant could scarcely believe that a people to whom it was the height of civilization could be a threat.

Around the timber structure sprawled the nomad wagons in filthy confusion. Their sloping canopies were shingled with cow droppings set out to dry in the wan sunlight before being burned for fuel. The light soot that had settled out of thousands of cooking fires permeated the camp with an unclean, sweetish odor. Nothing in the village but the untethered horses watching the patrol return looked cared for.

Long lances had been butted into the ground beside each wagon. As he stared back at the flat gazes directed at him by idle Sarmatians, Dama realized what was wrong with the scene. Normally, only a handful of each family group would have been armored lancers. The rest would be horse archers, able to afford only a bow and padded linen protection.

Most of their escort hung cased bows from their saddles, but all bore the lance and most wore scale mail.

"Lucius," the merchant whispered in Latin, "are all of these nobles?"

"You noticed that," Vettius replied approvingly. "No, you can see from their looks that almost all of them were just herdsmen recently. Somebody made them his retainers, paid for their equipment and their keep."

"Hydaspes?" the merchant queried.

"I guess. He must have more personal retainers than the king, then."

"You will be silent!" ordered the Sarmatian leader.

They had ridden almost completely through the camp and were approaching a tent of gaily pennoned furs on the edge of the plains. At each corner squatted an octagonal stump of basalt a few feet high. The stones were unmarked and of uncertain significance, altars or boundary markers or both. No wains had been parked within fifty paces of the tent. A pair of guards stood before its entrance. Dama glanced at the streamers and said, "You know, there really is a market for silk in this forsaken country. A shame that—"

"Silence!" the Sarmatian repeated as he drew up in front of the tent. He threw a rapid greeting to the guards, one of whom bowed and ducked inside. He returned quickly, followed by a tall man in a robe of fine black Spanish wool. The newcomer's face was thin for a Sarmatian and bore a smile that mixed triumph and something else. On his shoulder, covered by the dark hood, clung a tiny monkey with great brown eyes. From time to time it put its mouth to its master's ear and murmured secretly.

"Hydaspes," Vettius whispered. "He always wears black."

"Have they been disarmed?" the wizard questioned. The escort's leader flushed in embarrassment at his oversight and angrily demanded the Romans' weapons. Vettius said nothing as he handed over his bow and the long cavalry sword he carried even now that he commanded an infantry unit. The merchant added his crossbow and a handful of bolts to the collection.

"What is that?" Hydaspes asked, motioning his man to hand him the crossbow.

"It comes from the east where I get my silk," Dama explained, speaking directly to the wizard. "You just drop a bolt into the tall slot on top. That holds it while you pull back on the handle, cocking and firing it all in one motion."

"From the east? I get weapons from the east," the Sarmatian said with a nasty quirk of his lip. "But this, this is only a toy surely? The arrow is so light and scarcely a handspan long. What could a man do with such a thing?"

Dama shrugged. "I'm not a warrior. For my own part, I wouldn't care to be shot with this or anything else."

The wizard gestured an end to the conversation, setting the weapon inside his tent for later perusal. "Dismount, gentlemen, dismount," he continued in excellent Greek. "Perhaps you have heard of me?"

"Hydaspes the wizard. Yes," Vettius lied, "even within the Empire we think of you when we think of a powerful sorcerer. That's why we've come for help."

"In whose name?" the Sarmatian demanded shrewdly. "Constantius the emperor?"

"Celsus, Count of Dacia," Vettius snapped back. "The Empire has suffered the bloody absurdities of Constantius and his brothers long enough. Eunuchs run the army, priests rule the state, and the people pray to the tax gatherers. We'll have support when we get started, but first we need some standard to rally to, something to convince everyone that we have more than mere hopes behind us. We want your giants, and we'll pay you a part of the Empire to get them."

"And you, little man?" Hydaspes asked the merchant unexpectedly.

Dama had been imagining the count's face if he learned his name was being linked with raw treason, but he recovered swiftly and fumbled at his sash while replying, "We merchants have little cause to love Constantius. The roads are ruinous, the coinage base; and the rapacity of local officials leaves little profit for even the most daring adventurer."

"So you came to add your promise of future gain?"

"Future? Who knows the future?" Dama grunted. Gold gleamed in his hand. A shower of coins arced unerringly from his right palm to his left and back again. "If you can supply what we need, you'll not lament your present payment."

"Ho! Such confidence," the wizard said, laughing cheerfully. The monkey chittered, stroking its master's hair with bulbous fingertips. "You really believe that I can raise giants from the past?

"*I can!*"

Hydaspes' face became a mask of unreason. Dama shifted nervously from one foot to the other, realizing that the wizard was far from the clever illusionist they had assumed back at Naisso he must be. This man wasn't sane enough to successfully impose on so many people, even ignorant barbarians. Or was the madness a recent thing?

"Subradas, gather the village behind my tent," Hydaspes ordered abruptly, "but leave space in the middle as wide and long as the tent itself."

The leader of the escort dipped his lance in acknowledgement. "The women, Lord?"

"All—women, slaves, everyone. I'm going to show you how I raise the giants."

"Ho!" gasped the listening Sarmatians. The leader saluted again and rode off shouting. Hydaspes turned to reenter his tent, then paused. "Take the Romans, too," he directed the guards. "Put them by the flap and watch them well.

"Yes," he continued, glancing back at Vettius, "it is a very easy thing to raise giants, if you have the equipment and the knowledge. Like drawing a bow for a man like you."

The Hell-lit afterimage of the wizard's eyes continued to blaze in the soldier's mind when the furs had closed behind the black figure.

As the rest of the Sarmatians dismounted and began to jostle them around the long tent, Dama whispered, "This isn't working. If it gets too tight, break for the tent. You know about my bow?"

Vettius nodded, but his mind was chilled by a foretaste of death.

As the prisoner had said, eleven long trenches bristled outward from the wall of Hydaspes' tent. Each was shallow but too extensive for the wizard to have dug it in the frozen ground in one night. Dama disliked the way the surface slumped over the ditches, as if enormous corpses had clawed their way out of their graves . . .

Which was what the wizard seemed to claim had happened.

The guards positioned the two Romans at the center of the back wall of the tent where laces indicated another entrance. Later comers crowded about anxiously, held back in a rough circle by officers with drawn swords. Twenty feet to either side of the Romans stretched the straight walls of the tent paralleled by a single row of warriors. From the basalt posts at either corner curved the rest of the tribe in milling excitement, warriors in front and women and children squirming as close as they could get before being elbowed back.

The Sarmatians were still pushing for position when Hydaspes entered the cleared space, grinning ironically at Vettius and Dama as he stepped between them. A guard laced the tent back up. In the wizard's left hand was a stoppered copper flask; his right gripped a small packet of supple cowhide.

"The life!" Hydaspes shouted to the goggle-eyed throng, waving the flask above his head from the center of the circle. He set the vessel down on the dirt and carefully unrolled the leather wrappings from the other objects.

"And the seed!" the wizard cried at last. In his palm lay a pair of teeth. They were a dull, stony gray without any of the sheen of ivory. One was a molar, human but inhumanly large. The other tooth, even less credible, seemed to be a canine fully four inches long. With one tooth in either hand, Hydaspes goatfooted about the flask in an impromptu dance of triumph.

His monkey rider clacked its teeth in glee.

The wizard stopped abruptly and faced the Romans. "Oh, yes. The seed. I got them, all thirteen teeth, from the Chinese—the people who sell you your silk, merchant. Dragons' teeth they call them—hee hee! And I plant them just like Cadmus did when he built Thebes. But I'm the greater prince, oh yes, for I'll build an empire where he built a city."

Dama licked his lips. "We'll help you build your empire," he began, but the wizard ignored him and spoke only to Vettius.

"You want my giants, Roman, my darlings? Watch!"

Hydaspes plucked a small dagger from his sash and poked a hole in the ground. Like a farmer planting a nut, the wizard popped the molar into the hole and patted the earth back down. When he straightened he shouted a few words at the sky. The villagers gasped, but Dama doubted whether they understood any more of the invocation than he did. Perhaps less—the merchant thought he recognized the language, at least, one he had heard chanted on the shores of the Persian Gulf on a dead, starless night. He shuddered.

Now the wizard was unstoppering his flask and crooning under his breath. His cowl had fallen back to display the monkey clinging fiercely to his long oily hair. When the wizard turned, Dama could see the beast's lips miming its master obscenely.

Droplets spattered from the flask, bloody red and glowing. The merchant guessed wine or blood, changed his mind when the fluid popped and sizzled on the ground. The frozen dirt trembled like a stricken gong.

The monkey leaped from Hydaspes' shoulder, strangely unaffected by the cold. It faced the wizard across the patch of fluid-scarred ground. It was chanting terrible squeaky words that thundered back from Hydaspes.

The ground split.

The monkey collapsed. Hydaspes leaped over the earth's sudden gape and scooped up the little creature, wrapping it in his cloak.

Through the crack in the soil thrust an enormous hand. Earth heaved upward again. The giant's whole torso appeared, dribbling dirt back into the trench. Vettius recognized the same thrusting jaw, the same high flat eyesockets, as those of the giant he had killed.

The eyes were Hydaspes' own.

"Oh yes, Roman," the wizard cackled. "The life and the seed—but the mind too, hey? There must be a mind."

The giant rose carefully in a cascade of earth. Even standing in the trench left by his body, he raised his pointed skull eight feet into the air.

"My mind!" Hydaspes shrieked, oblivious to everyone but the soldier. "Part of me in each of my darlings, you see? Flowing from me through my pet here to them."

One of the wizard's hands caressed the monkey until it murmured lasciviously. The beast's huge eyes were seas of steaming brown mud, barely flecked by pinpoint pupils.

"You said you knew me," continued the wizard. "Well, I know you too, Lucius Vettius. I saw you bend your bow, I saw you kill my darling—

"I saw you kill me, Roman!"

Vettius unclasped his cape, let it slip to the ground. Hydaspes wiped a streak of spittle from his lips and stepped back to lay a hand on the giant's forearm. "Kill me again, Roman," the wizard said softly. "Go ahead; no one will interfere. But this time you don't have a bow."

"Watch the little one!" he snapped to the guard on Dama's right. The Sarmatian gripped the merchant's shoulder.

Then the giant charged.

Vettius dived forward at an angle, rolling beyond the torn-up section of the clearing. The giant spun, stumbled in a ditch that had cradled one of his brothers. The soldier had gained the room he wanted in the center of the open space and waited in a loose-armed crouch. The giant sidled toward him splayfooted.

"Hey!" the Roman shouted and lunged for his opponent's dangling genitalia. The giant struck with shocking speed, swatting Vettius in midair like a man playing handball. Before the Roman's thrusting fingers could make contact, the giant's open-handed blow had crashed into his ribs and hurled him a dozen feet away. Only the giant's clumsy rush saved Vettius from being pulped before he could jump to his feet again. The soldier was panting heavily but his eyes were fixed on the giant's. A thread of blood dribbled off the point of his jaw. Only a lip split on the hard ground—thus far. The giant charged.

Two faces in the crowd were not fixed on the one-sided battle. Dama fingered the hem of his cloak unobtrusively, following the fight only from the corners of his eyes. It would be pointless to watch his friend die. Instead the merchant eyed Hydaspes, who had dug another hole across the clearing and inserted the last and largest tooth into it. The wizard seemed to ignore the fighting. If he watched at all, it was through the giant's eyes as he claimed; and surely, mad as he was, Hydaspes would not otherwise have turned his back on his revenge. For the first time Dama thought he recognized an unease about the monkey which rode again on the wizard's shoulder. It might have been only fatigue. Certainly Hydaspes seemed to notice nothing unusual as he tamped down the soil and began his thirteenth invocation.

Dama's guard was wholly caught up in the fight. He began to pound the merchant on the back in excitement, yelling bloodthirsty curses at Vettius. Dama freed the slender stiletto from his cloak and palmed it. He did not turn his head lest the movement catch the guard's attention. Instead he raised his hand to the Sarmatian's neck, delicately fingered his spine. Before the moth-light touch could register on the enthusiastic

Sarmatian, Dama slammed the thin blade into the base of his brain and gave it a twist. The guard died instantly. The merchant supported the slumping body, guiding it back against the tent. Hydaspes continued chanting a litany with the monkey, though the noise of the crowd drowned out his words. The wizard formed the inaudible syllables without noticing either Dama or the stumbling way his beast answered him. There was a look of puzzlement, almost fear, in the monkey's eyes. The crowd continued to cheer as the merchant opened the flap with a quick slash and backed inside Hydaspes' tent.

Inside a pair of chalcedony oil lamps burned with tawny light. The floor was covered with lush furs, some of which draped wooden benches. On a table at one end rested a pair of human skulls, unusually small but adult in proportions. More surprising were the cedar book chests holding parchments and papyri and even the strange pleated leaf-books of India. Dama's crossbow stood beside the front entrance. He ran to it and loosed the bundle of stubby, unfletched darts beside it. From his wallet came a vial of pungent tarry matter into which he jabbed the head of each dart. The uncovered portions of the bronze points began to turn green. Careful not to touch the smears of venom, the merchant slipped all ten missiles into the crossbow's awkward vertical magazine.

Only then did he peer through the tent flap.

Vettius leaped sideways, kicking at the giant's knee. The ragged hobnails scored his opponent's calf, but the giant's deceptively swift hand closed on the Roman's outer tunic. For a heartsick instant the heavy fabric held; then it ripped and Vettius tumbled free. The giant lunged after him. Vettius backpedaled and, as his enemy straightened, launched himself across the intervening space. The heel of his outstretched boot slammed into the pit of the giant's stomach. Again the iron nails made a bloody ruin of the skin. The titan's breath whooshed out, but its half-ton bulk did not falter at the blow. Vettius, thrown back by the futile impact, twisted away from the giant's unchecked rush. The creature's heels grazed past, thudded with mastodonic force. The soldier took a shuddering breath and lurched to his feet. A long arm clawed for his face. The Roman staggered back, barely clear of the spade-like talons. The monster pressed after him relentlessly, and Vettius was forced at last to recognize what should have been hopelessly obvious from the first: he could not possibly kill the giant with his bare hands.

A final strategem took shape. With desperate purpose Vettius began to circle and retreat before his adversary. He should have planned it, measured it, but now he could only trust to luck and the giant's incredible weight. Backed almost against a corner post, he crouched and waited. Arms wide, the giant hesitated—then rushed in for the kill. Vettius met him low, diving straight at his opponent instead of making a vain effort to get clear again. The Roman's arms locked about the great ankles and the giant wavered, then began to topple forward. As he fell his taloned fingers clamped crushingly on Vettius' ribs.

The unyielding basalt altar met the giant's skull with shattering force. Bone slammed dense rock with the sound of a maul on a wedge. Warm fluids spattered the snow while the Sarmatians moaned in disbelief. Hydaspes knelt screaming on the ground, his fists pummeling terror from a mind that had forgotten even the invocation it had just completed. The earth began pitching like an unmastered horse. It split in front of the wizard where the tooth had been planted. The crack raced jaggedly through the crowd and beyond.

"Lucius!" Dama cried, lifting the corner of the tent.

The soldier pulled his leg free from the giant's pinioning body and rolled toward the voice, spilling endwise the only Sarmatian alert enough to try to stop him. Dama dropped the tent wall and nodded toward the front, his hands full of crossbow. "There's horses waiting out there. I'll slow them up."

Vettius stamped on a hand that thrust into the tent.

"Get out, damn you!" the merchant screamed. "There aren't any more weapons in here."

A Sarmatian rolled under the furs with a feral grimace and a dagger in his hand. The soldier hefted a full case of books and hurled it at his chest. Wood and bone splintered loudly. Vettius turned and ran toward the horses.

The back flap ripped apart in the haste of the Sarmatians who had remembered its existence. The first died with a dart through his eye as Dama jerked the cocking handle of his weapon. The next missile fell into position. The merchant levered back the bow again. At full cock the sear released, snapped the dart out into the throat of the next man.

The Sarmatian's life dissolved in a rush of red flame as the bolt pricked his carotid to speed its load of poison straight to the brain. The third man stumbled over his body, screamed. Two darts pinged off his mail before one caught the armpit he bared when he threw his hands over his face.

Relentless as a falling obelisk, Dama stroked out the full magazine of lethal missiles, shredding six screaming victims in the space of a short breath. The entrance was plugged by a clot of men dying in puling agony. Tossing his empty bow at the writhing chaos behind him, Dama ran through the front flap and vaulted onto his horse.

"We'll never get clear!" Vettius shouted as he whipped his mount. "They'll run us down in relays before we reach the Danube."

Wailing Sarmatians boiled around both ends of the tent, shedding helmets, weapons—any encumbrance. Their voices honed a narrow blade of terror.

"The control," Dama shouted back as the pair dodged among the crazy pattern of wagon tongues. "He used his own mind and a monkey's to control something not quite a man."

"So what?"

"That last tooth didn't come from a man. It didn't come from anything like a man."

Something scaly, savage and huge towered over the wreckage of the tent. It cocked its head to glare at the disappearing riders while scrabbling with one stubby foreleg to stuff a black-robed figure farther into its maw. Vettius twisted in his saddle to stare in amazement at the coffin-long jaws gaping twenty feet in the air and the spined backfin like that of no reptile of the past seventy million years.

The dragon hissed, leaving a scarlet mist of blood to hang in the air as it ducked its head for another victim.

The Trials and Tribulations of Tribulations of Myron Blumberg, Dragon

Mike Resnick

Sylvia's always after me.

"It's a skin condition," she says.
"It's a wart," I say.
"It's a skin condition and you're going to the doctor and don't touch me until he gives you something for it."

So I go to the doctor, and he gives me something for it, and she makes me sleep in the guest room anyway.

"Myron, you're green," she says.
"You mean like I don't know the ropes, or you mean like I got ptomaine poisoning from your tuna salad?" I ask.
"I mean like you're the same color as the grass," she says.
"Maybe it's the lotion the doctor gave me," I say.
"It doesn't come off on your shirts," she says.
"So maybe it all dried up," I say.

"Maybe," she says, "but stay in your room when I have the girls over for mahjong."

"I told you not to smoke in bed," she says.

"I know," I say.

"Well, then?" she says.

"Well, then, *what?*" I say.

"Well, then, why are you smoking in bed?" she says.

"I'm not," I say.

"Then how did your pillow get scorched?" she says.

"Not from the passion of your lovemaking, that's for sure," I say.

"Don't be disgusting," she says.

Then I belch, and out comes all this smoke and fire, and she says if I ever lie to her again she's going to give me a rolling pin upside my head, and then she walks out of the house before I can tell her I haven't lit up a cigarette in four days.

"It looks like a cancerous growth," she says.

"It's just a swelling," I say. "There must be a busted spring in the chair."

"You should see a doctor," she says.

"Last time you sent me to a doctor I turned green," I say.

"This time you'll see a specialist," she says.

"A specialist in swellings?" I ask.

"Whatever," she says.

"Well?" she asks.

"Well what?"

"What did he say?"

"He says it looks like a tail," I say.

"Hah!" she says. "I *knew* it!"

"I wonder if our insurance covers tails," I say.

"Is he going to amputate it?" she asks.

"I don't think so," I say. "Why?"

"Because even if our insurance covers getting rid of tails, it doesn't cover growing them," she says. "What am I going to do with you, Myron? We've got a bar mitzvah to attend this Saturday, and you're green and all covered with scales and you keep belching smoke and fire and now you're growing a tail. What will people say?"

"They'll say, 'There goes a well-matched couple,' " I answer.

"That is *not* funny," she says. "What am I going to do with you? I mean, it was bad enough when you just sat around the house watching football and reading *Playboy*."

"You might fix some dinner while you're thinking about it," I say.

"What do you want?" she asks. "Saint George?"

I am about to lose my temper and tell her to stop teasing me about my condition, when it occurs to me that Saint George would go very well with pickles and relish between a couple of pieces of rye bread.

It is when my arms turn into an extra set of legs that she really hits the roof.

"This is just too much!" she says. "It's bad enough that I can't let any of my friends see you and that we had to redecorate the house with asbestos wallpaper"—it's mauve, and she *hates* mauve—"but now you can't even button your own shirts or tie your shoes."

"They don't fit anyway," I point out.

"See?" she says, and then repeats it: "See? Now we'll have to get you a whole new wardrobe! Why are you doing this to me, Myron?"

"To *you?*" I say.

"God hates me," she says. "I could have married Nate Sobel the banker, or Harold Yingleman who's become a Wall Street big shot, and instead I married you, and now God is punishing me, as if watching you spill gravy onto your shirt for forty-three years wasn't punishment enough."

"You act like *you're* the one who's turning into a dragon," I complain.

"Oh, shut up and stop feeling sorry for yourself," she says. She holds out the roast. "It's a bit rare. Blow on it and make yourself useful." She pauses. "And if you breathe on me, I'll give you such a slap."

That's my Sylvia. One little cockroach can send her screaming from the house. She sees a spider, she calls five different exterminators. God forbid a mouse should come into the garage looking for a snack.

But show her a dragon, and suddenly she's Joan of Arc and Wonder Woman and Golda Meier, all rolled into one steel-eyed *yenta* with blue hair and a double chin.

*   *   *

"Where are you going?" she says.

"Out," I say.

Out where?" she says.

"Just *out*," I say. "I have been cooped up in this house for almost two months, and I have to get some fresh air."

"So you think you're just going to walk down the street like any normal person?" she says. "That maybe you'll trade jokes with Bernie Goldberg and flirt with Mrs. Noodleman like you always do?"

"Why not?" I say.

"Well, I won't hear of it," she says. "I'm not going to have the whole neighborhood talking about how Sylvia Blumberg married a *dragon*, for God's sake!"

I figure it is time to make a stand, so I say, "I am going out, and that's that!"

"Don't you speak to me in that tone of voice, Myron!" she says, and I stop just before she reaches for the rolling pin. She pauses for a moment, then looks up. "If you absolutely *must* go for a walk," she says, "I will put a leash on you and tell everyone you are my new dog."

"I don't look very much like a dog," I say.

"You look even less like Myron Blumberg," she answers. "Just don't talk to anyone while we're out. I couldn't bear the humiliation."

So we go out, and when Mrs. Noodleman passes by Sylvia tells me to hold my breath and not exhale any fire, and then we come to Bernie Goldberg, who is just coming home from shopping at the delicatessen, and Sylvia tells him I am her new dog, and he asks what breed I am, and she says she's not sure, and he says he thinks maybe I am imported from Ireland, and then Sylvia yanks on the leash and we walk to the corner.

"He's still looking at you," she whispers.

"So?" I say.

"I don't think he believes you're a dog."

"There's nothing we can do about that," I say.

"Yes, there is," she says, leading me over to a fire hydrant. "Lift your leg on this. That will convince him."

"I don't think dragons lift their legs, Sylvia," I say.

"Why do you persist in embarrassing me?" she says. "Lift your leg!"

"I can't," I say.

"Whoever heard of a dragon that couldn't lift its leg?" she insists. "You don't have to do anything disgusting. It's just to show that know-it-all Bernie Goldberg."

I try, and I fall over on my side.

"What good are you?" demands Sylvia as Bernie stares at me, blinking his eyes furiously behind his thick bifocals.

"Help me up," I say. "I'm not used to having all these legs."

"Myron," she says as she drags me to my feet, "the situation is becoming intolerable. Something's got to be done before you make me the laughing-stock of the entire neighborhood."

"This is the last straw!" she says, ripping open the envelope.

"What is?" I ask.

"The state has refused to extend your unemployment benefits. They don't care that you're a dragon, as long as you're an able-bodied one." She glares at me. "And you're going through twenty pounds of meat a day. Do you know how much that costs?"

I shrug. "What can I say? Dragons get hungry."

"Why are you always so selfish, Myron?" she says. "Why can't you graze in the backyard like a horse or something?"

"I don't think dragons like grass," I say.

"And that's it?" she demands. "You won't even try?"

"I'll try, I'll try," I say with a sigh, and go out to the backyard. It doesn't look like Caesar salad, but I close my eyes, lean down, and open my mouth.

Sylvia hides me in the basement just before the fire department comes to save what's left of the garage.

"You did that on purpose!" she says accusingly after the firemen have left.

"I didn't," I say. "It's just that my flame seems to be getting bigger every day."

"While our bank account is getting smaller," she says. "Either you get a job, or you'll have to ask your brother Sidney for a loan."

It is an easy choice, because when Sidney dies they will need a crowbar to pry his fingers off the first dollar he ever made, and every subsequent one as well, so I go out to look for work.

You would be surprised at how difficult it is for an honest, industrious dragon to find work in our neighborhood. Stuart Kominsky puts me on as a sand-blaster, but when I melt the stone he fires me after only half a day on the job. Herbert Baumann says maybe I could give kids rides on my back when he reopens the carnival, but it is closed until next spring. Phil Rosenheim, who has never struck me as a bigot before, says he won't hire anyone with green skin. Muriel Weinstein tells me she'll be happy to take me on, just in case some out-of-town dragons come by to look at some of her real estate listings, and she'll call me the moment that happens, but somehow I know that she won't.

Finally I latch on with Milt Fein's heating company. Winter's coming on and he's shorthanded, and when a furnace goes out he pays me thirty dollars an hour to go to the scene and breathe into the vents and keep the building warm until he can get there and solve the problem. The first week I make $562.35, which is more than I have ever made in my life, and the second week we are so busy I get time-and-a-half on the weekend and take home almost seven hundred dollars, and Sylvia is so happy that she buys a new dress and dyes her hair bright red.

And just when I am thinking that things are too good to last, it turns out that things *are* too good to last.

One day I start breathing into the ventilation shaft in an office building, and nothing happens, except that Milt Fein lays me off.

Two days later I wake up and I have hands again, and the next morning most of my scales are gone.

"I knew it!" screams Sylvia. "You finally find something you're good at, and then you decide not to be a dragon any longer!"

"I didn't exactly *decide*," I say. "It just kind of happened."

"Why are you doing this to me, Myron?" she demands.

"I'm not doing anything," I say. "I seem to be *undoing*."

"This is terrible," she says. "Look at you: you're hardly green at all. Why does God hate me so?"

Four days later I am the old Myron Blumberg again, which, as you can imagine, is quite a relief to me. Two weeks after that, Sylvia packs up her clothes and the portable TV and the Cuisinart and leaves without so much as a good-bye note. The divorce papers arrive six weeks later.

I still get cards from her every Yom Kippur and Chanukah. The last time I hear from her she has married a gorgon. Sylvia, who hates snakes and can't stand to be stared at.

Boy, do I not envy *him*.

St. Dragon and the George

Gordon R. Dickson

I

A trifle diffidently, Jim Eckert rapped with his claw on the blue-painted door.

Silence.

He knocked again. There was the sound of a hasty step inside the small, oddly peak-roofed house and the door was snatched open. A thin-faced old man with a tall pointed cap and a long, rather dingy-looking white beard peered out, irritably.

"Sorry, not my day for dragons!" he snapped. "Come back next Tuesday." He slammed the door.

It was too much. It was the final straw. Jim Eckert sat down on his haunches with a dazed thump. The little forest clearing with its impossible little pool tinkling away like Chinese glass wind chimes in the background, its well-kept greensward with the white gravel path leading to the door before him, and the riotous flower beds of asters, tulips, zinnias, roses and lilies-of-the-valley all equally impossibly in bloom at the same time about the white fingerpost labelled

384

S. CAROLINUS and pointing at the house—it all whirled about him. It was more than flesh and blood could bear. At any minute now he would go completely insane and imagine he was a peanut or a cocker spaniel. Grottwold Hanson had wrecked them all. Dr. Howells would have to get another teaching assistant for his English Department. Angie . . .

Angie!

Jim pounded on the door again. It was snatched open.

"Dragon!" cried S. Carolinus, furiously. "How would you like to be a beetle?"

"But I'm not a dragon," said Jim, desperately.

The magician stared at him for a long minute, then threw up his beard with both hands in a gesture of despair, caught some of it in his teeth as it fell down and began to chew on it fiercely.

"Now where," he demanded, "did a dragon acquire the brains to develop the imagination to entertain the illusion that he is *not* a dragon? Answer me, O Ye Powers!"

"The information is psychically, though not physiologically correct," replied a deep base voice out of thin air beside them and some five feet off the ground. Jim, who had taken the question to be rhetorical, started convulsively.

"Is that so?" S. Carolinus peered at Jim with new interest. "Hmm." He spat out a hair or two. "Come in, Anomaly—or whatever you call yourself."

Jim squeezed in through the door and found himself in a large single room. It was a clutter of mismatched furniture and odd bits of alchemical equipment.

"Hmm," said S. Carolinus, closing the door and walking once around Jim, thoughtfully. "If you aren't a dragon, what are you?"

"Well, my real name's Jim Eckert," said Jim. "But I seem to be in the body of a dragon named Gorbash."

"And this disturbs you. So you've come to me. How nice," said the magician, bitterly. He winced, massaged his stomach and closed his eyes. "Do you know anything that's good for a perpetual stomach-ache? Of course not. Go on."

"Well, I want to get back to my real body. And take Angie with me. She's my fiancée and I can send her back but I can't send myself back at the same time. You see, this Grottwold Hanson—well, maybe I better start from the beginning."

"Brilliant suggestion, Gorbash," said Carolinus. "Or whatever your name is," he added

"Well," said Jim. Carolinus winced. Jim hurried on. "I teach at a place called Riveroak College in the United States—you've never heard of it—"

"Go on, go on," said Carolinus.

"That is, I'm a teaching assistant. Dr. Howells, who heads the English Department, promised me an instructorship over a year ago. But he's never come through with it; and Angie—Angie Gilman, my fiancée—"

"You mentioned her."

"Yes—well, we were having a little fight. That is, we were arguing about my going to ask Howells whether he was going to give me the instructor's rating for next year or not. I didn't think I should; and she didn't think we could get married—well, anyway, in came Grottwold Hanson."

"In *where* came *who?*"

"Into the Campus Bar and Grille. We were having a drink there. Hanson used to go with Angie. He's a graduate student in psychology. A long, thin geek that's just as crazy as he looks. He's always getting wound up in some new odd-ball organization or other—"

"Dictionary!" interrupted Carolinus, suddenly. He opened his eyes as an enormous volume appeared suddenly poised in the air before him. He massaged his stomach. "Ouch," he said. The pages of the volume began to flip rapidly back and forth before his eyes. "Don't mind me," he said to Jim. "Go on."

"—This time it was the Bridey Murphy craze. Hypnotism. Well—"

"Not so fast," said Carolinus. "*Bridey Murphy . . . Hypnotism . . .* yes . . ."

"Oh, he talked about the ego wandering, planes of reality, on and on like that. He offered to hypnotize one of us and show us how it worked. Angie was mad at me, so she said yes. I went off to the bar. I was mad. When I turned around, Angie was gone. Disappeared."

"Vanished?" said Carolinus.

"Vanished. I blew my top at Hanson. She must have wandered, he said, not merely the ego, but all of her. Bring her back, I said. I can't, he said. It seemed she wanted to go back to the time of St. George and the Dragon. When men were men and would speak up to their bosses about promotions. Hanson'd have to send someone else back to rehypnotize her and send her back home. Like an idiot I said I'd go. Ha! I might've known he'd goof. He couldn't do anything right if he was paid for it. I landed in the body of this dragon."

"And the maiden?"

"Oh, she landed here, too. Centuries off the mark. A place where there actually were such things as dragons—fantastic."

"Why?" said Carolinus.

"Well, I mean—anyway," said Jim, hurriedly. "The point is, they'd already got her—the dragons, I mean. A big brute named Anark had found her wandering around and put her in a cage. They were having a meeting in a cave about deciding what to do with her. Anark wanted to stake her out for a decoy, so they could capture a lot of the local people—only the dragons called people *georges*—"

"They're quite stupid, you know," said Carolinus, severely, looking up from the dictionary. "There's only room for one name in their head at a time. After the Saint made such an impression on them his name stuck."

"Anyway, they were all yelling at once. They've got tremendous voices."

"Yes, you have," said Carolinus, pointedly.

"Oh, sorry," said Jim. He lowered his voice. "I tried to argue that we ought to hold Angie for ransom—" He broke off suddenly. "Say," he said. "I never thought of that. Was I talking dragon, then? What am I talking now? Dragons don't talk English, do they?"

"Why not?" demanded Carolinus, grumpily. "If they're British dragons?"

"But I'm not a dragon—I mean—"

"But you *are* here!" snapped Carolinus. "You and this maiden of yours. Since all the rest of you was translated here, don't you suppose your ability to speak understandably was translated, too? Continue."

"There's not much more," said Jim, gloomily. "I was losing the argument and then this very big, old dragon spoke up on my side. Hold Angie for ransom, he said. And they listened to him. It seems he swings a lot of weight among them. He's a great-uncle of me—of this Gorbash who's body I'm in—and I'm his only surviving relative. They penned Angie up in a cave and he sent me off to the Tinkling Water here, to find you and have you open negotiations for ransom. Actually, on the side he told me to tell you to make the terms easy on the georges—I mean humans; he wants the dragons to work toward good relations with them. He's afraid the dragons are in danger of being wiped out. I had a chance to double back and talk to Angie alone. We thought you might be able to send us both back."

He stopped rather out of breath, and looked hopefully at Carolinus. The magician was chewing thoughtfully on his beard.

"Smrgol," he muttered. "Now there's an exception to the rule. Very bright for a dragon. Also experienced. Hmm."

"Can you help us?" demanded Jim. "Look, I can show you—"

Carolinus sighed, closed his eyes, winced and opened them again.

"Let me see if I've got this straight," he said. "You had a dispute with this maiden to whom you're betrothed. To spite you, she turned to this third-rate practitioner, who mistakenly exorcized her from the United States (whenever in the cosmos that is) to here, further compounding his error by sending you back in spirit only to inhabit the body of Gorbash. The maiden is in the hands of the dragons and you have been sent to me by your great-uncle Smrgol."

"That's sort of it," said Jim dubiously, "only—"

"You wouldn't," said Carolinus, "care to change your story to something simpler and more reasonable—like being a prince changed into a dragon by some wicked fairy stepmother? Oh, my poor stomach! No?" He sighed. "All right, that'll be five hundred pounds of gold, or five pounds of rubies, in advance."

"B-but—" Jim goggled at him. "But I don't have any gold—or rubies."

"What? What kind of a dragon are you?" cried Carolinus, glaring at him. "Where's your hoard?"

"I suppose this Gorbash has one," stammered Jim, unhappily. "But I don't know anything about it."

"Another charity patient!" muttered Carolinus, furiously. He shook his fist at empty space. "What's wrong with that auditing department? Well?"

"Sorry," said the invisible bass voice.

"That's the third in two weeks. See it doesn't happen again for another ten days." He turned to Jim. "No means of payment?"

"No. Wait—" said Jim. "This stomach-ache of yours. It might be an ulcer. Does it go away between meals?"

"As a matter of fact, it does. Ulcer?"

"High-strung people working under nervous tension get them back where I come from."

"People?" inquired Carolinus suspiciously. "Or dragons?"

"There aren't any dragons where I come from."

"All right, all right, I believe you," said Carolinus, testily. "You don't have to stretch the truth like that. How do you exorcize them?"

"Milk," said Jim. "A glass every hour for a month or two."

"Milk," said Carolinus. He held out his hand to the open air and received a small tankard of it. He drank it off, making a face. After a moment, the face relaxed into a smile.

"By the Powers!" he said. "By the Powers!" He turned to Jim, beaming. "Congratulations, Gorbash, I'm beginning to believe you about that college business after all. The bovine nature of the milk quite smothers the ulcer-demon. Consider me paid."

"Oh, fine. I'll go get Angie and you can hypnotize—"

"What?" cried Carolinus. "Teach your grandmother to suck eggs. Hypnotize! Ha! And what about the First Law of Magic, eh?"

"The what?" said Jim.

"The First Law—the First Law—didn't they teach you anything in that college? Forgotten it already, I see. Oh, this younger generation! The First Law: *for every use of the Art and Science, there is required a corresponding price.* Why do I live by my fees instead of by conjurations? Why does a magic potion have a bad taste? Why did this Hanson-amateur of yours get you all into so much trouble?"

"I don't know," said Jim. "Why?"

"No credit! No credit!" barked Carolinus, flinging his skinny arms wide. "Why, I wouldn't have tried what he did without ten years credit with the auditing department, and *I* am a Master of the Arts. As it was, he couldn't get anything more than your spirit back, after sending the maiden complete. And the fabric of Chance and History is all warped and ready to spring back and cause all kinds of trouble. We'll have to give a little, take a little—"

"GORBASH!" A loud thud outside competed with the dragon-bellow.

"And here we go," said Carolinus dourly. "It's already starting." He led the way outside. Sitting on the greensward just beyond the flower beds was an enormous old dragon Jim recognized as the great-uncle of the body he was in—Smrgol.

"Greetings, Mage!" boomed the old dragon, dropping his head to the ground in salute. "You may not remember me. Name's Smrgol— you remember the business about that ogre I fought at Gormely Keep? I see my grandnephew got to you all right."

"Ah, Smrgol—I remember," said Carolinus. "That was a good job you did."

"He had a habit of dropping his club head after a swing," said Smrgol. "I noticed it along about the fourth hour of battle and the next time he tried it, went in over his guard. Tore up the biceps of his right arm. Then—"

"I remember," Carolinus said. "So this is your nephew."

"Grandnephew," corrected Smrgol. "Little thick-headed and all that," he added apologetically, "but my own flesh and blood, you know."

"You may notice some slight improvement in him," said Carolinus, dryly.

"I hope so," said Smrgol, brightening. "Any change, a change for the better, you know. But I've bad news, Mage. You know that inch-worm of an Anark?"

"The one that found the maiden in the first place?"

"That's right. Well, he's stolen her again and run off."

"*What?*" cried Jim.

He had forgotten the capabilities of a dragon's voice. Carolinus tottered, the flowers and grass lay flat, and even Smrgol winced.

"My boy," said the old dragon reproachfully. "How many times must I tell you not to shout. I said, Anark stole the george."

"He means Angie!" cried Jim desperately to Carolinus.

"I know," said Carolinus, with his hands over his ears.

"You're sneezing again," said Smrgol, proudly. He turned to Carolinus. "You wouldn't believe it. A dragon hasn't sneezed in a hundred and ninety years. This boy did it the first moment he set eyes on the george. The others couldn't believe it. Sign of brains, I said. Busy brains make the nose itch. Our side of the family—"

"*Angie!*"

"See there? All right now, boy, you've shown us you can do it. Let's get down to business. How much to locate Anark and the george, Mage?"

They dickered like rug-pedlars for several minutes, finally settling on a price of four pounds of gold, one of silver, and a flawed emerald. Carolinus got a small vial of water from the Tinkling Spring and searched among the grass until he found a small sandy open spot. He bent over it and the two dragons sat down to watch.

"Quiet now," he warned. "I'm going to try a watch-beetle. Don't alarm it."

Jim held his breath. Carolinus tilted the vial in his hand and the crystal water fell in three drops—*Tink! Tink!* And again—*Tink!* The sand darkened with the moisture and began to work as if something was digging from below. A hole widened, black insect legs busily in action flickered, and an odd-looking beetle popped itself halfway out of the hole. Its forelimbs waved in the air and a little squeaky voice, like a cracked phonograph record repeating itself far away over a bad telephone connection, came to Jim's ears.

"*Gone to the Loathly Tower! Gone to the Loathly Tower! Gone to the Loathly Tower!*"

It popped back out of sight. Carolinus straightened up and Jim breathed again.

"The Loathly Tower!" said Smrgol. "Isn't that that ruined tower to the west, in the fens, Mage? Why, that's the place that loosed the blight on the mere-dragons five hundred years ago."

"It's a place of old magic," said Carolinus, grimly. "These places are like ancient sores on the land, scabbed over for a while but always breaking out with new evil when—the twisting of the Fabric by these two must have done it. The evilness there has drawn the evil in Anark to it—lesser to greater, according to the laws of nature. I'll meet you two there. Now, I must go set other forces in motion."

He began to twirl about. His speed increased rapidly until he was nothing but a blur. Then suddenly, he faded away like smoke; and was gone, leaving Jim staring at the spot where he had been.

A poke in the side brought Jim back to the ordinary world.

"Wake up, boy. Don't dally!" the voice of Smrgol bellowed in his ear. "We got flying to do. Come on!"

II

The old dragon's spirit was considerably younger than his body. It turned out to be a four-hour flight to the fens on the west seacoast. For the first hour or so Smrgol flew along energetically enough, meanwhile tracing out the genealogy of the mere-dragons and their relationship to himself and Gorbash; but gradually his steady flow of chatter dwindled and became intermittent. He tried to joke about his long-gone battle with the Ogre of Gormely Keep, but even this was too much and he fell silent with labored breath and straining wings. After a short but stubborn argument, Jim got him to admit that he would perhaps be better off taking a short breather and then coming on a little later. Smrgol let out a deep gasping sigh and dropped away from Jim in weary spirals. Jim saw him glide to an exhausted landing amongst the purple gorse of the moors below and lie there, sprawled out.

Jim continued on alone. A couple of hours later the moors dropped down a long land-slope to the green country of the fenland. Jim soared out over its spongy, grass-thick earth, broken into causeways and islands by the blue water, which in shallow bays and inlets was itself thick-choked with reeds and tall marsh grass. Flocks of water fowl rose here and there like eddying smoke from the glassy surface of one mere and drifted over to settle on another a few hundred yards away. Their cries came faintly to his dragon-sensitive ears and a line of heavy clouds was piling up against the sunset in the west.

He looked for some sign of the Loathly Tower, but the fenland stretched away to a faint blue line that was probably the sea, without showing sign of anything not built by nature. Jim was beginning to wonder uneasily if he had not gotten himself lost when his eye was suddenly caught by the sight of a dragon-shape nosing at something on one of the little islands amongst the meres.

Anark! he thought. And Angie!

He did not wait to see more. He nosed over and went into a dive like a jet fighter, sights locked on Target Dragon.

It was a good move. Unfortunately Gorbash-Jim, having about the weight and wingspread of a small flivver airplane, made a comparable amount of noise when he was in a dive, assuming the plane's motor to be shut off. Moreover, the dragon on the ground had evidently had experience with the meaning of such a sound; for, without even looking, he went tumbling head over tail out of the way just as Jim slammed into the spot where, a second before, he had been.

The other dragon rolled over onto his feet, sat up, took one look at Jim, and began to wail.

"It's not fair! It's not fair!" he cried in a (for a dragon) remarkably high-pitched voice. "Just because you're bigger than I am. And I'm all horned up. It's the first good one I've been able to kill in months and you don't need it, not at all. You're big and fat and I'm so weak and thin and hungry—"

Jim blinked and stared. What he had thought to be Angie, lying in the grass, now revealed itself to be an old and rather stringy-looking cow, badly bitten up and with a broken neck.

"It's just my luck!" the other dragon was weeping. He was less than three-quarters Jim's size and so emaciated he appeared on the verge of collapse. "Everytime I get something good, somebody takes it away. All I ever get to eat is fish—"

"Hold on," said Jim.

"Fish, fish, fish. Cold, nasty fi—"

"Hold on, I say! SHUT UP!" bellowed Jim, in Gorbash's best voice.

The other dragon stopped his wailing as suddenly as if his switch had been shut off.

"Yes, sir," he said, timidly.

"What's the matter? I'm not going to take this from you."

The other dragon tittered uncertainly.

"I'm not," said Jim. "It's your cow. All yours."

"He-he-he!" said the other dragon. "You certainly are a card, your honor."

"Blast it, I'm serious!" cried Jim. "What's your name, anyway?"

"Oh, well—" the other squirmed. "Oh well, you know—"

"*What's your name?*"

"Secoh, your worship!" yelped the dragon, frightenedly. "Just Secoh. Nobody important. Just a little, unimportant mere-dragon, your highness, that's all I am. Really!"

"All right, Secoh, dig in. All I want is some directions."

"Well—if your worship really doesn't . . ." Secoh had been sidling forward in fawning fashion. "If you'll excuse my table manners, sir. I'm just a mere-dragon—" and he tore into the meat before him in sudden, terrified, starving fashion.

Jim watched. Unexpectedly, his long tongue flickered out to lick his chops. His belly rumbled. He was astounded at himself. Raw meat? Off a dead animal—flesh, bones, hide and all? He took a firm grip on his appetites.

"Er, Secoh," he said. "I'm a stranger around these parts. I suppose you know the territory . . . Say, how does that cow taste, anyway?"

"Oh, terrubble—mumpf—" replied Secoh, with his mouth full. "Stringy—old. Good enough for a mere-dragon like myself, but not—"

"Well, about these directions—"

"Yes, your highness?"

"I think . . . you know it's your cow . . ."

"That's what your honor said," replied Secoh, cautiously.

"But I just wonder . . . you know I've never tasted a cow like that."

Secoh muttered something despairingly under his breath.

"What?" said Jim.

"I said," said Secoh, resignedly, "wouldn't your worship like to t-taste it—"

"Not if you're going to cry about it," said Jim.

"I bit my tongue."

"Well, in that case . . ." Jim walked up and sank his teeth in the shoulder of the carcass. Rich juices trickled enticingly over his tongue . . .

Some little time later he and Secoh sat back polishing bones with the rough uppers of their tongues which were as abrasive as steel files.

"Did you get enough to eat, Secoh?" asked Jim.

"More than enough, sir," replied the mere-dragon, staring at the white skeleton with a wild and famished eye. "Although, if your exaltedness doesn't mind, I've a weakness for marrow . . ." He picked up a thighbone and began to crunch it like a stick of candy.

"Now," said Jim. "About this Loathly Tower. Where is it?"

"The wh-what?" stammered Secoh, dropping the thighbone.

"The Loathly Tower. It's in the fens. You know of it, don't you?"

"Oh, sir! Yes, sir. But you wouldn't want to go there, sir! Not that I'm presuming to give your lordship advice—" cried Secoh, in a suddenly high and terrified voice.

"No, no," soothed Jim. "What are you so upset about?"

"Well—of course I'm only a timid little mere-dragon. But it's a terrible place, the Loathly Tower, your worship, sir."

"How? Terrible?"

"Well—well, it just is." Secoh cast an unhappy look around him. "It's what spoiled all of us, you know, five hundred years ago. We used to be like other dragons—oh, not so big and handsome as you, sir. Then, after that, they say it was the Good got the upper hand and the Evil in the Tower was vanquished and the Tower itself ruined. But it didn't help us mere-dragons any, and I wouldn't go there if I was your worship, I really wouldn't."

"But what's so bad? What sort of thing is it?"

"Well, I wouldn't say there was any real *thing* there. Nothing your worship could put a claw on. It's just strange things go to it and strange things come out of it; and lately . . ."

"Lately what?"

"Nothing—nothing, really, your excellency!" cried Secoh. "Your illustriousness shouldn't catch a worthless little mere-dragon up like that. I only meant, lately the Tower's seemed more fearful than ever. That's all."

"Probably your imagination," said Jim, shortly. "Anyway, where is it?"

"You have to go north about five miles." While they had eaten and talked, the sunset had died. It was almost dark now; and Jim had to strain his eyes through the gloom to see the mere-dragon's foreclaw, pointing away across the mere. "To the Great Causeway. It's a wide lane of solid ground running east and west through the fens. You follow it west to the Tower. The Tower stands on a rock overlooking the sea-edge."

"Five miles . . ." said Jim. He considered the soft grass on which he lay. His armored body seemed undisturbed by the temperature, whatever it was. "I might as well get some sleep. See you in the morning, Secoh." He obeyed a sudden, birdlike instinct and tucked his ferocious head and long neck back under one wing.

"Whatever your excellency desires . . ." the mere-dragon's muffled voice came distantly to his ear. "Your excellency has only to call and I'll be immediately available . . ."

The words faded out on Jim's ear, as he sank into sleep like a heavy stone into deep, dark waters.

When he opened his eyes, the sun was up. He sat up himself, yawned, and blinked.

Secoh was gone. So were the leftover bones.

"Blast!" said Jim. But the morning was too nice for annoyance. He smiled at his mental picture of Secoh carefully gathering the bones in fearful silence, and sneaking them away.

The smile did not last long. When he tried to take off in a northerly direction, as determined by reference to the rising sun, he found he had charley horses in both the huge wing-muscles that swelled out under the armor behind his shoulders. The result, of course, of yesterday's heavy exercise. Grumbling, he was forced to proceed on foot; and four hours later, very hot, muddy and wet, he pulled his weary body up onto the broad east-and-west-stretching strip of land which must, of necessity, be the Great Causeway. It ran straight as a Roman road through the meres, several feet higher than the rest of the fenland, and was solid enough to support good-sized trees. Jim collapsed in the shade of one with a heartfelt sigh.

He awoke to the sound of someone singing. He blinked and lifted his head. Whatever the earlier verses of the song had been, Jim had missed them; but the approaching baritone voice now caroled the words of the chorus merrily and clearly to his ear:

> "A right good sword, a constant mind,
> A trusty spear and true!
> The dragons of the mere shall find
> What Nevile-Smythe can do!"

The tune and words were vaguely familiar. Jim sat up for a better look and a knight in full armor rode into view on a large white horse through the trees. Then everything happened at once. The knight saw him, the visor of his armor came down with a clang, his long spear seemed to jump into his mailed hand and the horse under him leaped into a gallop, heading for Jim. Gorbash's reflexes took over. They hurled Jim straight up into the air, where his punished wing-muscles cracked and faltered. He was just able to manage enough of a fluttering flop to throw himself into the upper branches of a small tree nearby.

The knight skidded his horse to a stop below and looked up through the spring-budded branches. He tilted his visor back to reveal a piercing pair of blue eyes, a rather hawk-like nose and a jutting generous chin, all assembled into a clean-shaven young-man's face. He looked eagerly up at Jim.

"Come down," he said.

"No thanks," said Jim, hanging firmly to the tree. There was a slight pause as they both digested the situation.

"Dashed caitiff mere-dragon!" said the knight finally, with annoyance.

"I'm not a mere-dragon," said Jim.

"Oh, don't talk rot!" said the knight.

"I'm not," repeated Jim. He thought a minute. "I'll bet you can't guess who I really am."

The knight did not seem interested in guessing who Jim really was. He stood up in his stirrups and probed through the branches with his spear. The point did not quite reach Jim.

"Damn!" Disappointedly, he lowered the spear and became thoughtful. "I can climb the dashed tree," he muttered to himself. "But then what if he flies down and I have to fight him unhorsed, eh?"

"Look," called Jim, peering down—the knight looked up eagerly—"if you'll listen to what I've to say, first."

The knight considered.

"Fair enough," he said, finally. "No pleas for mercy, now!"

"No, no," said Jim.

"Because I shan't grant them, dammit! It's not in my vows. Widows and orphans and honorable enemies on the field of battle. But not dragons."

"No. I just want to convince you who I really am."

"I don't give a blasted farthing who you really are."

"You will," said Jim. "Because I'm not really a dragon at all. I've just been—uh—enchanted into a dragon."

The man on the ground looked skeptical.

"Really," said Jim, slipping a little in the tree. "You know S. Carolinus, the magician? I'm as human as you are."

"Heard of him," grunted the knight. "You say *he* put you under?"

"No, he's the one who's going to change me back—as soon as I can find the lady I'm—er—betrothed to. A real dragon ran off with her. I'm after him. Look at me. Do I look like one of these scrawny mere-dragons?"

"Hmm," said the knight. He rubbed his hooked nose thoughtfully.

"Carolinus found she's at the Loathly Tower. I'm on my way there."

The knight stared.

"The Loathly Tower?" he echoed.

"Exactly," said Jim, firmly. "And now you know, your honor as knight and gentleman demands you don't hamper my rescue efforts."

The knight continued to think it over for a long moment or two. He was evidently not the sort to be rushed into things.

"How do I know you're telling the truth?" he said at last.

"Hold your sword up. I'll swear on the cross of its hilt."

"But if you're a dragon, what's the good in that? Dragons don't have souls, dammit!"

"No," said Jim, "but a Christian gentleman has; and if I'm a Christian gentleman, I wouldn't dare forswear myself like that, would I?"

The knight struggled visibly with this logic for several seconds. Finally, he gave up.

"Oh, well . . ." He held up his sword by the point and let Jim swear on it. Then he put the sword back in its sheath as Jim descended. "Well," he said, still a little doubtfully, "I suppose, under the circumstances, we ought to introduce ourselves. You know my arms?"

Jim looked at the shield which the other swung around for his inspection. It showed a wide X of silver—like a cross lying over sideways—on a red background and above some sort of black animal in profile which seemed to be lying down between the X's bottom legs.

"The gules, a saltire argent, of course," went on the knight, "are the Nevile of Raby arms. My father, as a cadet of the house, differenced with a hart lodged sable—you see it there at the bottom. Naturally, as his heir, I carry the family arms."

"Nevile-Smythe," said Jim, remembering the name from the song.

"Sir Reginald, knight bachelor. And you, sir?"

"Why, uh . . ." Jim clutched frantically at what he knew of heraldry. "I bear—in my proper body, that is—"

"Quite."

"A . . . gules, a typewriter argent, on a desk sable. Eckert, Sir James—uh—knight bachelor. Baron of—er—Riveroak."

Nevile-Smythe was knitting his brows.

"Typewriter . . ." he was muttering, "typewriter . . ."

"A local beast, rather like a griffin," said Jim, hastily. "We have a lot of them in Riveroak—that's in America, a land over the sea to the west. You may not have heard of it."

"Can't say that I have. Was it there you were enchanted into this dragon-shape?"

"Well, yes and no. I was transported to this land by magic as was the uh—lady Angela. When I woke here I was bedragoned."

"Were you?" Sir Reginald's blue eyes bulged a little in amazement. "Angela—fair name, that! Like to meet her. Perhaps after we get this muddle cleared up, we might have a bit of a set-to on behalf of our respective ladies."

Jim gulped slightly.

"Oh, you've got one, too?"

"Absolutely. And she's tremendous. The Lady Elinor—" The knight turned about in his saddle and began to fumble about his equipment. Jim, on reaching the ground, had at once started out along the causeway in the direction of the Tower, so that the knight happened to be pacing alongside him on horseback when he suddenly went into these evolutions. It seemed to bother his charger not at all. "Got her favor here someplace—half a moment—"

"Why don't you just tell me what it's like?" said Jim, sympathetically.

"Oh, well," said Nevile-Smythe, giving up his search, "it's a kerchief, you know. Monogrammed. E. d'C. She's a deChauncy. It's rather too bad, though. I'd have liked to show it to you since we're going to the Loathly Tower together."

"We are?" said Jim, startled. "But—I mean, it's my job. I didn't think you'd want—"

"Lord, yes," said Nevile-Smythe, looking somewhat startled himself. "A gentleman of coat-armor like myself—and an outrage like this taking place locally. I'm no knight-errant, dash it, but I *do* have a decent sense of responsibility."

"I mean—I just meant—" stumbled Jim. "What if something happened to you? What would the Lady Elinor say?"

"Why, what could she say?" replied Nevile-Smythe in plain astonishment. "No one but an utter rotter dodges his plain duty. Besides, there may be a chance here for me to gain a little worship. Elinor's keen on that. She wants me to come home safe."

Jim blinked.

"I don't get it," he said.

"Beg pardon?"

Jim explained his confusion.

"Why, how do you people do things overseas?" said Nevile-Smythe. "After we're married and I have lands of my own, I'll be expected to raise a company and march out at my lord's call. If I've no name as a knight, I'll be able to raise nothing but bumpkins and clodpoles who'll desert at the first sight of steel. On the other hand, if I've a name, I'll have good men coming to serve under my banner; because, you see, they know I'll take good care of them; and by the same token they'll take good care of me—I say, isn't it getting dark rather suddenly?"

Jim glanced at the sky. It was indeed—almost the dimness of twilight although it could, by rights, be no more than early afternoon yet. Glancing ahead up the Causeway, he became aware of a further phenomenon. A line seemed to be cutting across the trees and grass and even extending out over the waters of the meres on both sides. Moreover, it seemed to be moving toward them as if some heavy, invisible fluid was slowly flooding out over the low country of the fenland.

"Why—" he began. A voice wailed suddenly from his left to interrupt him.

"No! No! Turn back, your worship. Turn back! It's death in there!"

They turned their heads sharply. Secoh, the mere-dragon, sat perched on a half-drowned tussock about forty feet out in the mere.

"Come here, Secoh!" called Jim.

"No! No!" The invisible line was almost to the tussock. Secoh lifted heavily into the air and flapped off, crying. "Now it's loose! It's broken loose again. And we're all lost . . . lost . . . lost . . ."

His voice wailed away and was lost in the distance. Jim and Nevile-Smythe looked at each other.

"Now, that's one of our local dragons for you!" said the knight disgustedly. "How can a gentleman of coat armor gain honor by slaying a beast like that? The worst of it is when someone from the Midlands compliments you on being a dragonslayer and you have to explain—"

At that moment either they both stepped over the line, or the line moved past them—Jim was never sure which; and they both stopped, as by one common, instinctive impulse. Looking at Sir

Reginald, Jim could see under the visor how the knight's face had gone pale.

"In manus tuas Domine," said Nevile-Smythe, crossing himself.

About and around them, the serest gray of winter light lay on the fens. The waters of the meres lay thick and oily, still between the shores of dull green grass. A small, cold breeze wandered through the tops of the reeds and they rattled together with a dry and distant sound like old bones cast out into a forgotten courtyard for the wind to play with. The trees stood helpless and still, their new, small leaves now pinched and faded like children aged before their time while all about and over all the heaviness of dead hope and bleak despair lay on all living things.

"Sir James," said the knight, in an odd tone and accents such as Jim had not heard him use before, "wot well that we have this day set our hands to no small task. Wherefore I pray thee that we should push forward, come what may, for my heart faileth and I think me that it may well hap that I return not, ne no man know mine end."

Having said this, he immediately reverted to his usual cheerful self and swung down out of his saddle. "Clarivaux won't go another inch, dash it!" he said. "I shall have to lead him—by the bye, did you know that mere-dragon?"

Jim fell into step beside him and they went on again, but a little more slowly, for everything seemed an extra effort under this darkening sky.

"I talked to him yesterday," said Jim. "He's not a bad sort of dragon."

"Oh, I've nothing against the beasts, myself. But one slays them when one finds them, you know."

"And old dragon—in fact he's the granduncle of this body I'm in," said Jim, "thinks that dragons and humans really ought to get together. Be friends, you know."

"Extraordinary thought!" said Nevile-Smythe, staring at Jim in astonishment.

"Well, actually," said Jim, "why not?"

"Well, I don't know. It just seems like it wouldn't do."

"He says men and dragons might find common foes to fight together."

"Oh, that's where he's wrong, though. You couldn't trust dragons to stick by you in a bicker. And what if your enemy had dragons of his own? They wouldn't fight each other. No. No."

They fell silent. They had moved away from the grass onto flat sandy soil. There was a sterile, flinty hardness to it. It crunched under the hooves of Clarivaux, at once unyielding and treacherous.

"Getting darker, isn't it?" said Jim, finally.

The light was, in fact, now down to a grayish twilight, through which it was impossible to see more than a dozen feet. And it was dwindling as they watched. They had halted and stood facing each other. The light fled steadily, and faster. The dimness became blacker, and blacker—until finally the last vestige of illumination was lost and blackness, total and complete, overwhelmed them. Jim felt a gauntleted hand touch one of his forelimbs.

"Let's hold together," said the voice of the knight. "Then whatever comes upon us, must come upon us all at once."

"Right," said Jim. But the word sounded cold and dead in his throat.

They stood, in silence and in lightlessness, waiting for they did not know what. And the blankness about them pressed further in on them, now that it had isolated them, nibbling at the very edges of their minds. Out of the nothingness came nothing material, but from within them crept up one by one, like blind white slugs from some bottomless pit, all their inner doubts and fears and unknown weaknesses, all the things of which they had been ashamed and which they had tucked away to forget, all the maggots of their souls.

Jim found himself slowly, stealthily beginning to withdraw his forelimb from under the knight's touch. He no longer trusted Nevile-Smythe—for the evil that must be in the man because of the evil he knew to be in himself. He would move away . . . off into the darkness alone . . .

"Look!" Nevile-Smythe's voice cried suddenly to him, distant and eerie, as if from someone already a long way off. "Look back the way we came."

Jim turned about. Far off in the darkness, there was a distant glimmer of light. It rolled toward them, growing as it came. They felt its power against the power of lightlessness that threatened to overwhelm them; and the horse Clarivaux stirred unseen beside them, stamped his hooves on the hard sand, and whinnied.

"This way!" called Jim.

"This way!" shouted Nevile-Smythe.

The light shot up suddenly in height. Like a great rod it advanced toward them and the darkness was rolling back, graying, disappearing. They heard a sound of feet close, and a sound of breathing, and then—

It was daylight again.

And S. Carolinus stood before them in tall hat and robes figured with strange images and signs. In his hand upright before him—as if it was blade and buckler, spear and armor all in one—he held a tall carven staff of wood.

"By the Powers!" he said. "I was in time. Look there!"

He lifted the staff and drove it point down into the soil. It went in and stood erect like some denuded tree. His long arm pointed past them and they turned around.

The darkness was gone. The fens lay revealed far and wide, stretching back a long way, and up ahead, meeting the thin dark line of the sea. The Causeway had risen until they now stood twenty feet above the mere-waters. Ahead to the west, the sky was ablaze with sunset. It lighted up all the fens and the end of the Causeway leading onto a long and bloody-looking hill, whereon—touched by that same dying light—there loomed above and over all, amongst great tumbled boulders, the ruined, dark and shattered shell of a Tower as black as jet.

III

"—why didn't you wake us earlier, then?" asked Jim.

It was the morning after. They had slept the night within the small circle of protection afforded by Carolinus' staff. They were sitting up now and rubbing their eyes in the light of a sun that had certainly been above the horizon a good two hours.

"Because," said Carolinus. He was sipping at some more milk and he stopped to make a face of distaste. "Because we had to wait for them to catch up with us."

"Who? Catch up?" asked Jim.

"If I knew *who*," snapped Carolinus, handing his empty milk tankard back to emptier air, "I would have said *who*. All I know is that the present pattern of Chance and History implies that two more will join our party. The same pattern implied the presence of this knight and—oh, so that's who they are."

Jim turned around to follow the magician's gaze. To his surprise, two dragon shapes were emerging from a clump of brush behind them.

"Secoh!" cried Jim. "And—Smrgol! Why—" His voice wavered and died. The old dragon, he suddenly noticed, was limping and one wing hung a little loosely, half-drooping from its shoulder. Also, the eyelid on the same side as the loose wing and stiff leg was sagging more or less at half-mast. "Why, what happened?"

"Oh, a bit stiff from yesterday," huffed Smrgol, bluffly. "Probably pass off in a day or two."

"Stiff nothing!" said Jim, touched in spite of himself. "You've had a stroke."

"Stroke of bad luck, *I'd* say," replied Smrgol, cheerfully, trying to wink his bad eye and not succeeding very well. "No, boy, it's nothing. Look who I've brought along."

"I—I wasn't too keen on coming," said Secoh, shyly, to Jim. "But your granduncle can be pretty persuasive, your wo—you know."

"That's right!" boomed Smrgol. "Don't you go calling anybody your worship. Never heard of such stuff!" He turned to Jim. "And letting a george go in where he didn't dare go himself! Boy, I said to him, don't give me this *only a mere-dragon* and *just a mere-dragon*. Mere's got nothing to do with what kind of dragon you are. What kind of a world would it be if we were all like that?" Smrgol mimicked (as well as his dragon-basso would let him) someone talking in a high, simpering voice. "Oh, I'm just a plowland-and-pasture dragon—you'll have to excuse me, I'm only a halfway-up-the-hill dragon—*Boy!*" bellowed Smrgol, "I said, you're a *dragon*! Remember that. And a dragon acts like a dragon or he doesn't act at all!"

"Hear! Hear!" said Nevile-Smythe, carried away by enthusiasm.

"Hear that, boy? Even the george here knows that. Don't believe I've met you, george," he added, turning to the knight.

"Nevile-Smythe, Sir Reginald. Knight bachelor."

"Smrgol. Dragon."

"Smrgol? You aren't the—but you couldn't be. Over a hundred years ago."

"The dragon who slew the Ogre of Gormely Keep? That's who I am, boy—george, I mean."

"By Jove! Always thought it was a legend, only."

"Legend? Not on your honor, george! I'm old—even for a dragon, but there was a time—well, well, we won't go into that. I've something more important to talk to you about. I've been doing a lot of thinking the last decade or so about us dragons and you georges getting together. Actually, we're really a lot alike—"

"If you don't mind, Smrgol," cut in Carolinus, snappishly, "we aren't out here to hold a parlement. It'll be noon in—when will it be noon, you?"

"Four hours, thirty-seven minutes, twelve seconds at the sound of the gong," replied the invisible bass voice. There was a momentary pause, and then a single mellow, chimed note. "Chime, I mean," the voice corrected itself.

"Oh, go back to bed!" cried Carolinus furiously.

"I've been up for hours," protested the voice, indignantly.

Carolinus ignored it, herding the party together and starting them off for the Tower. The knight fell in beside Smrgol.

"About this business of men and dragons getting together," said Nevile-Smythe. "Confess I wasn't much impressed until I heard your name. D'you think it's possible?"

"Got to make a start sometime, george." Smrgol rumbled on. Jim, who had moved up to the head of the column to walk beside Carolinus, spoke to the magician.

"What lives in the Tower?"

Carolinus jerked his fierce old bearded face around to look at him.

"What's *living* there?" he snapped. "I don't know. We'll find out soon enough. What *is* there—neither alive nor dead, just in existence at the spot— is the manifestation of pure evil."

"But how can we do anything against that?"

"We can't. We can only contain it. Just as you—if you're essentially a good person—contain the potentialities for evil in yourself, by killing its creatures, your evil impulses and actions."

"Oh?" said Jim.

"Certainly. And since evil opposes good in like manner, its creatures, the ones in the Tower, will try to destroy us."

Jim felt a cold lump in his throat. He swallowed.

"Destroy us?"

"Why no, they'll probably just invite us to tea—" The sarcasm in the old magician's voice broke off suddenly with the voice itself. They had just stepped through a low screen of bushes and instinctively checked to a halt.

Lying on the ground before them was what once had been a man in full armor. Jim heard the sucking intake of breath from Nevile-Smythe behind him.

"A most foul death," said the knight softly, "most foul . . ." He came forward and dropped clumsily to his armored knees, joining his gauntleted hands in prayer. The dragons were silent. Carolinus poked with his staff at a wide trail of slime that led around and over the body and back toward the Tower. It was the sort of trail a garden slug might have left—if this particular garden slug had been two or more feet wide where it touched the ground.

"A Worm," said Carolinus. "But Worms are mindless. No Worm killed him in such cruel fashion." He lifted his head to the old dragon.

"I didn't say it, Mage," rumbled Smrgol, uneasily.

"Best none of us say it until we know for certain. Come on." Carolinus took up the lead and led them forward again.

They had come up off the Causeway onto the barren plain that sloped up into a hill on which stood the Tower. They could see the wide fens and the tide flats coming to meet them in the arms of a small bay—and beyond that the sea, stretching misty to the horizon.

The sky above was blue and clear. No breeze stirred; but, as they looked at the Tower and the hill that held it, it seemed that the azure above had taken on a metallic cast. The air had a quivering unnaturalness like an atmosphere dancing to heat waves, though the day was chill; and there came on Jim's ears, from where he did not know, a high-pitched dizzy singing like that which accompanies delirium, or high fever.

The Tower itself was distorted by these things. So that although to Jim it seemed only the ancient, ruined shell of a building, yet, between one heartbeat and the next, it seemed to change. Almost, but not quite, he caught glimpses of it unbroken and alive and thronged about with fantastic, half-seen figures. His heart beat stronger with the delusion; and its beating shook the scene before him, all the hill and Tower, going in and out of focus, in and out, *in* and *out* . . .

. . . And there was Angie, in the Tower's doorway, calling him . . .

"*Stop!*" shouted Carolinus. His voice echoed like a clap of thunder in Jim's ears; and Jim awoke to his senses, to find himself straining against the barrier of Carolinus' staff, that barred his way to the Tower like a rod of iron. "By the Powers!" said the old magician, softly and fiercely. "Will you fall into the first trap set for you?"

"Trap?" echoed Jim, bewilderedly. But he had no time to go further, for at that moment there rose from among the giant boulders at the Tower's base the heavy, wicked head of a dragon as large as Smrgol.

The thunderous bellow of the old dragon beside Jim split the unnatural air.

"*Anark!* Traitor—thief—inchworm! Come down here!"

Booming dragon-laughter rolled back an answer.

"Tell us about Gormely Keep, old bag of bones! Ancient mudpuppy, fat lizard, scare us with words!"

Smrgol lurched forward; and again Carolinus' staff was extended to bar the way.

"Patience," said the magician. But with one wrenching effort, the old dragon had himself under control. He turned, panting, to Carolinus.

"What's hidden, Mage?" he demanded.

"We'll see." Grimly, Carolinus brought his staff, endwise, three times down upon the earth. With each blow the whole hill seemed to shake and shudder.

Up among the rocks, one particularly large boulder tottered and rolled aside. Jim caught his breath and Secoh cried out, suddenly.

In the gap that the boulder revealed, a thick, slug-like head was lifting from the ground. It reared, yellow-brown in the sunlight, its two sets of horns searching and revealing a light external shell, a platelet with a merest hint of spire. It lowered its head and slowly, inexorably, began to flow downhill toward them, leaving its glistening trail behind it.

"Now—" said the knight. But Carolinus shook his head. He struck at the ground again.

"Come forth!" he cried, his thin, old voice piping on the quivering air. "By the Powers! Come forth!"

And then they saw it.

From behind the great barricade of boulders, slowly, there reared first a bald and glistening dome of hairless skin. Slowly this rose, revealing two perfectly round eyes below which they saw, as the whole came up, no proper nose, but two airslits side by side as if the whole of the bare, enormous skull was covered with a simple sheet of thick skin. And rising still further, this unnatural head, as big around as a beach ball, showed itself to possess a wide and idiot-grinning mouth, entirely lipless and revealing two jagged, matching rows of yellow teeth.

Now, with a clumsy, studied motion, the whole creature rose to its feet and stood knee-deep in the boulders and towering above them. It was manlike in shape, but clearly nothing ever spawned by the human race. A good twelve feet high it stood, a rough patchwork kilt of untanned hides wrapped around its thick waist—but this was not the extent of its differences from the race of Man. It had, to begin with, no neck at all. That obscene beachball of a hairless, near-featureless head balanced like an apple on thick, square shoulders of gray, coarse-looking skin. Its torso was one straight trunk, from which its arms and legs sprouted with a disproportionate thickness and roundness, like sections of pipe. Its knees were hidden by its kilt and its further legs by the rocks; but the elbows of its oversize arms had unnatural hinges to them, almost as if they had been doubled, and the lower arms were almost as large as the upper and near-wristless, while the hands themselves were awkward, thick-fingered parodies of the human extremity, with only three digits, of which one was a single, opposed thumb.

The right hand held a club, bound with rusty metal, that surely not even such a monster should have been able to lift. Yet one grotesque hand carried it lightly, as lightly as Carolinus had carried his staff. The monster opened its mouth.

"He!" it went. "He! He!"

The sound was fantastic. It was a bass titter, if such a thing could be imagined. Though the tone of it was as low as the lowest note of a good operatic basso, it clearly came from the creature's upper throat and head. Nor was there any real humor in it. It was an utterance with a nervous, habitual air about it, like a man clearing his throat. Having sounded, it fell silent, watching the advance of the great slug with its round, light blue eyes.

Smrgol exhaled slowly.

"Yes," he rumbled, almost sadly, almost as if to himself. "What I was afraid of. An ogre."

In the silence that followed, Nevile-Smythe got down from his horse and began to tighten the girths of its saddle.

"So, so, Clarivaux," he crooned to the trembling horse. "So ho, boy."

The rest of them were looking all at Carolinus. The magician leaned on his staff, seeming very old indeed, with the deep lines carven in the ancient skin of his face. He had been watching the ogre, but now he turned back to Jim and the other two dragons.

"I had hoped all along," he said, "that it needn't come to this. However," he crackled sourly, and waved his hand at the approaching Worm, the silent Anark and the watching ogre, "as you see . . . The world goes never the way we want it by itself, but must be haltered and led." He winced, produced his flask and cup, and took a drink of milk. Putting the utensils back, he looked over at Nevile-Smythe, who was now checking his weapons. "I'd suggest, Knight, that you take the Worm. It's a poor chance, but your best. I know you'd prefer that renegade dragon, but the Worm is the greater danger."

"Difficult to slay, I imagine?" queried the knight.

"Its vital organs are hidden deep inside it," said Carolinus, "and being mindless, it will fight on long after being mortally wounded. Cut off those eye-stalks and blind it first, if you can—"

"Wait!" cried Jim, suddenly. He had been listening bewilderedly.

Now the word seemed to jump out of his mouth. "What're we going to do?"

"Do?" said Carolinus, looking at him. "Why, fight, of course."

"But," stammered Jim, "wouldn't it be better to go get some help? I mean—"

"Blast it, boy!" boomed Smrgol. "We can't wait for that! Who knows what'll happen if we take time for something like that? Hell's bells, Gorbash, lad, you got to fight your foes when you meet them, not the next day, or the day after that."

"Quite right, Smrgol," said Carolinus, dryly. "Gorbash, you don't understand this situation. Every time you retreat from something like this, it gains and you lose. The next time the odds would be even worse against us."

They were all looking at him. Jim felt the impact of their curious glances. He did not know what to say. He wanted to tell them that he was not a fighter, that he did not know the first thing to do in this sort of battle, that it was none of his business anyway and that he would not be here at all, if it were not for Angie. He was, in fact, quite humanly scared, and floundered desperately for some sort of strength to lean on.

"What—what am I supposed to do?" he said.

"Why, fight the ogre, boy! Fight the ogre!" thundered Smrgol—and the inhuman giant up on the slope, hearing him, shifted his gaze suddenly from the Worm to fasten it on Jim. "And I'll take on that louse of an Anark. The george here'll chop up the Worm, the Mage'll hold back the bad influences—and there we are."

"Fight the ogre . . ." If Jim had still been possessed of his ordinary two legs, they would have buckled underneath him. Luckily his dragon-body knew no such weakness. He looked at the overwhelming bulk of his expected opponent, contrasted the ogre with himself, the armored, ox-heavy body of the Worm with Nevile-Smythe, the deep-chested over-size Anark with the crippled old dragon beside him—and a cry of protest rose from the very depths of his being. "But we can't win!"

He turned furiously on Carolinus, who, however, looked at him calmly. In desperation he turned back to the only normal human he could find in the group.

"Nevile-Smythe," he said. "You don't need to do this."

"Lord, yes," replied the knight, busy with his equipment. "Worms, ogres—one fights them when one runs into them, you know." He considered his spear and put it aside. "Believe I'll face it on foot," he murmured to himself.

"Smrgol!" said Jim. "Don't you see—can't you understand? Anark is a lot younger than you. And you're not well—"

"Er . . ." said Secoh, hesitantly.

"Speak up, boy!" rumbled Smrgol.

"Well," stammered Secoh, "it's just . . . what I mean is, I couldn't bring myself to fight that Worm or that ogre—I really couldn't. I just sort of go to pieces when I think of them getting close to me. But I could—well, fight another dragon. It wouldn't be quite so bad, if you know what I mean, if that dragon up there breaks my neck—" He broke down and stammered incoherently. "I know I sound awfully silly—"

"Nonsense! Good lad!" bellowed Smrgol. "Glad to have you. I—er—can't quite get into the air myself at the moment—still a bit stiff. But if you could fly over and work him down this way where I can get a grip on him, we'll stretch him out for the buzzards." And he dealt the mere-dragon a tremendous thwack with his tail by way of congratulation, almost knocking Secoh off his feet.

In desperation, Jim turned back to Carolinus.

"There is no retreat," said Carolinus, calmly, before Jim could speak. "This is a game of chess where if one piece withdraws, all fall. Hold back the creatures, and I will hold back the forces—for the creatures will finish me, if you go down, and the forces will finish you if they get me."

"Now, look here, Gorbash!" shouted Smrgol in Jim's ear. "That Worm's almost here. Let me tell you something about how to fight ogres, based on experience. You listening, boy?"

"Yes," said Jim, numbly.

"I know you've heard the other dragons calling me an old windbag when I wasn't around. But I *have* conquered an ogre—the only one in our race to do it in the last eight hundred years—and they haven't. So pay attention, if you want to win your own fight."

Jim gulped.

"All right," he said.

"Now, the first thing to know," boomed Smrgol, glancing at the Worm who was now less than fifty yards distant, "is about the bones in an ogre—"

"Never mind the details!" cried Jim. "What do I do?"

"In a minute," said Smrgol. "Don't get excited, boy. Now, about the bones in an ogre. The thing to remember is that they're big—matter of fact in the arms and legs, they're mainly bone. So there's no use trying to bite clear through, if you get a chance. What you try to do is get at the muscle—that's tough enough as it is—and hamstring. That's point one." He paused to look severely at Jim.

"Now, point two," he continued, "also connected with bones. Notice the elbows on that ogre. They aren't like a george's elbows. They're what you might call double-jointed. I mean, they have two joints where a george has just the one. Why? Simply because with the big bones they got to have and the muscle on them, they'd never be able to bend an arm more than halfway up before the bottom part'd bump the top if they had a george-type joint. Now, the point of all this is that when it swings that club, it can only swing in one way with that elbow. That's up and down. If it wants to swing it side to side, it's got to use its shoulder. Consequently if you can catch it with its club down and to one side of the body, you got an advantage; because it takes two motions to get it back up and in line again—instead of one, like a george."

"Yes, yes," said Jim, impatiently, watching the advance of the Worm.

"Don't get impatient, boy. Keep cool. Keep cool. Now, the knees don't have that kind of joint, so if you can knock it off its feet you got a real advantage. But don't try that, unless you're sure you can do it; because once it gets you pinned, you're a goner. The way to fight it is in-and-out—fast. Wait for a swing, dive in, tear him, get back out again. Got it?"

"Got it," said Jim, numbly.

"Good. Whatever you do, don't let it get a grip on you. Don't pay attention to what's happening to the rest of us, no matter what you hear or see. It's every one for himself. Concentrate on your own foe;

and *keep your head*. Don't let your dragon instinct get in there and slug run away with you. That's why the georges have been winning against us as they have. Just remember you're faster than that ogre and your brains'll win for you if you stay clear, keep your head and don't rush. I tell you, boy—"

He was interrupted by a sudden cry of joy from Nevile-Smythe, who had been rummaging around Clarivaux's saddle.

"I say!" shouted Nevile-Smythe, running up to them with surprising lightness, considering his armor. "The most marvelous stroke of luck! Look what I found." He waved a wispy stretch of cloth at them.

"What?" demanded Jim, his heart going up in one sudden leap.

"Elinor's favor! And just in time, too. Be a good fellow, will you," went on Nevile-Smythe, turning to Carolinus, "and tie it about my vambrace here on the shield arm. Thank you, Mage."

Carolinus, looking grim, tucked his staff into the crook of his arm and quickly tied the kerchief around the armor of Nevile-Smythe's lower left arm. As he tightened the final knot and let his hands drop away, the knight caught up his shield into position and drew his sword with his other hand. The bright blade flashed like a sudden streak of lightning in the sun, he leaned forward to throw the weight of his armor before him, and with a shout of "*A Nevile-Smythe! Elinor! Elinor!*" he ran forward up the slope toward the approaching Worm.

Jim heard, but did not see, the clash of shell and steel that was their coming together. For just then everything began to happen at once. Up on the hill, Anark screamed suddenly in fury and launched himself down the slope in the air, wings spread like some great bomber gliding in for a crash landing. Behind Jim, there was the frenzied flapping of leathery wings as Secoh took to the air to meet him—but this was drowned by a sudden short, deep-chested cry, like a wordless shout; and, lifting his club, the ogre stirred and stepped clear of the boulders, coming forward and straight down the hill with huge, ground-covering strides.

"Good luck, boy," said Smrgol, in Jim's ear. "And Gorbash—" Something in the old dragon's voice made Jim turn his head to look at Smrgol. The ferocious red mouth-pit and enormous fangs were frighteningly open before him; but behind it Jim read a strange affection and concern in the dark dragon-eyes. "—Remember," said the old dragon, almost softly, "that you are a descendant of Ortosh and Agtval, and Gleingul who slew the sea serpent on the tide-banks of the Gray Sands. And be therefore valiant. But remember, too, that you are my only living kin and the last of our line . . . and be careful."

Then Smrgol's head was jerked away, as he swung about to face the coming together of Secoh and Anark in mid-air and bellowed out his own challenge. While Jim, turning back toward the Tower, had only time to take to the air before the rush of the ogre was upon him.

He had lifted on his wings without thinking—evidently this was dragon instinct when attacked. He was aware of the ogre suddenly before him, checking now, with its enormous hairy feet digging deep into the ground. The rust-bound club flashed before Jim's eyes and he felt a heavy blow high on his chest that swept him backward through the air.

He flailed with his wings to regain balance. The over-size idiot face was grinning only a couple of yards off from him. The club swept up for another blow. Panicked, Jim scrambled aside, and saw the ogre sway forward a step. Again the club lashed out—*quick!*—how could something so big and clumsy-looking be so quick with its hands? Jim felt himself smashed down to earth and a sudden lance of bright pain shot through his right shoulder. For a second, a gray, thick-skinned forearm loomed over him and his teeth met in it without thought.

He was shaken like a rat by a rat terrier and flung clear. His wings beat for the safety of altitude, and he found himself about twenty feet off the ground, staring down at the ogre, which grunted a wordless sound and shifted the club to strike upward. Jim cupped air with his wings, to fling himself backward and avoid the blow. The club whistled through the unfeeling air; and, sweeping forward, Jim ripped at one great blocky shoulder and beat clear. The ogre spun to face him, still grinning. But now blood welled and trickled down where Jim's teeth had gripped and torn, high on the shoulder.

—And suddenly, Jim realized something:

He was no longer afraid. He hung in the air, just out of the ogre's reach, poised to take advantage of any opening; and a hot sense of excitement was coursing through him. He was discovering the truth about fights—and about most similar things—that it is only the begin-

ning that is bad. Once the chips are down, several million years of instinct take over and there is no time for thought for anything but confronting the enemy. So it was with Jim—and then the ogre moved in
on him again; and that was his last specific intellectual thought of the
fight, for everything else was drowned in his overwhelming drive to
avoid being killed and, if possible, to kill, himself. . . .

IV

It was a long, blurred time, about which later Jim had no clear
memory. The sun marched up the long arc of the heavens and crossed
the nooning point and headed down again. On the torn-up sandy soil
of the plain he and the ogre turned and feinted, smashed and tore at
each other. Sometimes he was in the air, sometimes on the ground.
Once he had the ogre down on one knee, but could not press his advantage. At another time they had fought up the long slope of the hill
almost to the Tower and the ogre had him pinned in the cleft between
two huge boulders and had hefted its club back for the final blow that
would smash Jim's skull. And then he had wriggled free between the
monster's very legs and the battle was on again.

Now and then throughout the fight he would catch brief kaleido-
scopic glimpses of the combats being waged about him: Nevile-Smythe
now wrapped about by the blind body of the Worm, its eyestalks
hacked away—and striving in silence to draw free his sword-arm,
which was pinned to his side by the Worm's encircling body. Or there
would roll briefly into Jim's vision a tangled roaring tumble of flailing
leathery wings and serpentine bodies that was Secoh, Anark and old
Smrgol. Once or twice he had a momentary view of Carolinus, still
standing erect, his staff upright in his hand, his long white beard flowing forward over his blue gown with the cabalistic golden signs upon it,
like some old seer in the hour of Armageddon. Then the gross body of
the ogre would blot out his vision and he would forget all but the
enemy before him.

The day faded. A dank mist came rolling in from the sea and fled
in little wisps and tatters across the plain of battle. Jim's body ached

and slowed, and his wings felt leaden. But the ever-grinning face and sweeping club of the ogre seemed neither to weaken nor to tire. Jim drew back for a moment to catch his breath; and in that second, he heard a voice cry out.

"Time is short!" it cried, in cracked tones. "We are running out of time. The day is nearly gone!"

It was the voice of Carolinus. Jim had never heard him raise it before with just such a desperate accent. And even as Jim identified the voice, he realized that it came clearly to his ears—and that for sometime now upon the battlefield, except for the ogre and himself, there had been silence.

He shook his head to clear it and risked a quick glance about him. He had been driven back almost to the neck of the Causeway itself, where it entered onto the plain. To one side of him, the snapped strands of Clarivaux's bridle dangled limply where the terrified horse had broken loose from the earth-thrust spear to which Nevile-Smythe had tethered it before advancing against the Worm on foot. A little off from it stood Carolinus, upheld now only by his staff, his old face shrunken and almost mummified in appearance, as if the life had been all but drained from it. There was nowhere else to retreat to; and Jim was alone.

He turned back his gaze to see the ogre almost upon him. The heavy club swung high, looking gray and enormous in the mist. Jim felt in his limbs and wings a weakness that would not let him dodge in time; and, with all his strength, he gathered himself, and sprang instead, up under the monster's guard and inside the grasp of those cannon-thick arms.

The club glanced off Jim's spine. He felt the arms go around him, the double triad of bone-thick fingers searching for his neck. He was caught, but his rush had knocked the ogre off his feet. Together they went over and rolled on the sandy earth, the ogre gnawing with his jagged teeth at Jim's chest and striving to break a spine or twist a neck, while Jim's tail lashed futilely about.

They rolled against the spear and snapped it in half. The ogre found its hold and Jim felt his neck begin to be slowly twisted, as if it were a chicken's neck being wrung in slow motion. A wild despair flooded through him. He had been warned by Smrgol never to let the ogre get him pinned. He had disregarded that advice and now he was lost, the battle was lost. *Stay away*, Smrgol had warned, *use your brains* . . .

The hope of a wild chance sprang suddenly to life in him. His head was twisted back over his shoulder. He could see only the gray mist above him, but he stopped fighting the ogre and groped about with both forelimbs. For a slow moment of eternity, he felt nothing, and then something hard nudged against his right foreclaw, a glint of bright metal flashed for a second before his eyes. He changed his grip on what he held, clamping down on it as firmly as his clumsy foreclaws would allow—

—and with every ounce of strength that was left to him, he drove the fore-part of the broken spear deep into the middle of the ogre that sprawled above him.

The great body bucked and shuddered. A wild scream burst from the idiot mouth alongside Jim's ear. The ogre let go, staggered back and up, tottering to its feet, looming like the Tower itself above him. Again, the ogre screamed, staggering about like a drunken man, fumbling at the shaft of the spear sticking from him. It jerked at the shaft, screamed again, and, lowering its unnatural head, bit at the wood like a wounded animal. The tough ash splintered between its teeth. It screamed once more and fell to its knees. Then slowly, like a bad actor in an old-fashioned movie, it went over on its side, and drew up its legs like a man with the cramp. A final scream was drowned in bubbling. Black blood trickled from its mouth and it lay still.

Jim crawled slowly to his feet and looked about him.

The mists were drawing back from the plain and the first thin light of late afternoon stretching long across the slope. In its rusty illumination, Jim made out what was to be seen there.

The Worm was dead, literally hacked in two. Nevile-Smythe, in bloody, dinted armor, leaned wearily on a twisted sword not more than a few feet off from Carolinus. A little farther off, Secoh raised a torn neck and head above the intertwined, locked-together bodies of Anark and Smrgol. He stared dazedly at Jim. Jim moved slowly, painfully over to the mere-dragon.

Jim came up and looked down at the two big dragons. Smrgol lay with his eyes closed and his jaws locked in Anark's throat. The neck of the younger dragon had been broken like the stem of a weed.

"Smrgol . . ." croaked Jim.

"No—" gasped Secoh. "No good. He's gone. . . . I led the other one to him. He got his grip—and then he never let go. . . ." The mere-dragon choked and lowered his head.

"He fought well," creaked a strange harsh voice which Jim did not at first recognize. He turned and saw the Knight standing at his shoulder. Nevile-Smythe's face was white as sea-foam inside his helmet and the flesh of it seemed fallen in to the bones, like an old man's. He swayed as he stood.

"We have won," said Carolinus, solemnly, coming up with the aid of his staff. "Not again in our lifetimes will evil gather enough strength in this spot to break out." He looked at Jim. "And now," he said, "the balance of Chance and History inclines in your favor. It's time to send you back."

"Back?" said Nevile-Smythe.

"Back to his own land, Knight," replied the magician. "Fear not, the dragon left in this body of his will remember all that happened and be your friend."

"Fear!" said Nevile-Smythe, somehow digging up a final spark of energy to expend on hauteur. "I fear no dragon, dammit. Besides, in respect to the old boy here"—he nodded at the dead Smrgol—"I'm going to see what can be done about this dragon-alliance business."

"He was great!" burst out Secoh, suddenly, almost with a sob. "He—he made me strong again. Whatever he wanted, I'll do it." And the mere-dragon bowed his head.

"You come along with me then, to vouch for the dragon end of it," said Nevile-Smythe. "Well," he turned to Jim, "it's goodby, I suppose, Sir James."

"I suppose so," said Jim. "Goodby to you, too, I—" Suddenly he remembered.

"Angie!" he cried out, spinning around. "I've got to go get Angie out of that Tower!"

Carolinus put his staff out to halt Jim.

"Wait," he said. "Listen . . ."

"Listen?" echoed Jim. But just at that moment, he heard it, a woman's voice calling, high and clear, from the mists that still hid the Tower.

"*Jim! Jim, where are you?*"

A slight figure emerged from the mist, running down the slope toward them.

"Here I am!" bellowed Jim. And for once he was glad of the capabilities of his dragon-voice. "Here I am, Angie—"

—but Carolinus was chanting in a strange, singing voice, words without meaning, but which seemed to shake the very air about them. The mist swirled, the world rocked and swung. Jim and Angie were caught up, were swirled about, were spun away and away down an echoing corridor of nothingness . . .

. . . and then they were back in the Grille, seated together on one side of the table in the booth. Hanson, across from them, was goggling like a bewildered accident victim.

"Where—where am I?" he stammered. His eyes suddenly focused on them across the table and he gave a startled croak. "Help!" he cried, huddling away from them. "Humans!"

"What did you expect?" snapped Jim. "Dragons?"

"No!" shrieked Hanson. "Watch-beetles—like me!" And, turning about, he tried desperately to burrow his way through the wood seat of the booth to safety.

V

It was the next day after that Jim and Angie stood in the third floor corridor of Chumley Hall, outside the door leading to the office of the English Department.

"Well, are you going in or aren't you?" demanded Angie.

"In a second, in a second," said Jim, adjusting his tie with nervous fingers. "Just don't rush me."

"Do you suppose he's heard about Grottwold?" Angie asked.

"I doubt it," said Jim. "The Student Health Service says Hanson's already starting to come out of it—except that he'll probably always have a touch of amnesia about the whole afternoon. Angie!" said Jim, turning on her. "Do you suppose, all the time we were there, Hanson was actually being a watch-beetle underground?"

"I don't know, and it doesn't matter," interrupted Angie, firmly. "Honestly, Jim, now you've finally promised to get an answer out of Dr. Howells about a job, I'd think you'd want to get it over and done with, instead of hesitating like this. I just can't understand a man who can go about consorting with dragons and fighting ogres and then—"

"—still not want to put his boss on the spot for a yes-or-no answer," said Jim. "Hah! Let me tell you something." He waggled a finger in front of her nose. "Do you know what all this dragon-ogre business actually taught me? It wasn't to be scared, either."

"All right," said Angie, with a sigh. "What was it then?"

"I'll tell you," said Jim. "What I found out . . ." He paused. "What I found out was not, not to be scared. It was that scared or not doesn't matter; because you just go ahead, anyway."

Angie blinked at him.

"And that," concluded Jim, "is why I agreed to have it out with Howells, after all. Now you know."

He yanked Angie to him, kissed her grimly upon her startled lips, and, letting go of her, turned about. Giving a final jerk to his tie, he turned the knob of the office door, opened it, and strode valiantly within.